It Had To Be You

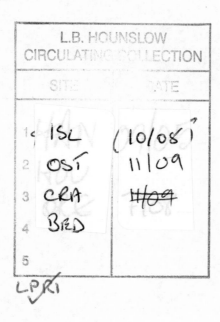

It Had To Be You

SARAH WEBB

ISIS
LARGE PRINT
Oxford

62 065 026

10/05

Copyright © Sarah Webb, 2004

First published in Great Britain 2004
by
Macmillan,
an imprint of Pan Macmillan Ltd

Published in Large Print 2005 by ISIS Publishing Ltd,
7 Centremead, Osney Mead, Oxford OX2 0ES
by arrangement with
Pan Macmillan Ltd

British Library Cataloguing in Publication Data
Webb, Sarah
    It had to be you. – Large print ed.
    1. Female friendship – Ireland – Fiction
    2. Bookstores – Ireland – Fiction
    3. Large type books
    I. Title
    823.9'2 [F]

ISBN 0–7531–7425–1 (hb)
ISBN 0–7531–7426–X (pb)

Printed and bound in Great Britain by
T. J. International Ltd., Padstow, Cornwall

This one's for my sisters, Kate and Emma.

Thanks

To all my family and friends, especially Mum and Dad, Kate and Richard; Emma, Peter, Luan and Charlie; Ben, Sam and Amy-Rose; Nicky, Andrew and Tanya.

To my agent Ali Gunn, for her advice and enthusiasm. And to Milly Gosworth for all her help.

To all in Macmillan — especially my editor, Imogen Taylor, David North, Emma Bravo, David Adamson and Trisha Jackson. And to Cormac Kinsella in Repforce.

To Councillor Mary Elliott and Deputy Fiona O'Malley for the invaluable insights into the world of local councillors and Irish politics.

To the staff at Dalkey library, especially Trish Byrne and Niall Brewster for all the help in finding just the books I needed for my research, and for never asking why I desperately needed information on dating, shoes and pregnancy all on the same day!

To all my writing friends — especially Martina Devlin, Martina Murphy, Clare Dowling and all the Irish Girls. It's a pleasure knowing you and thanks for all the fun lunches, dinners, e-mails and phone calls.

To all those in the Irish book trade who have always been so encouraging — especially Tom Owens, Eoin McHugh, David O'Callaghan, Alan Johnson, Maria Dickenson, Cathal Elliot, Bert Wright and all the Eason gang.

And to all the booksellers I met on my last book tour — especially Seamus Duffy in Westport — thanks for all the support and kindness.

And finally to you, the reader. I hope you enjoy reading *It Had To Be You* as much as I enjoyed writing it. I love hearing from my readers so do drop me an e-mail. You can contact me through my website — www.sarahwebb.info.

After writing *It Had To Be You*, my sister, Emma, told me about an area near Greystones, Co. Wicklow called "The Burnaby". I've become so attached to my own fictional village, Burnaby Village, that it would break my heart to change it — so Burnaby Village it stays. But, for the record, there's no Happily Ever After in "The Burnaby", or anywhere else in Ireland for that matter — and more's the pity!

"Make good use of bad rubbish"
Elizabeth Beresford

CHAPTER ONE

Molly

The minute Anita walked through the door of Happily Ever After bookshop that fateful Monday morning, Molly knew that something was up. Although Anita looked perfectly normal — her long red hair tied back in its customary loose chignon, her floor-sweeping black jersey dress clinging in all the wrong, bumpy places — there was a strange expression on her face. Her usual Monday wrinkled brow looked a little less furrowed and her gait was loose and almost girlish, unlike her more normal heavy-footed loaf. She smiled at Molly as soon as she swung open the door, sending the small bell into wild reverberations.

"Hi Molly, how are you this fine morning?"

Molly studied her boss carefully. Was Anita *really* smiling? It suited her: more's the pity that she didn't do it more often.

"Anita. You're early. I wasn't expecting you until lunchtime."

Although Anita lived in an apartment directly above the bookshop, she wasn't know to be an early riser. She rarely lifted her head from her anti-allergy pillow until after ten, and without exception never made it down the stairs and through the shop door before noon, though she was usually just in time to be taken out to lunch by whichever publisher's rep was currently courting her. Anita was crotchety and ill-tempered at the best of times but she also had an unerring talent for spotting bestsellers. Every day she received at least ten couriered packages or jiffy bags containing manuscripts and proofs from various publishers — some from as far away as America and Canada. She was the best-kept secret in Irish bookselling and, as publishers had been telling her for years, she'd missed her calling as an editor. What they didn't know and what she'd never divulged was that she *had* worked as an editor for a large British publisher many moons ago and the experience had been enough to put her off the publishing business for life.

Anita sniffed. "Yes, well, I have some news. Where's the other poor unfortunate?"

"In the back going through the Eason's order."

"I see," Anita said dreamily.

Molly looked at her carefully — Anita was behaving most strangely this morning.

The bell on the door finally stopped ringing and Molly breathed a sigh of relief, grateful for the peace once again. As if to compensate, Anita picked up a stapler off the counter and began to play with it — pressing it together and watching as closed staples fell uselessly onto the fake pine with whispery rattles.

Molly coughed. Anita looked at her. She knew how much Molly hated her fidgeting. They'd had many minor arguments about it over the past few years.

Molly had been working in Anita's bookshop for nearly six years now — ever since she'd left college — progressing from lowly part-time assistant to the lofty heights of shop manager. She and Anita were like chalk and cheese and it was amazing that they hadn't killed each other yet.

Molly brushed the wasted staples onto her right hand and dropped them purposefully into the bin under the counter. She resisted the temptation to pull out the duster to polish the fake pine. It was only ten o'clock after all and they'd only just opened. Not even one greasy customer fingerprint to warrant such action yet.

"Felix came in especially early this morning to get the new orders processed," Molly said. Felix was the other full-time staff member. "It's really busy at the moment what with the Rosemary Hamilton reading and the Book Club meeting, both on the same day." She looked at Anita pointedly.

Anita ignored her and instead picked up yesterday's copy of the *Sunday Ireland* newspaper and began to flick through it. Molly sighed and went back to cutting up *The Times* book pages, continuing her usual Monday morning review selection for the bookshop's large notice board. Anita had booked Rosemary to read and sign, forgetting that it would clash with the Book Club, which met religiously on the first Saturday morning of every month. And by the time Molly had realized the mistake, it had been too late to cancel Rosemary's event. Meaning yet more work for Molly.

Still, she was looking forward to meeting the popular American writer.

Rosemary Hamilton was starting to break through in Ireland and the UK. She wrote big, generous, kind-hearted romantic sagas, exactly the kind of books that both Anita and Molly liked to read. It was one of the few things that they actually had in common. Rosemary had been described as an "American Maeve Binchy" and there had been terrific response to the event which they'd advertised in the local press and which had been picked up by some of the nationals, even the *Irish Daily* who weren't exactly renowned for their love of romantic fiction.

Anita Vickers had opened Happily Ever After to cater for readers like herself — voracious readers of popular fiction, especially romantic fiction, thrillers and crime novels. And although the shop had a decidedly female slant, including its very own pink-couched "Romance Room" packed full of all kinds of women's fiction from Mills and Boon to Jane Austen, they also had many loyal male customers who travelled to Burnaby Village, to find books by their favourite American crime writers which were difficult to come by in mainstream bookshops.

Happily Ever After was just off Burnaby's main street, tucked between Coffee Heaven, and Slick Harry's — Irish floral-design legend Harry Masterson's shop which specialized in unusual plants and shrubs and catered to the well-heeled market. Burnaby Village, nestled on the south Dublin coast, was a Mecca for shoppers with a taste for the unusual. Hidden within its windy, cobbled laneways was the tiny yet perfectly formed print and art gallery, Halo; Presents of Mind, a gift shop crammed full of all kinds of delights including a miniature stone Buddha carved from pink, black and white marble; funky American cloth bags decorated with Andy Warholesque prints for the discerning grocery shopper; not to mention Baroque, the uber-trendy shoe emporium stocking everything from Converse and Camper, to Gina and Jimmy Choo.

The bell rang and Molly looked up. Their first customer of the day.

"Morning." She smiled at the tall, white-haired woman.

"Hello. Have you got the new Ivy White book? I believe it came out today."

"You might be in luck. We've just received an order of new titles and it should be in one of the boxes. Let me check for you."

"Thanks," the woman said gratefully. "I'm going on my holidays today and I was hoping to take it with me." Molly went into the back room to find it for her.

"It's good," said Anita thoughtfully while the customer waited. "She writes wonderfully about affairs of the heart, don't you think?"

"Yes." The woman nodded. "Quite."

Molly came out smiling, holding the spanking-new book out in front of her. "Here we are. The very first copy. We haven't even priced it yet."

After the woman left, happily swinging her dark pink Happily Ever After bag by her side, Molly looked at Anita. "What were you saying about having news? I got

5

distracted by a scathing review of Paddy O'Hara's new thriller."

"I'm not surprised, it was very harsh indeed," said Anita. "And completely undeserved, poor man."

"Your news?" Molly pressed.

"Ah, yes. I was just coming to that. Can you get Felix?"

"Can't you tell me first? Please."

"Of course." Anita smiled easily, unnerving Molly yet again. "I've just sold the shop."

"You've what?" Molly stared at her incredulously.

"Sold the shop."

"You can't have."

"Ah, but I did."

"To who?"

"To whom, you mean?"

"Anita!" Molly was reeling with shock and didn't need a lesson in grammar right now.

The bell on the door rang again and Molly cursed inwardly. This was unbelievable. Anita *was* Happily Ever After, the bookshop wouldn't exist without her. And Anita almost wouldn't exist without the shop — the shop was her whole life.

Molly heard a discreet cough. Anita was staring at her. Patricia Simons, the Trinity publisher's sales rep was standing in front of them, glammed up to the teeth as usual in a perfectly-pressed navy suit with cream and red pipe-edging, a dazzling sheen on her immaculately bobbed blonde hair and her lips painted a perfect rosebud pink. "Penny for them," Patricia smiled.

6

Molly looked at Anita's face which somewhat unnervingly wasn't betraying any emotion at all, and back at Patricia. "Sorry, I was miles away," she said. "Anita just told me some rather surprising news."

"Oh, really?" Patricia's eyes lit up. She loved news, and she loved being the purveyor of it to all her customers. Nothing like a juicy bit of gossip, ahem, news to make the day go a little faster.

Anita glared at Molly. Had Molly taken leave of her senses? Telling Patricia anything guaranteed that it would be all over town in the blink of an eye. Bush fires had nothing on this publisher's rep.

"Well?" Patricia tapped her red nails on the counter-top impatiently.

Molly could feel the heat of Anita's stare and chose to ignore it. She wasn't stupid — she knew exactly how big Patricia's mouth was and she had no intention of telling the woman anything. She just wanted to make Anita sweat. "Harry Masterson is thinking of opening a lap dancing club in the basement of Slick Harry's. What do you think of that?"

"Really?" Patricia asked with unabashed interest. "But that's just beside you. It could bring in some interesting new business, I suppose."

Molly laughed. "Could do. But I'm only joking! Harry isn't exactly the lap dancing type."

Patricia frowned. Molly often poked fun at her expense and she didn't like it one little bit. She sniffed. "He's a business man though. It wouldn't be the worst idea in the world."

"Would you like some coffee?" Anita interrupted. She knew there was no love lost between the two women.

"Love some," Patricia smiled gratefully. "But why don't we pop next door? My treat. I have a manuscript that I'd love you to read. A young Irish author straight out of college that Trinity's looking at acquiring."

Anita looked at Molly who shrugged her shoulders. "We'll have that meeting as soon as I get back," promised Anita. "I won't be long."

"Fine. I have plenty to be getting on with." Molly turned towards Patricia. "Are we doing the order for the December new titles today?"

"I'll do the order with Anita if that's all right. There's nothing of much importance, to tell the truth. December is a pretty dead month for us."

"Fine," Molly said curtly. It was her job to order the new titles for the shop from the sales reps and Patricia knew this. Patricia was no fool. The experienced rep knew she'd get a far larger order than was strictly necessary from Anita — who always got carried away in the face of glossy new fiction titles and blew their budget for the month with one single publisher. Which was precisely why Anita and Molly had agreed years ago that Molly would do all the "front list" or new title ordering.

As soon as Anita and Patricia had left the shop Molly picked up the phone and dialled nine for an outside line.

"Paige? Pick up if you're there. It's Molly."

Paige, a Burnaby County Councillor and Molly's best friend, was notorious for screening her calls. She said it was a necessity in her business when all the local nutters had both her work and home numbers and were likely to call at all hours of the day to complain about anything that took their fancy — from blocked drains and leaking pipes, to noisy neighbours and dog poo on the streets.

"Hi, Molly. How are you this fine morning?"

"Do you have me on speaker phone again?"

"No."

"You do, don't you?"

"Well yes, but I'm in the middle of typing a document and . . ."

"No buts. I demand your 100 per cent concentration. It's important."

Paige picked up the receiver. "OK, you have it. Now what's up?"

"I can't believe you never told me about Anita selling the shop."

"Happily Ever After?"

"Yes! What other shop would I be talking about?" snapped Molly.

"Keep your shirt on. I didn't know. I would have told you if I'd heard anything."

"But you know everything about Burnaby!" Molly protested. "That's your job."

"And you're sure she's sold it?"

"Yes! She told me herself only a few minutes ago."

"Why didn't you ask her who she sold it to then?" Paige said trying not to sound condescending. She regretted the question as soon as she'd asked it.

"I would have if she hadn't left the building. She's gone out for coffee with Patricia Simons who walked in as soon as Anita had broken the news to me, bloody nuisance of a woman. And she'll be gone for a while I imagine. I'm dying of curiosity here. I thought you might be able to put me out of my misery."

Paige sighed. "I'm sorry I can't be more help. It must have been a private sale. But it seems a bit out of the blue. Two weeks ago she was telling me about her plans for the October events. Is she selling it as a going concern?"

"A what?" Molly was confused.

"You know — will it still be trading as a bookshop?"

"Goodness, I hadn't even thought of that." Molly sat down on the stool behind the counter and began to run her left fingers up and down the coiled flex nervously. "You mean the new owners might close the shop? And I might lose my job? I'm hardly qualified to do anything else. That would be terrible. What would I do?"

"Stop right there," commanded Paige. "There's no point worrying about things that may never happen. Anita's no fool. There's no way she'll see you out in the street — or Felix for that matter. Talk to her as soon as she comes back. I'm sure she'll put your mind at rest."

"You're probably right. But what if . . ."

"Molly!"

"Sorry. Listen, I'd better go. I can see a customer approaching out the window."

"Ring me when you've talked to Anita."

"OK."

"Promise?"

10

"Promise."

"And Molly?"

"Yes."

"Stop worrying. I'm sure your job is safe."

The bell on the shop door rang, interrupting their conversation.

"I'll try. I have to go." Molly put down the phone and smiled at the man in front of her. "Hello, how can I help you?"

"Are you Molly?"

She studied the short, shiny-headed man in front of her. He was wearing an expensive-looking black wool polo neck and dark brown cords and as he held out his hand, a heavy gold bracelet slid down his wrist towards his hairy hand. She nodded. How on earth did this stranger know her name?

"Yes, how can I help you?"

"I'm Milo Devine, the new owner of this shop, since you ask. And the question is — how can I help *you*?"

Molly stared at him without saying a word. She could feel the blood drain from her face and her palms began to feel cold and clammy.

"Are you all right?" Milo asked with concern. "You seem a little pale."

"Um, yes, fine," she mumbled.

"I'm sorry, my dear, has Anita not told you about me?"

Molly shook her head. "No. Not a word."

"Ah, I see." He looked a little embarrassed. "Maybe I should have waited . . . but still, now that I'm here, why don't you show me around? Tell me about the kind of

11

books you stock. I'm not much of an expert on romance I must admit, but I have seen *Gone With the Wind*."

Molly had been decidedly unsettled by Milo's unannounced visit and, in Anita's continued absence, had rung her friend Paige again to discuss it. Paige had sighed, saved her half-written document on the computer and picked up the receiver. Molly gave her a description of the man — gold chains, wide Hollywood smiles and all — and told her what he'd said in one breathless gasp.

"Milo Devine, first of all, what kind of name is that?" Paige scoffed when she'd heard the details. "Sounds like a dodgy American detective."

Molly laughed. "It does rather, I suppose, but he's actually Irish. He gives me the creeps to be honest. He reminds me of a wide-boy car salesman — all smiles and platitudes but always on the make. I have a bad feeling about him, Paige, I really do. He mentioned a few of his plans for the shop, but it's what he didn't say that I'm worried about."

"When's Anita back?" asked Paige looking at her watch and biting her lip. Much as she loved talking to Molly she really did have rather a lot of work to do today.

"Soon, I hope. I have a lot of questions to ask her." The bell rang again. "Damn, I have to go."

"Ring me later," Paige insisted. "But not for about an hour if you don't mind, I have to get this bloody document finished before lunchtime. This is better than *EastEnders*. I'm dying to hear more."

"Excuse me. Have you seen my dad?" a deep, treacle-rich voice asked Molly as soon as she'd put the receiver down.

Molly looked up. This day was getting stranger and stranger. There in front of her was the face of an angel — a rugged, no-shoes and dirty-faced kind of angel, but an angel nonetheless. His dark blonde hair hung in messy curls around his strong square face. Molly had read about "chiseled cheekbones" in many of her romantic novels but she'd never come face to face with them in real life. His must have been carved by Michelangelo — they were that sharp and that perfect. One of his front teeth was slightly chipped and his full dark-pink lips were lopsided — all adding to his attraction in Molly's eyes.

Stop staring and say something, she told herself.

"Um, your dad?" Brilliant, Molly, just brilliant. Inspired.

"Milo Devine?" The man smiled. "I was supposed to meet him in here but I'm running a bit late." He coughed nervously and glanced at his watch. "Well, very late actually."

The new owner's son. This was all she needed. "He was here but he left a while ago," Molly said. "Sorry."

"I see. I'm Sam. And you are . . . ?"

"Oh, sorry." She could feel hot prickles running up the back of her neck and spreading towards her cheeks. "I'm Molly," she managed eventually. "Molly Harper. I'm the manager."

"Ah, yes, of course. I've heard all about you from Anita." He smiled again.

Molly noticed that the pocket on his dark blue shirt was torn and had an irrational urge to touch it, and an even more irrational urge to offer to take it home and mend it. What was happening to her?

"This must all have come as a bit of a surprise to you — the shop being sold and everything," he said kindly. She nodded. "Yes."

"But Dad's only going to make one or two minor changes. And I'll just slot in — you'll see. You won't even notice me. Of course I'll need your help at first — I've never run a bookshop before. But I'm sure I'll get the hang of it quickly enough."

Molly felt decidedly faint. What did he mean — run a bookshop? She was the manager here. Did he not know that? She'd had enough. Was no one going to tell her anything? Wait until she got her hands on Anita, she'd had an emotional roller coaster of a morning thanks to her.

"Have I said something wrong?" He looked at Molly carefully. She was staring at him and her large blue eyes seemed to be swimming with moisture.

A large tear dropped from her right eye and twinkled down her cheek. She wiped it off swiftly with the back of her hand, mortified. "Sorry," she murmured. "Something in my eye. Excuse me." She brushed past him, pushed open the door at the back of the shop and stepped through it.

Felix looked over. He was sitting outside the back door catching a few surreptitious rays of morning sun.

He stood up quickly. "Are you all right, Molly? I'm just waiting for the Macmillan delivery. The driver rang to say he was on his way."

"I'm fine, thanks. I don't want to disturbed." Molly walked past him and into the office, closing the door behind her.

14

Felix shrugged his shoulders and sat back down. He'd been working in the bookshop for almost five years now, so was well used to Molly and knew to keep out of her way when she was angry or upset. After a moment, he heard a knock on the door which led on to the shop floor. "Hello, is anyone there? Molly?" A tall figure walked through the doorway and blinked in the brightness. Felix stood up again. "Can I help you?"

"Do you know where Molly went?" the man asked.

Felix gestured towards the wide open back door. "She went out, mate," he lied smoothly. "Gone to get a coffee, I'd say. I'm just on my way in to look after the shop. Can I help you?"

"No, never mind," he said. "Tell her Sam said goodbye."

"Sam. Sure thing."

Sam turned swiftly on his heels, took one last lingering look at the dark pink bookshelves and left the shop, the bell ringing loudly behind him.

As soon as Molly heard the bell she gingerly opened the office door a slit. "Is he gone?" she asked Felix in a low voice.

"Sam?"

"Yes."

Felix nodded. "He said to say goodbye."

"Thanks," she said. What a relief. The tears had stopped just as soon as they'd started and she felt stupid. It was just a reaction to the sudden news, she told herself, nothing to worry about, just shock. She still felt a little funny though.

"I'll look after the shop for a while," Felix said, noticing the slightly manic look in her red-rimmed eyes. "You stay in the office. I'm sure you have work to do."

"Thanks." She smiled gratefully. Felix never asked questions, that was one of the reasons she liked him so much. A silver-haired early retiree from the civil service who had got bored at home, he'd been working in Happily Ever After for almost as long as she had, pottering along at his slow yet solid pace, getting everything done and rarely making a mistake.

Half an hour later Anita opened the door of the office and found Molly rifling through one of the drawers of the tall grey filing cabinet — the top drawer where Anita kept all her private papers.

Anita coughed quietly. Molly jumped.

"I was just looking for . . ." Molly began and then stopped.

"For what?" prompted Anita.

Think of something, Molly willed herself. Anything. She couldn't — her mind had gone completely blank. "I was looking for information about the sale," she said truthfully. "About Milo and his son. About my job." She stared at the dark blue carpet tiles, bit her lip and willed the tears away. Could this day get any worse?

Anita put her hand on Molly's shoulder. "I'm so sorry," she said. "Sam rang my mobile and left a message. He was worried that he might have upset you."

Molly pushed her back against the drawer, sending it clattering home. "When were you going to tell me about the new owner?"

"This morning," Anita said gently. "You know that. Milo just pre-empted me, that's all. He's quite . . . um, how will I put this?"

"Pushy?" Molly suggested.

"Not exactly the word I was going to use. Forthright I suppose."

"Pushy," Molly said again.

Anita ignored her. "His son seems nice though — Sam. Did you like him?"

"Sam, the new manager, you mean?" Molly glared at her.

"Is that what he told you?"

Molly nodded silently.

"I see. You'd better sit down." Anita waved at the sofa opposite the desk.

Molly did as requested.

"Sam will be working here with you. You will be the Book Manager — in charge of everything to do with the books and the events — just as you are now. Sam will do what I've been doing — staff rotas, holidays, the accounts, tax returns, that kind of thing. His official title will be Shop Manager, but it doesn't mean he's over you. Not at all. Milo promised me that we'd all keep our jobs and that the shop would stay as it always has been with one or two minor changes, nothing drastic, he promised."

"We?" asked Molly. "Are you staying?"

"Yes, I'll be working at the weekends and on Thursday evenings. Just to keep my hand in. And I'll still be living upstairs so you'll see me all the time. Now do you feel any better? I'm so sorry you've had such a stressful morning, my dear. I didn't mean for it all to come out this way."

"I understand. But you should have told me earlier."

"I know."

Molly cocked her head to one side. "One more question. Why did you sell to him?"

"He offered me a good price," said Anita honestly. "He's taken early retirement and has always wanted to own a bookshop in the area."

"And?"

"And what?"

"Don't give me that, Anita. There must be another reason. You love this place."

"No other reason, honestly."

"There is, and I know it. And if you won't tell me I'll find out anyway."

Anita smiled. "You'll be disappointed."

"We'll see."

"Feeling better now?" Anita asked. She put her hand on Molly's shoulder and gave it an affectionate squeeze.

"Yes," Molly said. "Much better. But please tell Felix before Milo or Sam get to him, OK?"

"I'll tell him right now." Anita smiled. "I promise."

CHAPTER
TWO

Kate

Kate looked up, sipping her lukewarm coffee and saw the man she assumed to be her new client, Angus Cawley. He'd described himself on paper as "tall and dapper, with an eclectic dress sense". Eclectic, she thought, looking him up and down, more like downright bad. He was wearing what she presumed were once black jeans but which had now turned an unsavoury shade of greeny-grey, a grey cotton polo neck and the pièce de résistance — a black silk waistcoat decorated with what looked like bright red cherries. To top it all he was also wearing red suede brothel creepers on his large feet and some of his hair was greased back in a type of poor man's duck's-ass, the rest falling lankly around his face. Kate sighed. She had her work cut out for her with this one.

Kate had been running "Dublin Dummy Dates" ("Dummy Dates" for short) for over six months now and it hadn't been quite the "nice little earner" she'd imagined when she'd set it up. In fact, most days it was downright disheartening — there were a lot of sad lost male souls out there all too in need of her services. After an initial consultation, like this morning's

19

meeting, she took men out on dummy dates and put them through their paces — from grooming and clothes, to conversational openers (otherwise known as "chat-up lines") and learning to listen without interrupting — building their confidence and preparing them for future "real" dates. Many of the men on her books had gone on to have successful "real" dates and one, Ken, had even announced an engagement a month after meeting his "ideal woman", a dog groomer from Rialto, which, although it had been cancelled after three weeks, still counted as an engagement (on Kate's promotional blurb anyway).

Her plan had been to start the company, get it running smoothly and then fade back into a purely administrative role, allowing her hand-picked employees to deal with the actual dates. But herein lay the problem. The company hadn't actually made enough money for Kate to employ anyone, so she'd ended up taking out all the clients herself, which wasn't exactly ideal. Alex and Matty O'Connor, the sibling owners of Coffee Heaven where she held most of the initial meetings with the prospective dates, thought she was some sort of compulsive man-eater until Kate had explained what her work entailed.

In the afternoons and on Saturdays, too, Kate worked in Baroque, the local designer shoe shop, but mornings and evenings she turned into Ms Dummy Date. She advertised her services in the local newspaper, Burnaby People, and in several Dublin magazines. The phone hadn't stopped hopping from the second week on after she'd appeared on the Brenda

Jackson morning radio show talking about her services. Brenda had been intrigued and had sent her intrepid reporter Missie O'Donaghue along on a dummy date with Kate and one of her clients — a rather showy man from Howth called Bryan — "Bryan with a y, mind, not an i, mind". Bryan had turned out to be a compulsive liar, the most sexist man either woman had ever encountered and was basically a lost cause. Awful as he was, he had made compulsive radio listening and the company had gained the best free nationwide advertising ever. After the show, Kate had been interviewed by *Sunday Ireland*, the *Irish News* and the *Dublin People*.

She raised her hand and waved at her new client who was looking around the coffee shop anxiously. He caught her eye and smiled. Kate smiled back. He made his way towards her, tripping over a buggy and slopping a mug of coffee all over a table. "Sorry," he murmured to the owner of the coffee who was glaring at him.

Kate tried not to sigh. An awkward, socially inept specimen — she'd seen it all before. He probably had a stutter or a stammer and voted Green Party to boot. Stop it! She chastised herself. That's not nice. You are here to help this man, not to make fun of him. Just because you had a disagreement with Trina already this morning doesn't mean you can take it out on this poor individual, even if he is pathetic.

Trina was the rich and rather batty owner of Baroque whose taste in shoes was, as Kate liked to say rather crudely, "up her ass", and who couldn't tell a Manolo Blahnik from a Gina Couture — quite a failing in a designer shoe buyer. She had far more money than sense and Kate was convinced that Trina's husband, Dublin and London property magnate Farrell de Barra, only bankrolled the shop to keep his darling wife out of his hair and away from his office. Trina ran the shop with the help of her "VBF", Cathy Philips, another trophy wife, married to snooker hall and leisure plex owner "Flames" Philips. Unlike Trina, who was Burnaby old-money born and bred, Cathy was from Limerick and had worked as an Aer Lingus air hostess for three years before serving "Flames" champagne on a memorable trans-Atlantic trip. He'd whisked her away from her life in green, but after two children ("Axel", boy and "Lolita", girl) she'd decided she needed to get out of the house more and going into cahoots, otherwise known as "business" with Trina seemed like a good idea at the time.

Shoes, after "Flames", were Cathy's great passion — and the more expensive the better. Kate had no complaints about Cathy's taste, it was Trina who had chosen the bright orange '70s inspired wedge sandals and the chunky "Bjork" inspired white tap dancers with the thick dark brown heels and soles for this season, when all their customers were clamouring for was sexy dark pink stiletto sandals and neat '50s peep-toes with kitten heels.

Angus stuck out his hand in front of her face. "Kate, I presume? Sorry I'm late."

"Not to worry. Please sit down. I've ordered you a coffee."

He pulled the chair back from the table, catching the back legs on the wooden floor with a loud dragging noise. "Sorry. I'm a bit nervous."

"No need to be." Kate said kindly. "I'm here to help you. Think of me as your sister."

"I haven't got a sister," he admitted as he sat down.

"Your aunt then."

He shook his head again.

This man was beginning to annoy her and he'd only just arrived. "Your mother then." She fixed a smile on her face. "You have one of them, don't you?"

Angus looked down at the table. "I did. She died last year."

Kate's heart sank. Please let him not be a crier, she pleaded. I couldn't deal with that today.

"But she was a great woman," he continued looking up and smiling back.

"You have nice eyes," she said, studying him properly for the first time. His quiff had collapsed, dark brown hair tumbled shapelessly around his face. His steel-rimmed Germanic glasses did nothing for him, but his dark brown eyes shone brightly and intelligently from his slightly sallow skin. Maybe Angus wasn't going to be such a difficult nut to crack after all. She glanced at her watch and jotted down the time at the top of her foolscap sheet. "Bang on quarter past ten — let's get started shall we?"

"Fine."

Alex arrived at the table with a large mug of coffee and placed it on the table in front of Angus. Terminally nosy, she always enjoyed having a look at Kate's latest client. "Enjoy," said Alex looking him up and down. She wasn't impressed. Too skinny and what was with that hair?

"Thanks," he said, oblivious to Alex's critical gaze.

"Thanks, Alex," added Kate.

Alex lingered within hearing distance, flicking a cloth ineffectually at the table beside them and rearranging the milk jug and sugar bowl several times. But Kate was having none of it. She waited patiently until Alex had sniffed audibly and retreated into the kitchen, allowing Angus to take a few calming sips of his coffee before continuing. She promised her clients absolute confidentiality and that was what she gave them.

"I just need to get one or two details from you before we begin our session," she said poising her pen at the top of the page. "How old are you, Angus, if you don't mind me asking?"

"Not at all," he said. "I'm twenty-nine."

"Really?" she raised her eyebrows. Her clients had a habit of stretching the truth a little and he looked a lot younger than that.

"OK," he admitted, "I'm twenty-six. But I much prefer women who are a few years older than me, so I usually say twenty-nine just to be on the safe side."

Kate looked him in the eye. "Let's get this straight from the very start. I'm here to help you. You're paying me to be honest with you. The process won't work unless you tell me the truth — do you understand?"

He nodded. "Yes, I'm sorry, I understand, really. Please continue."

24

She tried not to laugh. He really did look rather contrite; his head hung low, almost disappearing into his shoulders and his hands were clasped on the table in front of him.

"Do you work?" she continued.

"Yes, um, well no."

"Which is it — yes or no?"

"I'm not sure. I went back to college to take my teaching diploma which I've nearly finished. I'm working part-time in a primary school at the moment as work experience — does that count as work or not?"

"Yes, I guess so. Are you training to be a primary school teacher?"

He nodded sheepishly.

"You're embarrassed by this?" she asked.

"A little."

"Why?"

He shrugged his shoulders. "Not very manly is it — teaching four- and five-year-olds?"

"I don't know," Kate said thoughtfully, "some women like men with a sensitive side. It's a very useful job and you're obviously not in it for the money." She looked him in the eye. "Why are you in it exactly?"

He held her gaze for a few minutes and then looked away. "My mother was a primary school teacher. I like children and I think I'll be a good teacher. I know it's not very fashionable and to be honest, I get more than my fair share of snide comments from people who don't know me, which frankly I find a little upsetting. Implying . . . well, things."

"I can imagine," Kate said. She was ashamed that she'd been thinking along the same lines herself. "I'm sorry, but I need to get to know you a little so that I can help you."

"I understand. But honestly, I want to be a teacher for all the right reasons. Trust me."

Something in those eyes made her believe him without question. She scribbled some preliminary notes on the foolscap pad. In this job, her two years studying psychology in UCD came in extremely useful — not that she could remember many of the technical terms. *Training to be primary school teacher*, she jotted down. *Wears heart on sleeve. Over sincere? Could be a problem. Too intense? Scaring women away? Mother complex? Oedipus thingy?*

"What are you writing?" asked Angus.

"Just notes, nothing for you to worry about."

"I'll stop trying to read upside down, then."

She smiled. "Yes. Better not to. Where are you studying?"

"Trinity College."

"And your last date was?"

"Excuse me?"

"Your last date — when was it exactly?"

"That's a bit personal isn't it?"

"Angus, it's only me you're talking to." She lowered her voice. "Kate from 'Dummy Dates', remember? I'm not here to judge you. I'm just trying to help, honestly."

"Sorry," he murmured. "I know. OK, it was last year."

"Can you give me some of the details? How do you feel it went?"

"Terribly. We had nothing to talk about and halfway through the meal she excused herself to go to the Ladies." He stared at his hands.

"And?" Kate asked gently.

"She never came back. I waited for half an hour and then left. I never saw her again."

"Right," Kate said a little more brightly than she'd intended. "That does happen. Two of my other clients have had exactly the same experience. One in a cinema and one in Wales."

"In Wales?"

"Yep. They went over to Wales on the ferry to spend a romantic weekend in a hotel. My client's date excused herself while they were having a drink in the hotel bar and Bob's your uncle."

"What happened?" he asked with interest.

"She'd gone upstairs, packed her bag and got the last ferry back to Dublin."

"No!"

"Honestly. He was devastated. Poor man."

"I can imagine."

"But he got over it. In fact he got engaged to a lovely girl only two months later."

"Really?"

"Yes, really. So, you see, there's hope for you all." She thought it prudent not to mention that the engagement had been broken after only a few weeks.

Angus considered this for a brief moment. "For us all, you mean?"

"No, for you all. All my clients."

"Have you already found your own true love then?" he asked.

"My own true love?" she repeated slowly. She had a right one on her hands here.

"Yes, you know, your soulmate."

Kate smiled indulgently. "Let's crack on, shall we?"

"Maybe you'll tell me later?"

She raised her eyebrows and ignored him. "Can you tell me a little about your previous dating history? Before the one who did the legger."

"OK, point taken. We're here to talk about me not you, right?"

She nodded curtly. "Dating history?"

"Right, well, there hasn't been a huge amount of it to tell the truth. I find it very difficult to talk to women. I tend to get nervous and clam up."

"You're talking to me," she pointed out.

"But that's different. You told me to pretend I was talking to my mother."

"True. Sorry, continue."

"There was Sandy in school, we went out for two weeks just before the debs. She was in the Computer Club with me."

"And what happened?"

"She dumped me at the debs for a guy from the debating team. Then there was Dina."

"Dina? Tell me about her?"

"She was from Bangor. I studied Computer Science in college and I met her there. We were together for two years. Dina was special."

His voice became wistful and Kate allowed him time to collect his thoughts.

"She married my best friend last summer. I'd asked him to keep an eye on her while I was in Germany for two months working on my Master's. I never believed he'd betray me like that. Anyway he did and after that, there was the legger woman as you called her and that's about it."

Let down and hurt badly by friend and ex-girlfriend ("Dina"), Kate jotted down, *self-esteem problems?, honest, seems sincere.*

"Thank you for sharing that with me," she said, putting down her foolscap pad. "And now can I ask you — what are you looking for in a woman? What qualities do you find important?"

Angus considered for a moment. "Honesty," he began hesitantly. "I'd like someone I can trust, and someone kind. She'd have to like children, I guess, and have a big heart. Someone a bit pretty maybe, but I'm not too bothered."

"You said you liked older women?"

Angus shrugged his shoulders. "I don't know why I said that to tell the truth. I just thought someone a little older might be less inclined to judge me and might accept me for who I am."

"And is that important to you — acceptance?"

"Of course, isn't that what everyone wants — to be accepted and loved for who they are?"

"I suppose so."

He stared at the table and then looked up again. "This isn't how I thought it would be, you know."

"What?" she asked.

"You, I suppose. All this. I thought you'd just give me some hints on how to dress and some killer chat-up lines."

"But you could get that from a book or a magazine. I try to get a little deeper, get down to the root of the problem."

"And what's my problem, Doctor?"

"I'm not sure yet," she said honestly. "You seem a very decent young man and . . ."

"Why did you call me that?"

"What?"

"Young man? You can't be much older than me."

"I don't know why," she replied. "I don't suppose I am."

"To establish professional distance?" he suggested.

"Maybe."

"What age are you anyway?" he said. "If you don't mind me asking."

"Actually I do. And as I keep reminding you, I'm not the one we're here to talk about, am I?"

"Sorry, I just find other people far more interesting than myself, I guess."

"So do I. But I get paid for finding out about other people and you don't. So let's move on." She glanced at her watch. "We only have another ten minutes before this session is over."

"What's next?"

"I'm going to advise you on your appearance and then we're going to set up a dummy date so that I can get a feel for how you behave on a first date. Then I'll give you a full report with some recommendations."

"And then?"

"It's up to you to use the information I've supplied."

"And will the dummy date be with you?"

"I'll have to check my diary. I think all my employees are pretty much booked up for the next few weeks. I presume you'd like the date as soon as possible?"

"Yes."

"Well then it will be me all right."

"Good." He smiled.

"So, appearance," she said trying to veer the conversation back onto safer ground. "What do you think women like men to wear?"

"I'd say they like them to look smart and coordinated. And clean," he added as an afterthought.

"Good. And what type of clothes do you wear generally?"

"This kind of thing," he said gesturing to his chest. "Although I keep this waistcoat for special occasions. Normally it's just the polo neck or maybe a checked shirt."

"I see." Kate bit the top of her pen.

"You don't approve of the waistcoat, do you?"

"No."

"Why not?"

"Honestly?"

He nodded.

"It's too loud. And not very fashionable."

"Oh. Mum made it for me. It's my lucky waistcoat."

"Right." She could hardly tell him how awful it was now.

"If I said it was a post-modernist joke would I get away with it?" He tilted his head to the side.

"Not really."

"I see. I won't wear it again then."

"I didn't say that. Just don't wear it on the first date, OK?"

"Understood. And how about the shoes? You don't like them either, do you?"

"Truthfully?"

He nodded again.

"No, I think they're terrible," she said.

"They're going in the bin then. I've no major attachment to them and besides they're not all that comfortable. What about the jeans?" He looked at her face. She was wrinkling her nose slightly. "Another no-no. So give it to me straight — what should I be wearing?"

"On a first date you want to look smart yet not too formal. Clean, classic, ironed clothes always impress. As you're twenty-six I'd suggest something fashionable but not too over the top. Think Next or TopMan rather than cutting edge. A nice white shirt, a pair of jeans that fit properly — Levis, or something like that, not cheap chain store jeans, girls hate them; brown or black boots, and, if the budget will stretch to it, a nice simple well-made leather or suede jacket. And you'll need to get a haircut and maybe think of changing the frames of your glasses for something less severe."

Angus whistled. "Serious make-over stuff. I'm way off the mark, aren't I, Kate?"

"Just a little," she admitted.

"And does all that really make a difference — the haircut and the clothes?"

"Yes, it really does. Most people judge on first appearances whether they admit to it or not. It can make or break a first date."

"Well, I'll have a go. I have jeans that might be OK and runners, are runners acceptable?"

"Not really. They can be a bit scruffy."

"I think the budget might just about stretch to a pair of boots and a haircut. I have a white shirt — I'll get it pressed in the dry cleaners. And I have contacts instead of the glasses, should I wear those?"

"Definitely."

"Then I'm pretty much set." He smiled widely. "This is going to change my life, Kate, I can feel it in my bones."

"Great. Your time's up, I'm afraid. When would you like your dummy date?"

"How about next Wednesday night?"

"Fine."

"Where would you suggest?"

"It's usually best to go somewhere casual on the first date. I wouldn't always suggest dinner, unless you're confident that you can eat and talk without getting too nervous. Women do like to be taken out to dinner but sometimes a drink can be a little less intimidating for you both. Arrange it for the early evening — say sevenish — and if you're getting on well with your date you can always suggest dinner after the drink. Or maybe she'll even suggest it — if she's interested."

"And how will I know that?"

"I'll explain how to read the signs on the dummy date."

"Great. So how about seven in O'Connor's pub on Wednesday?"

"Perfect. I look forward to it."

"Really?"

She smiled at him. "Sure. Now I'm afraid I have a lunch appointment so you'll have to excuse me."

"A date?"

"Angus!" She laughed. Maybe she should try setting him up with Alex — they were as bad as each other.

"Sorry." He stood up and held out his hand.

She took it in hers and shook it. His grip was surprisingly firm. "Bye, Kate. See you on Wednesday."

"See you." She watched as he walked towards the door, managing to reach it safely and without incident this time.

Alex buzzed over to Kate's table as soon as he'd left. "Well, what's he like?"

"As always, Alex, I'm afraid I can't tell you. Client confidentiality and all that. But I would like a Chicken Caesar Salad and a fresh cup of coffee, thanks."

Alex sniffed. "Fine," she said and flounced away.

Kate reached into her bag and fished out her *Irish Times*. She loved Thursday's edition — the property pages and the new film reviews — lots to interest her. She began to read about a bijoux cottage in Burnaby, which sounded about as big as a shoebox, which was selling for over three hundred thousand euro. She'd never be able to afford to buy in Burnaby at this rate. The townhouse she shared with Molly was tiny and they spent the whole time trying not to get under each other's feet — which was difficult as there wasn't even enough room to pass comfortably in the hall and they shared a tiny shower-room. Damn, she remembered, I promised Molly I'd get a new bulb. The bathroom had no window and they'd been having showers by candle light for the last two days — romantic but not very practical. She got on well with her housemate but sometimes Molly could be a little anal about cleanliness and tidiness. It was best just to keep out of her way when she was on one of her regular "spring, summer, autumn or winter" cleaning sprees.

Kate had arrived back in Dublin nearly a year ago, after ten years living and working in Boston. But that was all in the past. Her new life lay in Burnaby — making enough money to buy a house in the area that felt like home, near her beloved Granny Lily. She got on fine with her mum and dad who had moved to Connemara after her dad had retired, but it was Lily who she'd always felt closest to. Her parents had had a rather tempestuous marriage when Kate was growing up, and she had loved staying in her granny's peaceful and cosy Burnaby house, away from her parents' continuous arguments and shouting matches. Her father, Billy, had always been a bit of a bully, with a furious temper, which had mellowed with age, than goodness, and Cleo, his wife and Kate's mum, had walked out on him several times over the years. But she always came back and they'd stayed together, mainly for their daughter's sake. Now, in their early sixties, they seemed to have come to some sort of strained truce.

Kate had written to Lily every week when she was in the States, and once her granny had learnt how to use the Internet at evening classes there was no stopping her. They conversed every day on-line, sometimes several times a day. In fact, it was Lily who had advised her to come home to Ireland before "all the good men are snapped up", as she'd put it. If only Lily knew the whole story. Kate had no intention of letting a man get close to her ever again — American, Irish or any other nationality for that matter. But she was enjoying being home and knew she'd made the right decision. Besides, Lily hadn't been all that well recently and Kate wanted to be there for her — especially as she was her only grandchild.

"Here you are," said Alex.

Kate moved the newspaper to allow Alex to place the steaming mug of coffee and large white plate in front of her. The plate was heaped full with light green lettuce, croutons and strips of juicy looking chicken. The dish was topped with a generous amount of Parmesan shavings and dusted with freshly ground black pepper — just the way Kate liked it.

"Thanks, Alex," she said. "That looks great."

"Have you any more clients coming in today?" asked Alex hopefully.

"No." Kate smiled.

"Pity," Alex said, walking away.

Kate tucked into her salad with relish and thought about Angus. He was an interesting one all right. She really was quite looking forward to Wednesday to tell the truth — in her professional capacity of course. She wondered what he'd look like with a haircut and contacts. As she speared a piece of chicken with her fork she remembered that she'd have to talk to Trina again today about the shoe lines that weren't selling. She'd tried talking sense into the woman earlier this morning, but they'd ended up arguing. Kate had pointed out that it made no sense waiting until the end of the summer season to sell skimpy sandals and white shoes — they might as well cut their losses early. Maybe that way they'd shift them all before July was out but Trina was having none of it, control freak that she was.

Sometimes Kate wished she had Molly's job — books could be returned to their publisher with no questions asked. Light bulb! she thought suddenly. She'll kill me if I forget again. She pulled a blue ballpoint out of her bag and wrote the word in capital letters on the back of her left hand. *LIGHTBULB!!*

CHAPTER
THREE

Paige

"What do you mean you're closing 'Little Orchard' for August?" Paige demanded. "You can't close for a whole month — what will I do?"

Clodagh sighed. "I'm sorry, Paige, but we can't get staff to cover us in August, and me and Ethel badly need a holiday."

"What about Connie? Will she not be around? You must be able to do something!"

"Connie's going back to Sydney for the month. And before you ask, Marta's English isn't good enough yet to run the place. Even if it was, she's only been here three months and she'd need at least six staff to keep the place open. We just can't do it — I'm sorry — we have tried, believe me."

Paige felt bad — it was hardly Clodagh's fault she had to close. "No, I'm sorry. I didn't mean to jump down your throat. It's just I rely on you to be able to work, that's all."

"I understand, honestly. But there's nothing we can do." Clodagh, who ran the crèche and after-school club had had this exact conversation with many of the parents. But her hands were tied — she had to give her staff holidays. She couldn't afford to pay them as well as she would like to, so a month's holidays in the summer was the least she could do.

"Do you have any suggestions?" Paige asked. "Is there somewhere else open that you can recommend?"

"Not really," said Clodagh. "You could try Nora Hilton's place in Sandybay but I think it's full to tell the truth."

"Do you have the number? I'll give it a try."

Clodagh flicked through the large desk diary, wrote down Nora's number on a yellow sticky note and handed it to Paige.

"Thanks, I appreciate it," said Paige. "And you're open again . . .?"

"Monday the third of September. The first day of school for most of the older children. I've booked Alfie and Callum in already — Alfie into the baby room and Callum into Montessori and afternoon care — is that right?"

"Yes." Paige nodded. "We'll see you on Monday. And sorry for being short with you."

Clodagh smiled. "Not to worry. I know how busy you are, Paige. I read all about the proposed refugee centre on Burnaby Crescent. Good luck with it anyway."

"Thanks. I hope it gets resolved soon. Everyone's getting a little heated about the whole thing."

"But the Crescent would be ideal for the families wouldn't it? I know a lot of them have young children and it's just beside the park. I can't really see what the problem is."

"Not everyone sees it like that," Paige said evenly. "I have to represent all my constituents and they have all kinds of views. Especially the Crescent residents."

"I can imagine. Mrs Calloway from the gallery lives there, doesn't she?"

Paige nodded but said nothing. Connie Calloway was the current thorn in her side and the over-opinionated woman was calling into Paige that very evening — a prospect that didn't exactly fill her with joy. "Anyway, I'd better collect my little monsters before they think I've abandoned them."

Clodagh led her towards the baby room at the back of the building. Paige looked through the glass at the top of the door and studied the row of baby seats, looking for Alfie. She spotted him almost immediately. He was crying and Marta was crouching beside him, offering him a bottle. He hit her hand away, sending the bottle flying across the room.

"He's been a bit cranky today," said Clodagh leading her in. "Teeth coming through I expect."

Paige sighed. "Tell me about it. He was like a demon last night — wouldn't settle at all. His poor little gums were sore and he was dribbling like a dog. We didn't get a wink of sleep. I was hoping he'd be better today."

"You never know," Clodagh said kindly as they walked towards him. "He might be all right by this evening. Fingers crossed."

Paige bent down, unclipped Alfie from his chair and lifted him up. "There, there, little man. What's bothering you?" He'd obviously been crying for a while — his face was red and blotchy and his breath was uneven. Paige felt a stab of guilt pierce her heart. She shouldn't have left him here all day. He hadn't been happy this morning when she'd got him ready and he'd cried all the way to "Little Orchard". She was a terrible mother. She held him close to her.

Marta handed her another bottle. "Try this one," she said gently in her accented English, "it's nice and warm."

"Thanks, Marta." Paige swung Alfie around so that he was nestled in the crook of her left arm and put the teat in his mouth. He sucked immediately, his crying forgotten.

"He would have been the same at home," said Clodagh, as if reading Paige's mind. "He's just having a bad day. Marta's been great with him — rocking him in his seat and walking him around the room in the buggy. He was in good hands."

Paige could feel tears prick the back of her eyes. Clodagh really was a find — she knew exactly the right thing to say at exactly the right moment. "Thanks," she murmured gratefully.

Clodagh smiled. She knew how difficult it was for working mums. "That's what I'm here for. Now, let's find Callum, shall we?"

Clodagh helped Paige gather together all Alfie's bits — baby bag, bottles, food containers, buggy and baby seat. She clicked the seat into the buggy expertly and pushed it in front of Paige who was still holding Alfie.

As they entered the other, larger room Callum came crashing towards them and hurled himself at his mother's legs.

"Callum!" she scolded. "You nearly knocked me over and I'm holding Alfie."

"Sorry, Mum." He looked up at her, beaming. "Can I see Alfie?"

"Sure." She bent down and showed Callum his brother's face. "Now don't poke him or anything, he's not a very happy camper today."

"Why not?" asked Callum. "Does he have a poo in his nappy?"

"No, he doesn't!" Paige tried not to laugh. "His little teeth are coming through his gums, that's all. But if he did have a smelly nappy I'd make you change it."

Callum wrinkled his nose. "Yucky!"

"Let's get you both to the car," said Paige. "Say goodbye to Clodagh now and go and put your coat on, there's a good fellow."

"Bye, Clodagh Woda," he shouted as he ran towards the coat pegs. "See you later, alligator. Not too soon, you big baboon."

"Hey, that's my line." Clodagh laughed.

"Sorry," Paige said. "His manners are getting really bad."

"I'm quite used to it. He's by no means the worst. He's just lively."

Paige smiled. "I'd love to ask you who was but I'm sure you wouldn't tell me."

"Try guessing," Clodagh suggested with an evil glint in her eyes.

Paige lowered her voice. "I'd say Axel and Lolita Philips, am I right?" naming the ultra-spoilt children of one of Burnaby's best know socialites, Cathy Philips, co-owner of Baroque shoe shop.

"I couldn't possibly say." Clodagh gave a tiny nod and grinned widely.

"You've made my day." Paige laughed. "I'll see you on Monday morning."

"Bright and early." Clodagh opened the main door for Paige and helped her down the three steps with Alfie's buggy.

"Bye poo-face," Callum said loudly as soon as she closed the door behind them.

Paige glared at him. "I hope she didn't hear that. You are a very rude little boy and there'll be no telly for you this evening. Do you hear me? Tea, bath and straight to bed."

"Muuumm!" he moaned. "That's not fair."

"Quiet!" she snapped. "Mummy's tired and she won't take any more nonsense from you, young man, do you hear me?"

He nodded.

Alfie began to cry again.

"Now look what you've done." Paige pushed the buggy down the gravel drive towards the car. Callum trailed behind her. "Sorry, Mummy. Can I have a treat on the way home?"

"What do you think, Callum?"

"Yes?" he asked, his little face upturned hopefully.

She ignored him, unlocked the car, unclicked Alfie's seat from the buggy and lifted it onto the back seat, all the while listening to his ever-increasing roars. "Please, let me just get home sane," she murmured. "You're

OK, Alfie," she soothed, lodging his bottle into his mouth and cupping his plump pink hands around it. "Here's your bottle. There's a good boy." He looked at her for a moment, contemplating whether to continue crying or not, then decided he was actually quite hungry and began to suck. "Thank you, baby." Paige let out a sigh of relief. She turned around to tell Callum to get in beside his brother but he'd disappeared. She put her hand to her head. Not again. Callum had a habit of playing hide-and-seek at the most inopportune moments. Her nerves were frayed enough as it was today, she didn't know if she could take any more.

"Callum!" she shouted. "Come here right now or there'll be trouble. Do you hear me?"

She leant her back against the car. It was just as well that she wasn't premenstrual or she'd have started crying right about now. In fact, she thought suddenly, have I had my period this month? I must have had, but I don't remember it. She heard gravel crunching on the far side of the car.

"Come on, Callum. Get into the car, please."

"Boo!" He jumped in front of her and waved his hands above his head.

"Very funny, now what have I told you about wandering off?"

"But I was beside the car, you just couldn't see me. I was doing good hiding."

Paige held him by the arm to stop him running off again.

"That hurts, Mummy!" he protested. "Leave me alone."

44

"I'll give you hurt if you don't get into the car this instant, young man, do you hear me?"

He climbed in and sat on the booster seat.

"Keep still, I'm trying to fasten your seat belt."

"I hate seatbelts!" He wriggled again.

"The guards will arrest you if you don't wear your seatbelt," she threatened.

"They never wear theirs," he retorted. "I've seen them."

"Yes, they do," Paige lied, thinking that her son had a point. "Most of the time anyway. But sometimes they need to be able to jump out of cars quickly to catch robbers and things, that's all."

"I need to catch robbers," he said, wriggling again.

"No you don't," she said firmly. "And for the last time, stay still." She finally managed to click him in, tucking the seatbelt clasp under the upholstery of the back seat just as her husband Tom had shown her. It was the only way to stop Callum unclicking himself as soon as she started driving. They'd had to use duct tape over the clasp up until last weekend when Tom had made the loose upholstery discovery while cleaning her car for her.

As Paige sat behind the steering wheel and turned the key in the ignition she could feel pressure building behind her temples. Great, she thought, a tension headache. Just what I need before a meeting with Madame Calloway.

"Tom, are you in?" Paige shouted as she walked into the hall. "Tom?"

"In here."

She walked into the kitchen. "Be an angel and give me a hand with the kids, will you? They're still in the car and Connie Calloway will be here any minute."

He groaned. "Could she not have met you earlier or this evening? Dinner time is not exactly convenient, is it?"

"I know, and I'm sorry. But she insisted on meeting me today and she has some kind of gala charity do later this evening."

"So as usual you're expected to bend over backwards to suit her, is that it?"

"Something like that." Paige smiled wryly. "I'm sorry. But with the elections coming up soon . . ."

"I know, she's a well respected member of the community with a lot of contacts, I understand. But the sooner the bloody elections are over the better."

"Not long now," Paige promised. "The polling date is due to be announced any day, it's only a matter of time."

"Good! I've saved up all my holidays to help you, but at this stage I'm getting itchy feet."

"I know and I really appreciate it, my love. You'll make a great campaign manager."

"I don't know about . . . is that Alfie screaming?"

They ran outside the house.

"Callum, what are you doing?" asked Tom.

Callum quickly took Alfie's bottle out of his mouth and hid it behind his back. He smiled sheepishly. "I was having a drink, I was thirsty. Mummy wouldn't get me a treat in the shops."

"Give your brother back his bottle this instant," said Paige testily. "Will you take Callum inside, Tom? I'll deal with Alfie."

"Sure." Tom unbuckled the seatbelt and let Callum free. Callum jumped up, sprung out of the car and ran into the house. Tom immediately followed him. Callum on the loose in this kind of humour was no joke.

"He's not allowed any telly," Paige shouted to their disappearing backs.

"Come on, little man," she said to Alfie, "let's get you out."

"Connie, how nice to see you, won't you come in?"

Connie Calloway stepped over the bulging baby bag which had been unceremoniously dumped in the hall, past the litter of outdoor shoes and overcoats heaped to one side and noted the broken radiator cover that was hanging from the wall by a single hinge.

Paige led her into the sitting room to the right. Connie studied the seat of the leather sofa carefully before she sat down. She took in the small painting beside the window — a reasonable attempt at a still life, practically worthless, of course, but pleasant enough, and the random pieces of rather fine antique furniture — gifts from relatives no doubt. She wouldn't have thought of Paige as a collector.

"Would you like some coffee?" asked Paige politely.

"Please, black, no sugar."

As Paige walked into the kitchen she frowned. Callum was sitting at the kitchen table, eating some toast and watching television.

"Sorry," Tom said sheepishly. "I said he could watch one episode of *Rugrats*. I need to get Alfie ready for bed." Alfie was sitting in his little chair with a fresh white Babygro and vest by his feet.

"Don't worry about it," Paige said mildly. "I probably would have done the same myself." She flicked on the kettle, luckily still warm from Tom's cup of tea and put some biscuits on a plate. "I was talking to Clodagh today. They're closing 'Little Orchard' for August. She can't get extra staff to cover the holidays."

Tom whistled. "Not good news for us. Any ideas?"

"She gave me the number of a place in Sandybay, I'll try that tomorrow."

"Otherwise?"

Paige shrugged her shoulders.

"My mum might help if we asked her," Tom suggested. "She'd take Alfie anyway."

"That would be great but Callum's the problem," said Paige.

"I'm not a problem," Callum insisted.

"Little pitchers and all that." Tom smiled. He turned towards Callum. "No love, we were talking about another Callum."

"Oh." Callum accepted this immediately and went back to watching *Rugrats*.

"Would there be any students around for the month do you think?" asked Tom. "We could pay them well."

"I'm not sure," Paige said doubtfully. "Do you think they'd be able to cope?"

"You never know. If we found the right person."

"It's a possibility. I'll put an ad up in the supermarket tomorrow. Can you type something up for me later?"

"No problem. I have a bit of work to do anyway after dinner."

"Not again," Paige sighed. The kettle boiled, she poured the steaming water into the cafetière, lowered the plunger, pulled out a tray and put the coffee, two mugs and the biscuit plate on it.

"Sorry, love. August will be quieter, I promise." Tom was a manager in the Castle Building Society in Dun Laoghaire, in charge of the mortgage department. It was a highly responsible and very busy job, and one he was becoming less and less enamoured of as time went on. He'd love to spend more time with the children but it just wasn't possible these days. He had to cover their own mortgage after all. Not to mention the bills. As a local councillor, Paige was only paid a nominal salary. She got reasonably generous expenses on top of this but, in total, it didn't even cover the crèche fees. It was Tom's salary that supported the household, a fact he never alluded to, being the kind and decent man that he was.

"Into the fire." She kissed him on the cheek before picking up the tray.

"Here you go, Connie," Paige said, walking through the door.

"Thank you. I thought you'd forgotten all about me."

"Sorry, had to wait for the kettle to boil." Paige placed the tray on the coffee table, sat down in front of it and began to pour.

Connie said nothing.

"So," Paige opened, "you wanted to see me."

"Yes. And I'm sure you know exactly what it's about."

"The refugee centre?"

"Precisely. We just can't allow it to happen in the Crescent. You understand that, don't you, my dear?"

Paige refused to be drawn. "Why don't you explain your objections and I'll just jot them down." She took a notebook and pen from the desk by the window.

"Right, first of all, they're all foreigners, aren't they? We don't know what kind of diseases they may have brought with them, do we?" Connie sniffed.

"Objection number one: foreign diseases. Any foreign diseases in particular, Connie, or just diseases in general."

Connie looked at her. Was Paige trying to be funny? She wasn't smiling but Connie got the distinct impression that she wasn't exactly taking this matter as seriously as she should. "Aids, my dear girl, for one. And malaria and typhoid, things like that. And smallpox."

Paige wrote everything down.

Connie continued, "And the Crescent doesn't have the car parking spaces for lots of extra cars. It's already a big problem."

"I don't think the refugees will own many cars, to tell the truth," Paige said evenly. "Most of them won't have been in the country very long."

"Well then," said Connie, "they won't even have any English, will they?"

"Probably not. The centre would offer English lessons to all age groups, including children."

"Another problem. Children. It's a busy road and there's no pedestrian crossing to the park."

"And will I put down house prices?" Paige suggested.

Connie stared at her. "That isn't one of our main reasons, but it is a factor, yes. The residents are worried that it would affect the value of their properties."

"Especially you, I would imagine, as you're right next door to the proposed centre."

"*All* the residents," Connie stressed.

"And is everyone in agreement on this?" Paige asked. "The objections, I mean."

"Everyone except one or two," Connie admitted. "But they're new to the area, they don't really count."

"Who are new?"

"Harry Masterson and Darcy Wallis."

"Darcy has lived in Burnaby for years," said Paige. "She's hardly a newcomer."

"But she's only been on the Crescent for three," Connie pointed out. "Making her a newcomer."

"Right, I see." Paige glanced at her watch. She was starving. "Any more objections, Connie? I know you have a dinner to go to later."

"My dear, I've only just started. The dinner can wait. This is far more important."

Paige sighed inwardly. It was going to be a long evening.

CHAPTER
FOUR

Molly

Molly slipped the key into the lock of Happily Ever After and turned it. She stepped inside, closed the door behind her and quickly made her way to the office where she disabled the alarm. It wasn't even eight yet and the rest of the staff wouldn't be in for at least another hour but she'd slept really badly — tossing and turning all night and finally waking up for good at six a.m. She'd lain in bed for a while but had only got to worrying about the future of the bookshop and about last night's rather unnerving phone call from her ex-boyfriend, Denis — both good reasons for her fretful slumber.

Molly sat down at the desk she shared with Anita. She'd come in early to try to get some writing done. For several years now she'd been cutting her teeth on a succession of short stories — building up her confidence and learning how to make her characters and stories come to life. What she really wanted to write was a big, romantic saga, like *Gone With the Wind*, only set in nineteenth-century Ireland, encompassing all the sweeping political and social changes that had taken place at that time. She had a main character in mind — a feisty heroine who would start off as a kitchen maid and go on to become actively involved in the 1916 Easter rising, finally meeting and marrying a fictional tragi-hero, not unlike Michael Collins. She even had a title — "The Price of Gold".

Molly had only told two people in the whole world about her writing — Anita, who had been hugely supportive and had offered to read her work at any time, and Denis, who had laughed, patted her on the head and said "Stick to the book-selling, Molly, you're not a writer. You don't have it in you".

After fifteen long minutes staring at a blank computer screen, Molly gave up and pulled a blank yellow-sheeted foolscap pad towards her. If she couldn't write, she may as well do some work instead. She found a pen in the top drawer and wrote "Saturday 12th July — Book Club Meeting and Rosemary Hamilton Event" on the top of the first sheet in large capitals, intending to make a list of all the things she needed each member of staff to do as soon as they all came in. She then put the pen down, sat back and sighed. Her brain just wouldn't click in this morning. Coffee, she thought, that's what I need, strong, black coffee. Matty would definitely be in Coffee Heaven baking or making soup or something, even if they didn't open till nine. He always was. You could set your watch by him. She stood up, took her wallet out of her bag and walked out of the office. She decided against setting the alarm — she'd only be a few minutes after all.

"Morning, Molly, I was wondering who was banging so insistently on my door," Matty smiled. He brushed his sandy-blonde hair out of his eyes, sprinkling flour onto his freckled temples in the process.

"Sorry, Matty," said Molly. "Hope I wasn't interrupting anything."

"Just the usual early-morning scone-making, nothing important. Coffee is it?"

She nodded and smiled. "How did you guess?"

"Come on in. I've just put on the first brew of the day — Columbian all right?"

"Perfect."

He poured the rich steaming-hot liquid into a large paper cup, popped on a plastic lid and handed it to her.

"Thanks, how much do I owe you?"

He waved his hand at her. "Nothing. On the house."

"Are you sure?"

"Yes. Sorry I can't stop and chat but I have soup to prepare."

"That's OK. Thanks again."

As she unlocked the bookshop for the second time she got the distinct feeling that someone was watching her. She turned around and looked up and down Burnaby's main street. It was completely empty. She must have been imagining it. Although Denis had been known to follow her. In fact that was how they'd first met.

The Molly and Denis saga had begun almost twelve years ago. When Molly and Paige reached the ripe old age of sixteen they were finally allowed to take the train home from school — Loreto Convent in Killiney — on their own. There were one or two rules, of course. They weren't allowed to talk to strangers, including the boys from the neighbouring Christian Brothers' College, Killiney (CBC) and had to come straight home after their after-school activities. What their collective parents didn't know was that neither of the girls were actually members of the debating club, the school magazine, or the choir. They both played hockey all right for the Senior Thirds, and now and again Molly wrote articles for "The Loreto Killiney News", usually detailed and somewhat hyperbolic accounts of hockey matches — *The crowd went wild as Paige Brady flicked the ball into the back of the opponent's net with all the grace and fury of an African gazelle . . .* — mainly to throw the parentals off the scent. Because after school all the Loreto girls congregated under the green bridge in the train station, on the southbound platform, shielded from nosy neighbourhood eyes, and smoked until they were green in the face, matching their putrid-coloured green uniforms perfectly. The station platform was also where they met the CBC boys — small in height compared to themselves, kitted out in purple and grey, and far more nervous of the girls than the convent girls were of them, however cool and together they seemed.

Molly always felt a bit of an outsider with the station gang. She didn't smoke for one thing — she didn't see the point really. It tasted nasty and made you feel ill — what was to like? Paige made it look cool of course. She could even French inhale, inhaling the smoke through her nose. The CBC boys were very impressed. When

Paige learnt how to blow large smoke rings, she was considered the bee's knees.

Paige had lots of boyfriends — she changed regularly and was currently working her way through fifth year CBC after cutting her teeth on the boys her own age. Molly had never had one, apart from Garvan Evans, if you could count him. He'd only gone out with her for two hours in order to talk to Paige. But Paige had been so unimpressed with his treatment of her best friend that she'd completely ignored him when he'd introduced himself. But Denis was different.

Paige had noticed him first, not in the way she usually noticed boys though. Denis wasn't exactly what you'd call good-looking. Smallish and thin, with wispy dark brown hair that always looked as if it could do with a good wash, and eyes that were almost permanently fixed on the ground in front of him. The other boys pretty much ignored him at the train station but he always insisted on standing only a few feet away from them, as if some of their social skills with the convent girls might be transferred to him by osmosis if he stood close enough. Paige had also noticed him because, according to her, he was always staring at Molly. Molly refused to believe this of course. Why would he be staring at her for goodness sake? She was plain and didn't wear any make-up unlike the other girls. Her skirt was the regulation length, instead of hiked up towards her armpits, and even her shoes were boring — sensible brown lace-ups instead of the kitten-heeled black suede stilettos of her peers. Or, if you were very cool like Paige, flat black impossibly pointy winkle pickers with dinky fake silver zips adorning the toes.

One day when Paige was at the dentists getting fitted for a brace (which, to Molly's knowledge, she wore once then hid at the bottom of the kitchen rubbish bin, under some carrot and potato peelings and claimed she'd lost it) Molly was left to make the journey home alone. It was a nice enough day and she didn't mind too much to tell the truth. It meant she could go straight home instead of pretending to have debating. She'd just started a new Virginia Andrews novel and was dying to get stuck into the strange and warped world, which she found totally addictive. Her head was stuck in her book at the station and on the train. Two stops later she'd arrived in Burnaby, crossed the railway bridge and had started to make her way home, her nose still stuck in her book. She'd discovered many years ago that if she progressed slowly, she could read whilst walking. Once she'd walked into a concrete bollard and grazed her knees and she'd often narrowly missed being mowed down by a fast-travelling baby buggy, but generally she got home in one piece after managing to read a chapter or two of the current favourite.

Today, as she read, she could hear footsteps behind her. She waited for the person to catch up with her and overtake her plodding pace but it didn't happen. They stayed behind her. This began to unnerve her and she began to walk even more slowly, tucking herself into the side of the pavement, willing them to pass. But they didn't. Finally she'd had enough. She was nervous, scared and more than a little cross. Who was trying to keep her from her book? She took a deep breath and turned around.

"Oh," she squeaked in surprise.

"Hello," said Denis, blushing furiously.

"Are you following me?"

He coughed nervously. "Um, no."

"What are you doing then?"

"Um, I don't really know."

She put her finger in her book to keep her place and stood up straight. "Are you a stalker?"

"A what?"

"You know — do you follow people all the time? A stalker. Famous people have them."

He still looked confused.

"Never mind," she sighed. "Do you live in Burnaby?"

"No, Bray."

"So you are following me!"

"Maybe." He shrugged his shoulders and stared at the pavement in front of him.

"Why?" she asked in amazement. She'd never been followed home before, except by a lost dog, but that didn't count. In fact, even Paige hadn't been followed home.

"Because I wanted to meet you," he said still staring down. "You look nice. Not like the other girls."

"Oh!" Molly was completely taken aback. She hadn't expected that at all.

From that moment on they were inseparable — almost thirteen years in total.

Until April this year that was, when Molly had had a change of heart and Denis, in turn had his heart broken. She'd made the decision that there must be more to life than having a safe, comfortable relationship and a safe, comfortable job. She wasn't even sure she still loved Denis, and she'd stopped fancying him ages ago, so being with him had just become a habit. And encouraged by Paige, after several long, agonizing days she'd finally managed to convince Denis that she really meant it when she said she didn't want to be with him any more. When he'd called into her house and proposed in May after a month apart and daily phone calls, her heart had sunk to the pit of her stomach, leaving her even more convinced that she'd made the right decision. It was only then that he'd left her alone.

But last night he'd rung her mobile, knowing that it was rarely on in the evenings and had left an extraordinary message. "Hi, Molly. Just to say, you don't have to worry any more, I'm completely over you. I've met a lovely girl called Carrie and things are going great. We're getting quite serious. I just thought I should tell you. Bye . . ." Bastard! He knew Molly had a jealous streak as green as the Incredible Hulk. But this wasn't going to make any difference this time, her mind was set. She was very happy that he'd met someone else and she wanted the best for him. And she was going to ring him later and tell him so.

"Molly, Molly." Anita's voice rang out loud and clear as a bell from the shop floor.

She raised her head from the computer where she'd been reordering books for the crime department and looked at her watch. Ten to nine, almost time to open.

Seconds later the office door swung open. She'd taken to rising earlier now that she was no longer in charge of the shop.

"There you are," said Anita. "Did you not hear me?"

"I did, I was finishing an order."

"Already? How long have you been in?"

"A little while," Molly admitted. "We have a busy day ahead and I wanted to be prepared."

"Milo and Sam are coming in this afternoon for the event. Just to warn you."

"Checking up on us?" Molly saved her work, sent the order down the line and stood up.

Anita ignored her. "They won't be here for the Book Club but said they'd both try to make the next one."

She stared at Anita. "Why would they do that?"

"I don't know, out of interest I suppose. What's wrong?"

"Reading is not a spectator sport. If they want to attend a meeting they'll have to read the book, same as everyone else."

"Fine, I'll tell them. I won't ask what's wrong with you this fine morning as you'll only bite my head off."

"Sorry. I didn't sleep very well, that's all. I'll be fine in a while, honestly."

"You'd better be. I think I hear Felix at the door, I'll just let him in." She turned on her heels leaving Molly in the office.

Molly leant against the desk. She thought of ringing Paige but didn't want to wake her up. Tom usually took the two boys for a walk to the shops on Saturday morning, leaving Paige to have a lie-in before the Book

Club meeting. Still, she'd see her later and maybe they could have coffee together before the Rosemary Hamilton event kicked off at three. The phone rang, interrupting her thoughts.

"Hello, I wanted to find out about the event this afternoon. Is it booked out?"

"No, not quite," Molly replied. "Will I take your name and reserve you a seat? It starts at three."

"Please."

Molly scribbled down the woman's details. "Thanks for ringing. See you later."

The phone rang again almost instantly. She sighed. At least it would keep her mind off Denis, she thought.

"Is everyone here?" Paige asked the rest of the Book Club members, looking around the room.

"Harry's not coming, he sent his regrets," said Anita. "He has a wedding today and they want seven extra cactus arrangements for the tables apparently. He's doing his nut."

"Cactus arrangements at a wedding?" sniffed Trina. "Surely not? Whose wedding exactly?"

"No idea," Anita replied.

Kate came flying into the side room where the Book Club meetings were held. "Sorry I'm late, guys, have you started?"

"No," Paige said. "Out late were you? Another dummy date or a real one?"

"Dummy," Kate said.

"She doesn't do the normal kind, remember?" added Trina who thought that Kate's other job was very peculiar indeed. She'd much prefer if the girl would commit to Baroque on a full-time basis but there was no talking to her on the subject. She'd threatened to leave completely if Trina didn't stop going on at her. And that was the last thing Trina wanted. Kate might be odd but she was a damned fine salesperson whatever way you looked at it, and she sure as hell knew her shoes.

Kate ignored her. "I've only got halfway through the book, I'm sorry," she admitted as she squeezed in between Molly and Anita.

"That's OK," Paige said quickly before Trina had a chance to butt in. "Let's get going, shall we? Who'd like to start?" She looked around the table. This month's choice had been a sweeping literary saga by Booker award nominee, Francesca Scata.

"I will," said Cathy, "as I chose it. I was a bit disappointed to tell the truth. I loved her other books, which is why I suggested this one. But it's not as strong. I found the main character Elena a little unbelievable. I mean, if she was as stunningly beautiful as the author portrayed her, why didn't anyone realize that she was a woman masquerading as a man? It didn't make sense."

"You're right." Anita nodded. "It was a little unbelievable."

"But in those times wouldn't it have been so unbelievable that she would have got away with it?" Molly suggested. "It would have been such an outrageous thing to do in the nineteenth century, especially in England, to pose as a man and work in a newspaper, maybe it just wouldn't have crossed anyone's mind to question it. Nowadays, yes, she would have been questioned, but perhaps not then."

"But what about Oliver, her eventual husband?" Cathy demanded. "Surely he would have copped? He said he was attracted to her from the moment he realized she was a woman — that's rubbish! How can he suddenly have feelings like that? It doesn't make sense."

"Again, maybe not now, but this was set almost two hundred years ago," said Molly. "Things have changed. It wouldn't have been acceptable then to admit that you found a person who you thought was the same sex as you attractive."

"Maybe," Cathy allowed. "But the way their relationship was described and the sex scenes . . . I mean really, what baloney."

"I liked those," Anita said. "They were gentle and tender. We're just used to stronger stuff in modern books. But I thought the sex scenes were very much in keeping with the period. And I love her writing, it's so descriptive."

"She has a way with words all right," Paige said. "Remember that scene set in the corn field — that was stunning."

An hour and a half later they'd finished dissecting the book and were trying to decide on a text for the following meeting, which always provoked much discussion.

"Not Anita Shreve again, please," Trina moaned. "I know you like her, Cathy, but we've read her to death."

"Trina has a point," said Kate. "How about Anne Tyler? She had a new one out."

"Harry's not that keen on her, remember?" Molly said.

"But he's not here, is he?" Paige smiled. "How about something different? Alan Frost has a new book out — *Stradbrook* — we could try it. It would be more literary than some of the books we read."

"Wouldn't mind giving it a go," Cathy said. "He's a Booker winner, isn't he?"

"That's right — for one of his earlier books. *Stradbrook* sounds interesting, have you heard much about it, Anita?" asked Molly

Anita nodded. "The book's been getting some rave reviews in the press all right, but that doesn't always mean much. The book's out in paperback next month but I might be able to get early copies off the rep if I ask nicely."

"Excellent!" Paige looked around the table. "Now are we all agreed?"

Everyone nodded.

"I'll order it and ring you all when it comes in," Anita promised.

"How much will it be?" Trina asked.

"About ten euro, I think."

"Fine."

"You'll treat us all then, Trina, I presume?" Cathy said smiling. Rich as she was, Trina was known for her Scrooge-like tendencies.

Trina kept quiet. She knew Cathy was only teasing her.

"Who's coming for coffee?" asked Paige. "It's on me."

"We have to get back to the shop," Cathy said, looking at Trina pointedly. "We're supposed to open at twelve."

"Only on Book Club days." Trina sniffed. "Otherwise it's strictly ten o'clock, that's what we agreed." Although if she'd had her way she would have made Kate miss Book Club and open up on Saturdays without them. Kate had Cathy wrapped around her little finger.

Molly turned to Anita. "Is it OK if I pop out for a few minutes?"

"Of course," Anita said. "But don't be too long. Milo and Sam will be here soon."

"Don't remind me," Molly groaned. "I'll be back before one, I promise."

"So, how are things at home?" Molly asked Paige as they walked into Coffee Heaven. "Tom has the kids, I presume."

"Yes, poor man. Callum's being rather difficult these days. He was like a devil this morning. He took a swipe at me with his shoe earlier and really hurt me."

Molly's eyes widened.

"Don't look at me like that," said Paige. "He's five. Five-year-olds do that sort of thing, it's quite normal."

"But maybe you should . . ."

"Drop it," said Paige. "I'm not bringing him to see anyone, especially to some child psychologist who will make him even worse. He'll grow out of it."

Molly wasn't so sure. He was due to start school this September and she pitied his poor teacher.

"How are my favourite Saturday customers?" Alex smiled at the small group. "I've booked a table for you in the back."

"Thanks, Alex," said Molly.

"No Harry today?" Alex asked.

"Busy with a wedding," Molly explained.

"I see. And what can I get you all?" Alex pulled out her small notepad and pencil.

"The usual, I'd say," Kate said, "two cappuccinos and a latte, is that right, ladies?"

They all nodded in the affirmative.

As soon as they'd settled into their coffees, Paige heard a familiar shrill voice behind her.

"I need to talk to you urgently, Paige," Connie Calloway mock whispered. "It's about . . . well, you know."

"The refugee centre," Paige said, trying not to sigh.

"The proposed centre," Connie corrected her.

"Would you mind terribly if I finished my coffee? I'm with my Book Club friends you see."

"Not at all," Connie replied. "I'll just sit behind you here and wait." She pulled a chair over and did exactly that — sat directly behind Paige, Kate and Molly, tapping her fingers together impatiently. After a few minutes Paige admitted defeat and moved to a table at the far side of the shop to talk to her in private.

"Poor Paige," Kate said to Molly after she'd gone. "Does that happen a lot?"

"Unfortunately yes." Molly drained her coffee cup and placed it back down on the table. "She's far too nice to people like that if you ask me. I'd tell them where to go."

Kate laughed. "You wouldn't go very far in politics then, my girl. Paige is contesting the next election, isn't she?"

"How do you know that? It's supposed to be a secret."

"Cathy told me. Her husband is backing Annette thingy apparently and Annette thinks Paige will be her main opposition."

"Annette Higgins? Wasn't her dad done for tax evasion a few years ago?"

"I believe he paid it all back, according to Cathy anyway."

"Let off by his political cronies more like."

"Shush, someone will hear you."

"Don't care if they do. Paige is so decent and hard working. It makes my blood boil that someone like Madame Higgins can swan in and win elections on her father's rather dodgy name."

"She was a councillor for a while, like Paige," Kate pointed out.

"Yes and a pretty terrible one from all accounts," Molly snapped.

"I didn't realize you felt so strongly about politics," Kate said. "It's a whole new side of you."

"I don't really, except when it comes to Paige."

"Fair enough. Listen I'd better get going or Trina will have my guts for garters. Will I see you this evening?"

"I'm having dinner at Paige's but I won't be too late. Have you anything planned?"

"If you're going to be out I'll probably call into Granny Lily and make her dinner."

Molly smiled to herself. Kate was so good to her gran, it was quite something. "Why don't I get a video and we can watch it when I get back. Something lame and girly."

"You're on. But to be honest I'd prefer a thriller if you don't mind."

"Not at all. I can pick something up from the video shop later. She you around tennish, OK?"

"Perfect, see you later. Tell Paige I said goodbye."

"Will do." Molly watched her housemate leave. She'd known Kate vaguely when they were both teenagers as they'd played hockey against each other, and Kate and Paige had liked the same boy at one stage. Luckily there had been no hard feelings when Paige had won the particular boy's heart, as usual. Molly had been pleasantly surprised when Kate had arrived at her doorstep one evening after answering an ad for a housemate — Molly thought she'd recognized the voice on the phone but hadn't been sure at the time as she hadn't asked for her surname.

They'd hit it off from the very beginning — it was nice to have someone to do things with, especially after breaking up with Denis. But Molly always felt there was something that Kate wasn't telling her — there was something about her return from Boston that didn't quite fit. Molly wasn't one to meddle and so she'd let it lie and Kate was very private and rarely volunteered any personal information about her past, or her present for that matter — especially when it came to men. And as time went on she'd almost forgotten about it. Until now. Because Molly had had a rather strange phone call from someone with a decidedly American accent. Someone looking for a "Cat". It was only afterwards that she'd realized that maybe the "Cat" he'd been looking for was actually Kate. But as she hadn't even got a name from him it would be foolish to even mention it to Kate — wouldn't it?

As Molly walked back into the bookshop she was surprised to find Sam and Anita behind the front desk.

"I'm just showing Sam how to work the till," said Anita. "Then maybe you could show him how to take a special order."

"Um," Molly murmured noncommittally. He still looked stunning. His hair was falling foppishly over his face and he was biting his lip in concentration. She walked past them towards the side room where Felix was unstacking the folding chairs.

"Hi, Molly." Felix looked up. "How do you want the room set up? How many are you expecting?"

"About sixty, I think, but there could be a few extra latecomers who haven't booked. If you put the lectern at the far end of the room and curve the chairs around it in a semi-circle. It will look less formal that way. Rosemary said she'd like a comfortable chair for signing afterwards, one with arms."

"I'll get one of the chairs from the office for the singing, will I?" asked Felix. "No need to take it out yet."

"Perfect." Molly surveyed the room. Felix had adorned the room with pink and purple balloons and large banner-style posters advertising Rosemary's new book, and he had also placed a large glass vase of white lilies on the table beside the lectern.

"Is it OK?" Felix asked. "Anita said just to fire ahead with the posters and balloons."

"It looks great," Molly replied. "Couldn't have done better myself. I'll do a display of her books on the front table as you come in the door and then we should be pretty much set."

"Is she a Ripley Barker do you think?" he asked nervously. "Or is she normal?"

Molly smiled. Ripley Barker was an American crime writer, one of three writers who had taken part in last year's "Murder on Burnaby Street" crime event. The other two authors had been charming but Ripley had been an eye-opener. Arriving in a black stretch limousine, wearing an Armani three-piece suit and a black Stetson, he looked like a Hollywood film star. He'd had three minders with him — two from the publishers and one from the film company who had optioned his latest book — and had demanded ultra-special treatment from the minute his silver-tipped cowboy boot had stepped in the door of the bookshop. Felt tip pens in dark blue only, no biros — he couldn't write with them; no flowers — he was allergic to them; French mineral water, not Irish, and only in blue bottles, not green — he hated the colour green; and vegetarian food with no mushrooms or peppers.

"And M&M's with all the brown ones taken out, I suppose," Anita had quipped to his American publicist, who had not been amused.

"No," Molly smiled at Felix. "Not another Ripley. Rosemary's lovely apparently."

"Good." He breathed a sigh of relief. It had been his job to source the vegetarian food and the French mineral water in a blue bottle and he'd never forgotten it. Ripley hadn't even said thank you and had asked Felix not to look at him while he was eating as it interfered with his digestive system.

Molly felt a tap on her shoulder and jumped.

"Sorry," Milo beamed. "Didn't mean to startle you." His eyes lingered on the balloons and the posters. "Very pink, isn't it?"

"The cover of Rosemary's new book is pink," Molly explained. "They tend to use the same image and colour scheme on the posters and display material."

"I was talking about the shelves. Have they always been pink?"

"Not always. They were natural brown to start with but Anita updated them several years ago when the shop started specializing in romantic fiction."

Milo nodded slowly, a thoughtful expression on his face. "I see. What type of bookshop was it previously?"

"A general one really. It stocked a bit of everything. But we decided it was a good idea to specialize, as most of our customer base was female. It made sense really.

So we have a large range of fiction mainly aimed at the female market plus most things you'd expect in your average bookshop as well — books on gardening, health, reference books, children's books and a very strong crime section of course."

"But the figures have been slipping slightly in recent months, do you think it's time for another change?" he asked. His thick black eyebrows rose. "Say a crime bookshop for example, or a literary bookshop?"

She hesitated for a moment. Was he fishing for a reaction or was he serious? "There's already a crime bookshop in Dublin — 'Murder Books' on Callow Street."

"Is there a literary bookshop?" he asked.

"No, for very good reason. It's not . . ."

"Molly, are you ready to show Sam how to take a special order?" Anita interrupted. "I have to help a customer with children's books." She looked from Molly to Milo and back again. "Sorry, were you in the middle of something?"

"Milo was just asking me what I thought of changing the shop into a literary bookshop. You know, Anita, lots of serious hardbacks, Booker novels, IMPAC nominees, black shelves, jazz music, that sort of thing. What do you think?"

Milo put his hand on Molly's shoulder before Anita had a chance to reply. "Now, Molly, it was only a thought. No need to get hot under the collar, my dear."

She shrugged off his hand. "I'm glad to hear it."

"As long as the figures start improving you have no need to worry," Milo continued.

"And if they don't?" Anita demanded. He hadn't said anything about drastically changing the shop when he'd made his offer.

"We'll have to see, won't we?"

"I think we need to talk, Milo," Anita said gravely. "There are one or two things about Happily Ever After that you don't seem to understand."

"Ah, yes," Milo smiled a little too widely, showing two large gold-capped wisdom teeth, 'Happily Ever After', now as names go . . ."

"We'll talk later, Milo," Anita snapped, interrupting him mid-flow. "Right now we have a shop to run. Why don't you help Felix and Declan with the chairs?"

"As long as I don't get dirty, I'd be happy to." Milo brushed his hand over the front of his black polo neck. "Cashmere does have a habit of picking up dust."

"There are several publisher's T-shirts in the back," Anita said. "I can get you one if you like. Save your good clothes." She emphasized the word good, trying not to wrinkle her nose in the process. Milo might be an attractive man for his age and most charming when he wanted to be but today he was seriously starting to annoy her.

He held up his hands. "That won't be necessary."

"Then let's get back to work, shall we?"

Molly led Sam towards the back desk where the second computer lay waiting.

"Customer orders are an important part of our business," she began. "We can order books from America or the UK in a matter of days but you have to be careful not to promise too much."

"I'm sorry about Dad," Sam said, not really listening to her spiel on special orders. "When he gets an idea into his head he can be quite bullish."

"I just hope he doesn't change the bookshop for the sake of it," she said. "We've spent the last few years building the business up and tweaking things to get it just right."

"I understand, really I do," Sam said. "But he's got it into his head that the figures should be better."

"What line of business was he in before he retired?" Molly asked.

"Property. Money isn't a problem. He's just a stubborn old businessman who wants the shop to be as profitable as it can be."

"I see. He's the owner. And you're his son. And to be honest, I don't feel all that comfortable talking about this with you. Can we just drop it?"

"Of course. But one last thing."

She looked at him with interest. Damn, he had the loveliest eyes. But maybe in time she'd become immune to his physical charms. "Yes?"

"Stand up to him. He likes a challenge."

"OK." And his son? Does he like a challenge? Please tell me I didn't say that out loud, Molly begged. Please, please. "OK," she said again, realizing that blessedly she hadn't. "I'll stand up to him."

"Good. Now what were you saying about special orders?"

"Do you really want to know?"

"Honestly?" he asked.

She nodded.

He smiled broadly, his eyes wrinkling most attractively around the edges. "Not today, if you don't mind. I'm sure it's all very interesting and everything . . ."

"It's not," Molly laughed. "Why don't I show you around the different sections instead and how to tell if a book's in stock or not. You'll need to be able to find the books if you're going to be working here, won't you?"

"Absolutely! And you can tell me all about yourself in the process."

"Another day," she said. "First, the crime shelves."

He felt deflated but he tried not to show it. He was only trying to be friendly. Molly Harper was proving to be the Brazil nut of all nuts to crack.

"How did your event go?" Paige asked Molly that evening while standing over the sink. "Sorry I couldn't make it, I had council business."

"Not to worry, it was packed," said Molly. "Just over eighty people in total. And Rosemary was a pet. She stayed around for ages after the talk — signing people's books and chatting to them." She picked a black olive from the bowl on the table and popped it in her mouth.

"Good. And how's Anita? It must be strange for her working in the shop when she's no longer the owner."

"Especially when the new owner's the spawn of the devil." Molly licked her fingers.

"Molly! You don't mean that."

"Yes, I do," she said. "He's terrible. A big greasy lump of a man, in his cashmere polo necks and his bloody literary bookshop."

75

"Hold it right there, what are you talking about?" Paige stopped washing the cherry tomatoes and turned around.

"He wants to change Happily Ever After into a literary bookshop."

"You can't be serious?"

"He said unless the figures improved he was going to make changes. I'm telling you. Ask Anita."

"Unless the figures improve?"

Molly nodded.

"Are they bad?"

"Not especially. The whole book trade is in a bit of a slump at the moment — it happens sometimes. There haven't been as many big titles as there usually are in the first half of the year and people are spending their money on other things, that's all."

"No new Harry Potter or footballer spilling his guts you mean?" Paige asked.

"Exactly!"

Paige for silent for a few minutes.

"Paige?" Molly asked eventually. "What are you cooking up in that brain of yours? I know you."

"Nothing." Paige smiled broadly. "Absolutely nothing. Now let's eat. Tom!" she shouted out the door. "Dinner's ready!"

"Coming!" he shouted back. A minute later he joined them in the kitchen. "Callum's locked himself in the bathroom and I can hear all the taps running. Can you talk to him? I've tried till I'm blue in the face but he won't listen to me."

"I'll give it a go," Paige sighed. "What's wrong with him?"

Tom shrugged his shoulders. "I have no idea. And I'll kill him if he wakes up Alfie, I've just got him to sleep again."

Paige kissed him on the cheek. "You're an angel and I don't deserve you, do you know that?"

"I do." He flopped down on the kitchen bench beside Molly.

"Keep an eye on the lasagne," Paige said. "I'll be as quick as I can."

As soon as she'd left the room Molly turned towards Tom. He was slumped over the table, his head in his hands.

"You have to talk to her about Callum," Molly began. "He's getting worse and it's draining you both."

Tom sat up and rubbed his eyes with his knuckles. "I know, but she won't listen to me. Why don't you try again?"

"It won't do any good. What about her mum?"

"She said she doesn't want to get involved. And mine's as bad. Sometimes I think Paige is right — maybe he will grow out of it — but he may send one of us to an early grave in the process."

"Tom! Don't say that."

"You haven't had the day I've had. First he punched Alfie in the stomach on the way to the shops, then he had a tantrum in the supermarket, and then he ran across the road without looking and nearly got himself killed. It's no joke looking after him, Molly, believe me."

She put her hand on his. "I know, I understand, honestly. But unless Paige is prepared to do something about it nothing will change, you know that."

"I know."

"And I don't really want to be having this conversation with you for the rest of his childhood."

"I'll talk to her again."

"Promise?"

"Yes."

"Good. Now you'd better check the lasagne. I'm the guest, I'm not allowed to move. I have to sit here and eat all these delicious olives."

"Do you now?"

"Yes. And I'd love another glass of wine while you're up."

"You're early. How was dinner?" Kate asked as Molly walked into their small sitting room.

"Great. Except for Callum." She sat down in the armchair, flicked off her runners and curled her feet under her body.

"What did he do this time?"

"Flooded the bathroom. Paige had to break the lock to get in."

"Poor Paige."

"No kidding."

"I hope you don't mind but I mentioned Callum to Granny the other day. I thought she might know someone who could help." Granny Lily knew everyone in Burnaby and the surrounding area, and was a fountain of knowledge when it came to almost every subject from gardening to psychology.

"I don't mind at all. But don't tell Paige for heaven's sake. You know how touchy she is about Callum."

"I know. But Lily would never say anything to anyone, you know that. She's the soul of discretion."

"Did she have any ideas?" Molly asked hopefully.

"Not really, but she said she'd have a think about it."

"Tell her thanks."

"I will," Kate replied. "Now are you ready to watch Ben Syles?" Ben was the latest Hollywood hunk.

"Always. Bring on the eye candy."

CHAPTER
FIVE

Kate

On Wednesday evening, Kate checked her profile in her full-length mirror, and was satisfied that she looked presentable. Her Dummy Date clients always made a huge effort to spruce up and she saw no reason to let them down. This evening she was wearing a plain white cotton wrap-around shirt, neatly ironed and starched, and a dark pink silk skirt, which clung to her slender frame in all the right places. She was also wearing her favourite pink shoes — delicious leather and canvas sandals with sky-scraper heels that had cost her two week's wages even with her generous discount. But they were worth it — she always felt like a million dollars when she wore them and they were exceptionally comfortable for such a high shoe. She was a little overdressed for the local but to hell with it, she thought as she looked in the mirror again, who cares?

It was only ten minutes on foot to Burnaby and, as it was a dry and reasonably warm evening she decided to walk, heels or no heels. She clicked her way towards the village, past her Granny's ambling Georgian cottage with its slightly haphazard-looking front garden. Her Granny did have an on-off gardener who was almost the same age she was, but he was decidedly more off than on these days because of a clicky hip. She'd have to find someone else or the garden would go to pot, Kate thought. Maybe Harry would have some local contacts.

As she walked into O'Connor's pub she looked around. There were several couples sharing drinks, a group of men and women in suits — an office crowd no doubt — but no men on their own, apart from one with very short hair and his head buried in a newspaper. She sat down at one of the tables overlooking the street and ordered an orange juice from one of the lounge girls. From experience, she needed all her wits about her this evening if she was to be of use to her client and even one glass of wine had a bad effect on her as she had no tolerance for alcohol. To tell the truth she was a little tired — Trina had been her usual obstreperous self this afternoon and they'd had several disagreements about the winter stock.

Trina wanted to stock leather boots in all colours of the rainbow for the winter season. Kate was trying to reason with her — all women really wanted was the perfect black or dark brown boot. They didn't want purple, cream, pink or green. It would be a waste of time stocking the whole colour spectrum. Trina wouldn't see reason. Eventually she'd said "we'll see what Cathy has to say" and Kate had dropped it. She happened to know that Cathy had already bought most of the entire winter collection — including lots of different styles of brown and black boot as suggested by Kate — while Trina was on holiday in South Africa for three weeks in the spring, and she couldn't wait to see the sparks flying when Trina found out.

Kate pulled out her Filofax and checked her appointments for the following week. She had a Monday morning meeting with Ralph, a new client who worked with animals and sounded all right; and two evening dummy dates, one on Wednesday and one on Thursday. She was going to be busy. She looked at her watch. Angus was now officially late. She looked around the room again, her gaze settling on the man reading. As if sensing her, he raised his head. She recognized the eyes, even if they weren't hidden this time behind Germanic frames. It was Angus. He smiled over at her and waved.

"Stay there," she said loudly. "I'll come over."

He nodded and folded up his newspaper.

She put her Filofax back in her bag, picked up her drink and made her way towards him.

"I didn't recognize you," she said, standing in front of him. "You look very . . . um . . . different."

"Different good or different bad?" he asked, an anxious edge creeping into his voice.

"Good," she said decidedly. "Nice haircut."

He ran his hand self-consciously over his head. "I asked the hairdresser what she'd recommend and she scalped me. I'm not sure about it at all. I look like I'm in the army."

"You're lucky, you have an evenly shaped head. Some men have lumpy heads and they can't carry it off. But you're head isn't bumpy at all."

"Thanks, I think," he said smiling.

"Now, aren't you forgetting something?" she asked.

He thought for a second. "My glasses?"

"No, not your glasses, although now that you mention it, you look much better without them. You have nice eyes, there's no point in hiding them."

He thought again. "A drink, I haven't offered you a drink."

"No you haven't. But that would come next. You need to greet me first. Pretend this is a proper date, remember?"

"I'm so sorry, how rude of me." He stood up suddenly. "Lovely to see you Kate, won't you sit down?"

"That's better. Standing up was a nice touch."

"Now would you like a drink?" he said, relieved that he'd got over the first hurdle, albeit retrospectively.

"I already have one, thanks, but you can get the next one."

"Do I have to pretend you're my date right now or can you just be Kate for a while?"

"I'm your date from the very beginning," she said firmly. "You can call me Betty if you like, would that make it easier?"

"Not really. I'd prefer Kate if you don't mind. Can I start again then? You've caught me a little off guard."

"OK, if you think it would help. Pretend you've just greeted me and I've just sat down. Start from there."

"Have I offered you a drink yet?"

"Yes."

"So we're actually at exactly the same place as we were before I asked could you be Kate for a while?"

She looked at him intently. It was going to be a long evening if he insisted on analysing every little detail as they went along. "OK, how about this? I'll be Kate for a few minutes, you can get any pressing questions out of the way and then I'll be your date again."

"Great!" He beamed. "First of all, what do you think of the clothes? I took your advice."

She looked him up and down. White shirt tucked loosely into faded Levis, dark-brown lace up boots, dark brown leather belt. He was slim and toned, she noticed, with a real waist. She wondered did he work out? Most men of his age were starting to lose their waists unless they were actively fighting against it. "So I see," she said finally. "The belt is a nice touch. It matches your boots perfectly."

"So the lady in the shop said. It cost me an arm and a leg but she said it was a good investment."

"She was right."

"So you approve?"

"Yes, quite a transformation. As I said, I didn't recognize you."

"And you look lovely too. I like the sandals."

She smiled. She loved it when people noticed her shoes and it didn't happen that often, especially not with men. "Thank you. Now do you have any other questions or will we press on?"

"If I think of more can I ask them as we go along?"

"Not really, it would interrupt the flow of the date."

He seemed disappointed. "Oh, I see."

"But you can save them up and ask me at the end."

"I might not remember them all."

84

"Well, they can't be important if you can't remember them."

"I don't know, I haven't thought of them yet."

Kate said nothing. She couldn't win.

"You're annoyed with me, aren't you?" he asked. "I'm doing everything wrong."

"No, you're not," she said kindly. She hadn't meant to make him feel ill at ease. "Let's just have a conversation. And if you have questions ask away as they come to you. How's that? I don't normally allow it but I'll make an exception for you."

"Thanks, Kate," he said. "I appreciate it. So how will I start?"

"Ask me something about my day. About work, or if I don't work how I've spent the day."

"That's a good one. Will I tell you what I did first?"

"No, Angus, ask *me* first. It's much more polite."

"Oh, right. How was your day, Kate?"

"It was fine thank you, Angus."

He looked at her intently. "That's not a great answer. What am I supposed to ask now? I expected you to go on for at least a few minutes. I haven't even thought of my next question yet."

"No, you're right, it wasn't a great answer. But I'm testing you. Try saying — tell me a little about your work, Kate."

"OK."

"Well."

"Well, what?"

She sighed. "Say it."

"Again?"

"Yes, again."

"The thing you've just said about telling me about your work?"

"Yes, Angus!" She was trying not to get exasperated but he was starting to wear her down.

"OK, tell me about your work, Kate. Do you meet many interesting people during the day or is it boring?"

"It's boring."

"But there must be something interesting about it. Sure, aren't you working there? There must be some redeeming factors. Sorry to interrupt the flow, Kate but do I know where you work or not?"

"Yes, I work in a shoe shop and you met me at a party and we talked briefly. Does that make it easier?"

"Yes, thanks. Will I continue?"

She nodded.

"What are your favourite shoe designers?" he asked. "I've heard of Manolo Blahnik all right, do you sell his shoes?"

"Good," Kate said. "I love Manolo, these are actually his." She couldn't help raising her foot and pulling up her skirt slightly.

"You have lovely feet," he said admiringly. "Very dainty. And I like the pink nail polish."

"Thank you. Do you like shoes yourself?"

"Um, not particularly."

"What do you like?"

"Books, films."

"Anything else?"

"I thought I was supposed to be asking the questions."

"At first, to get things going. After the first few minutes conversation will hopefully just come naturally. But don't worry if it doesn't. Just keep talking and letting her talk."

"OK. What do I say next?"

Kate looked at the table for inspiration. This was one of the hardest dummy dates she'd ever had. Usually her clients got the swing of it much more quickly and treated her as a real date. Angus seemed to be having problems getting his head around the whole concept. Her eyes fell on his newspaper. "Tell her about something you read in the newspaper."

"Her?"

"Me! Tell me! Your date!"

"Sorry. Are you annoyed with me again?"

"No," she lied. "So was there any interesting news today?"

"A man in his eighties swam the English Channel for charity. Is that interesting?"

"Yes, very," she said. "Go on."

"Um, I only read the headline, I'm afraid. But he's someone famous's grandfather, I remember that much. Um, do you have any grandparents?" he asked, floundering for something to say.

"Yes, actually I do. One granny — she's nearly eighty. And she swims in the sea every day. She's never swum the Channel though."

He whistled. "Impressive. I don't have any unfortunately — more's the pity. They all died quite a few years ago. I always felt closer to them in a way than

87

to my own parents. I could really talk to them, you know, without being judged."

"I know exactly what you mean. It's an easier kind of relationship, isn't it?"

"Yes. Do you get on with your own parents?"

Kate drained the last of her drink and put it back down on the table before answering. "Sort of. I don't see them that much to tell the truth. Dad took early retirement and they moved down to Connemara."

Angus leant forward, his head on his hands. "This is going well, isn't it?" he said in a low voice. "Do I ask you for dinner now or later?"

Kate laughed. "Angus!"

"Sorry, have I annoyed you again?"

"Stop asking me that! Please!"

"OK. But what about dinner?"

"Honestly?"

"Yes."

"If I was your date, yes, this is a good time to ask. We are getting on well. But as for me, I'd have to say I'm not so sure."

"Why?"

"I don't know if I have the energy to continue counselling you all night."

"Are you suggesting I need counselling? Am I that bad?" He seemed a little upset by her comment.

"No, of course not. It was the wrong word to use. I should have said helping, advising."

"I'm tiring you out."

"Yes. I'm afraid you are."

"Oh." He stared at the table, his hands clasped together in prayer position, the tops of his fingers touching lightly.

"Angus, I'm sorry. I didn't mean to upset you. I shouldn't have been quite so direct."

"You didn't upset me, not really. I was coming on too strong, wasn't I? You don't like me, do you?"

"That's not it at all. You were doing great. I do like you — as a client. And as I said, if I was your date I'd definitely go for dinner with you."

"Really?" He looked up, his brown eyes catching hers and reminding her of something. "How about we just go to dinner as friends?" he suggested eagerly. "We could drop all the dummy date thing and . . ."

"I don't think so, but thanks for the offer." She was often asked out by her clients and she made it a policy not to meet them outside "office hours".

"Have I overstepped the line again?" he asked.

"A little."

"I didn't mean a date. Just dinner."

"Stop right there," she said. "Please. I can't have dinner with you, OK? I have other plans."

"That's OK. I'm a complete loser, I know. Why would you want to have dinner with me?" He stared at the table.

"Ah, Angus, you're not a loser. You're just a little different. Tell you what — let's meet again next week and talk — for coffee this time. What do you think? I'll give you your report and we can talk it through. Usually I send the report out in the post but I'd be happy to meet you if you think it would help."

"Thanks," he said. "That would be great. I do appreciate your help, really I do. I'm finding this a bit difficult, that's all. Maybe dummy dating isn't for me. Please be nice about me in your report."

"I'll be honest," she said evenly. "That's all I can promise."

"Can I ring you to set up a time? I don't have my diary on me."

"Of course." She stood up. "It was nice to see you again, Angus. And you did well."

"Thanks. I'll see you next week."

"Yes. Ring me."

A bushbaby, Kate thought as she walked home. That's what his eyes remind me of, an African bushbaby — dark, chocolatey brown. All wide-eyed and innocent.

The following night Kate had an even stranger dummy date experience. She was sitting in O'Connor's pub again, this time with another client, Clive, chatting about cars and four-wheel drives (he was a car salesman who was trying to get his dating confidence back after coming out of a long relationship) when, out of the blue, a red haired woman poured a pint of cider over her head.

"What the hell!" Kate exclaimed standing up and leaning forward, her head dripping onto the carpet.

"Bitch!" the woman screamed. "I should have known there was some reason Clive was going off me."

"Going off you?" Clive demanded, standing up. "I loved you. You broke up with me, remember? Eight years and then wham, you said it was over."

"Only because I thought you didn't love me any more. You never told me, how was I to know?"

"Excuse me," Kate interrupted. "I'm going to the bathroom to dry off. Clive talk to . . . sorry what's your name. Tell her how you feel."

"Linda," Clive said.

"What are you talking about?" the woman demanded. "How do you know how he feels?"

"I'm his counsellor," Kate lied smoothly. "The electricity is off in my office so we had to meet here instead. He was just telling me how much he missed you at our session, weren't you Clive?" She stared at him, willing him to agree.

"Yes," he said, rather convincingly. "Kate has been great. A real professional."

"Shit, I'm so sorry," the woman said looking genuinely shocked. "I saw you both over here together and I realized how much I missed Clive. I thought . . ."

"Never mind," Kate said quickly. "No harm done. Now I'll leave you both to it, shall I?"

"Thanks, Kate," Clive said sincerely. "Thanks for everything."

"My pleasure. It's all part of the service."

The following morning there was a knock on the door and as Kate answered it she was almost knocked out by the heady smell of lilies.

"Kate Bowan?" the man holding the huge bouquet asked.

"Yes?"

He thrust the flowers towards her. "For you."

"Thanks." She stepped inside and managed to wrestle the tiny card out of its envelope.

"To Kate," she read. "Who's no dummy. Getting married to Linda in the spring. Thanks for everything, Clive."

She smiled to herself. Another happy customer. The same morning she got another surprise delivery — this time from the postman. She started as she recognized the familiar sharp, angular writing on the envelope and the American stamp. Her immediate reaction was to tear it up, but curiosity got the better of her. She walked into the kitchen, sat down at the table and stared at the envelope in her shaking hands. Just then the phone rang. She let the answering machine take it.

"Hi, Kate, hoping we could meet up on Tuesday at lunchtime. Say half twelve in Coffee Heaven? Give me a ring if it doesn't suit. Oh, this is Angus by the way. Your mad but keen client. Remember to say nice things about me in your report. Bye."

She put her head on the table and let the solid wood cool her brow. Angus and a letter from America. She didn't know which was worse.

"What's wrong with you?" Trina asked as soon as Kate had stepped in the door of Baroque that afternoon. "You have a real sourpuss face on you."

"Thank you very much, Trina," she said evenly. "Nice to see you too."

"Out late last night, were you? Had a few tequilas too many?"

"No, I just have a lot on my mind. Where's Cathy?"

"She'll be back in a minute. She's gone out with Flames for coffee and then I'm off. There's this charity lunch in aid of some local arts thingy that Connie's running. I promised I'd go for a while."

"You can go now if you like, I'll hold the fort. But don't forget we all have to finish talking about the summer sale and the winter collection later." Kate would be glad to see the back of her for a while — sarky cow.

"I won't forget." Trina grabbed her black leather coat and Gucci bag. She kissed her hand and blew it at Kate. "*Ciao!*"

"Bloody *Ciao* to you too," Kate said as soon as Trina had breezed out the door in her wafts of Gucci perfume. She looked at the desk and on the floor. As usual there were at least twenty assorted shoeboxes to be put away. Trina never cleared away after herself, leaving Kate and Cathy to do all the real work. She got stuck in, replacing the toe-stiffeners and foam in all the shoes and wrapping them back into their tissue cocoons before closing them into their boxes. At least it would keep her occupied. The letter this morning had really unnerved her.

At half past four Trina flung open the door and staggered in. Her eyes looked wild — her pupils dilated and the whites blood-shot. She was a terrible drinker —

she couldn't take a glass of wine without looking like the mad Lady Macbeth.

"Uh-oh," Cathy whispered. "I'll run out and get some black coffee. Want anything?"

"No, thanks. But don't leave me with her in that state," Kate said. "I'll go."

Cathy patted her arm. "She'll be fine. She's a pussy cat really." She turned towards Trina who was tottering towards them. "Sit down, darling. I'm going on a coffee run. Back in a tick."

Trina plonked herself down on one of the two large red-velvet covered sofas which ran down the centre of the shop, back to back.

"That's better," she said, kicking off her impossibly high gold sandals. "My feet are killing me."

"Don't say that if any customers walk in," said Kate. "Those sandals are one of our best sellers."

"Crappy things." Trina ignored her. She began to massage the ball of her right foot. "What have you been doing all afternoon anyway? Talking on your phone as usual, I suppose. Anyone would think you had a boyfriend the way you carry on."

Kate stared at her but said nothing.

"Oh, no, too high and mighty for that sort of thing, aren't you? Think you're so superior with your vamps and your uppers and moulded soles — who gives a damn how shoes are made as long as they fit? I certainly don't."

Kate ignored her again. She'd seen Trina drunk before, but she'd never been this bad.

"Answer me, girl!"

Kate had had enough. "Don't speak to me like that, Trina, I have no intention of answering you, you stupid woman. Look at the state of you, it's embarrassing. You should go home."

"No, I won't go home. And don't *you* speak to *me* like that. I'm your boss, remember? Now get me some water, I want some water."

"Get it yourself, you know where the cooler is."

"How dare you! Get me some water."

Kate turned away and began to price some sale stock.

"Damn you!" Trina shouted.

Kate felt something hit the back of her head and then her shoulder. "Ow!" she looked down. Trina's shoes were lying on the floor beside her. She turned around and glared at the woman angrily.

Trina had a nasty smile on her lips.

"Did you just throw your shoes at me?" asked Kate angrily.

Trina threw her head back and laughed manically.

"What's going on here?" Cathy asked walking in the door with two large cups of coffee in her hands.

"She threw her shoes at me and hit me on the head," Kate explained.

"What?" Cathy stared at Kate in amazement. She looked down at Trina. "Did you?" she asked crossly.

Trina nodded, still smiling.

"What's got into you? I'm ringing Farrell."

"Don't do that. He'll be cross. I'm not supposed to be drinking — the injections . . ." She tailed off sheepishly.

Cathy stared at her again. "Are you having fertility treatment again?" Silence. "Answer me!"

Trina looked down at the floor.

"You stupid thing, you know you can't drink when you're having treatment, you know that. I'm ringing Farrell." She put the coffee down on the counter, pulled out her mobile and had a quick conversation with Trina's husband. "He's coming straight over. Could you get her some water, Kate? I'll lock the door and put the blinds down. I don't want anyone to see her like this. I'm sorry I left you, I hadn't realized how bad she was."

"Yes, get me some water," Trina cackled.

"Trina!" Cathy scolded. "Not one more word out of you, do you hear?"

"OK."

Kate felt like refusing but she knew none of this was Cathy's fault. She went into the office and came back a minute later with the water.

"Thanks, I appreciate it. Would you like to go home now? You look a little shell-shocked if you don't mind me saying. And take tomorrow and Saturday off."

"Are you sure?"

"Yes. I'll be fine on my own in the morning and Trina will be in in the afternoon whether she likes it or not. And all day Saturday."

Trina groaned beside her. "Don't feel too well," she said.

"I'm not surprised," Cathy handed her the water. "Drink this."

"'S'not alcohol is it?"

"No, most certainly not."

Trina drained the cup. "Didn't know you designed shoes, Kate," she slurred. "Lady at the lunch told me you used to work for Sin in Boston. You were one of their top designers." She hiccupped loudly. "And then you left suddenly to come back to Ireland."

"She must have me confused with someone else," Kate said calmly. She walked into the back room and collected her jacket and bag.

"Ring me if you need me tomorrow, Cathy," she said before she left. "Otherwise I'll see you on Monday."

"See you then," Cathy said to Kate's back. A shoe designer at Sin, the most cutting-edge of the American shoe design houses, now that was interesting, Cathy thought. And it made sense.

"So, Angus, how are you?" Kate asked after they'd sat down in Coffee Heaven.

"Good thanks. And what did you get up to over the weekend?"

"This and that."

He cocked his head to one side. "Why don't you answer the question? It wouldn't kill you."

She shrugged her shoulders. "Would you like some coffee?"

He nodded.

She caught Alex's eye. "Two coffees," she said loudly. "Thanks, Alex."

Alex smiled. "Coming up."

"You're very evasive," said Angus, picking up a sugar packet from the table and playing with it, rolling it backwards and forwards in his fingers. "What are you hiding?"

"Angus! I'm not hiding anything. We're here to talk about you, not me, OK?"

"Fine. I was just trying to be friendly. That's all."

"Sorry . . ."

"Sorry what?" he asked.

"Angus!"

"I thought you were going to say something else there," he explained. "You know, like sorry but I don't find it easy to open up to people. Or sorry, but I prefer to keep my private life to myself, or sorry . . ."

"I get the picture. And if you must know I was going to say — sorry, I'm not in great form today."

"Why?" he asked gently. "If you don't mind me asking. Although I know you probably do. But I'm asking anyway because I like you, Kate and I'm genuinely . . ."

"Stop! OK, I'll tell you if you're really interested." Anything to shut him up, she thought. "There was a bit of an incident with my boss on Friday — I work in a shoe shop some days, did I tell you that?"

"Yes, on our date."

"Dummy date."

"Sorry, of course, dummy date. Although I wasn't sure if it was you who worked in the shop or Betty."

"Betty?" What is he talking about, Kate wondered.

"You know, you asked me did I want to call you Betty."

"Right." Kate was losing patience. "Do you want me to tell you or not?"

"Yes, sorry. Go on."

"Well, she's been trying to contact me all weekend. It's been driving me nuts. She sat in her jeep outside my house for ages on Sunday waiting for me. I had to get my housemate to go outside and tell her I was away for the whole day."

"What did she do on Friday?" Angus asked, intrigued.

Kate sighed. "I shouldn't really tell you."

"I'm not likely to know her," he pointed out. "And I'm very discreet, honestly."

She studied his face. For some reason she trusted him — he was kooky, said all the wrong things and was most inappropriate with his questions — but she had a gut feeling that he wouldn't betray a confidence.

"OK then. She threw a pair of shoes at me and hit me on the back of the head. Oh, and she verbally abused me."

"Wow! Supermodels eat your heart out. Welcome to the spicy and vindictive world of Kate's shoe shop. Why did she do that?"

"A heady cocktail of alcohol and fertility drugs apparently. Gets them every time."

"Are you serious?" he asked.

She nodded. "The lives of Burnaby's rich and famous — who needs Hollywood?"

"No kidding. And are you all right? It must have really shaken you up."

"It did," she admitted. "But I'm OK now."

"And you haven't talked to her since — allowed her to apologize?"

"No, I'll see her later though. Unfortunately."

"I presume you're not going to sue her. You don't seem the type."

"No, I'm not. Life's too short."

Alex put two large mugs of coffee on their table.

"Sorry about the delay," she said. "We're pretty short staffed at the moment. Rona's just gone on holiday for the whole month and Peter's out sick."

"Not to worry." Kate smiled up at her.

Alex leaned towards her. "Heard about the shoe incident. Cathy told me. Are you all right?"

"Fine," she said shortly. She hoped Trina didn't think it was *her* spreading the gossip. She would have to have words with Cathy. "I think it would be best if you kept it to yourself, Alex, if you don't mind. For Trina's sake."

Alex looked at her for a second. "You're a good person, Kate. I won't say a word."

"Thanks." As Alex walked away Kate focused her eyes on her coffee cup — adding milk and sugar and stirring furiously.

"You should talk to Trina," Angus said, breaking the silence. "Clear the air."

She raised her eyes. He was smiling gently at her. "It would make work easier. You need to allow her to atone and to make amends."

"You're probably right. I don't know why I'm worrying about it, it's her who should be embarrassed, not me."

"I'm sure she is." Angus picked up the small ceramic jug on the table and poured more milk into his already very white coffee.

Just then, Molly came in the door and bustled over towards their table.

"Thank goodness," she said breathlessly. "I thought you might be here. I couldn't get through on your mobile and I've been home already in case you weren't answering the phone."

Kate gestured towards Angus. "I'm having coffee with Angus. Angus, this is my friend, Molly."

He smiled up at her. "Hi, Molly."

"Hi, Angus. Nice to meet you. Sorry to interrupt, Kate, but you need to get to St John's Hospital as soon as you can. It's Lily."

"Granny?" Kate asked faintly.

Molly nodded. "Yes. She fell over this morning after swimming and she broke her ankle. But I think she also bumped her head."

"Is she all right?"

"I'm not sure. They seemed a little concerned about concussion and wanted you to get there as soon as possible."

"Why did the hospital ring you?" Kate asked in confusion.

"Lily suggested it when they couldn't get through to you. Your mobile was off apparently."

Kate pulled her phone out of her bag and was greeted by a blank screen. "No wonder, stupid thing is out of juice again." She banged the phone ineffectually on the top of the table.

"I can get an hour off if you need a lift over," Molly said, aware that her friend was in a bit of a state. "I'll call into Anita — I'm sure she'll cover for me."

Kate stood up and picked up her bag. "OK. Thanks."

"Listen, I'll take her," Angus offered. "I'm not working at the moment and I wouldn't mind, honestly."

Molly looked at Kate. She was pale and seemed very shaken, but she didn't protest at the man's offer. Molly didn't recognize him but she presumed he was a good friend of Kate's to offer his services like that. Maybe even a new boyfriend. As Kate never shared her private life with Molly she had no idea if Kate had met someone recently. "Is that all right with you, Kate? I'll call over to the hospital straight after work. Would you like me to call into Cathy for you and tell her what's happened?"

"Yes, if you wouldn't mind."

"Not at all. And, Kate, ring me if you need anything later, understand," said Molly. "Anything."

"Thanks."

Molly looked at Angus. "And you're sure this is all right?"

"Honestly, it's fine. I'll drive her over and stay with her for a little while to check she's OK."

"Great, I appreciate that. Kate, I'll see you later."

After Kate and Angus had left Molly ordered three coffees from Alex.

"He seems nice," Molly said as she watched Alex pour. She was fishing for information and felt sure that Alex would know something. "Kate's friend. Haven't met him before."

"He's actually one of her clients," Alex said. "They left very suddenly. Everything all right?"

"Kate's granny's been taken into hospital with a broken ankle. She might have concussion too."

"Granny Lily? I hope she's OK. Lovely woman. Mum knows her from the church flowers."

"I should have driven Kate to St John's myself," Molly said a little anxiously. "I hadn't realized he was a client. But she seemed happy enough to let him drive."

"Then don't worry. He seems sweet. He's been in here a lot over the last two weeks. Must have moved into the area."

"You're right. I'll stop fretting and get back to work." She paid and picked up the tray of paper cups. "Thanks for the coffee."

"Any time." Alex smiled. "Give my best wishes to Lily when you see her."

"Will do."

It was only a twenty-minute drive to St John's Hospital in Sandybay but Kate worried the entire journey. Angus tried to talk to her and keep her mind off her granny's fall but she was so preoccupied that he gave up after a few minutes and flicked on the radio instead. The presenter was discussing people who had strange collections — the lady he was talking to collected ceramic toads.

"Do you collect anything, Kate?" Angus asked as he negotiated a large pothole on Burnaby Hill Road. The hill between Burnaby and Sandybay, nicknamed "Swiss Cheese" by the locals, was notorious for its lumps and bumps. He may as well give conversation one more go — he had nothing to lose.

"Sorry?" she murmured.

"Do you collect anything?" he repeated. "You know — like model cars or cacti?"

"Shoes," she said absent-mindedly.

"What kind of shoes?"

"All kinds," she replied, still staring out the passenger window.

"Like what? New shoes, old shoes. Borrowed shoes, blue shoes? Blue suede shoes, dancing shoes?" he was trying to lighten the mood but it didn't seem to be working.

"Old ones," she said after a long pause. "Foreign ones. I pick them up on the internet and at car boot sales and sales of work."

"What's your favourite pair?"

"I have some nineteenth-century Lotus shoes my granny gave me for my birthday a few years ago."

"Lotus shoes?"

She sighed. "Do you really want to know or are you just making conversation? Because if you're not really interested I'd prefer not to talk if you don't mind."

"I was just making conversation to begin with," Angus said, ignoring her short tone. "But now I'm interested. Very interested. Please go on."

"Fine. Lotus shoes were worn by Chinese women. You've heard of foot binding?"

"Yes," said Angus. "Mao banned it in 1949."

"Did he? How do you know that?"

"Read it somewhere. I'm a mine of useless information. Go on anyway."

"A 'Golden Lotus' was a foot measuring three inches or less. That's where the name of the shoe came from."

"So they're basically tiny shoes."

"Mine are tiny black shoes covered in pink and white embroidery to be exact."

"Where did your granny find them?"

"In an antique shop in town. It was pure luck."

"How long have you collected shoes for?"

"Years."

"How many pairs do you have?"

"I'm not sure really. Lots."

"What is your second favourite pair?"

"Angus! Enough! Stop the questions, please. I'm not in the mood for talking this morning, I'm sorry."

"Worried about your granny?"

Kate said nothing.

"Sorry, stupid question." He kept quiet until they drove into Sandybay.

"You can drop me outside St John's," said Kate evenly. "I'm fine from there."

"I'll bring you in, it's no trouble."

"But . . ."

"Kate, you might need me to go and get something for your granny. You probably won't want to leave her."

"Like what?"

"Coffee or a newspaper."

"Angus, she might have concussion, and if she has, she'd hardly be able to read a paper, would she?"

"Sorry, I wasn't thinking." He sounded subdued.

"That's all right. I shouldn't have snapped at you. You're only trying to help."

"I'm coming in with you whether you like it or not. You're in shock. I insist."

"Fine." She didn't have the energy to argue.

As they walked into Lily's ward Kate thought she could hear her granny's laughter from behind some drawn flowery curtains which encircled one of the hospital cubicles.

"Excuse me, I'm looking for Lily Bowan," she said to a nurse.

The nurse pointed to the curtains. "In there, love, talking to Dr Martin."

"Thanks." Kate pulled back the curtains and looked in. A white haired doctor was sitting on a stiff-backed hospital chair. Her granny was sitting upright in the bed, a blue cotton hospital gown covering her tanned chest.

"Hello, love." Lily beamed. "Coming to join the party? This is nice Dr Miles Martin. He'll be operating on my ankle in a few days. Isn't that right, Miles?"

"You must be Kate," Miles said. "Lily was telling me all about you."

"That's right," Kate faltered. "And is Granny all right? I was told she might have concussion."

"Not me." Lily knocked her knuckles against the side of her head. "Tough old nut, I have."

"We think your granny passed out from the pain of breaking her ankle. We can't find any evidence of concussion but we're keeping an eye on her just in case."

"That's a relief," said Kate. "And her ankle?"

"Cooee, I'm still here," Lily reminded them, "you can ask me, you know."

Miles stood up. "I'll let Lily fill you in on all the details. She knows almost as much about the procedure as I do from all accounts. Who was it had the same operation, Lily?"

"Old Mr Carmody from swimming," Lily replied. "Old fool slipped on seaweed a couple of years ago. Went into all the details at the time, let me tell you."

"Thanks, Doctor," Kate said.

"No problem. I'll be back to check on her later. Your granny is a great friend of my mother's, you know."

"From the chess club," Lily explained. "See you later, Miles." She waved at him.

"Granny, were you flirting with that poor doctor?" Kate smiled as she sat down on the bed.

"Ow," Lily squealed sharply.

Kate jumped up immediately. "Oh, my God! Did I sit on your bad ankle?"

Lily winked at her. "Only joking," she said, her eyes twinkling mischievously.

Kate frowned. "I'll sit on the chair just in case."

"What's ailing you, love?" asked Lily. "You seem a little out of sorts."

"I was worried about you. I thought you were concussed. I wasn't sure what to expect."

Lily patted her hand. "Sorry to disappoint you, chicken, but apart from my ankle I'm as fit as a fiddle."

"And what will they have to do with it exactly — your ankle I mean?"

"Put pins in it," Lily said. "I'll be like the bionic woman. When you cremate me you'll have to take out the pins before you sprinkle my ashes on the sea."

"Granny, don't talk like that!"

"Why not? Everyone dies in the end. Not much we can do about it. Might as well just enjoy ourselves while we're here. Kate, is there someone outside the curtains? I can feel something. Can you have a look?"

Kate got up and pulled the yellow and pink curtain open. Angus was standing patiently against the wall at the far end of the ward. She'd forgotten that he'd followed her up.

"One second, Granny." She walked towards him. "What are you doing?" she asked a little crossly. "I'm here now and everything's fine. There's no need for you to wait for me."

"I'll go then," he said. "I just wanted to make sure . . ."

"Bring the lad over," Lily said in a loud voice. "I'd like to meet him." Kate hadn't closed the curtain behind her and she and Angus were in full view of Lily's hospital bed.

Angus immediately made his way towards Lily.

"You can't stay," Kate hissed following closely behind him. "She's very weak."

"She looks it," Angus said just before he reached the curtain. "Hello, you must be Lily." he smiled. "I'm Angus. I'm . . ."

"Angus is a friend of mine," interrupted Kate. "Before you ask, he's a primary school teacher and he's on his summer break. He very kindly drove me over and he's just about to leave, aren't you, Angus?"

"No, I can stay for a little while." Angus beamed angelically at Kate.

Kate felt like hitting him. Why was he being so obstinate? This was her granny, her hospital visit, her life for goodness sake. What the hell was he doing interfering?

"That's nice," Lily said. "I'm a bit bored to tell the truth. The nurses are pets but they're much too busy to chat. And all the other old dears in the ward are a bit doddery if you know what I mean."

Angus stayed standing. "Sit down, Kate. I'll go downstairs and fetch us all some tea, will I? Make myself useful. I'm sure you'd like to talk to your granny on your own."

"I've tea coming out my ears. Do you know what I'd love, young man?" asked Lily.

"A nice big gin and tonic?"

Lily laughed delightedly. "Apart from that. Some nice cold bottled water. The water they give you in here is lukewarm and tastes mouldy." She pointed at the plastic water jug by her bed. "And I'd love some sweets, toffees if you can find them."

"Your wish is my command." He bowed. "And for you, mademoiselle?" he looked at Kate.

Really he was too much. "I'd like a bottle of water too. Still please. And Granny likes sparkling."

"Matches my personality," Lily winked at him.

"I think you're right." He laughed.

As soon as he'd left the ward, Kate sensed that the second interrogation of the day was about to begin.

"He's adorable!" Lily enthused. "Such a thoughtful lad. Very endearing and such good manners. Where did you meet him?"

Kate thought quickly. "Tell me about the operation, Granny. All the gory details."

Lily was torn — she wanted to find out all about Angus but she knew she wouldn't get another chance to tell her usually hypersqueamish granddaughter about her operation. She opted for the blood and guts.

"I won't bore you with too many details — but first of all they give you some sleeping pills, then the anaesthetist puts you to sleep," Lily began. "An injection. Hate them. They can never find my veins. I'm too slim you see, my toned figure is a curse." She snorted and Kate smiled. "They'll be paranoid putting me under, of course — convinced I won't wake up again on account of my age, you see."

"Granny!"

"Then they'll cut through the skin and the . . ."

Kate tried to block out the procedure her gran was describing while still appearing interested. Maybe she should have told her about Angus after all and got it over with. But what was there to say — he's a lost cause, Granny, and I'm trying to help him get a girlfriend. Still, he had brought her to the hospital and he was doing an errand for them. But it didn't redeem his peculiar behaviour. And it wasn't lovable or endearing, not one little bit.

110

"Are you listening, Kate?" Lily asked. "You seem a bit away with the fairies."

"I'm fine, just a bit preoccupied with things at work, that's all. Please, continue. We got to the bit where the doctor was fitting the pins."

CHAPTER
SIX

Paige

"Hi, Molly, you'll never believe what happened at the council meeting this evening," Paige began. She was picking up Callum's clothes from the kitchen floor, the portable phone jammed between her shoulder and her ear. He'd insisted on warming his naked body in front of the aga before putting on his pyjamas and had dumped his clothes unceremoniously on the tiles. "Davorka Ferata arrived."

"The Bosnian opera singer?" Molly asked intrigued.

"The very same. Apparently she's also an award-winning photographer. She's in Ireland for the Wexford Opera Festival and one of her old friends, Besnik something or other is living in a B&B just outside Burnaby. He's a famous tenor in his own country."

"What's he doing here?"

"He's an asylum seeker. He and his family were forced out of their home by the Serbian army."

"Was Connie Calloway at the meeting?"

"She was."

"You are infuriating sometimes. Where is all of this leading?"

112

"It was amazing. Davorka stood up and . . . Shit! What's that smell? Hang on a second, Molly." Paige ran up the stairs and sniffed the air in the upstairs landing. The strong, heady odour was coming from Callum's room. She put her hand over the receiver. "Callum, what are you doing in there?" There was no answer.

"Paige!" Molly protested.

"I have to go," said Paige. "There's a really strong smell coming from Callum's bedroom, suspiciously like Chanel No 5. I'll kill him if it is. He's supposed to be asleep."

"Paige, you can't leave me hanging like this. Tell me what Davorka said. Please."

"I'll ring you back in a few minutes," she promised. "I really have to go." She put down the receiver, took a deep breath and walked into Callum's room.

He was nowhere to be seen. There was a telltale puddle of dark yellow liquid on the floorboards and as she bent down to investigate she was nearly knocked out by the fumes. It was her Chanel all right, but where was the bottle?

"Callum? I know you're in here. Are you under the bed?" She pulled up his duvet which was hanging over the side of his lower bunk bed and looked underneath. He wasn't there. However she did spy the pieces of broken glass and the plastic spray insert and metal top amongst the dust balls, once her perfume bottle. He'd obviously kicked them under there to hide the evidence. She stood up and pulled open his closet, another of his favourite hiding places. He smiled up at her nervously, knowing he'd done something very bad

113

this time, but at the same time shocked at his own audacity and bravery.

"Get out," she said in a dangerously low voice. She pointed at the pool of perfume on the floor. "What happened?"

"I was on the top bunk and the bottle kind of slipped out of my hand," he explained. "It wasn't my fault."

"And whose fault was it then exactly?"

"Um, Alfie's."

"Why was it Alfie's fault?"

"He was annoying me."

"But he's in his room asleep, Callum."

"He was still annoying me. He's a shit."

"Callum! Don't use that language in this house."

"You do. I just heard you on the phone."

"That's different."

"Why?"

"It just is." She sighed deeply. "And what were you doing with my perfume anyway? You know you're not allowed to take things from Mummy and Daddy's bedroom, don't you? And why does the hall smell of perfume too? Tell me the truth. It'll be a lot better for you if you do. I know when you're lying to me, young man."

He had the good grace to look a little contrite. "I was using it as a magic potion. You know, like Harry Potter. I was making myself grow bigger. I put some on my head. It didn't work. I was standing on the stairs so I could listen to you on the phone, then I came up to my room. I dropped the bottle when I was climbing onto the top bunk."

She leant down and smelt his hair. It reeked of perfume. "Oh, Callum, what am I going to do with you?"

"Smack me?" he said nervously.

"No, I'm not going to smack you. We don't smack in this house, you know that. But you have to understand that you can't take things without asking and then break them. Or listen in to my phone calls." She sat down on the side of the bed. "I'm tired of all this, love. Can't you just be good for a change?"

"I'll try, Mummy."

"You need a bath and a hair wash. Your hair stinks."

"Can we use Fruit Alive Shampoo for Kids — 'Makes hair washing fun for all the family'?" He sang the shampoo's distinctive jingle loudly.

"No, we'll use the normal shampoo. You watch too much telly, Callum."

"No, I don't!" he shouted.

"Why did you just shout at me?" she asked in exasperation. "You said you were going to be good."

"Sorry, Mummy."

"Now, I'm going downstairs to get some kitchen roll and a plastic bag to put the glass into. And then you can help me mop up the perfume, OK? Now sit on your bed and wait for me like a good boy."

He nodded eagerly.

When she walked back into Callum's room three minutes later she found him crouched over the perfume puddle.

"What are you doing?" she asked.

"Helping." He smiled up at her.

She looked down at the floor and to her horror saw that he'd been mopping up the perfume with his new white towelling dressing gown.

"Callum! What the hell are you doing? You'll ruin your dressing gown, you idiot." She knelt down on her hunkers and put her head in her hands.

"Are you crying, Mummy?" he asked with interest.

"No! But I will be in a minute. You're driving me mad! Get out of here."

"Where will I go?"

"I don't care. Out!"

"I'll go and watch telly, will I?"

"Yes, whatever. Just get out!"

"You shouldn't really shout at me, Mummy. Daddy doesn't like it."

"Daddy isn't here. He's at the gym. And if you know what's good for you, you'll get out right now, Callum and stop annoying me. And stop answering me back, do you hear? Go!"

Callum skipped down the stairs to the television room. His mummy got a bit tired sometimes, she didn't mean to shout, that's what Daddy said.

Paige sat on her son's floor, moving her legs from beneath her as they started to get pins and needles. She heard a faint cry coming from Alfie's room, then a stronger one. I know exactly how you feel, Alfie, she thought. She pulled some kitchen paper off the roll and began to mop up the perfume. She'd become immune to the strong smell by this stage. But as for Callum, she was far from immune to his fatal charms at the moment. As soon as Tom got home their son would get a strong talking to, she'd see to that. She didn't have the energy to do it herself. Besides, after cleaning the mess up and soothing Alfie back to sleep she'd be fit for nothing except her bed.

Paige rang Molly back an hour later.

"Is Callum OK?" Molly asked gently.

"No comment," said Paige. She explained what had happened to her favourite bottle of perfume.

"Is he asleep now?"

"Yes, Tom gave him a bath and settled him down."

Molly took a deep breath. "It might be time for you talk to someone about Callum. For your own sake if not for his. He's wearing you down and it's not right."

Paige didn't reply.

Molly broke the silence. "I'm sorry, I shouldn't have said anything, you're probably exhausted. Bad timing."

"No, you're right," Paige said finally. "It's getting beyond a joke and he doesn't seem to be growing out of it, in fact he's getting worse."

"I hope you don't think I'm interfering because I'm not. I just care . . ."

"Stop! Honestly, it's all right."

"Good. And you never finished the story about Davorka," Molly reminded her.

"OK. To cut a long story short, she's going to hold a fundraising concert in St John's Church next month to raise funds for the refugee centre."

"I bet Connie is only too thrilled." Molly snorted.

"No kidding. But she seems to have had a bit of a change of heart."

"Oh?"

"Davorka's no fool. Apparently her friend Besnik filled her in on the details. Davorka called into Connie's gallery and offered her the very first showing of her photographs in Ireland. Connie was delighted and accepted immediately. But Davorka had one condition."

"Let me guess. That Connie drops her objections to the refugee centre."

"Darling," Paige drawled in her best "posh" Connie voice, "now that a famous tenor is involved in the arts centre how could I refuse?"

"Arts centre?"

"Gas, isn't it? Connie agreed on the condition that the refugee centre be called the Burnaby Arts Centre and that Davorka be its patron."

"Brilliant! But they'll still be teaching English and helping the refugees find jobs, like you wanted."

"Yes. As well as holding multicultural music and drama evenings, exhibitions, festivals and events for children. So everyone wins."

"Including you."

"Exactly!"

"Another triumph for Councillor Brady."

"Why, thank you, Molly."

The following day Paige visited Lily in hospital.

"Hi, Lily, I hear this place is driving you bonkers." She smiled, leant down and kissed Lily's cheek. "I thought I'd come in and say hi."

"How lovely to see you, Paige. And how is your mum? Still teaching the flower arranging? I haven't seen her for a while."

"She's great, thanks. And yes, still teaching, mainly evening classes these days. It keeps her out of trouble."

"I took one of her classes last year, it was a one-off thing in the church hall for the Flower Festival. She was very good. Very organized. Perfectly symmetrical arrangements — amazing. I was useless of course, mine kept drooping to one side."

Paige sat down on the chair beside Lily's bed. "So how are they treating you in here?"

"Very well. My doctor is a dear — Miles Martin — do you know him?"

Paige shook her head.

"Lovely man. His mother is an old friend of mine."

Paige smiled to herself. Lily knew everyone in Burnaby and had more friends than anyone she knew.

"And how are you, Paige? You look a little tired."

"Things are busy enough, Lily. Alfie was teething last night so I didn't get much sleep to tell the truth."

"And how's Callum?"

"Fine. Still a handful."

Lily looked at Paige carefully, tapped the tips of her fingers together and then smiled knowingly. "And when's the next one due? Kate didn't say anything to me so it must be early days yet. No wonder you're tired."

Paige could feel the blood drain from her face and she became suddenly lightheaded. She swayed dangerously in her chair.

"Put your head between your knees and take deep breaths," Lily commanded. "That's it, good girl, take it easy."

Paige sat back up after a few minutes and Lily handed her a glass of water. "I'm sorry, I shouldn't have said anything," Lily said. "Forgive me."

"No, it's not your fault, really. I just . . . I hadn't realized to tell the truth. But I think you're right. No, I know you're right. It all makes sense. I've been really tired in the last few weeks and I've had to eat all the time or I've felt faint and sick. How could I have been so stupid? What lousy timing!" Fat tears began to roll down Paige's cheeks.

Lily pulled some tissues out of a box on the cluttered bedside table and handed them to her. "It will all work out, you'll see."

"But the elections are coming up soon and I've no one to mind the children in August and . . ." She began to cry, her sobs catching in her throat and making it hard to breathe.

Lily patted her on the shoulder. "There, there, love. Things are never as bad as they seem. Stop crying now and we'll see if Lily can help, will we? I know a lovely primary school teacher who might be available. A young man called Angus who would be wonderful with Callum I think, from all appearances a kind and gentle soul. Don't cry, Paige, we'll sort it all out, you'll see."

Paige looked at Lily, her eyes still full of tears. "A primary school teacher. Do you think he'd be interested? It would be a godsend, really it would. I've interviewed all kinds of people, mostly college students, and older women, but none of them were quite right. Some had no experience of children at all, and there's no way they'd be able to cope with Callum. Mum has offered to take Alfie, but . . ."

"Let's just see, will we?" Lily smiled. "God moves in mysterious ways. Leave it with me." She patted Paige's hand. "Now you go home and have a little lie down. You've had a bit of a shock. Ring that nice husband of yours."

A couple of hours later Kate rang Paige on her mobile.

"Granny says you're looking for Angus's number," she said, a slight edge to her voice.

"Are you OK, Kate? You sound a little strange," Paige asked.

"It's nothing." Kate had had a flaming arguement with Lily less than an hour ago and it was still affecting her. She couldn't believe that her granny wanted to ring Angus. She knew it was in a good, no an excellent cause, and she knew in her heart that her granny was right — Angus could be just what the doctor ordered for Callum — but Lily had no right to involve Angus in their lives. He'd actually had the nerve to visit Lily off his own bat the previous day — bringing her grapes and two bottles of sparkling water. It wasn't on. He was a paying client — nothing more and nothing less and she was damned if she was going to start treating him as a real person. "Here's the number. Granny's already had a chat with him and apparently he is available in theory. But he said to give him a ring."

"Brilliant! Kate, Lily is an amazing woman. If you see her this evening tell her how much I appreciate this."

"I will." Kate put down the phone, her blood boiling. Yes, Granny was amazing — amazingly interfering. And she'd had almost enough. She had a good mind not to visit her this evening out of spite. Her mobile phone beeped. It was a text message from her. She should never have bought Lily a phone in the first place — it was a bad idea. But after her fall, she'd been worried, and had presented her with a brand new mobile the day after her ankle operation and making her promise faithfully that she'd carry it whenever she left the house. Now she was using it to harass her — typical.

Can u bring in your posh moisturizer this eve? Skin drying out — bloody hospital. Granny.

That evening while lying in bed, Paige filled Tom in on all the events of the day. Callum and Alfie were both asleep, much to their parents' relief. She had tried to ring Tom earlier but he'd been in meetings all afternoon and evening. She'd decided to save the momentous news — the news about the baby — till last. She had no idea how he was going to take it and she was afraid that he'd be annoyed and upset. After all, it did have huge consequences for both of them, and the way things were at the moment, they were just about hanging on to their sanity by the thinnest of threads.

"So you talked to this Angus guy and he's agreed to come and meet Callum?" Tom asked with interest.

"Yes. He said it was up to Callum. They would spend some time together and if Callum liked him he'd do it."

Tom smiled and shook his head. "The man has no idea what he's letting himself in for, does he?"

Paige glared at him. She didn't appreciate Tom's flippancy. "Callum's not that bad. I'm sure he'll be on his best behaviour when Angus meets him."

Tom said nothing. In his opinion, Callum was likely to play up when confronted with Angus — he'd be Denis the Menace and Just William all rolled into one just out of mischief.

"And he'll bring over his references. He was working in the local national school in Killiney last term and has several character references — including one from the priest in Sandybay."

"Sounds good," said Tom. "You'll check them all out, of course."

"We'll check them all out, you mean," Paige said, her voice dangerously low. Tom had a habit of leaving things for her to do and she wasn't in the mood for his passing the buck, not today. "You can't be too careful. And he is a man after all."

"If I'd said that you would have accused me of being sexist," Tom pointed out.

"You're right, I probably would."

"Did he sound nice on the phone?"

"Very."

"Well, I'm happy if you're happy. And it certainly solves the babysitting problem for August. Mum's already agreed to take Alfie, bless her. And Paige, I heard on the news on the way home that they announced the date for the general elections. I would have rung you but . . ."

"I know, I know. You don't like using the phone in the car. As I keep telling you, you have a handset, Tom, it's legal you know. Anyway I heard about the elections earlier."

"And as I keep telling *you*, I still prefer to concentrate 100 per cent on my driving. There are an awful lot of nutters on the roads these days and talking on the phone while driving is a distraction no matter how legal it is."

Paige sighed. When Tom got an idea into his head there was no budging him on it. Besides, he was probably right. "We'll have to start getting organized," she said. "I've already ordered the printing of the posters and flyers. And I'll have to start the doorstepping next week if I want to get around the whole neighbourhood by early September."

Tom nodded. "You're probably right. At least we've drawn up the provisional plan of action so we're fairly on top of things. And the Arts Centre issue has been a bonus. You managed to keep everyone happy and come out of it smelling of roses in the process, clever woman."

"And I have a few more tricks up my sleeve which should keep the media interested," she added.

"Really, and they would be?" Tom asked. This was news to him.

"I'll tell you tomorrow. I don't have any energy left right now."

"No energy at all?" He smiled wickedly at her, his blue eyes flashing.

"Well, maybe a little," she admitted. She flicked off the reading light on her bedside table and turned towards him. She had hoped to tell him about the baby but that could wait until tomorrow.

He kissed her firmly on the mouth and she responded instantly. No matter how often she kissed Tom she never tired of it. She was lucky she'd found him — a best friend and a lover all rolled into one. And what a lover. He was kind and considerate, yet powerful and strong when she wanted him to be. This evening she wanted to feel loved and cherished and he sensed this — taking things slowly and languorously, his hands moving expertly over her smooth skin with lingering, caressing touches.

Suddenly they heard something.

"What was that?" Tom asked.

"I don't know, it sounded like a thump."

Tom sighed. "I'd better go and see." He pulled on a pair of boxer shorts and went into the hall.

"It was only Callum," he told Paige as he got back into bed a few minutes later.

"Did he fall out of bed?"

"No, he'd pulled his mattress onto the floor so that he could play magic carpets."

"What?"

"Don't ask. I remade his bed on the floor and told him he could stay there as long as he went straight to sleep."

125

Paige smiled despite herself. "Let's hope he stays there. Now where were we?"

"Right about here, Councillor," Tom said, kissing her again.

The following day Molly rang Paige just before nine. "Have you seen the local newspaper yet?" she asked.

"No, why?"

"I think you'd better take a look. Ring me back as soon as you've bought a copy. And try not to worry, it's only a newspaper. I have to run, the shop's about to open. Bye."

"Molly, what are you talking about?" But her friend had cut her off.

Paige was intrigued. She made two pressing phone calls — one about rubbish collection or lack of it on one of Burnaby's cobbled pedestrian side streets, and the second about a gas leak on Collins Avenue — and then she walked down to the newsagents to buy a copy of the *Burnaby News*. She could have sworn that the young girl behind the till smirked at her as she bought her copy but Paige decided she was just being paranoid. She flicked through the pages as she walked home. The banner headline read "Proposed Burnaby Rubbish Dump — Local Councillor Says No". Was this what Molly was talking about? She stopped on the path and read on. No, this article was all about Paddy Burns, the local People's Party councillor and election candidate. Paddy was a decent man and Paige had a lot of time for him. He was a little "old school" for her taste but he wasn't easily swayed and was a good ally to have. She

126

was standing as an independent candidate and as soon as Paddy had heard the news he had rung to wish her good luck. "We could do with some fresh blood in the constituency," he'd said. "But is there any chance you might stand for the People's Party, Paige, do you think? Any chance at all? A woman like you would live long and prosper in the party, mark my words." She'd been flattered but unmoved.

Paige turned the page. Immediately the offending photograph struck her straight between the eyes. She felt like she'd been slapped in the face — her cheeks began to burn and she turned around her to see if anyone was staring at her, feeling distinctly paranoid. This was what Molly had been talking about. She closed the newspaper quickly and had to stop herself from running home. Once back in the house, she closed the hall door behind her, hurried into the kitchen, opened the newspaper on the table and stared at page three. How could this have happened and where on earth did they get that photograph? She felt sick to the stomach. She sat down and forced herself to read the tabloid-like headline. *Councillor and Election Candidate in Flashing Shocker.*

Local County Councillor and independent election candidate, Paige Brady, has quite a checkered past as this recent photograph clearly shows. Is this the type of person we want representing Burnaby at national level? Councillor Brady was unavailable for comment when we contacted her last night, but Councillor Annette Higgins,

127

another independent election candidate, had this to say — "I think it's a disgrace, Ms Brady exposing herself like that. I have no idea where the picture was taken but I just pray there were no children present." Ms Brady who lives in Burnaby has two young children and Ms Higgins feels that she should not be putting herself forward as a candidate in the September election in light of this exposé.

Paige stared at the photograph. It was her all right. Football shirt pulled up, showing a rather nice lacy white bra. She remembered the occasion only too well — the UCD team, under her captaincy had just won the all-Ireland university title and had been chosen to represent their country in France the following month. The whole team was over the moon and had pulled their shirts over their heads in true football fashion to celebrate. Unfortunately the shot had been taken as her shirt was on its way to her head and not covering her face. But why had they printed only her mug shot — where was the rest of the team? And why had they given so much space to Annette Higgins' rants? And most importantly — where had they got the photograph?

Paige sat down at the table and took a deep breath. This is only the beginning, she thought. I've put myself on the line by becoming an election candidate. I have two choices — I can fall at the first hurdle or I can fight back. Her mobile phone rang and she pulled it out of her pocket. It was Tom.

"Oh, Paige. It's all my fault, they rang last night. You were working on the computer and I never gave you the message, I'm so sorry," he said all in one rush.

"The newspaper you mean?"

"Yes, they rang and I forgot to give you the message."

"It's most certainly not your fault, Tom," she said firmly. "Who rang exactly?"

"The editor — Millie thingy."

"Millie O'Shea?"

"Yes."

Paige knew Millie from way back. She was a decent enough sort but very ambitious. Paige knew she'd do anything to sell papers but she hadn't expected this. She made a quick decision. "I'm going to ring her. Tell her the real story behind the photograph. Insist that she print the whole photograph and not just the cropped version. That will put everything in context. I have a strong feeling that Annette is behind this whole thing, Tom, mark my words."

"You're an amazing woman," Tom said in admiration. "And if Annette is behind this she'd better watch her back. No one messes with my wife and gets away with it."

"Thanks, Tom. Now I'd better get moving 'cause I want them to run a front page retraction tomorrow."

"Are you sure you're all right, Paige? Is there anything I can do?"

"No. I'm fine, honestly. For a brief moment there I was a bit upset to tell the truth, but I've decided not to let this get to me. I'm stronger than that. And this is

129

only the start of it, Tom. I intend to win a place in the elections — I deserve it — I've worked bloody hard for this constituency and no one is going to deny me the chance."

"Good woman, I'm proud of you. And Paige?"

"Yes?"

"I love you."

"Love you too." She clicked the phone off with a smile on her lips, walked into the sitting room which she also used as a study, bringing the copy of the *Burnaby News* with her. She dialled calmly.

"Hello, is that the *Burnaby News*? I'd like to speak to Millie O'Shea please. Tell her it's Councillor Brady and that it's urgent. She's in a meeting? Well you can tell Ms O'Shea that it's in her best interest to talk to me right now, or she can deal with my lawyers instead. Because I'm sure she doesn't want a libel case on her hands now, does she?"

CHAPTER
SEVEN

Molly

Molly smiled widely as she read the lead story in the following day's *Burnaby News* — *"Councillor Brady All-Ireland Soccer Hero"*, which was accompanied by the large and extremely striking photograph of the UCD Ladies' Soccer team, each team member with her shirt lifted over her face in celebration of their all-Ireland victory. She read on:

Councillor Brady is proud of her impressive sporting achievements, including three all-Ireland medals and one European silver medal. At only twenty-two she was awarded the most prestigious college sporting award in existence — the Golden Griffin — for her dedication and tireless promotion of the sport. Councillor Brady, an independent candidate in the forthcoming election, says she will wholeheartedly support all the local GAA and soccer clubs if elected, and might even be cajoled into coaching the ladies' youth team. We think that Councillor Brady is just the sort of politician needed to represent Burnaby on a national level, and we apologize unreservedly for any embarrassment caused by yesterday's unfortunate photograph, which had been cropped in error, and the corresponding article. Ms Brady has graciously accepted our apology.

Molly immediately rang Paige. "Paige, that's a brilliant article — how on earth did you get them to print it? You're a miracle worker."

"I threatened them with a libel suit, no more and no less. Millie O'Shea is no fool — the paper isn't exactly rolling in it and a libel suit is the last thing she needs on her CV."

"You'll make some politician," Molly said with respect. "There'll be no messing with you."

Paige laughed. "That's what Tom said. Let's hope I get in. So, are you free for lunch? I feel like celebrating."

"I surely am. Coffee Heaven at one, or would you like to go somewhere more swanky, you sports hero, you?"

"Coffee Heaven is perfect. See you later."

As Molly put down the phone and folded up the paper which was lying on her desk, she murmured jauntily "Hi ho, hi ho, it's back to work we go". As she walked out of the office and onto the shop floor she found Sam on his hands and knees in the small children's section at the back of the shop, sorting through picture books. He looked up at her.

"What are you smiling about?" he asked. "Must have been a good joke."

She told him all about Paige's article.

"Phew." He whistled. "She sounds like a tough cookie, your friend. But she's dead right — the press shouldn't get away with printing things like that. Good on her."

"And what are you up to?" Molly asked. "Are they not a bit young for you?" She nodded at the picture books fanned out on the floor.

"I'm alphabetizing them," he explained. "I wouldn't have started if I'd realized what a big job it was."

"No kidding. Now you see why it doesn't get done as often as it should."

He smiled. "At least I now know what we have in stock. So it hasn't been a complete waste of time."

"I wouldn't tidy them too well or you'll be stuck doing it till kingdom come. Unless you like children's books, of course."

"I like all books. To paraphrase the late, great Dr Seuss — 'a book's a book, no matter how small.' "

Molly laughed. "Not bad, Mr Devine, not bad. And how are you settling in? I'm sorry I didn't have much time to spend with you over the weekend, but it was pretty hectic."

"Hectic but fun," Sam said. "And I liked Rosemary, she was a real lady. Are there any more events lined up?"

"Loads," Molly said. "So keep your diary free."

"Are they always at weekends?"

"Not always, why?"

"Weekends can be difficult for me, that's all."

Molly looked at him. Was he being funny? Weekends didn't exactly suit *her* either but she just got on with it,

133

along with the rest of the staff. She hoped he didn't expect special treatment just because he was the owner's son. Just when she'd started to like him too — typical.

"Sorry," he said after a moment. "That came out wrong. I know working weekends is part of the job. It's just . . ." The bell rang on the front door.

"Excuse me," Molly said to Sam as she broke away and strode towards the front of the shop.

"There you are!" It was Anita — looking in buoyant form — a huge grin plastered on her face. "How's my favourite bookseller?"

"Not too bad. And to what do I owe this honour? It's not often I see you so early on a Monday morning. Especially as Monday is now officially one of your many days off, you lady of leisure, you."

"I have news, my dear, good news. Paige tells me you're meeting her for lunch. I'll be joining you and we're going to talk about . . ." she leant towards Molly and whispered conspiratorially in her ear "our plan."

"What plan?" Molly asked in her normal voice. She refused to whisper. Anita was being very Nancy Drew-ish and she wasn't having it.

"Shush!" Anita hissed.

"Anita, what are you talking about? There's not a soul in the shop."

"What about Sam?" Anita whispered.

Molly stared at her. This time she did lower her voice. "*What* about Sam? What are you talking about?"

Anita put her finger to her lips. "Don't tell him a word."

"I can hardly tell him anything as you haven't exactly told *me* anything now, have you?"

Anita winked at her. "See you at one in Coffee Heaven." She walked towards the door.

"Oh, no, you're not leaving," Molly protested. "That's so unfair. Tell me what's going on. I want to know."

"See you later," Anita said breezily, completely ignoring her.

"Anita!" It was no use, Anita was strolling down the road, swinging her shopping basket at her side.

"Who was that?" Sam asked.

"Anita. She just called in to say hi."

"Nice woman." Sam smiled broadly but said nothing else.

"What?" Molly asked.

"Nothing."

"Why are you smirking?"

"Am I smirking? I don't mean to. Ignore me, it's nothing."

"Sam! Go on. It's something about Anita, isn't it? You'd better tell me or I'll jump to all sorts of conclusions." She studied his face carefully. He looked a little flushed. "You don't . . . no!"

"What?" he asked. "I don't what?"

"You know — like her."

"Me!" he spluttered. "Of course not. Not me. No offence, but she's at least twenty years older than me."

"So? Some men like older women. She's very attractive."

"I agree — she's just not my type."

"Really? And what is your type exactly?"

"How did I get myself into this?" He laughed. "You're a pretty straight shooter, aren't you, Molly?"

"Straight shooter?"

"You ask very direct questions."

"Does it bother you?"

"No, not really."

"So are you going to answer my question?"

"No, not today. Maybe some other time."

"Fair enough. But at least tell me about your father's crush on Anita."

"Molly! I never said that."

"Do you deny it? It's true, isn't it? If it's not you, it must be him. It's hardly Felix, he's very happily married."

He smiled. "I'm saying nothing. My lips are sealed."

"I'm going to be keeping a good eye on your dad, just in case," she said. "Smooth operator that he is."

"Promise you won't say a thing to Anita," he pleaded. "Dad would kill me."

"I promise. But you owe me one."

"I do not."

"You so do."

"OK, I'm not going to argue about this. Now shouldn't we do some work?"

"*You* should," she said. "The Panda rep is due in at any minute and we'll be in the office for about an hour ordering the new titles."

"Can I sit in?"

She shook her head. "Sorry, someone has to keep an eye on the shop and Felix won't be in until twelve."

136

"Fine." He seemed a little put out.

"Tell you what," Molly said. "You can sit in on the session with Dunwoody Press this afternoon? How about that?"

"Thanks. Is there anything you'd like me to do in the meantime?"

"Tidy the tables and put out the stock titles. They're on the trolley in the Romance room."

"Will do."

"I have a few things to do in the office, so can you send the Panda rep in when she arrives?"

"Sure. How will I know her?"

"She's tall with blonde hair. She's called Mona."

Molly sat down at her desk and stared straight ahead of her. Sam was definitely growing on her. Now if he hadn't been late this morning and given such a feeble excuse she might even . . . no, that was stupid. He was Milo's son for goodness sake. Just because Sam didn't wear cashmere polo necks it didn't mean that he wasn't another charmer. Like father like son. Still, he was nice and she missed having a man around. She liked her independence and enjoyed her evenings in with Kate or Paige, but it wasn't quite the same. She missed having someone to snuggle up to on the sofa, someone to bring her chips and bottles of wine, someone to watch videos with, someone . . . Stop it! She told herself. You're a disgrace to modern women. You are perfectly fine on your own and much better off without a man to complicate things. She turned her attention to the computer screen and checked her e-mails. One new message in her in-box jumped straight out at her. It was from Denis and the subject was "Missing You". She knew she should delete it immediately without reading it but curiosity got the better of her. As she opened the message she heard a gentle knock on the door.

"Come on in, Mona." She smiled up at the rep as she entered. "You're bang on time as usual."

"Creature of habit," Mona replied.

"Sit down," Molly said. "Make yourself comfortable."

"In this place?" Mona laughed. "Never!"

Molly liked Mona very much. She was a no-nonsense kind of woman with a razor-sharp mind and she was damn good at her job. Meetings with her were always a pleasure. Molly dragged her attention away from her e-mail and concentrated on the job at hand.

"Who's the new assistant?" Mona asked with interest. "Not bad."

"That's Sam Devine. The new owner's son no less. You've heard the news I presume?"

Mona nodded. "Patricia told me. I hope they don't change the shop — it's perfect as it is."

"Thanks." Molly smiled gratefully. "You say all the right things."

"That's my job, honey buns. What's he like — the new guy?"

"Sam? I haven't quite decided yet. I'll tell you when I have."

"He's a good-looking man. I wouldn't mind working with him myself, let me tell you."

"You're welcome to visit any time."

"Better get back to business," Mona sighed. "I have some crackers for Christmas too. Wait till you see."

"That's terrible!" Molly groaned.

"What?"

"Crackers for Christmas, Mona, I expect more from you."

"I'll try harder next time," Mona grinned. "Now, let's talk food — de-da!" She pulled a large hardback out of her large black-leather rep's bag. "The new, all singing, all dancing *Panda Sinful Chocolate Cook Book*."

As Molly walked towards the till a little later, passing several customers who were happily browsing, Sam was standing beside one of the front tables. "What do you think?" he asked as she approached.

She looked at the table. He'd changed the books around so that they faced the front of the shop, not all four sides as they usually did. He'd created a raised area in the center of the table with one of the most popular hardbacks of the week. "It looks great. Thank you."

"I quite enjoyed it. It's a bit like building, isn't it?"

"I suppose it is."

"Mona seemed nice. She introduced herself."

"Oh, really?" Molly said. "Your sort of woman, is she?"

He sighed deeply. "Molly! Stop. I was just saying she was nice, that's all. I'm not in the market for a girlfriend at the moment, thank you very much. And I'll keep my observations to myself in future." He looked at her with a serious expression on his face.

Molly felt that she'd overstepped the line and was mortified. She hadn't meant to embarrass him. "Look, I'm sorry, I promise I won't ask you any more personal questions, all right?"

"No, I'm sorry, I didn't mean that to come out the way it did." He stopped for a second as if deciding what to say next. "I had a bad experience with someone last year to tell the truth and I haven't quite got over it. That's all. So, go easy on me."

"I'm sorry," she said, contrite. "I really am. I don't know what to say."

"It's no big deal. Let's talk about something else. Where do you live, Molly? Is it near here?"

She smiled at him gratefully. She told him about the townhouse she rented in Burnaby Grove and about Kate, making sure she kept the whole conversation on level ground. They were interrupted once or twice by customers asking questions or paying for books but it didn't seem to interrupt the flow.

"And where do you live?" she asked him after she'd wrapped a book in gift paper for a customer.

"In Sandybay, near the beach. I own a little cottage — it used to be a railway worker's cottage — it's small but fine for one. I've spent the last few years doing it up, it was in a complete state when I bought it. It's handy for Burnaby too — I can walk or get the train if I'm feeling lazy."

"You're so lucky," Molly said enviously. "I love Sandybay beach. I often walk along it in the evenings."

"So do I. Maybe we'll bump into each other one of these days."

"Maybe." Another customer walked in. Molly smiled at them and then looked at her watch. "Listen, I have to fly. Felix said he'll come out onto the floor to give you a hand. I'm off for lunch with Anita and my friend, Paige. I'll be back in an hour."

"See you later."

Molly stopped outside Coffee Heaven for a moment. She turned around quickly. She could have sworn someone was staring at her, she could feel it, but that was stupid — there was no one there. She looked across the road. There were a few people on the far pavement — a young woman pushing a buggy and a well-dressed older man talking to Connie from Halo — none of whom were paying her the least bit of attention. She pushed open the door to the coffee shop, breathed in the familiar warm, coffee smell and felt better instantly. Paige and Anita waved at her from their favourite table at the back of the shop. She smiled and made her way over. I was just being stupid, she told herself. But the sensation of being watched had unnerved her and it took a few minutes to shake it off. But as she listened to the two women's plan unfold she forgot all about it. Their startling idea for the bookshop was quite something — but could they pull it off?

After their heady and productive lunch Paige walked Molly back to the bookshop.

"Come in and meet Sam," Molly insisted.

"Can't — I have to run. I've a meeting with . . . hang on, this is Sam Devine, the owner's son? Anita says he's very attractive. Maybe I'll just stick my head in for a minute. Just to be polite. Why didn't you tell me he was good looking?"

"It wasn't relevant," Molly sniffed.

"Since when are good-looking men in Burnaby not relevant?" Paige laughed. "Get a grip. It's not as if the place is exactly crawling with them."

"You're a married woman," Molly reminded her.

"Doesn't mean I can't admire a nice bod when I see it."

"Paige!"

Paige ignored her and waltzed in the door. She went straight to the front desk. "You must be Sam." She smiled warmly and held out her hand. "I'm Paige, a good friend of Molly's. Nice to meet you."

"Hi, Paige." Sam smiled back. "You're the 'Sport Billy'. Molly was telling me about the article this morning. Good on you — I like your style. Newspapers get away with too much these days. It's good to see someone fighting back."

"Thanks. Listen, I have to run. But welcome to Burnaby. Are you a local?"

"If you mean can I vote, then the answer is yes. And you have my vote, Councillor Brady."

"Fell straight into that one, didn't I?" Paige grinned. "You'll have to excuse me, it's election time after all."

"Best of luck with it. Hope you get elected."

"Thanks."

Molly had been listening to the whole exchange with interest. She walked Paige out. "You're shameless," she hissed at her outside the door.

"And he's lovely," Paige whispered back. "If I were you . . ."

"I don't want to hear it." Molly glared at her. "Talk to you later, Councillor."

"Later, lover." Paige winked at her.

"I wouldn't be winking at me like that. Annette Higgins might have you outed as a lesbian."

"Wouldn't put it past her. I wonder what she'll come up with next."

"Next?"

"Who do you think sent the *News* the photo?"

"No!" Molly exclaimed. "Really? How did you find out?"

Paige tapped her nose. "I have my sources." She glanced at her watch. "Now I really do have to go. Later, Babe."

As Molly turned towards the door she felt a hand on her shoulder and jumped.

"Sorry," a familiar voice said, "I didn't mean to frighten you."

"Denis," she said, staring at him in astonishment. "I thought we'd agreed . . ."

"I had to see you, Molly. It was a matter of life and death."

"Hardly. And I'm working, Denis. This is not a good time."

He looked at her carefully. "Tonight then. It's important, please."

"No, Denis. Not tonight and not any night, understand? We have to get on with our lives. We can't go backwards." She sighed. "We've been through all this. And anyway, I thought you'd met someone."

He looked sheepish. "Yes, well that's over now."

Molly stared at him in amazement. "That was quick." She narrowed her eyes. "Hang on, Denis, there never was anyone, was there? You were just trying to make me jealous."

"There was!" he protested. "It just didn't work out."

Molly knew better than to argue with him. "I have to go," she said firmly, walking away as she spoke.

"I'll drop in tomorrow." He turned on his heels and scooted away quickly before she had a chance to say anything.

"Denis," she called after him. "Don't come into my work again, please."

But to no avail. He'd rounded the corner and was now out of sight.

"Shit!" she muttered. Her hands were shaking. She leant against the shop front and took a deep breath. A few minutes later, when her heart had stopped thumping quite so hard in her chest, she went inside.

"Everything all right?" Sam asked. He'd seen her talking to a man outside and the exchange didn't seem too friendly. He didn't like to mention it, as he shouldn't have been spying on her.

"Fine," she lied. "Just fine and dandy."

Later Molly opened yet another e-mail from Denis. *Darling Molly, why don't you stop this madness? You know we belong together. Don't fight it. I won't give you up. I love you with all my being. Denis.* She

144

shivered. It was all going to start again, she could feel it. But this time would be different — this time she'd have the strength to say no. She'd made a promise to herself, not to mention to Paige. There was no way in high heaven she was going to get back with him. No way! It was time for her to move on — finally.

"Callum, please stop kicking my seat," Molly said crossly. She glanced at Paige. "Sorry," she mouthed at her. She didn't want to get him in trouble but it was getting annoying and she had asked him several times.

Paige swiftly pulled into a parking spot. "Callum, you'd better behave in the puppet show, I'm warning you," Paige turned around and told him. "Do you understand?"

"Yes, Mummy," he said with an angelic smile and nodded his head vigorously.

"I'll get you a treat afterwards if you're good," Molly said. Paige had been through a busy time in the last week, what with the unsavoury exposé in the *Burnaby News* and the corresponding aftermath and Molly was determined to make this afternoon as easy for her as she could. Paige had had to be convinced to come out in the first place — she was exhausted but felt guilty that she hadn't spent any time with Callum this week.

"Can I have Skittles?" he asked hopefully. His mummy never let him have Skittles and they were his favourite sweets.

"No," Paige said firmly. "They're full of E numbers, they always send you up the walls. You can have some popcorn or crisps."

"Pringles are crisps," he said firmly. "Aren't they, Molly?"

Molly said nothing. Most of the time it was best not to interfere when it came to Paige and Callum.

"We'll see how good you are," said Paige.

A few minutes later they were entering the large red wooden gate of the Hayward Puppet Theatre in Blackrock.

"I haven't been here since I was a child," Molly reminisced. "It's changed quite a bit but I remember it clearly. Dad used to take me every Christmas until I was seven. Then he said I was too old for puppets and he stopped. I remember being really upset and Mum having to comfort me. He didn't replace the trip with anything, you see, and I didn't understand. I thought I'd done something wrong and that he was punishing me."

"That's a shame," Paige said. "He can be quite . . . how will I put this — black and white, your dad."

"Tell me about it." Molly frowned. She didn't much like talking about her dad. Fergal Harper was a strong, overpowering man who had been deeply disappointed that his only daughter hadn't followed him into the family printing business. Even though she was twenty-eight, he still made Molly feel like a child when he talked at her. She got on well with her mother, Laura, but had never really forgiven her for not standing up to him more and for never taking her side when she was growing up. Molly, rightly or wrongly, blamed her lack of self-confidence and her feeling of inadequacy on her childhood.

"Have you seen your folks recently?" Paige asked as she paid for three tickets.

"Not really. I spoke to Mum last week, she seems fine. I sent her out the list of books we've read in the Book Club. She's just started one up with some of her Mothers' Union friends."

"I didn't think she was a great reader," Paige said, watching Callum, who was walking in front of them, like a hawk as they made their way towards the puppet theatre.

"She used to read a lot apparently, before she had me. Then she kind of got out of the habit."

"Callum!" Paige said loudly. "Sorry, Molly. I'll be back in one second." Callum had run on ahead, bumping into a tall man and his son and sending the young boy flying sideways. He came to a halt at the theatre door and leant against the wall to wait for his mother, oblivious to the trouble he'd caused.

"I'm so sorry about my son," Paige said to the man. He turned towards her. "Oh, it's you," she said in surprise.

"Sorry?" he asked.

"We met briefly last week in the bookshop. I'm Paige, Molly's friend. Molly's just . . ."

"Here," Molly finished for her.

"Of course. Paige. I didn't recognize you out of your suit. So this is what you do on your days off, Councillor." Sam smiled at Molly. "And Molly, not what I would have expected from you at all — going to puppet shows."

"I'm here with Paige and her son, Callum," Molly explained. "He's the one who knocked . . . um . . ."

The boy had been watching and listening to the adults with interest. He was small, with white-blonde hair and steel-rimmed round glasses, but from his face Paige reckoned he might be five or six.

"This is Hugh," Sam said. "My son. Say hello Hugh."

Hugh said nothing, clutched his dad's hand and hid behind his legs.

"He's a little shy."

"You didn't tell me you had a son," said Molly. She was more than a little taken aback to tell the truth. She'd presumed from what Sam had been saying over the last week that he was single. She was confused. Hadn't he said he lived on his own? She'd obviously got the wrong end of the stick. Still, it did explain some of his late mornings she figured — he was probably dropping his son to school. It also explained why working weekends might be difficult for him.

"You didn't ask," he said evenly in answer to her question.

Paige snuck a look at Molly. Molly seemed a little flushed and flustered.

"What age are you, Hugh?" Paige bent down and asked the boy.

Still no reply.

"He's nearly six," Sam answered for him.

"Mum!" Callum shouted from the doorway. "Hurry up."

148

"Sorry, I'd better go and get him," Paige said. "But we might see you both afterwards."

She and Molly walked towards Callum, excusing themselves to the people queuing in front of them.

"Mum!" Callum beamed as she reached him. "Who's the little boy you were talking to? I've been waiting ages."

"That's the little boy you knocked down when you dashed over here," she said sternly. "He's called Hugh."

"Sorry," he murmured, knowing from her tone of voice that he was in trouble again.

The woman taking the tickets smiled at Paige. "Go on in," she said. "The lad's dying for the show to begin. Can't wait, he told me, didn't you, pet? He's been as good as gold waiting for you."

Callum smiled up at his new friend.

"Thanks," Paige said gratefully, handing the woman the tickets.

"Enjoy the show, young man," the woman said to Callum.

As they sat down on the small wooden seats in the dim auditorium Paige leant over to Molly.

"You never told me he was married," she whispered.

"I didn't know he was. He's not wearing a ring and I could have sworn he told me he lived alone. Still, it makes no odds to me."

"Really?"

"Yes, really. And stop looking around. He'll think we're talking about him."

"We are."

Molly sniffed. "Not any more we aren't."

"Message received and understood." Paige smiled at her knowingly.

"My Action Man says that when you pull the string in his back," Callum said.

Paige grinned at Molly. "Little pitchers," she said.

"Have big ears," Callum finished for her.

"Yes, thank you Callum," said Paige. "That's what your daddy always says too. Now you tell me when the curtain opens, will you?"

"Do you not have eyes, Mum?"

"Just watch the curtain, Callum, OK?" Paige said curtly, ignoring his rudeness.

"OK, Mum. But can I go . . ."

"No!"

"OK, OK." He sat slumped with his arms folded in front of him and pulled his face into a huge scrunched-up frown. He started jiggling his feet up and down on the floor.

"What's wrong, Callum?" Paige asked with a sigh.

"I only wanted to ask could I go to the loo. I really need to pee. It's an emergency. If I don't go I'll wet —"

"Yes, thank you, Callum," Paige interrupted. "We get the picture."

"I'll take him," Molly offered quickly.

"Are you sure?" Paige asked. She could do with a few minutes' peace.

"Not at all. Come along, Callum."

"Tell her I'm allowed in the boys' loo, will you, Mum?"

"Is he?" asked Molly.

150

Paige shook her head. "Bring him into the Ladies with you, if you don't mind. He has a habit of talking to strangers and you wouldn't know . . ."

"I understand," said Molly. "You can't be too careful. Now, hurry up Callum or we'll be late for the show."

On the way back, Molly saw Sam and Hugh sitting on the right-hand side of the auditorium. Hugh had his head on his dad's knee and Sam was talking to him or telling him a story, she couldn't make out which. He noticed her and waved over. She waved back and took her seat again.

"Was Callum OK?" Paige asked.

"Fine," Molly replied biting her lip. He'd actually tried to soak her with water from the tap but her friend didn't need to know that.

After the show, they met Sam and Hugh again in the foyer.

"Did you all enjoy that?" Sam enquired.

"It was great," Callum answered. "I want to be the prince." He stood with his two hands together in front of him. "Look, I can cut down that forest for the princess lady, no trouble."

"Sleeping Beauty," Hugh said quietly. "She was called Sleeping Beauty."

"That's right," said Paige. "Did you like the show, Hugh?"

He nodded eagerly. "I have a puppet theatre at home. Daddy made it for me. It's wood."

Paige and Molly looked at Sam with interest.

"You made a puppet theatre?" asked Molly.

151

Sam shrugged his shoulders. "I like woodwork. I'm good with my hands."

"He made my bed too," Hugh added proudly. "And my desk and my shelves."

"Yes, well, we'd better be going." Sam put his arm around Hugh. "Have to get you home, young man."

"Do you need a lift?" Paige asked kindly.

"No, it's only around the corner, we'll walk. But thanks for the offer."

"Not at all. See you around."

"Yes, and see you tomorrow, Molly."

"Yes," she replied distractedly. "Tomorrow." She could have sworn he said he lived in Sandybay. How could they walk that far? It would take hours. It was all very strange.

"What's up?" Paige asked as they got onto the car. "You seem a little out of it."

"Nothing," Molly said. She had no intention of telling Paige that she'd been thinking about Sam. "Just work stuff, you know."

"Don't let it get you down. As I told you, once our plan is in action there'll be absolutely nothing to worry about. Honestly."

"Thanks," Molly said gratefully. "I'll stop worrying, I promise." Easier said than done, she thought. "And how are you?"

"Fine, well almost fine. We're a right pair, aren't we?"

Molly laughed. "That we are."

"At least I don't have to worry about Callum this month. Angus starts tomorrow."

"Kate told me. I don't think she's too thrilled to tell the truth. She doesn't like to mix business with pleasure."

"Is there something going on between them?" Paige asked. "Is that what you mean?"

"No! Sorry, pleasure was probably the wrong word to use. Angus is one of her dummy dating clients and . . . oops, you knew that, didn't you?"

"Not exactly. Lily said they were friends. She didn't say how they knew each other."

"Trust me to put my foot in it. I'm sorry, I should have kept my mouth shut. Kate is very particular about client confidentiality. Don't say anything to Angus, please?"

"I won't," Paige said. "And if Kate and Lily like him that's all that matters to me. The fact that he can't get a date and resorted to using Kate's help has no bearing on my views of him. No, none at all."

"Paige! Promise me you won't say anything."

"I already have. It just seems kind of sad though. Sad and funny at the same time."

"I guess it does," Molly said thoughtfully. Although the way her own arid love life was looking, she could probably do with a helping hand herself.

CHAPTER
EIGHT

Kate

Kate stood on the doorstep and put the key in the lock. She heard a noise behind her — a slight rustle in the bushes and she swung around to have a look. Nothing. Must have been a cat or something, she reasoned. Then she heard it again. It sounded bigger than a cat, more like a person moving through the leaves.

"Hello?" she said nervously. "Is anyone there?"

There was no reply. She turned the key quickly, let herself in and closed the door firmly behind her. Safely in the hall, she leant her back against the door, her breath catching in her throat and her heart thumping. Was there someone out there? She left the living-room light off, tiptoed towards the window and looked out. She gasped as she saw a shadowy figure crawl from under the rather scraggly hedge and walk towards the gate. Who the hell was that and what were they doing? The figure paused for a moment before walking out the gate and down the road. Kate watched him in astonishment. Because it certainly was a him and not a her. She noticed the lenses of his glasses flash under the street lamp as he sloped away.

"Molly?" she shouted upstairs. "Molly, are you in? Quick!"

She heard a muffled noise from upstairs. "Coming!" Molly yelled. She appeared at the top of the stairs, resplendent in her dark pink towelling dressing gown, her hair caught up in a clashing light pink towel. "I was washing my hair. Is everything OK?"

"Not really. There was a man hiding in the front garden. I opened the door and he went away. I saw him from the livingroom window."

"A man?" Molly asked with concern. "Where exactly in the garden?"

"Behind the big straggly bush."

Molly looked at her blankly.

"The one beside the gate."

"Oh, that one." She walked down the stairs and looked carefully at Kate. "Nothing happened did it? He wasn't a flasher or anything?"

"No, I don't know what he was doing. Just watching the house, I think. He just gave me a fright, that's all."

"And you're all right?"

"Fine. I think I should ring the guards though. He might be dangerous. He could be a burglar or something."

"Maybe," Molly said, a thought coming into her mind. "What did he look like? Did you recognize him?"

Kate shook her head. "No. He was quite tall and thin and wearing glasses, that's all I know."

"I see," Molly said slowly.

"What?" Kate demanded. "Do you know who it was?"

"I might," she replied slowly. "I'll find out. Give me one second." She walked quickly back up the stairs.

"Molly . . ." Kate shouted after her but it fell on deaf ears.

"I'll kill him," Molly muttered as she picked up her mobile from her dressing table and punched in the familiar number. "Denis, is that you? Where are you?"

"Um, nowhere," he said a little nervously. "Where are you?"

"You know damn well where I am. Just answer me this one question — are you spying on me? Were you outside the house a few minutes ago?"

"Um, no."

"What do you mean, no?" she asked, her voice rising to a dangerous level. "I know you're lying. And before you say anything you may like to know that my housemate saw you and is able to identify you."

"But I've never met her," he protested. "How could she . . ."

"Got you," Molly screamed. "Don't you ever, ever scare her like that again, do you hear me?"

"But I was just dropping in a letter," he said meekly. "Then I just thought I'd wait for a little while to see if you came out. I wanted to talk to you. You haven't been answering my phone calls and . . ."

"Too right I haven't, you nutcase. And if I ever catch you stalking me again I'll report you to the guards, do you understand?" She didn't wait for his answer.

She sat down on the bed and took a deep breath. Men! There was a knock on the door.

"Molly? Are you all right?" It was Kate.

156

"Come on in."

"I heard the shouting and I was worried."

Molly looked up at Kate. "I should explain — that guy in the bushes earlier was my ex — Denis. I'm so sorry he frightened you. I wouldn't say he'll do it again in a hurry. I gave him a right earful."

"At least it wasn't a burglar, I suppose. But he gave me a real fright. My heart is still thumping."

"I'm so sorry."

"It's OK, it's not your fault. And this was on the hall floor. It's addressed to you." Kate handed her a red envelope.

Molly handed it straight back. "It's from him. Bin it for me."

"Are you sure?"

"Positive."

Kate took it back, sat down on the bed beside her friend and cleared her throat. "Is Denis, how will I put this, a little highly strung?"

"As in totally crazy?"

Kate nodded. "Does he often do this kind of thing?"

"I'd have to say yes. But hopefully it's all over now."

"Hopefully," Kate murmured. She didn't want any more unnerving experiences — she got quite enough of those at work, thank you very much.

"I'm sorry about all this," Molly said. "I don't know what to say. He's a strange one."

"And I never even had the pleasure of meeting him," Kate said. "Listen, don't worry about it. I'm going to bed now. I'm tired to the bone."

"How was your date?"

"Brutal. He was a total male chauvinist and kept calling me babe."

"That good?"

"Sad thing is he'll probably have no problem finding a date — some women love that kind of thing. Plus from all accounts he's rolling in it."

"Always helps." Molly smiled.

"No kidding. The more I learn about men the less I like them."

"You don't mean that," Molly said. "You must have met some decent ones along the way. What about that Angus — Callum's nanny? Paige has been singing his praises."

"I'm sure he'd be delighted to be referred to as a nanny," Kate said. "I must tell him that. He's OK, I suppose."

"Only OK?" Molly looked at Kate, a smile lingering on her lips.

"What are you implying? Stop looking at me like that."

"Like what?"

"You know." Kate stood up abruptly. "I'm going to bed."

"Sweet dreams," Molly said, still smiling.

"Yeah, Yeah," Kate muttered. She walked into her room, the red envelope still in her hand. She threw it into her waste paper bin and stared at it. Men! What a waste of time and energy. She walked over to the window and stared out. No one lurking under the street lamp or in their garden as far as she could tell. She closed the curtains and sat down on the bed. Angus! As if she'd be interested in someone like Angus — what a joke!

The following lunchtime Kate called into Coffee Heaven before work. She'd had a blissfully free morning with no client meetings and was making the most of it. She'd gone for a long walk this morning up Killiney Hill, followed by a shower and some yoga and she hadn't felt this good in a long time. Last night's date was long forgotten and she even had a whole evening to herself — one of her clients had cancelled his date and she'd tried not to sound too delighted when he'd rung with his apologies.

"You look happy," Alex said as she placed a steaming bowl of carrot soup in front of her. She raised her eyebrows. "Anyone new on the scene?"

"Alex!" Kate scolded. "I don't need a man to be in a good mood."

"Sorry."

"Don't worry about it. So how are things? Any news?"

"Well actually," Alex leant down and lowered her voice, "I did want to talk to you about something, are you free in a few minutes? I won't keep you long."

"Sure." Kate was a little taken aback. She didn't know Alex all that well and wondered what on earth she wanted to ask her about.

"I'll be back in a minute. I'll just get Matty out of the kitchen to cover for me."

A few minutes later Alex sat down at Kate's table and smiled nervously at her. "How's the soup?" she asked.

"Good." Kate smiled back. "Is that what you wanted to ask me?"

"Um, no, not exactly." Alex blushed and leant forward. "I wanted to ask your advice on, um, dating, I suppose. There's this guy I like and I don't know what to do about it."

Kate put down her soup spoon and looked at Alex carefully. "I don't know if I'm the right person to ask. I normally help men, you see. I've never helped a woman before."

"I'd pay you," Alex said quickly. "What's the going rate?"

"Don't be silly."

"But you're a professional, Kate," Alex said firmly. "I insist."

"How about a month's supply of free coffee? And the odd bowl of soup?"

"Done!" Alex grinned. "So, will you help me?"

"I'll try. Tell me about this man. What's happened so far?"

"Well nothing's happened really. Nothing at all. In fact he never seems to notice me at all. He's very busy and . . . um, I'm sure I don't make much of an impression on him. He's only ever seen me in my apron."

"He's a customer?"

Alex nodded. "If I tell you will you promise to keep it a secret?"

"Of course, everything you say is completely confidential, you have my word."

"Thanks." Alex looked around to check there was no one listening and then whispered, "It's Harry from the plant shop."

"Harry Masterson?" Kate asked in amazement.

"Shush, lower your voice. Yes, that Harry. He's amazing and I'm totally mad about him. And Kate, he doesn't even know I exist."

"But he will," Kate said and patted her hand. "He most certainly will."

Ten minutes later, after arranging another meeting with Alex, Kate put the first germ of her plan into action. This was going to be an interesting one. Because just the previous day she'd taken on a new client — none other than Harry himself. Alex and Harry would be a rather unlikely couple — he lived his life at break-neck pace and personally Kate found him rather spiky. Alex was far more laid back, a nice girl with a good heart, if a little nosy — but stranger things had happened.

Swinging open the door of Slick Harry's after lunch she was greeted by a shout.

"Watch the bloody cactus!" Harry came running over. "Sorry, Kate. But I need it for the *Des and Shelly Show*. They are holding some sort of Western Special and I have to talk about cacti. That cactus is the centrepiece. So what can I do for you?"

"Two things," Kate said coming straight to the point, knowing how busy Harry always was. "Firstly, I'm looking for a new gardener for my gran, she's coming home from hospital next week but she has to rest her ankle for six weeks. I wanted someone to look after the garden for her. Someone who wouldn't mind being watched and advised."

"Might know the very woman," Harry said. "Cecily Hammond. She's from Bray — nice woman and very sensible."

"A woman? That would be great. Do you have a number for her?"

"Certainly." He strode towards the large stainless steel desk, flicked through his large Filofax and scribbled a mobile number on the back of one of his cards.

"Thanks," said Kate, pocketing it. "I appreciate it. And the other thing was that Alex in Coffee Heaven was looking for some new plants for the shop. I suggested she called in on Thursday morning to have a look. Will you be here?"

He flicked through his Filofax again. "Should be, yes, I think so. Is Alex the blonde girl?"

"Yes," Kate said, hoping she didn't sound a little too eager. "Lovely girl, great cook too."

"Thought it was her brother who did all the cooking?" asked Harry.

"In the shop, yes. But she trained at Dunmore House, with Rena Travis." Rena was a well-known Irish celebrity chef who ran her own cookery school.

"Really?" he seemed to be losing interest so she didn't push it.

"And I'll see you on Thursday evening for our, um, meeting," she said moving towards the door.

"Yes, indeed," he said a little nervously. "See you then."

162

As soon as she'd left he stared after her. To tell the truth he was a little embarrassed about using Kate's services, but as he'd had nothing but disasters on the dating front recently he'd decided that it was time to take matters into his own hands and do something positive about it. All he seemed to meet were models, television presenters and would-be actresses. And what he was really looking for was someone like his mother — a kind, decent girl who could take care of him and slow his life down. It had got far too fast for his liking and at times he longed to retire to the country with a Range Rover and a couple of dogs. And a nice, pretty wife and two adorable children — a boy and a girl. Not that he'd ever admit this to anyone of course. In everyone's eyes he was Harry Masterson, plant genius, daytime-television darling, and man about town.

"Hello, Kate," Cathy said looking up from the desk in Baroque. "Mind if I go on my lunch straight away? Trina's at the doctor's and I'm starving."

"No problem. Just give me a second to dump my bag in the back."

"You look well today," Cathy said to Kate she returned onto the floor. "I like the suede skirt."

"Thanks, it's Molly's. She claims it's too tight on her so she gave it to me."

"Listen Kate, Trina is a little, um, upset. She says she keeps trying to apologize to you but that you won't . . ."

"I don't really want to talk about it," Kate said firmly.

"I understand, but Trina is my friend. She may be an old boot some of the time but she's not that bad really underneath it all. She's been very good to me over the years."

"But she hasn't been good to me, has she Cathy? In all honesty?"

Cathy looked at the ground. "No, I suppose not," she admitted. "But people change. Give her a chance."

"That's just it, I don't believe they do. Not really."

"Just let her apologize properly, please? It would mean a lot to her. And it would make working here with the two of you a damn sight more bearable."

"Has it been awful?" Kate asked, suddenly realizing that it had probably been no picnic for Cathy over the while with the two of then sniping at each other.

"Yes, to tell the truth, it has."

Kate sighed. "I'll see what I can do. I'm not promising anything, mind."

Cathy smiled. "Thanks, Kate."

As soon as Trina opened the door of Baroque that afternoon Kate made a decision. What both Cathy and Angus had said had made her think. She stood just inside the door waiting in case she changed her mind. Trina looked pale and slightly frazzled. She looked at Kate expectantly.

"Yes?" Trina demanded. "Are you going to have a go at me already? Can you not wait till I'm in the door?"

"I want to talk to you," Kate said mildly, ignoring the barbed questions. She flicked the sign on the door from "open" to "closed" and pulled down the blinds.

"Oh? What about?" Trina asked, her interest piqued.

"Sit down," Kate replied firmly.

Trina did as she was told for once, without comment.

"I accept your apology," Kate began. "I know all about the fertility treatment — Cathy told me. The injections sound horrible and I'm sorry you have to go through all that."

Trina nodded, too stunned to say anything.

"I want to declare a truce," Kate continued. "I've had enough of the bickering, it's tiring and neither of us needs it right now. So can we agree to be civil to each other?"

Trina nodded. "Yes, absolutely."

"And no smart comments from either side?"

"Agreed. On one condition."

"What's that?" Kate asked.

"That you think about designing a shoe collection for Baroque."

Kate began to protest. "But . . ."

Trina put her hands up. "I just said think about it, OK? I have a contact in Italy who runs a shoe factory. They specialize in soft leathers. I know you were good, Kate, one of the best. I talked to my contacts in Boston and they remember you well. Let me know when you're interested."

"Don't hold your breath."

"And last thing," Trina added.

"Yes?"

"I think there's definitely a market out there for Irish designer baby shoes — soft leather ones. 'Baroque for Babies', what do you think?"

"I don't think it would work," Kate said calmly. She opened the blinds and let the sun back into the shop. Designer shoes for babies, now that would be a fun project — if she were interested, of course, which she was most certainly not. She hadn't designed a shoe for a very long time. Not since Boston. Not since . . . she blocked it out of her mind. No point thinking about the past, she had to move on.

Later that afternoon Cathy was delighted to find the two women working together at the desk at the back of the shop — putting the final touches to the sale banners and showcards.

"Looking good, ladies," Cathy said surveying the assorted dark pink signs. They'd had them printed in the local printers — dark purple lettering on a rich pink background, all in "Baroque"-style lettering of course — to which Kate and Trina were adding pink feathers and assorted sequins and plastic jewels. "How many more are you going to do?"

"We're almost finished," Kate said with a smile. "Thank goodness. I've glue all over my fingers."

A customer walked in the door. "I'll get it," Cathy said. "Councillor Higgins, how are you? How can I help?" Cathy knew that Annette Higgins liked to be referred to by her proper title and she tried not to smirk as she said it. It had been plain old Annette up until a year ago, before she'd gone all high flying. And now that she was on the verge of being elected to the Dail, the Irish government (in her own mind at least), Annette was becoming unbearably pompous.

"I'm looking for something comfortable but smart for canvassing," said Annette. "With a low heel, I think."

"I have just the shoe," Cathy said. "What colour — black, dark brown . . .?"

"Navy," Annette said firmly. "All my suits are navy."

"Fine," Cathy said. "And you're a size . . .?"

"Six."

"Right then. Give me a moment and I'll pull out the shoe I'm thinking of."

"Rather her than me," Trina murmured to Kate as Cathy walked past them into the small storeroom. "I bet her feet smell."

"Trina!" Kate giggled. "I'm sure they don't." She smiled to herself — maybe being nice to Trina wasn't going to be as difficult as she'd thought.

"Hi, Angus, thanks for coming." Kate gestured at him to sit down.

"Two coffees please, Alex," she shouted over.

"Coming right up," Alex shouted straight back.

"My pleasure." Angus sat down, nudging the table a little and spilling some milk from the small white jug. "Oops, sorry. So, am I in trouble? What does my report say — 'will never amount to much', 'if Angus spent as much time at his work as he did clown-acting he might do better in class'?"

"Report?" Kate murmured in confusion. Then she remembered. Of course — that was why they'd arranged to meet for coffee last week — before Molly had found them and they'd rushed off to hospital.

She'd forgotten all about it. "Sorry, I left it at home. I'll send it to you in the post. Is that all right?"

"Fine," he said. "So, you decided you couldn't live without me, it that it?"

"Not exactly." Kate stifled a laugh. "I wanted to talk to you about Paige. I understand she's asked you to mind Callum."

"Yes, I'm going over to meet him tomorrow. I hope he likes me."

Kate smiled. "I'm sure he will. But do you think it's such a good idea? I don't feel all that comfortable with it to tell the truth."

"What do you mean? Thanks," he mouthed to Alex as she put down their coffee. He added milk and four spoons of sugar to his cup.

Kate wrinkled her nose. "How can you drink it so sweet?"

He took a slurp and smiled. "Easy. But stop trying to change the subject. Why does it bother you? Because Paige is your friend? Because in some strange convoluted way you've got it into your head that it compromises your position? Because you're scared that if you see too much of me you actually might start liking me?"

"No!" she protested. "Nothing like that. I'm just thinking of you."

"Oh really?" He raised his eyebrows. "How's that?"

"As I'm sure Paige has pointed out, Callum is a bit of a handful. I just think you should know what you're letting yourself in for, that's all."

168

"That's not it, is it, Kate?" he said gently. "I know you better than that, even though you won't believe me. I know you care about Paige and Callum, too. And from what Lily told me the little lad could do with some attention right at the moment. And maybe I can help. Would you begrudge him that just because you feel uneasy about having me around?"

"I don't feel uneasy . . ." she began.

"Face it, Kate, you're beginning to like me and it scares you."

"Angus! That's not it at all. You're being ridiculous."

"Am I? Think about it, Kate. I'll see you around." He stood up, pushed the chair towards the table, spilling both cups of coffee in the process and strode away.

Kate watched him leave, dumbfounded.

"Is he coming back?" Alex asked a few minutes later as she wiped the table down.

"Um, no," Kate said. "I don't think so."

"Right, I'll take away his coffee so. Anything wrong, Kate? You look a little perturbed."

"Just thinking."

"Any news on Harry?" Alex asked in a low voice.

"Yes, actually. I forgot to tell you. He's expecting you to call in on Thursday morning about some plants for Coffee Heaven. So be sure to slap on some lip-gloss. Maybe put your hair up. You could bring him some muffins or biscuits or something. And make sure to tell him you made them yourself."

"That's a little extreme isn't it?" Alex said. "Bringing him food. He doesn't even know me."

"Ah, but he does," Kate corrected her. "He said some very complimentary things about you and he was most impressed when I told him about your Dunmore House training."

"Really?"

Kate could see this gave Alex confidence and made her more sure of herself. She nodded firmly. "Play it cool. Ask his advice on new plants for the shop, but don't decide on anything. That way you can call back another day."

"Great, thanks. I hope I don't go all red and get tongue-tied."

"If you do, just take a deep breath and smile at him. You have a lovely smile. No man minds a little blushing. In fact, they think it's quite sweet."

"Really?"

"Really. And it would do no harm to drop into the library and take out a few books on plants. Drop in a few Latin names to impress him. Show him you have a shared interest."

"I quite like gardening to tell the truth, and that's a great idea." She leant forward and kissed her on the cheek. "Thanks, Kate. I appreciate it."

On Thursday Kate had two unexpected visitors to Baroque.

"Harry," she said, surprised to see him as he walked in the door. "You know we only do ladies' shoes. Unless you're looking for something in a larger size." She winked at him.

"No, I'm not here for shoes. Although I'd love to try some on for the giggle. But someone might see me. You know how small Burnaby is."

"Don't I just."

"Are Trina or Cathy here?"

"No, I'm on my own this afternoon."

"Good." He sat down on the red sofa. "I think I'll cancel our meeting this evening, if that's OK with you."

"Fine," she said. "I'll refund the money."

"Why don't you just hang on to it, I might need you at a later date."

"And, if you don't mind me asking, what has changed your mind?"

"Um, I kind of met someone."

"Really?"

"The girl from the coffee shop, you know, Alex. She called in this morning and I haven't been able to get her out of my head."

Kate beamed. Yes! she thought. Instant success. You're good, Kate Bowan, damn good.

"She called into the shop and she looked so different. Her hair was pinned up with curly bits hanging around her face and she has the loveliest smile, Kate. I was trying to rush her through choosing some plants but she offered me one of these amazing chocolate bun things that she'd cooked — they'd just come out of the oven and they were still warm. I started to eat it on my feet and she said it wasn't good for my digestion to eat that way and that I should sit down."

Kate stifled a grin. Alex telling Harry what to do — now there was a first.

"She waited until I'd finished eating and then we talked about plants," he continued. "She's quite into gardening, you know. She's just signed up for an evening course in Sandybay Community College on indoor plants."

"Really?" Kate asked, most impressed. Alex had done her homework impeccably.

"And she even knew the Latin name of one of my favourites — the *Citrus mituis*."

"Sorry?" asked Kate.

"It's a small tree that grows baby oranges. I suggested it for the coffee shop. She was a real breath of fresh air to tell the truth. I wanted to ask your advice. Do you think she might like to go to the Burnaby Flower Festival with me? It's on over the next weekend. Do you think I should ask her?"

"Yes, I definitely think you should." Kate put her hand on his. "If she's interested in plants she'd really enjoy it and it would give you both a chance to get to know each other better. The Flower Festival sounds lovely."

"Thanks, Kate. I'll ask her tomorrow." He jumped up. "Must dash. Radio tomorrow morning and I haven't got anything prepared. I'm supposed to be talking about bushy succulents and their medicinal properties. Don't ask. See you."

"See you." Kate smiled to herself. Her plan had worked like a treat. Maybe she should take on more female clients. Pity she couldn't fix her own love life while she was at it. She popped herself onto the stool behind the desk to lodge the last two sales in the stock

172

book — one pair of pink strappy sandals and a pair of red size three boots left over from last spring that they thought they'd never get rid of. Cathy and Trina would be delighted. Another customer came in the door. Before she had a chance to raise her head she heard a familiar voice. "Cat? Cat?" She recognized the soft American accent instantly and her heart began to pound in her chest. She leant towards the desk, her eyes fixed on the stock book. The numbers and letters swam before her eyes. Was this some sort of elaborate nightmare? Would she wake up any second now sweating and head thumping.

"Cat?" The voice drew nearer.

She forced herself to look up. There he was, standing in front of her, smiling — the man who had almost ruined her life. Still as damn attractive as ever.

"Jay?" she whispered. "What the hell are you doing here?"

CHAPTER
NINE

Paige

Paige lay in bed wide awake. It was only six o'clock in the morning but she couldn't get back to sleep.

"Tom?" she whispered. "Are you awake?"

No answer. She nudged him in the side. "Tom. I need to talk to you."

He grunted.

"Tom!" she said again, a little louder this time.

"What's wrong?" he asked groggily. "Have we slept through the alarm?"

"No, it's still early. But I have to talk to you."

"Can't it wait?"

"No."

He sighed and rolled over to face her. "What is it then?"

She looked at him in the half light and wondered how he was going to react to the news about the baby. It was nearly a week since she'd visited the doctor and had had her home test confirmed and she'd been putting it off ever since. But she couldn't keep it to herself any longer.

"I'm pregnant," she blurted out.

"What?"

"Pregnant. We're having another baby."

Silence again.

"Tom? Say something."

"I can't. I'm in shock."

She started to cry. Getting the news off her chest was a relief but she'd hoped he'd be pleased.

"What's wrong, love?" he asked putting his arms around her. "Are you not pleased? It's great news. I know it's a bit quick after Alfie, but it'll be fine."

"Do you really mean that?" she asked. "You're not annoyed?"

"Annoyed? Why would I be annoyed? Of course not. I'm delighted. You know I want a big family. It's a bit of a surprise, that's all."

"No kidding." She sniffed. "Think of how I feel. What with the elections and everything."

"It doesn't change a thing," Tom said evenly. "How many months gone are you?"

"Three, I think. I'm not sure of the dates."

"So you're over the worst of the tiredness and the sickness, aren't you?"

"Yes, Dr Spock. Since when are you the great expert?"

"I've been through it twice before, remember? You won't be all that big for a while yet. And there's no reason to mention it to anyone until after the elections."

"Is that not lying by omission?"

"Not at all. Your health is your own business. If anyone asks you directly you can answer them honestly. If they don't ask don't proffer the information. It's as simple as that."

"Spoken like a true campaign manager."

"Absolutely. Speaking of which, in the circumstances, are you really up to doorstepping this week, love?"

"Yes," she said firmly. "I'm going to do everything I can to win this election, Tom. Everything. Including drawing the raffle at the Burnaby Flower Festival, opening the new library in Sandybay National School, and holding an open questions and answers session on my policies in the new Burnaby Arts Centre in the spirit of openness and transparency, as suggested by my campaign manager."

"Are you really sure?" Tom asked again.

"Yes, positive."

"Then I'm behind you all the way."

"Thanks," she said gratefully. "I love you, Tom. You're so good to me."

Tom held her hand to his lips and kissed it. "Anything for the mother of my soon to be three children. Now seeing as we're up so early, Councillor." He moved his hands over her arms and she could hear the smile in his voice. "And we don't have to worry about time, let's make the most of it." He nipped her ear playfully with his teeth.

"How about a big cuddle?" Paige asked. "I'm not really up to anything else this morning, to be honest."

"A cuddle it is." He smiled warmly. "Come here you." He put his arms around Paige and hugged her tightly.

She hugged him back and smiled to herself. Maybe Tom was right. If she could just get through the next

176

few tense and superhumanly busy pre-election weeks, then everything would be fine.

Paige and Tom started their first day of doorstepping at nine o'clock that very morning. "Come in, young lady, come in. I've just put the kettle on," said Mrs O'Brien, an elderly Burnaby Grove resident as they stood in her hall at ten o'clock. They'd already covered the High Burnaby estate and were now moving down Burnaby Avenue towards the village. "Would you like a cuppa?"

Paige looked at Tom who shrugged then nodded.

"That would be lovely, Mrs O'Brien," he said. "But we don't want to put you to any trouble."

"Not at all. I insist." She showed them into the sitting room, then toddled slowly out the door.

Tom smiled at Paige when Mrs O'Brien had left the room. "This doorstepping is taking longer than I'd planned. I hadn't realized how much people like to talk."

"I know. But it means a lot to some of them, especially the older ones."

"Next week Molly and Kate have promised to help. And I've roped in your mum too. And Lily's going to ring as many of her friends as she can. She said if she wasn't incapacitated at the moment she'd be burning shoe leather with us."

"Lily's such a sweetie. I must give her a ring."

After a few minutes, Mrs O'Brien returned carrying a tray. "Here we go," she said.

Tom jumped up. "Let me help you."

"It's fine, young man. But thank you anyway." She placed the tray carefully on a small coffee table in front of them and began to pour tea from the elegant light blue china pot with matching tea cups, sugar bowl and milk jug.

"What lovely china." Paige smiled. "Where did you get it?"

Mrs O'Brien beamed. "How kind of you to ask. My late husband gave it to me for our fiftieth wedding anniversary. I use it whenever I have special guests over. He was a wonderful man you know, such a gentleman. Let me tell you about our wedding day. When I saw him standing at the altar waiting for me I thought I'd pass out. He looked so handsome . . ."

As they left the house forty minutes later Tom smiled at Paige. "You only managed to tell her about one of your policies but she adored you. You've definitely got her vote."

"Wasn't she sweet? Imagine, they were married fifty-seven years, isn't that just something?"

"It is, quite something." Tom looked at the list on the wooden clipboard in his hands. "Burnaby Manor next. Should be interesting."

As soon as they walked in the door of the old people's home, they heard loud piano music which sounded suspiciously like "Knees Up Mother Brown".

"That's Lily Bowan playing." The matron smiled warmly. "She's here every Monday morning running the weekly sing-song. The residents love it."

"Isn't she supposed to be resting?" asked Paige. "She's just out of hospital."

178

"You try telling Lily to rest," the matron snorted.

Paige laughed. "I know what you mean."

"Paige!" Lily cried as she and Tom entered the large front room. "How nice to see you. I hope you're all voting for Paige, ladies and Mr Fowler. She's an old friend of mine."

"Give us a song and we'll vote for you," a woman with pink hair quipped.

"Yes, go on, give us a song," another added. "That Annette one refused. Said she didn't know any. But you do, don't you, Paige?"

Tom pushed her firmly towards the piano. "She's a wonderful singer," he assured them.

"Tom!" Paige hissed.

"Do the one you do for the kids. The one about the moon."

"'Moon River'?" she asked.

"That's the one."

"I don't think . . ."

"I know that," Lily surprised her. "Audrey Hepburn in *Breakfast at Tiffany's*, wasn't it? Let me see." She played a few notes on the keys. "Got it. On you go, girl."

Paige began to sing the opening bars, wobbling a little at first. She had a clear, low-pitched voice which suited the song perfectly. As she sang the residents began to sing along, some more than a little out of time but it didn't matter, they were obviously enjoying themselves. As she finished everyone gave her a rousing round of applause.

"Well done, Paige." Lily smiled widely. "That was great. And now Tom."

"Oh, no!" Tom protested.

"Go on," Paige said. "Do 'Summertime'."

"I know that one too." Lily started to play.

"Go on," Paige cajoled. "Do it for the votes, please," she whispered.

He smiled. "Just for you." He sang in his lazy, easy manner and many of the residents joined in.

"He's great," the matron whispered to Paige as he began the second verse. "Thanks for being such good sports, you've made their day. I think they found Annette a little dry. She kept droning on about her policies and bored them all stupid."

"I'll have to remember not to do that."

"I don't think you could bore people if you tried. You have a nice easy way with people. And Lily is always singing your praises."

Paige smiled. "That's lovely to hear."

"I hope you get in. Burnaby could do with someone like you. Best of luck."

"Thanks."

Leaving the home an hour later after more tea and more singing Paige felt like she was walking on air.

"That went really well, Paige," Tom said. "If you keep that up you'll have the whole of Burnaby voting for you in no time."

"Here's hoping," she replied. "Fingers crossed."

The following morning Paige was one of the guests on Chat FM's political and local news programme, *What's*

Going On. The presenter, Wella Davis was a tall, attractive blonde in her late twenties, who was known and loved by the listeners for her sharp tongue and her "take no prisoners" approach to interviewing. She was also known in the radio world for being brutally ambitious — many young producers and researchers had been cut to the quick by her bruising criticism and downright rude manner. Her current researcher, Rita Farrell, rumoured also to be Wella's girlfriend, had rung Paige the previous evening to ask her to appear on Wella's radio show.

"Late notice isn't it?" Paige had asked.

"Wella likes to spring things on people — it's part of her style," Rita explained.

"Who else will be in the studio?"

"Annette Higgins, Paddy Burns, Miles McGreinna, Mark Tine and Jackie Pile."

Paige whistled. "Bring on the heavy hitters. And you want me as well?"

"Wella likes some of your policies. She thinks you have a good chance of winning a seat if the liberal vote comes through for you."

"Really?" Paige was flattered.

"So we'll see you tomorrow at quarter to ten in the studio? Do you have the address?"

"Yes, I've been in a few times before. See you then. And thanks, Rita."

"No problem. See you tomorrow."

As Paige drove towards Dublin city on the way to the studio, she listened to Wella laying into a representative from an Internet company who had been less than scrupulous with their on-line competitions. The show started at nine, and Paige and her fellow politicians were on at ten. Apparently, the Internet company had been making quite a habit of giving their top prizes to friends and family, angering many of their on-line customers who, by all accounts, had really won the competitions and had documentary on-line proof of the same. Paige was impressed by Wella's technique. Her legal training obviously served her well — she cleverly extracted enough damning information from the interviewee to sink them and then stuck the knife in — making them admit to their wrongdoings. By the end of the piece the company had promised to recompense all the aggrieved parties and had given an unconditional apology to all their clients into the bargain.

Paige gripped the steering wheel tightly. Wella was not to be trifled with. She decided there and then that the only way to deal with Wella was to be open and honest — completely transparent — and to hope to goodness that Rita was right and that Wella really did like some of her policies. She wasn't going to get into any slanging matches no matter how tasty the bait.

Paige parked the car on Merrion Square, luckily finding a spot almost straightaway. She fed coins into the parking meter and stuck the ticket onto the inside of her driver's window. Bending down, she contorted her upper body to check her lipstick in the wing mirror. As she suspected — telltale dark cherry red stains on her teeth. She rubbed them with her finger, then popped a finger in her mouth, pursed her lips around it and drew it back out. That should deal with the rogue

182

lipstick, she thought, shouldn't have put it on so hastily. She brushed down the front of her slightly wrinkled black pencil skirt and began to walk towards the radio station's building.

"Hello," she said a little nervously into the intercom.

"Chat FM. How can I help you?" A disembodied female voice asked.

"Paige Brady. I'm on Wella's show at . . ."

The intercom gave an almighty screech and Paige heard the door lock click open.

"Push the door. We're on the third floor," the voice said crisply.

Standing in the dimly lit lift Paige stared at her reflection in the grimy mirror. She looked pale. She ran her hands over her stomach. It was starting to take on a gently rounded shape. Soon she'd be in maternity clothes but hopefully not too soon. Luckily it was looking hopeful — with both Callum and Alfie she'd never got huge. She always felt sorry for the women who looked like baby elephants — their swollen bellies causing them to waddle in a most ungainly fashion, their breath short and laboured.

As the lift door opened she walked into the hall and looked around. There was no obvious indication of where she should go. Wooden swing doors led in three different directions. Then she spotted a small Chat FM sticker on one of the doors. She took a deep breath and pushed it open. Sitting on the lurid green sofas in front of her were Annette, Paddy, Mark and Miles.

"Hi, Paige." A young woman with short dark hair came rushing towards her, her hand outstretched. "It's lovely to meet you. I'm Rita. I spoke to you on the phone." She turned towards the other guests. "And you know everyone, I presume?"

Paige nodded. "Yes, thank you."

"Would you like a cup of coffee before we start? We're just waiting for Jackie and then we'll move into the studio during the news."

"I'd love one," Paige said gratefully. She could feel her hands begin to shake.

"Come and sit down, Paige." Paddy smiled up at her. "Take the weight off your feet. Not that you have any weight of course. Young slip of a thing like you." He looked around the room. "Or am I allowed to say things like that in this day and age? Annette will probably accuse me of being sexist."

Annette scowled at him. "And are we allowed to make comments about your weight, Paddy?" she asked.

"You can if you like," he said mildly, holding his stomach in. He was fond of the good life and this had taken its toll on his girth and his jowls over the years.

"How's the anti-dump campaign coming on?" Mark Tine asked, aware that Paddy and Annette didn't exactly see eye to eye at the best of times. Mark was the local Green Party representative, an idealistic young man in his late twenties. This was his first time to contest an election.

"Good, Mark, good. And thanks for all your support, and yours, Paige." Paddy nodded at her and ignored Annette and Miles who had both deemed local environmental issues beneath them.

184

"I saw an interesting photograph of you in the paper last week, Paige," Miles said, his sharp nasal voice cutting through the air. Miles McGreinna was the local Irish Party representative and Paige didn't like him one little bit. He was fixated by "family values" and the destruction of morality by the liberal agenda. He'd spoken out vehemently against both divorce and abortion when the relevant referenda had come into play and he was firmly right of centre, a die-hard conservative and vocal Roman Catholic. His policies were positively prehistoric and Paige hated his creeping anti-working woman stance. Annette also took this stance. Which was unsettling since she was one in theory, although her children were grown up.

"Would that have been the one of my team winning the all-Ireland?" Paige said feigning innocence. She knew damn well which one he was referring to.

Before he had a chance to answer, Rita came flurrying back. "Everyone ready? Let's get you all into studio. Jackie rang to say she was stuck in traffic. We'll have to go ahead without her."

Miles led the way, followed by Annette and Paddy. Mark and Paige brought up the rear. The studio was small and they all had to clamber over wires, old jugs of water and discarded ring folders to get to their places around the large table. Rita handed each guest headphones.

"I hate these things," Paddy complained. "They always pinch my ears."

"Me too," Mark agreed.

Wella smiled at them. "Welcome. They're playing the ten o'clock news at the moment and we'll go into our slot straight afterwards. I'm going to ask each candidate a question on their policies and there will be a little time for open discussion at the end. Please try not to hog the air space and give everyone a chance to speak."

They all nodded.

"Here we go," Wella said. She leant in towards the large furry grey microphone in front of her. "Welcome back to *What's Going On*, the topical news programme on Chat FM, with myself, Wella Davis. This morning in the studio we are privileged to have the leading Dun Laoghaire Rathdown candidates in the forthcoming September election — Deputy Paddy Burns from the People's Party; Councillor Annette Higgins, Independent; Mr Miles McGreinna, from the Irish Party . . ."

Miles interrupted her. "Doctor Miles McGreinna," he said pompously.

"Ah, yes, I'd forgotten about your Open University doctorate in ancient history," she said cuttingly. "Sorry *Doctor* McGreinna."

"London School of Arts," he corrected her. "And it was in philosophy not ancient history."

Paige caught Mark's eye. He winked at her. She looked down at the table and tried not to laugh. Miles was so annoying.

"To continue," Wella said, "Mr Mark Tine from the Green Party and last but not least, Councillor Paige Brady, also Independent. I'd like to start with Deputy Burns. Deputy, there has been a lot in the papers recently about the proposed Burnaby dump, can you fill the listeners in on some of the issues please?"

"Certainly, Wella," Paddy said warmly. "Be glad to."

As Paddy explained the risks involved in locating a dump near a residential area, Paige's mind began to drift. She was dog-tired today and she could have done without the mad dash into town to tell the truth. She was due back in Burnaby in two hours to talk at a Lady's Lunch in the Burnaby Golf Club and then Angus was calling in that afternoon to meet Callum and she was a little worried about it. She so wanted them to get on and . . . She was brought back to earth with a bump when Wella asked her a question.

"What do you think, Paige?"

Damn, she thought, what were they talking about — the dump? Or had they moved on from that? Openness and honestly, she reminded herself.

"Can you repeat the question, Wella?" she asked with a smile.

Wella looked at her for a second, and noticing Paige's drawn, pale face and dark shadows around the eyes decided to cut her some slack. "Of course. Do you think you are a good role model for young people? I was thinking specifically about the recent photograph in the *Burnaby News*."

Paige had been dreading this question, but figured if Wella hadn't asked it, Miles would have weaseled it in somewhere anyway.

Paige took a deep breath. "Interesting photo, wasn't it?" She smiled at Wella.

Wella laughed. "Yes, it was."

"To answer your question in one word — yes. I am an excellent role model for young people. I was introduced to sport from an early age, thanks largely to my father, Lorcan Brady, who also played soccer for his country, and who set up the local Burnaby Soccer Club in his time. I've played soccer at the highest level and have also been involved in both college and school coaching. I am very involved in the community and was instrumental in setting up the new Burnaby Arts Centre."

"And you have two young children I believe, Councilor Brady, is that right?" Wella asked.

"Yes. And one of my key policies is to lobby the government to provide affordable childcare for all working women in the country. At present Irish parents pay out over twenty per cent of their wages on childcare, way above the European average of eight per cent."

Miles snorted at this.

"Do you have a problem with women working, Dr McGreinna?" Wella asked, knowing full well that he did.

"I have no problem with women working *per se*," he said smoothly. "It's women with young children who work I object to. Children shouldn't be abandoned to strangers for large portions of the day. It's causing huge problems in our society — teenage drinking, delinquency, rise in crime rates . . ."

"I agree," Annette interjected. "Women should take full responsibility for their offspring."

188

"What about men?" Mark asked. "Surely they should take equal responsibility."

"Quite," Miles said with a sneer on his face. "But you wouldn't know anything about taking responsibility, Mr Tine, would you?"

"Sorry?" Mark asked. "Would you care to explain that last comment?"

"Yes, Dr McGreinna," Wella said, delighted with the way things were heading. Nothing like a whiff of scandal to boost the ratings. "Please explain what you're trying to say. I for one would like to hear it."

"Mark Tine is having a baby out of wedlock with a married woman." Miles stared at Mark with an evil glint in his eye. "Deny it if you can."

Mark was silent for a moment. His eyes were flashing and there were two angry red spots on his cheeks. "Of course I don't deny it. I *am* having a child with my partner of four years, it's true. And for your information, Miles, she's divorced . . ."

"An English divorce," Miles said snidely. "Not recognized by the church in this state."

Mark stared at him. "She's Protestant, so her divorce is recognized by her own church. But of course you don't believe there is any other church in this country except for the Roman Catholic one, do you Miles?"

"The Roman Catholic church has a very important role to play in —" Miles began.

Wella held her right hand up. "We're not really interested in the church's role this morning, thank you. Now let's get back to Mr Tine. Is there anything else you'd like to say on this matter, Mr Tine?"

"Yes, Wella, there is. I'd like to say that I am overjoyed at the prospect of being a parent. My partner suffers from polycystic ovaries and she didn't think she'd ever have children, so it was a delightful surprise for both of us. And we hope to get married next year when we've found a new house."

"Thank you for being so honest, Mr Tine." Wella smiled at him.

"If I were you, Mr Tine . . ." Miles began.

"And do you have children yourself, Dr McGreinna?" Wella asked quickly.

"Um, no."

"Or a wife?"

"No."

"Then you're not really in a position to give advice are you, Doctor?"

"But . . ." Miles was livid. How dare that young pup speak to him like that?

"Can I cut in here?" Paddy Burns said.

"I haven't finished . . ." Miles blustered.

"Yes, you have," Wella said, glaring at him. "Please allow Deputy Burns to speak."

"I'd like to congratulate Mr Tine on the news and wish him and his family all the best in the future."

"Thank you," Mark said gratefully.

After the slot had finished, they all walked through into Chat FM's hall together.

"Outrageous," Annette said. "Call that a radio show? I only got to talk about my garden winning a prize in the Tidy Towns competition for a brief moment and

190

didn't get to mention the new computer call centre I have planned for Dun Laoghaire borough at all."

"Terrible woman, that Wella," Miles grumbled. "Most unprofessional."

Paige put her hand on Mark's arm. "Well done," she said in a low voice. "You handled that very well."

"So did you," he said. "Exhausting, wasn't it?"

She nodded.

There was an awkward silence as they all waited for the lift in the small hallway.

"So, who's for the Burnaby Flower Show on Saturday?" Paddy asked in a jovial voice, breaking the atmosphere. "You're doing the draw, aren't you, Paige?"

"That's right."

"Hardly fair," Annette muttered.

"Sorry, what was that, Annette?" asked Paddy.

"They should really have asked me you know. After all, my garden did win a prize . . ."

"At the Tidy Towns, yes, I think we all know that by now, Annette. But I'm sure you're going to go along anyway, aren't you? Shame to miss an opportunity to meet the punters."

"I might," Annette admitted sniffily.

"And I'm running the bottle stall for my sins," Mark said.

"Well, I'll definitely see you then, Mark." Paddy laughed and rubbed his hands together. "Hope you have some nice Irish whiskey. I feel a lucky streak coming on."

★   ★   ★

Paige opened the front door and smiled at Angus. She felt decidedly nervous. Callum was in high spirits and was currently dashing around upstairs with no clothes on, nothing new. "Come in." She led Angus into the kitchen. Bright sunlight was flooding in the windows and she gestured towards the small flowery sofa. "Please, sit down. Would you like tea or coffee? Or a soft drink?"

He smiled. "Nothing for me, thanks. I'm fine. This is a lovely house, is it Georgian?"

"Yes. It was in rag order when we bought it but Tom's a bit of a DIY nut — he did a lot of it himself. And luckily he works in a mortgage company or we never would have been able to afford it. This part's an extension. They weren't mad into big kitchens in those days. The one we replaced was small and didn't get much light."

"Liked keeping the servants in the dark, did they?" He grinned. "I'm sure they would have had servants in a house this size."

"You're probably right." She was beginning to feel more at ease. Angus had a nice calm manner and a wonderfully warm smile. It was impossible not to smile back. "I'll just go upstairs and get Callum."

After she'd left the room Angus looked around. The kitchen was country-style wood complete with dark blue Aga and had a warm and homely feel. In front of the sofa where he was sitting was a large Victorian dresser crammed full with books of all shapes and sizes, framed photographs, a jar full of coins, plastic toys in various states of distress and candles in wooden and

192

wrought iron holders. There were larger framed photographs on the walls, along with an attractive oil painting of Burnaby's coastal Martello tower, the sea stretching out shimmering blue in the background. The most striking photograph on the wall was of two laughing teenage girls in scary eighties outfits — one in a pink and blue ra-ra skirt, with legwarmers, lace-up boots, and a string vest over a yellow T-shirt; and the second fashion victim in a tiny stonewash denim miniskirt, her slim legs in fishnet tights and her hair piled up on top of her head and fastened with some sort of bright blue netting. Hang on a second. He got to his feet and walked towards the photograph. Leaning forward and looking even closer, he snorted. It was Paige and the girl from the bookshop, Molly.

Just then he heard a noise behind him and swung around. "Great, isn't it?" Paige asked.

"Sorry, I didn't mean to . . ." Angus stammered.

"Don't worry, it catches everyone's attention. Molly gave it to me for my birthday last year. It was taken when we were thirteen. We thought we were the bee's knees."

"Mummy looks silly, doesn't she?" a little voice piped up.

Angus smiled at the little boy who was holding his mother's hand tightly. He looked angelic with his white blonde hair and open, round face. "You must be Callum. I'm Angus."

"Mummy told me there'd be no telly if I was bold so I have to be nice to you," Callum said. He then gave an almighty sniff and wiped his nose on the sleeve of his red sweatshirt.

"Callum!" Paige glared at him. "That's nasty. If you need to wipe your nose go and get a tissue."

Callum let go of her hand and toddled off into the hall.

"Sorry about that . . ." Paige began.

"Paige, I'm here to help. I'm well used to it, remember? I usually have twenty five or so of the little darlings at the one time."

"Thanks," she said gratefully. Callum came back into the room pulling a long tail of toilet paper behind him. "Callum, what are you doing?" she asked in exasperation. "I told you to get a tissue."

"Couldn't find one. And the loo paper wouldn't break off."

"That's just not true, is it young man?" she asked.

"It is, honestly, Mummy."

She said nothing. What must Angus think? She tore off a piece of the white tissue paper, handed it to Callum with a stern look on her face and began to pick up the remainder of the roll off the floor. "I'll be back in a second," she said to Angus as she followed the paper out of the room.

As soon as she'd gone Angus looked at Callum. "Do you like the Andrex ad where the boy gets the toilet paper stuck in his jeans and runs it all around the house?" he asked calmly.

Callum smiled knowingly and nodded. "Are you going to give out to me?" he asked after a few seconds.

194

"Not at all," Angus said. "Sure, why would I? I'm only here to play with you, not to give out to you."

Callum's eyes widened. "Is that right?" he asked. "That's not what Mummy said. She said you were here to mind me and that I was to be good."

"You don't have to be good," Angus said. "Except at our games. You have to be good at them."

"What sort of games?" Callum asked with interest, cocking his head to one side.

"All sorts — hide and seek, mountain climbing, making a tree house, making a camp fire, bungee jumping . . ."

"Bungee jumping!" Callum was amazed. "I've seen that on telly. They jump off bridges and stuff. Mum would never let me do that."

Paige, who was standing in the hall listening to the conversation with interest, stiffened. Bungee jumping? Callum was quite right. What was Angus thinking of?

"It's not real bungee jumping," Angus explained. "It's a bungee trampoline. You're attached to these rubber pulleys and you can jump up and down and go amazingly high. They have one on Sandybay seafront."

Paige who suddenly realized that she'd been holding her breath, felt a huge wave of relief flood her body. For a second there she'd begun to wonder about Angus's suitability.

"Cool!" Callum grinned. "Can we go now?"

"So you want me to play with you when your mum and dad are at work?" Angus asked.

Callum nodded firmly. "Yes."

"There's just one thing, Callum. Every morning you'll have to tidy up your room before we play and do one nice thing for your mum and dad."

"Like what?" Callum asked suspiciously.

"Nothing major. Give your mum a kiss, pick up Alfie's toys for him, blow your own nose, get up and dressed yourself like a big fellow, that kind of thing."

Callum thought about it for a minute — it didn't sound too bad really. "And then you'll take me bungee jumping and all the other cool things?"

"Yes, I promise. Bungee jumping or one cool thing every day. I'll make up a star chart and every morning I'll ask your mum and dad to put a star up if you've been helpful and nice. And then we play for the whole day. Is it a deal?"

"Sure," Callum said. "As long as Mum doesn't mind."

Mind? Paige smiled to herself as she rested her forehead against the wall, the plaster deliciously cool against her skin. She felt weak with relief — had they finally found someone who understood how to deal with Callum?

Angus started on Monday and sure enough, encouraged by the idea of bungee jumping and other "cool" activities, Callum behaved himself on Monday morning. After staring intently at the new star chart for several minutes, which Angus had dropped in over the weekend, he ran over and kissed Paige on the bottom.

196

"Callum!" Paige squealed and whipped around. She was rinsing the cereal bowls in the sink at the time and was taken quite unawares.

Callum smiled up at her. "I kissed you, Mummy. Angus said that was being nice. Can I have my star now?"

Paige laughed. "Yes, I suppose so, but next time try kissing me on the cheek. OK?"

"OK, Mummy."

"He just got the wrong kind of cheek, love," Tom grinned.

"Talking of cheek," Paige said to Tom. "Less of that, you. You're supposed to be showing your son a good example. How's Alfie getting on with his breakfast?"

"He's nearly finished. I'll drop him off to Mum's this morning if that would help."

"That would be great, thanks. And you're all right for campaigning at the train station at five?"

"Grand, I'll meet you there. Looking forward to it."

"Being belted by commuters' brollies, I'd say you are."

"Surely it doesn't get violent."

"Not usually, no."

Tom looked at her and she broke into a smile. She walked over and kissed him on the cheek. She was feeling decidedly chipper this morning, all things considered. "I'm going into the office to make some phone calls. See you later, alligator."

"In a while, crocodile," said Tom.

"Not too soon, you big fat baboon," Callum joined in.

"Callum!" they both chorused.

"Have I lost my star?" he asked anxiously.

"No, but I'd watch it young man," Paige said ominously.

"I'll go and tidy my room." Callum ran out the door and thundered up the stairs.

"Whatever that Angus has done, God bless him," Tom said.

"No kidding," Paige agreed.

CHAPTER
TEN

Molly

"Who are we waiting for?" Paige asked the rest of the Book Club at the August meeting.

"Just Harry, I think. Trisha can't make it," Cathy said. "I'm not sure about Kate."

"No, Kate's not coming. She sent her apologies, she's watching Lily swim," Molly explained. "She doesn't trust her on her own."

"Is Lily's ankle better then?" Paige asked.

"Not quite. But there's no stopping her. She says she's having withdrawal symptoms from the lack of her daily swim."

"Hello, everyone. This is the Book Club I presume?" Milo asked.

Everyone looked up.

"This is Milo Devine, the new owner of the shop," Anita explained. "He's going to be joining us today."

"Have you read the book?" Molly asked a little too sharply.

"Yes," he said. "And I thought it was most . . ."

Paige put up her hands. "Stop! We haven't started yet."

"Sorry," Milo said. Duly chastised, he sat down beside Anita.

Molly nudged Paige in the side. She'd already told her about Milo's crush. Paige smiled back at her and nodded discreetly.

Harry came blustering in. "Sorry, sorry, last minute order came in. Sent the wrong bloody pots of course, idiots. Still, I'm here now." He sat down beside Molly. "And how are we all this fine day?" He looked around the table, his eyes stopping when they came to Milo. There hadn't been a new member of the Club for quite some time.

Paige noticed Harry's interested gaze. "This is Milo, Harry. He's the new owner."

Harry raised his hand and waved casually at Milo. "Hi, welcome. Nice to have another man on board."

"Will we get started then?" Paige asked. "Who'd like to begin? Anita?"

Anita grimaced. "I was hoping you wouldn't ask me first." She sighed theatrically. "I have to say I hated it. Absolutely hated it."

"Thank goodness," Cathy joined in. "I thought it was just me. I couldn't make head or tail of it at all. What nonsense."

"Pretentious rubbish," Molly agreed. "Practically unreadable in parts."

"What I can't understand," Harry added, "is how the man won the Booker a few years ago. Had the judges gone mad?"

"The one that won the Booker — *Regret* — wasn't so turgid," Anita said. "In fact it was excellent in parts. But this one . . . *Mamma Mia!*"

200

"Tell us why you didn't like it, Anita," Paige encouraged.

"Where to start? First of all — the plot was very weak. Nothing really happened the whole way through the book. It was supposed to be about the narrator revisiting the village he grew up in — a presumably fictional place called "Stradbrook" which sounded like a small town in the north of Ireland. But it was so bloody boring. I couldn't stand the narrator — he never stopped moaning about how his life had stagnated in the place and how he'd never been able to make anything of himself because of his upbringing. And the other characters were completely wooden. I couldn't empathize with any of them, let alone understand them."

"Old Mrs White was particularly unbelievable, wasn't she?" Cathy asked. "She was like something out of *Ryan's Daughter* with the white lace shawl and the thatched cottage. I mean, please."

"She was supposed to be the narrator's sort of surrogate mother, wasn't she?" Molly asked. "But she wasn't a very pleasant character."

"That's right," Harry said. "She had no time for her own children and when her youngest son died — what was his name?"

"Johnny," Anita said.

"That's right, Johnny," Harry continued. "She didn't seem too bothered."

"Another thing I can't understand is how the book got so many good reviews. It's complete hogwash,"

Anita said. "It would make you wonder what the reviewers were thinking about."

"May I say something?" Milo asked Paige.

"Of course," Paige said. "Sorry, it is hard to get a word in edgeways at times. Fire away."

"I thought the book was wonderfully written," Milo began. "So atmospheric. You could almost touch the mist on the bogs and smell the turf burning in the old hearths. I think Frost has a touch of genius when it comes to describing the way life was in Ireland in the last century."

"Really?" Anita asked a little scornfully. "Did you not think his descriptive passages went on a bit?"

"No, I enjoyed them. Some of the sentences were exquisitely crafted. You could almost smell the sweat that went into writing some of them."

"But surely writing shouldn't be like that!" Anita cried. "Over crafted and arty. Surely it should flow and be artless. I think the best writers are the ones who make writing look easy. Frost spends far too much time crafting perfect sentences and not enough time creating a strong plot and real, believable characters."

"I agree with Anita," Harry said. "I found his writing most frustrating. I just wanted him to get on with the story, not waffle on about dew catching the light on spider's webs."

"But this is literary fiction we're talking about here, not story-telling," Milo insisted. "Surely you see the difference. Maybe you're more used to reading popular fiction, that's all. Maybe your reading tastes are a little unformed, a little unrefined."

"Rubbish!" Paige said a little more vehemently than she'd intended. "We read all kinds of things in this Book Club, including some damn fine literary fiction."

"Indeed," Anita said angrily. "All kinds of things. But we also read good popular fiction, we're not snobbish. A good book is a good book no matter what genre — crime, sci fi, historical saga, fantasy, whatever. Maybe you just haven't read enough good books to recognize *Stradbrook* for what it is, pretentious rubbish."

"Well really!" Milo said looking a little red in the face. "I'm not here to be insulted about my reading tastes. Maybe I should leave."

"Please don't," Paige said. "And don't take anything personally. We often have quite heated arguments about books, it's quite normal. Stay. We'd all like you to. Please."

Milo looked around the table. Everyone nodded. Even Anita.

"Sorry," Anita mumbled. "I got a little carried away there."

"Yes, well . . ."

"Have I missed anything?" Sam asked, walking towards the table. Everyone stared up at him. "Sorry I'm so late."

Paige laughed. "Not much, Sam. Please do sit down. Welcome. Did you get a chance to read the book?"

He nodded. "Yes, but I only got about halfway through. There's not much of a story to it, is there? I got bored of it to tell the truth. Picked up *Lucinda's Tale* instead. Anita had recommended it to me when I started in the shop. Now, there's a book."

Within minutes, the group was eagerly and noisily discussing *Lucinda's Tale*, which had been an earlier Book Club choice. Paige breathed a sigh of relief. She had enough squabbling children to deal with at home.

"So, what did you think of your first meeting?" Paige asked Milo after the meeting had finished.

"Interesting," he said. "Very interesting. I learnt a lot."

"About books?" Paige asked.

"Among other things," he said quietly. He looked over towards Anita who was deep in conversation with Cathy about next week's book. "I don't think she likes me," he said, gesturing towards the two women.

"Anita?"

He nodded.

"You'd be surprised," Paige said. "She just gets very passionate about books, that's all. I honestly don't think it was anything personal."

He said nothing.

After lunch, Anita and Molly met in Coffee Heaven to discuss their plan for the bookshop. Paige had excused herself — she had an interview with one of the radio stations and a photo call for the Flower Festival.

"I'm worried about pulling off a Book Festival of this size," Molly began. "I know you and Paige are confident but there are so many things that could . . ."

"Molly, have some faith." Anita smiled at her. "It's going to be a lot of work but it'll all come together, you'll see. Especially now that we've found such a great second venue. Paige has arranged everything with Tara, the new arts administrator in the Burnaby Arts Centre and she's mad keen to get involved. She wants to run a special Love Bean event for the children with African storytelling and dancing. And best of all, she'll organize the whole thing herself."

"What's a Love Bean when it's at home?"

"It's an African friendship token. It's literally a large, brown bean. You give it to someone you like."

Molly sighed. "I just don't . . ."

"Molly! What's wrong with you?"

She sighed again. "I don't know. Sorry, I'm all over the place today."

"Is that ex-boyfriend of yours pestering you again?"

"Not really. He's been fairly subdued this week to tell the truth."

"Good. Don't let him get to you. Be strong."

"I'll try."

"And how's the writing coming along?"

"Not great," Molly admitted. "I haven't been able to concentrate for a few weeks now. Maybe I'm not cut out to be a writer."

"Maybe not. But you should at least give it a go. You'll regret it if you don't."

"I suppose."

Anita put her hand on Molly's. "Have some courage, Molly. Be brave for once in your life. You have it in you, I know you do. Reach inside yourself and find your inner strength. I really do think that there's a writer in there."

Molly felt like crying. She had no idea why Anita believed in her but it was comforting to know that she did.

"Now, let's go over our list," Anita said gently, sensing Molly's emotionally fragile state of mind. "Who do we have for Saturday morning?"

Molly studied the sheet in front of her. "We blast off with two of the biggies — Rose Lovett and Jennie Tracker." Rose and Jennie were the American and British Queens of romantic fiction.

Anita whistled. "That should draw the crowds. Followed by . . .?"

"The Literary Lunch."

"Of course, that should be fun. And Matty and Alex have agreed to do the catering?"

Molly nodded. "And Harry has offered to decorate the tables for free."

"How sweet of him."

"It is decent of him, isn't it? After lunch we have the panel discussion on 'Getting Published — Tips from the Top'."

"Has Bonnie Evans agreed to sit on the panel?" Anita asked.

"She has." Molly smiled. "Should be interesting." Bonnie was one of Burnaby's most famous locals — a flamboyant romantic saga novelist who spent most of her time in the South of France. She was well known for her strong opinions on everything from writing to poker and horse racing and always had something outrageous to say. The media loved her — a glamorous woman in her early fifties, she ate interviewers for breakfast and had rendered even Terry Wogan and Gay Byrne speechless in her day.

"Should be," Anita agreed. "It's going to be wonderful, really Molly. You and Paige have done Trojan work putting it all together."

"Thanks, I hope it will work."

"It will. No doubt about it. Especially now that Brenda Jackson's researcher has confirmed Rose and Jennie for the radio show the week before the Festival to talk about their work."

"That's great news."

"Isn't it?" Anita said. "And talking about the media, did Millie from the *Burnaby News* get back to you?"

"She did," Molly said. "She agreed to run a short story competition to tie in with the festival. And she'd like you to be one of the judges, along with Bonnie."

"No problem, could be a bit of fun. I hope you're going to enter, Molly."

Molly wrinkled her nose. "I couldn't. It might be a conflict of interests."

"Perhaps. But think about it. Is there anything in the rules to say you can't?"

"Don't know," Molly said thoughtfully. "You haven't written them yet."

Anita laughed. "Then we'll have to see what we can do."

"There's no need, I'm not going to enter."

"OK." Anita knew better than to push her. She looked at her watch and sighed. "I suppose we'd better get back to the shop."

"One last thing. Cathy and Trina have offered to sponsor Jennie's flights. And they said they'll do a window advertising the event in their shop. And Harry and Alex offered to put up posters in their shops too."

"Excellent!" Anita beamed and put her hand on Molly's. "It's all coming together. I knew we could do it Molly. Now let's see if the press will sit up and take notice, shall we?"

"And Milo," Molly added.

"And Milo." Anita nodded solemnly.

That evening Molly decided that some fresh air would do her good. She grabbed a fleece and headed out the door straight after her dinner. Kate was out on yet another dummy date and as it was a sunny, warm evening there was nothing to keep Molly in the house. As she walked down Burnaby Lane towards Sandybay beach she thought about a short story she'd been working on. It was set on a beach in West Cork and involved a chance encounter between a lobster fisherman and an American tourist. Molly wanted to use the Selkie story as a basis for her tale — the legend of how seals came out of the sea and became women on land. But she was having difficulties sewing the traditional strands into her own short story without it being too "clunky" and obvious.

Crossing over the railway bridge, she stood for a moment gazing at the sea stretched out in front of her. It glistened in the evening sun — the light dancing merrily on the tips of the waves. There was a good breeze which whipped at her hair, threatening to pull it out of its loose ponytail. She walked down the steps and her feet crunched onto the stony beach. She strolled down the beach at a brisk pace in the direction of Wicklow, swinging her arms by her sides and taking in deep breaths of the tangy, salty air.

After a while, she heard a familiar voice behind her.

"Hey! Molly! Wait up!"

She turned around and shielded her eyes from the sun. She smiled as she saw Sam being pulled along by a large black Labrador.

"Are you walking him or is he walking you?" She laughed.

"I'm not altogether sure." The dog stopped at Molly's feet and began to jump up, putting it's wet paws on her thighs.

"Sorry," Sam said. "This is Tara, she belongs to my neighbour. She's just been playing in the waves, she's a bit wet."

"So I can see." Molly bent over and patted her head. "Hello, Tara. Are you enjoying your walk?"

Tara wagged her tail eagerly and began to bark.

"I think she likes you," Sam said. "Sorry, are we interrupting your walk?"

"Not at all, it's nice to have the company."

"In that case, mind if we join you?"

"Not at all."

Molly began to walk and Sam fell into step beside her.

"You like going at a fair lick, don't you?" he asked after a moment.

"I know. Paige is always complaining. Sorry, I'll slow down."

"Don't on my account. Tara likes it and I'll get used to it. I've been looking out for you when I'm walking but this is the first time I've seen you."

"I've haven't been walking in ages," Molly explained. "Too busy. You know how it is."

"Don't I just? But Hugh loves the beach. So we're usually here every weekend whether I like it or not."

Molly said nothing. She hadn't asked any questions about Sam's private life since she'd touched one of his raw nerves in the shop — she'd been too nervous of annoying him again.

"You can ask me if you like," Sam said, sensing her unease. "I won't bite your head off this time, I promise."

"About what?"

"About Hugh."

"I'm sorry — you must think I'm awfully nosy."

Sam laughed. "You're not the worst. Must be the writer in you. I hear you're all a very curious bunch."

"How do you know I write?" she asked quickly.

"Anita told me."

"Anita?"

"Sorry, I didn't realize it was a secret. I'd love to read some of your work if you'd let me."

Molly stared at the sea.

"Molly? Sorry, have I said something wrong?"

She shook her head. "I just don't like anyone knowing about my writing, that's all. Anita shouldn't have said anything to you. Not that's there's much to

210

know to tell the truth. I haven't written a word for weeks."

"Why not?" he asked gently.

She shrugged her shoulders. "Haven't felt in the right frame of mind I suppose."

"Not centred enough? I have the same problem myself sometimes."

She looked at him in surprise. "You write too?"

He laughed. "Me? Heavens, no. I make furniture, that's all. But I can only do it if I'm in a good mood." He picked up a stone and kicked it into the sea.

"I remember now, Hugh said you made him a puppet theatre."

"That's right. I make other things too. It's my hobby I suppose — I dabble in it. Not like your writing."

"What do you mean?"

"Well, Anita told me you're quite serious about your writing. How many short stories have you finished?"

"Twenty-seven," she mumbled. "And half a novella."

He whistled. "That's really something. Twenty-seven. I'm impressed."

"Don't be. It's won't come to anything."

"Why do you say that?"

"I just know."

"You should have some confidence in yourself. Maybe some of them are good."

She frowned. "I doubt it."

"Let Anita read one or two. At least you'd know then."

"Maybe I'm happier not knowing. Have you thought of that?"

Sam stopped walking and looked at her. She continued on without him, realized that he wasn't beside her, and stopped. "What?" she asked sharply. "What are you smiling at? Tell me."

"You," he said finally. "You're one big mass of contradictions, Molly. Do you know that?"

"I have no idea what you're talking about." Molly was getting more than a little uncomfortable at the direction this conversation was heading. She decided to change the subject. "Tell me about Hugh."

"What do you want to know?" Sam let Tara off the lead to play in the surf again, put the lead in his pocket and caught up with Molly.

"Are you married?" she asked before she could stop herself.

"Married!" He laughed. "I suppose it's a fair enough question. No, I'm not married. I thought about it at one stage — to Hugh's mum in fact, but it wouldn't have worked out. What about yourself?"

"I was asked once," Molly admitted. "But like you, it wouldn't have worked out."

"The guy outside the bookshop?" Sam asked astutely.

"You saw us?" she asked, embarrassed.

Sam nodded. "He seemed a little upset."

"That was my ex, Denis. He's all right really. Just gets a bit over-emotional at times."

"I know the feeling, Brona is a bit like that."

"Brona?"

"My ex, Hugh's mum."

"What happened? If you don't mind me asking?"

212

"No, it's fine. We were in college together — Arts in UCD. She was in my philosophy class and we met on the very first day of term. She was wearing the most amazing yellow coat with a huge furry yellow collar — you could hardly miss her."

"Love at first sight then?"

"You could say that. She sat down in the row in front of me during the very first lecture and I couldn't take my eyes off her. Afterwards I asked her for coffee and one thing led to another."

"And Hugh?"

Sam was quiet for a moment. "He wasn't exactly planned. Brona was in bits when she found out. Her family are quite strict Catholics and she was dreading telling them. At one stage she considered not having it but neither of us felt it was the right thing to do."

"What age were you?" asked Molly.

"I was twenty-two and Brona was twenty-one."

"It must have been hard."

"It was I suppose, but we managed. We lived together for a while but things didn't work out. She moved back in with her parents nearly two years ago. She and Hugh live in a self-contained apartment in their basement now — so it's all worked out for the best really. He gets to see his grandparents every day while Brona's working and I get to see him every weekend."

"What does she do?"

"She's an actress. She does voice-over work, radio ads mostly and she has a small part on *City Lights* as Jude's on-off girlfriend. You know, the soap opera."

"Don't watch it I'm afraid."

"Neither do I." He took Tara's lead out of his pocket and walked towards the edge of the water. "Here, girl!" he shouted. "You've had enough now." Tara barked and stayed in the water.

Molly laughed. "You have great control over her."

"I know. Still, she probably has the right idea." He sat down on the stones and began to untie his boots.

"What are you doing?" Molly asked.

"Going paddling. Come on!"

"No way. It'll be freezing."

"No it won't." He pulled off his boots and socks and rolled up the bottom of his jeans. He walked boldly into the water, trying not to wince as the icy water lapped his ankles.

"Told you," Molly said.

"It's not that bad," he insisted. "Come on. I dare you."

Molly looked at the water which was rippling and bubbling over the shingle. It did look rather inviting. "OK." She joined him, dipping in one foot gingerly, followed by the other.

"You liar, it is freezing." She grinned.

"Freezing but fun."

After two minutes Molly's toes had had enough. She stepped out of the water and walked slowly towards her shoes and socks. "My feet are practically numb," she said. "I blame you."

"It's good for you," he said. "Toughen you up."

She sat down on the shingle, waved her feet in the air to get rid of the drips and pulled her socks over her damp feet. As she tied the laces of her runners, Sam sat down beside her.

"When was the last time you paddled?" he asked.

She shrugged her shoulders. "No idea. Ages ago."

"You should do it more often, keeps you young."

"Is that right? What happened to you then?"

"Very funny," he grinned back. "Um, what are you up to this evening?"

"Do you know, I think I might attempt to do some writing."

"Good idea." He jumped up and walked towards the sea. "Here, Tara," he shouted at the dog who was still enjoying the waves. "Come on, girl. You'll freeze if you don't get out now."

Molly watched him from her seated position as Tara ran towards Sam, her tongue lolling out of her mouth. He wrestled with her good-naturedly on the stones, Tara yelping enthusiastically as he held her down and rubbed her tummy. He looked over at Molly and smiled, his eyes crinkling attractively at the corners.

Damn, Molly thought. I do believe Sam was going to ask me out. And I blew it. She looked at Tara and back at Sam. Oh, to be a dog, she thought. Life would be so much simpler.

CHAPTER
ELEVEN

Kate

"Hello. There are no free tables anywhere, mind sharing?"

Angus looked up in surprise at the attractive blonde woman in front of him. "Um, no, not at all. Please sit down."

"Thanks." She said, placing her coffee mug on the table and sat down. "It's busy in here today, isn't it?"

"Um, yes, very. Saturday shoppers, I suppose."

"Yes, of course." She looked at him and smiled. "I've seen you in here a few times." She held out her hand. "I'm Patricia. Patricia Simons. And you are . . .?"

Angus took a deep breath. Stay calm, he told himself. "Angus Cawley." He shook her hand firmly. "Nice to meet you."

"And you." Patricia smiled again.

Angus smiled at her shyly and was about to go back to reading his newspaper when she asked him another question.

"Are you working today?"

"Sorry?"

"Working?" Patricia asked again.

"Oh, no. Just having lunch."

"I see. I'm working."

"Oh."

"I'm a publisher's rep. Do you like reading yourself?"

"Yes, I suppose so. I don't get much time to read books though. Not whole ones anyway."

"You are a scream." She patted his arm playfully.

Angus wasn't sure why what he'd said was funny, but he played along with it anyway. He thought Patricia was a little pushy and there was something slightly off-putting about her perfectly set hair and immaculately made-up face but talking to her would be good practice. He was sure that Kate would approve.

"Your job sounds interesting," he said, remembering Kate's advice on talking to women. "Tell me about it."

Patricia was only too pleased to oblige. She loved talking about herself. And Angus was really rather good-looking, with those lovely chocolate brown eyes. There was a Booksellers' Ball being held the following weekend and she just might ask him to escort her.

"What?" Kate asked incredulously. "Angus is going out with who?"

"Patricia," Molly said evenly. "Patricia Simons. I'm sure I've told you about her before — she's one of my least favourite publisher's sales reps — she has a mouth the size of a car boot. She called into the shop this afternoon to drop in some catalogues and some car stock. Apparently she met Angus in the coffee shop, they got talking and she asked him to the Booksellers' Ball next weekend."

"Are *you* going?" Kate asked.

"I wasn't planning to. Why?"

"No reason." Kate was silent for a few moments. She tapped her teaspoon against the side of her mug. They were sitting at the kitchen table, having just finished sharing a Chinese takeaway.

"You're not jealous, are you?" Molly asked, trying not to smile.

"No!" Kate insisted. "Of course not. What's she like anyway? This Patricia woman."

Molly described the elegant, blonde sales rep.

Kate listened in stony silence. "Good for him," she said curtly before standing up. "I'm glad he's met someone."

"Where are you going?" Molly asked. "I thought you were staying in this evening."

"I've changed my mind. There's something I have to do."

"But I rented a video."

"Sorry. We can watch it tomorrow evening. How about that?"

"Fine." Molly folded her arms across her chest. Kate had been in a funny mood all week. Molly had blown out dinner at Paige's to stay in with her this evening in the mistaken belief that Kate might like the company. Kate was a strange one sometimes. There was obviously something bothering Kate but she didn't seem to want to talk about it. "Whatever," Molly sighed to herself.

Kate strode into the lobby of the Killiney Arms appearing a lot more confident than she felt. She'd made a special effort to look nice — light brown on-the-knee suede skirt, brown leather high-heeled boots, fitted black shirt. Her hair was freshly blow-dried and she'd carefully applied a layer of foundation, glittery gold eye shadow and strong, red lipstick — her "war paint". Because this evening, above all other evenings she was certainly going to war.

She sat down in an armchair where she had a good vantage point of the whole lobby and glanced at her watch. Good, she was five minutes early, enough time to collect her thoughts. Because she knew exactly what she was going to say — she'd been rehearsing it over and over for the past week. But as a familiar dark suited figure walked down the stairs, caught her eye, smiled and walked towards her, she was rendered speechless. Damn, she thought, he always does this to me.

"Cat." He grinned at her, his impossibly white teeth gleaming. "You look a million dollars. Let me look at you." He held both her hands firmly and looked her up and down. He whistled softly. "Still a beauty."

"Um, thanks," she managed to say.

"Would you like a drink? A glass of white wine?"

She nodded wordlessly.

"Wait there," he commanded her.

Kate watched as he walked towards the bar to the right of the lobby. His suit was immaculately cut, his smart black leather boots shone as if they'd just been polished, and his dark-brown hair was freshly shorn. As always, Jay Sweetman looked good, too damn good.

One of the top American fashion promoters, Jay's job took him all over Europe and he always dressed to impress. In fact, he was so stylish if you didn't know him you'd think he was Italian or Spanish, not Boston-Irish. Kate had first met him two years ago in the Diva, a glitzy hotel in Boston, at the launch party of a new range of Sin "streetwear for feet", which included several of her designs for funky pink, light blue and moss green sneakers. She'd caught his eye across a crowded room and had blushed as Jay had smiled and winked blatantly at her.

Later that evening, to her delight and after several hours of heavily loaded exchanged looks, he'd asked her to dance. They hit it off immediately. He was her ideal man — charming and polite, strong-willed and intelligent. They had talked all night and once he'd kissed her in their shared taxi home, her fate was sealed. He kissed like an angel. Or should that be a devil? Either way, he kissed too well to be strictly human.

"Here you are." Jay put a full glass of wine down in front of her. He sat down beside her, put the bottle in its silver cooler and his own glass on the table and put his hand on hers. She pulled it away quickly.

"Don't be like that," he said. "It's good to see you again. I've missed you, Cat."

As soon as he uttered his pet name for her again, the way he always said it, lingering over the "C" and caressing it with his tongue, Kate knew she shouldn't have come here this evening. Her stomach was already full of butterflies. She tried to keep calm and looked at him squarely in the eye.

"What are you doing here, Jay?"

"I came to see you." He lifted his glass and took a long sip of wine.

"And?"

"And I have a couple of business meetings in Dublin."

"Why did you want to see me?"

He raised his eyebrows, his normally baby-smooth forehead wrinkling slightly. "Why do you think, Cat?" His eyes bored into hers, dark pools of intensity, burning straight into her soul. She looked away quickly and stared at the table.

"I'll cut the bullshit and get straight to the point. I still love you, Cat. Surely you know that. We had something, something real, something . . ."

"Stop!" Kate insisted. He'd always had the gift of being able to throw himself full force into every conversation and completely catching her off guard. "We can't go back, Jay. You know that."

He was silent for a moment. "But things have changed. I've changed."

"No you haven't."

"How would you know? You vanished off the face of the earth. Never even said goodbye. I was distraught." He ran his finger up the stem of his glass. "I had a terrible time trying to find you. But I'm here now and . . ."

"How did you find me exactly?" she asked.

"Reena at Sin. You asked her to forward on your last pay cheque. It took me months to get your new address out of her."

Kate winced. She thought she could trust Reena but obviously she'd been wrong. Although knowing Jay, he'd woven Reena some elaborate tale to cajole the address out of her. He had a way of doing that as Kate knew only too well.

"You shouldn't have bothered." She gulped back the last of her drink.

Jay poured her another glass of wine. She didn't protest — she sure as hell needed some Dutch courage right now.

"I haven't been in Ireland for nearly two years," Jay said ignoring her last comment. "I've missed it."

She said nothing.

"Would you like to go for a walk?" he asked. "It's a beautiful evening. We could climb Killiney Hill."

"I'm not really dressed for it." She nodded at the heels on her boots.

"Why don't we go somewhere a little more private then? I have a hot tub on my balcony — and it has fantastic views."

Kate stared at him. Had he been listening to a word she was saying? She wanted nothing more to do with him — couldn't he get that into his thick skull. "I don't think so," she muttered. "I'm going." She stood up abruptly.

"Leaving without saying goodbye, Cat?" he asked smoothly. "Again? Your manners are appalling."

"Don't talk about my manners." She'd had quite enough of his arrogant behaviour. "Manners! I'll give you manners." She picked up her glass and poured the contents over his head.

222

"Cat! What the hell!" He grabbed her wrist, his hair and jacket soaked. "What's all that about? You left me, remember? Or have you conveniently forgotten?"

"Yes, I did. And you remember why of course?" her voice was raised to a dangerous level.

"Let's take this upstairs," he said calmly. "People are beginning to stare." He brushed his wet hair back with his hand, tendrils beginning to cling around his flushed face. Even soaked in wine he still looked good and remained poised and composed. Typical, Kate thought.

"Let them." She looked around. He was right, the two women at the table beside them were staring wide-eyed and the reception staff had also noticed the commotion. It would be just her luck if someone she knew was listening. She suddenly remembered that Trina's husband owned half the hotel and she was reluctant to have her personal life gossiped about all over Burnaby Village but she hadn't finished with Jay quite yet. "OK then," she decided quickly. "Let's go. Your room, now! I have one or two things I want to say to you, Jay Sweetman, in private."

He strode ahead of her towards the stairs, drips of wine still falling from his head, and powered up them at break-neck speed. Kate found it difficult to keep up in her heels and tight skirt but she was determined not to let him get the better of her. That was Jay, always too impatient to wait for the lift. On the third floor, he stopped outside a door and opened it with a card swipe. Kate was relieved; her heart was pounding in her chest both from the exertion and from the bubbling anger she felt.

Jay held the door for her. She walked in and looked around. It was a stunning room, dominated by a huge bed dressed in sparkling white linen, with a mountain of different sized velvet and satin cushions in shades of gold and beige, and a luxurious fur throw draped over the foot. The dusky evening light bounced off the white walls and Kate could see the large sunken hot tub on the balcony, steam rising in swirling snakes from the top of the water.

"Great view, isn't it?" Jay asked calmly. He gestured towards the balcony. "I'm going outside for a smoke. Care to join me? Then you can lay into me."

Kate looked at him incredulously. Was he serious? She followed him out wordlessly.

"You're some piece of work, Jay, you know that?"

He nodded but said nothing. He took a rolled cigarette out of his inside jacket pocket, lit it and inhaled deeply.

"What's that?" Kate asked, smelling the air suspiciously.

"Don't act the innocent." He smiled at her. "Would you like some?"

"No! You know I don't smoke."

"Sometimes you do. At least the old Cat used to. Or have you become a cheerleader, *Kate*?"

She ignored him, folded her arms in front of her chest and stared out at Killiney Bay, stretching out in front of them as far as the eye could see. The hotel was practically on the beach and Kate could smell the tang of salt in the air. Jay handed her the joint. She looked at it for a few seconds before deciding what the hell? She

224

took it from him without looking at him, and took an almighty drag, the thick smoke hitting the back of her throat, making her cough.

Jay patted her on the back. She felt the smoke fill her lungs and she immediately began to feel a little lightheaded.

"So what did you want to say to me?" Jay asked mildly.

She shook her head, took another calming drag, then began. "I hate you. You fed me a long line of bullshit and like a fool I believed you. I left Boston because I had to. I wanted to have people I could trust around me, decent people. Honest people."

"I never treated you badly, Cat, it's just . . ."

"It's just what?" she asked. "You were married, Jay. Married! And you never told me. I had to find out the hard way."

"I never meant to hurt you, Cat. My marriage was over, *is* over. Cindy and I were never meant to be but I couldn't leave her. Not just then. You never let me explain."

"Explain what?" Kate demanded.

"Cindy was pregnant. She broke the news to me soon after I'd met you and I didn't know what to do. We'd been trying for kids for a few years but it looked as if it was never going to happen. I knew even before I met you that I didn't love her any more. I was on the verge of telling her about you and me, but after she broke the news about the baby — what could I do, Cat? It's what she'd been dreaming of all that time — a baby of her own. I couldn't leave her, not then. I'm not that

225

big a bastard. But I loved you so much, not seeing you would have broken me. I had no choice, I had to keep Cindy and the baby a secret. Don't you see?"

Kate listened to him, staring at the sea and not knowing what to think. All kinds of things were racing through her mind.

She looked him in the eye. "So, as I keep asking, what are you doing here, Jay? What about Cindy? What about your child?"

Jay stared at his hands. "She lost the baby," he whispered. "Just after you left Boston. Things were difficult after that. Cindy was distraught. I couldn't help her get through it, although I did try. She moved back to Maine to be with her family and met up with her childhood sweetheart, a dentist. They fell in love and the rest is history. I lost my baby and I lost you, all in one fell swoop. I was completely alone." He paused for a moment to compose himself and swallowed. "As you can imagine I was devastated."

Kate didn't know what to say. Whatever explanation she'd expected, it hadn't been this. She was bowled over by anger and something else, something bordering on sympathy. He'd made her feel sorry for him and she hated him for it. How dare he?

"Why are you telling me all this?" she demanded. "Are you under the impression that I still care about you, Jay? Because as you've probably realized by now, I don't."

Jay looked at her. "You've asked me what I'm doing here. Well, I could ask you the same question, Cat. If that's true, what are *you* doing here? Why did you come here?"

"That's easy, Jay!" Kate said, her voice raised to a dangerous level. "I loved you, really loved you. When you asked me to marry you I was so happy. And then that Christmas Eve . . ." She took a deep breath. Tears threatened and she was damned if she was going to let him see her cry. Not like this. "I came here this evening to tell you to keep away from me. Pure and simple. I never want to see you again, do you understand? I didn't think I could do it on the phone. Not properly."

She looked at Jay and was shocked to see that he was crying. Unashamedly. Tears were pouring down his face and he wasn't even bothering to brush them away. "I'm sorry." He shook his head. "I'm so sorry you had to find out the way you did, it was unforgivable. But Cat, don't give up on us, please. I beg you. I love you. I've missed you so much."

"How can you say that?" She stubbed out the joint in a plant pot and sat on the edge of the hot tub as she was feeling decidedly strange — hot and light-headed. "You asked me to marry you when you had a wife already! That's bigamy, Jay. What were you thinking? You don't love me. You don't know the meaning of the word. And you certainly never respected me, or your wife for that matter."

"Yes, I do," he whispered. "I love you, honestly." He put his head in his hands. "But I've lost you, haven't I?"

"Yes. I'm afraid you have."

"The one person in the whole world who means the most to me. How could I have been so stupid? If only

I'd met you earlier, before, things would have been different."

"But you didn't," Kate pointed out. "Did you? And then you lied to me."

He shook his head. "And now that I've given up everything to be with you, you don't want me. How ironic is that?"

"What did you just say?" Kate asked.

He looked her straight in the eye. "I'm in the middle of a divorce settlement and I'm selling the apartment. I came over here to tell you. In a few weeks, I'll be a free man. My meetings in Dublin are about moving over to Ireland. I thought that we could buy a house, be together, get married as we'd planned. Maybe have a family. Start again. I know how much you want to be near your granny and I respect that, Cat. Family means everything and I thought we could start our own family here in Dublin."

Kate felt as if she'd been hit by a train. How dare he bring Lily into this? And what the hell was he talking about? She hadn't contacted him since coming home and now this. Was he mad? "What?" she cried. "I don't understand. Is this some sort of sick joke?"

"It's not a joke. You heard me. I'm free to marry you now. And I'll move to Ireland to be with you." There was a strange intensity in his eyes. "So I'm asking you again, Cat — will you marry me?"

"Are you serious?" she asked furiously. "After everything you've done, you still think I'll come running? Are you crazy? We haven't spoken for almost a year, did it not occur to you that I want nothing more to do with you? Well, Jay?"

"Don't be like that, Cat."

"Like what? You're some piece of work."

"Cat, I know you're scared and you have every right to be angry with me. But this time it's different, trust me. I'm a free man. No more deceit, I promise. Just you and me, we were made for each other, you know that. I love you."

Kate stared at him. "Don't," she whispered. She put her hand into the hot tub and moved her fingers through the clear warm water. She should never have come here this evening, it was a mistake.

He walked over and sat down beside her. "I know you still love me, Cat. I can see it in your eyes. And I love you so much. Why can't you trust me?"

Kate sighed deeply. She felt suddenly exhausted. "Jay, stop! I can't do this again. It nearly broke me the last time, but I'm OK now. Please, just let it go." She could feel her defences weaken. He always had this effect on her, Jay was her one big weakness. But she wasn't going to give in, not this time.

He put his arm around her shoulders but she immediately shrugged it off.

"Cat," he said softly, brushing her hair back with his hand.

"Don't touch me!" she insisted tetchily.

He ignored her and continued stroking her hair. "Let me take care of you. It could be like it was in Boston, the way it was before. We belong together. Do you remember what you used to call us, 'soulmates'?"

"I remember," she murmured, feeling her resistance starting to fade even more. The joint and the wine weren't helping. Why didn't I refuse it and stay clear-headed? she chastised herself. Stupid, stupid, Kate. Always so stupid. Her mind raced. Wouldn't it be easier just to give in to him? I think about him all the time, from the moment I wake up, to last thing at night. I thought I was over him, prayed I was over him, but who am I kidding? And what does it matter anyway? He's going to win in the end, she thought woozily, he always does. Or why not have one last night with him, get him out of my system? She laughed out loud.

"Why are you laughing, Cat?" he asked.

"I'm laughing at you," Kate replied woozily. "At us."

He ran his hand along the side of her face. "My beautiful Cat." He kissed her on the cheek.

She felt her heart somersault. "Don't," she said softly.

He silenced her with a firm kiss on the lips.

"Jay!" she protested and pushed him away. But he wasn't giving up that easily.

"Let me love you, Cat," he said. He cupped her head in his hand, and smiled at her. "Don't fight it."

The next time he leant forward to kiss her, Kate couldn't help herself. She could feel her lips respond to his kisses, and a delicious warmness spreading from her lips, down her neck and suffusing through her body.

He put both arms around her and held her tightly. "Cat," he whispered in between kisses, "my lovely Cat." She felt powerless to resist, overcome by her own pent-up emotions. At that precise moment she didn't care about anything other than Jay's hands and lips, both sending her whole being into divine ecstasy and leaving her wanting more. God, how she'd missed him. He was right — she'd never stopped loving him — no matter what he'd done, the lies he'd told, the fool he'd made of her. And she still wanted him — more than anything. But she certainly didn't trust him.

While still kissing her, he gently and expertly pulled her top over her shoulders and undid her bra.

"Jay," she said nervously, crossing her arms over her full, naked breasts. "We can't do this. Please . . ."

"Just getting into the hot tub, my sweet, that's all," he promised her. "It will relax you, then we can talk some more." He slipped off his own jacket and shirt, took off his boots and socks, leant over and kissed her bare shoulder. She felt a delicious shiver down her spine. As if in a trance, she pulled off her boots, socks and skirt, feeling exposed in just her black lacy G-string. Although it was a warm evening, she still shivered.

"Everything off." Jay grinned at her. "That's cheating."

"What about you?" she asked.

He shrugged his shoulders, dropped his trousers, stepped out of them and whisked off his pristine white boxers. "As naked as a jay-bird." He laughed.

He moved towards her, lifted her up in his strong arms and dumped her unceremoniously into the tub.

"Jay!" she spluttered.

He laughed again and stepped in. "Come here."

She stayed where she was, the water suddenly sobering her up. "Jay, this isn't right. I can't . . ."

He moved towards her and kneeled in front of her. Cupping her face in his hand once more he kissed her on the forehead, on both cheeks and then ever so gently on her lips. She could feel them tingle beneath his.

"You know you want me, Cat. Let yourself go. Just concentrate on how you feel right now. Let go of everything else. Just let go." He put his hands on her shoulders and pressed her against the back of the hot tub. "Lie very still," he whispered. He pressed a button behind her and jets of warm water began to fill the tub, snaking upwards and hitting her back, her buttocks and the tops of her thighs. "Now open your legs."

"Jay!" she cried.

"Just humour me, it'll be worth it. Please?" He kissed her again, this time his tongue caressing and teasing her lips and tongue and making her gasp. Her heart was racing and her whole body felt warm and on tenterhooks. As he nuzzled her neck, he moved his hands down her body, removed her G string and spread her legs. Then he lifted her up slightly in the water and repositioned her over a firm, strong jet of water. Kate could feel the warm, forceful jets against her most sensitive area. She closed her eyes and gave in to the delicious sensations. Jay held both her hands in his and kissed her all over her face and neck, whispering into her ears.

"That's it, Cat," he crooned. "I knew you wanted me. Just like I want you."

232

After a little while the jets began to feel stronger and stronger, warmer and warmer, until Kate's body had taken its fill. Her back arched and then she flopped forwards as limp as a rag doll, completely sated.

She opened her eyes and Jay smiled at her. Without saying a word he turned to sit, lifted her body onto his knee, light in the warm water. She wrapped her legs around his torso, pulled him close and began to kiss him ravenously, clutching and massaging his muscular shoulders and back in her hands.

"Cat!" he said. "You're back." She'd always been the most passionate and exciting woman he'd ever been with.

"Yes, I am," she murmured. "Now, shut up and kiss me." For old times sake, she thought as she kissed him passionately, there's no way I'm letting Jay back into my life, no way in high heaven.

"Cat, I have to go now, I have a meeting in town."

Kate opened her eyes and rolled over. Jay was standing in front of her, fully dressed in his signature dark suit. He looked fantastic as usual.

She looked up at him, rubbing her eyes. They hadn't had much sleep the previous evening and she felt a wave of regret that she had let things escalate to such an extent. She should have left straight after the hot tub. In fact she should never have been in the hot tub in the first place. Or in the hotel for that matter. What was she doing? She should have been stronger — the joint and the fact that she hadn't had sex since the last time she'd been with him in Boston were some excuse, but

Kate was ashamed of herself. "What time is it?" she asked.

"Eight," he said. "Don't get up. I'm sorry I can't stay but you know how it is. I have a breakfast meeting in The Morrison Hotel at nine."

"On a Sunday?" she asked.

"I know, tell me about it," he said, ignoring her suspicious tone. "But I'm only over for the next three days and you know what us Americans are like about breakfast meetings."

"It's fine, I understand."

"I'll see you this evening. Dinner here at eight? I'll book the restaurant."

"I don't think so, Jay."

"Please, Kate, it would mean a lot to me. I know what happened last night wasn't . . ."

"I don't really want to talk about it, Jay, OK? Just leave it."

"Can I at least ring you later?"

She sighed. "I suppose so."

He pulled out his mobile and stood waiting, his fingers hovering over the keys.

She dictated her mobile number.

He smiled at her. "I'll see you later."

"Jay . . ."

He kissed his fingers and lay them gently on her lips. "Just humour me," he said with a grin.

Soon after he'd left, Kate fell into a deep dreamless sleep. When she woke she felt deliciously refreshed. Standing in the shower, powerful jets of hot water spiking her body, she thought about Jay and about the previous night. And much to her disgust she felt happy. Happy that he still loved her, happy that he still wanted her. Because she knew deep down that she'd never stopped loving him. Lies or no lies. What was she going to do?

"You're in good form," Lily said as she and Kate walked down the steps towards Forty Foot bathing place in Sandycove that afternoon. "You haven't stopped smiling all day. What's up?"

Kate shrugged her shoulders. "Nothing in particular." She looked at the greyish-blue water stretched out in front of them. "I can't believe you've talked me into this." She laughed. "I must be mad." There were several people of all ages in the water — from young children with their parents to groups of teenagers and older swimmers. Some were jumping and diving in and others were sitting on the edge of the steps, chatting amicably in bathing suits with towels draped around their shoulders. The sun was hiding behind thick cloud cover but the air was warm.

"You'll enjoy it once you're in," Lily said. She led them towards the right where there were concrete seats. Several people nodded or said hello to Lily as she walked past. She sat down.

"How's the ankle today?" Kate asked, sitting down beside her.

"Not too bad. Healing nicely. I should be able to go naked in the next week or so."

"Naked?" Kate asked with interest.

Lily smiled. "Without a bandage." She opened her bag and pulled out her togs and towel. "Come along," she said to Kate. "Don't just sit there. Unless you intend to swim in your clothes."

"Maybe I'll just watch," Kate said uncertainly. "It looks a bit cold and . . ."

"A bit of cold never hurt anyone," Lily said dismissively. "Now that you're here you may as well try it."

"I suppose so." Kate was still very reluctant. To tell the truth her legs were still a little shaky after last night. She tried not to smile as she thought of Jay but it was proving difficult. Jay had held her in his arms and promised her that everything would be all right. Last night Kate had blocked out the voices in her head telling her that she was mad to get involved with Jay again. That he was a liar and a cheat, and a danger to her mental health. That he'd hurt her again, just like he did the last time. Today, as the afternoon had progressed the voices were becoming dimmer and dimmer. In fact she almost couldn't hear them any more. And one more evening with him couldn't hurt, could it? He was hardly serious about moving to Dublin and, after all, he was single this time — if he was telling the truth about his ex-wife and the loss of his baby. But Kate was sure that even Jay wouldn't lie about something like that.

"Kate? What do you think?" Lily asked again.

"Sorry, I was miles away. What did you say?"

"Would you like to go out for dinner this evening? To Bistro Nova?"

"I have to meet an old friend, Gran. Maybe next weekend."

"Who?" Lily cocked her head. "Anyone I know."

Kate shook her head. "No."

"It's not that nice Angus is it?" Lily persisted.

"No!" Kate laughed. "What made you think that?"

"He's a decent young man. And he seems very keen on you. Whenever he calls he always asks all about you."

"He still calls in?"

"Yes. This week Callum was with him. Lovely child — he's really growing into himself. Angus is working wonders with him."

"Well, I'm certainly not dining with Angus."

Lily smiled gently. "You could do worse. He's a good lad. You could trust him, Kate. He wouldn't break your heart like that American. What was his name again?"

"Gran!" Kate wanted to change the subject right now. She didn't feel at all comfortable with the direction this conversation was heading. "You know I don't like talking about him. Just drop it, OK? It's all in the past."

Lily looked at Kate carefully. "Is it?"

"Gran! Are we going swimming or not?" Kate pulled her togs and towel out of her bag and began to get undressed, using her towel to protect her modesty. She winced as her bare feet hit the concrete but decided it was her penance for last night's excesses. They'd polished off three bottles of champagne between them, although a large part of the third bottle hadn't been drunk — it had been liberally sprayed over each other and over the sheets.

"We most certainly are," Lily said. As she changed, Lily thought about Kate. She had a strong feeling that the American was back in town. She noticed a couple of fresh scratches and bruises on her granddaughter's arms, back and inner thighs. She wasn't born yesterday. And if it was the American and she was under his spell again — it spelt trouble for Kate. Trouble with a capital "T".

CHAPTER
TWELVE

Paige

Paige lowered herself onto the sofa. The house was blissfully quiet and, if she was lucky, she could catch a few minutes shut-eye before Callum and Angus arrived home. She rested her head against the side cushions and let her weary eyelids droop closed. A little while later she was wakened by a loud bang in the hall. It was the front door being slammed shut.

"Callum!" she heard Angus scold. "What did I say?"

"Close the door gently," Callum replied.

"And was that gently?"

"No," Callum admitted. "Please don't tell Mum and Dad. I've been really good today, haven't I?"

"Yes. And I'll let you off this time. But run upstairs and hang your coat on the back of the door, there's a good lad. And change your trousers, those ones are filthy."

Paige heard Callum scamper up the stairs. Angus walked into the living room.

"Sorry," he said, noticing her stretched out on the sofa. "Did we wake you?"

"That's OK." She yawned. "I have to get up anyway. More doorstepping this evening, I'm afraid. Are you still all right for babysitting?"

Angus nodded. "Fine."

Paige sat up slowly, rubbing her eyes. "Thanks. You've saved my life. Mum was supposed to do it but . . ."

"It's no trouble, honestly. I could do with the money to tell the truth."

"So what did you both get up to today?" asked Paige.

"We went to Bray on the train. Walked along Bray head and then had a few dodgem rides at the amusement park. Callum got a bit muddy rock climbing so I sent him upstairs to change."

"Callum was rock climbing?"

"Sure. Rock scrambling more like. He's pretty talented — he has great balance and he's very agile."

Angus looked at Paige's face. She looked a little anxious.

"It's good to stretch him, Paige. Don't look so worried, I'd never take him anywhere that wasn't safe, honestly."

"Sorry, I know you wouldn't. So what's the plan for tomorrow?"

"The waterfall at Powerscourt. Thought we could do some dam building in the stream. There's a great playground there too — should run off some of Callum's steam."

Paige smiled. "You're full of great ideas, Angus. We were lucky to find you. Callum hasn't been so easy to deal with for I don't know how long. We really appreciate it, you know that."

"I know. And he's a good kid — lively but bright. Just needs some one on one attention."

240

Paige sighed. "I wish me and Tom had more time to spend with him, but with the election coming up, and Tom's work . . ."

"It's difficult to juggle everything but . . ." Angus began.

"But what?" asked Paige.

He shook his head. "Nothing. Forget it."

"Please. Tell me what you were going to say."

Their conversation was interrupted by Tom. "Hello, everyone. How's my favourite councillor? Ready to visit some mad constituents?" He strode into the room and kissed Paige on the top of her head.

"Are you all right, love?"

"Fine. Just resting."

Callum came bounding down the stairs and threw his arms around his dad's waist. "Hi, Dad!"

"Hi, Callum. Have you been good today?"

"Very. Angus promised to show me how to use the washing machine this evening. How to put in the cleaning stuff and everything. All by myself. So I can help Mummy with the washing."

Tom looked at Angus. "Is Callum serious?"

Angus nodded. "He's really interested in machines. I'd be surprised if you didn't have a little engineer on your hands, mate."

"Sounds good to me," Paige said. "They're never too young to learn. I'll show you how to put on the dishwasher next young man, if you're good."

"Thanks, Mum!"

Tom glanced at his watch and sighed. "We'd better get something to eat, Paige. We need to leave in twenty minutes or so. The Killen Estate is huge — it will take us all evening to cover it."

"Molly and Kate offered to cover some of it with us. And Molly said that Alex and Harry have also offered to help."

"Harry from the plant shop? The guy from your book club?"

Paige smiled. "Gas, isn't it? We should send him round the houses with the big gardens. Maybe he'd hand out some free gardening tips — that might win us some brownie points."

Tom smiled back. "No kidding, he's really popular on the radio. I wouldn't have thought he was the political type though."

"Molly was saying it has more to do with Alex's influence than anything else. Kate worked some sort of magic there apparently. I'll tell you all about it when we're walking."

"Sounds interesting." He turned towards Angus. "You know Kate, don't you?"

"Yes." Angus blushed slightly. "Yes, I do. Lovely girl. I haven't seen her for a while but I called into her granny's a few days ago with Callum. I hope that was all right."

"Of course," Paige said. "Lily's a pet, isn't she? And Callum adores her."

"I'm hungry," Callum interrupted. "What's for tea?"

"Callum!" Angus, Paige and Tom said in unison.

"Sorry," Callum replied meekly.

"How about we make some toasted sandwiches for everyone?" Angus suggested kindly. "And then your mum and dad can have a sit down for a few minutes."

242

"OK," Callum said. "Can we use the whirr thing to grate the cheese?"

"The food processor?"

"Yes!" Callum said eagerly.

Angus looked at Paige, who nodded assent. "I suppose so. But you'll have to help me wash all the bits afterwards, deal?"

"Deal."

The doorbell rang shrilly.

"That must be Mum with Alfie," Paige groaned. "No rest for the wicked."

"I'll get it!" Callum ran out of the kitchen, past his parents and towards the door.

Tom patted Paige's hand and smiled at her. "And we're having another? Are we quite mad?"

She laughed. "I think we just might be."

"You take this side of the road and I'll take the far one," said Tom. "Try not to spend too much time with each person. We have a hell of a lot of houses to call on this evening."

"Right," Paige replied. "I'll try to keep focused and not get sidetracked." She looked at the number of the house in front of her and checked her clipboard. "I'll start with the Kavanagh household."

"Good luck. I'll wave at you from across the street."

Paige walked up to the door and rang the bell. A thin, darkhaired girl of about nine answered the door.

"Yes?" She stared at Paige suspiciously. "What are you selling?"

"Um, nothing. I'm Paige Brady, one of your local councillors. I'm looking for your support in the forthcoming general election."

"I'll get Mam. Mam!" she shouted into the house.

"Coming." A dark-haired woman appeared at the door from a doorway at the back of the hall. She looked at Paige. "You're the one who's campaigning for childcare, aren't you?"

Paige nodded. "That's right. Among other things."

The woman said nothing.

"Do you have any questions for me?" Paige asked evenly.

Again nothing. The woman was completely tongue-tied.

"Anything at all?"

Her daughter nudged her mother. "Ask her about a playground," she hissed. "Go on."

"Oh, yeah. We need a playground in the estate. The kids have nowhere to play since the green was taken over by the council for new housing. I have five kids and the garden is tiny."

Paige jotted down a note in her diary. "I'll certainly check it out for you, Mrs Kavanagh. As they haven't started building yet, maybe some sort of arrangement can be made with the builders. Insurance is usually the big problem with playgrounds, but I'll do my best. I promise."

"Fair enough." The woman was about to close the door when Paige stopped her.

"I'll make some enquiries and I'll ring you back within the next two weeks about it. Maybe in the

244

meantime you could talk to some of the other parents, and if they feel the same way you could start a petition."

"Good idea." The woman looked a little taken aback. "You're really going to ring me?"

"Yes," Paige promised. "I really am."

"I'll vote for you if you do."

"Thank you," Paige said. "But you don't have to."

"No, you're grand, I will. And I'll make sure my husband does too. He works nights but he votes before he comes home."

"Thank you, Mrs Kavanagh."

As Paige walked away from the house she put two discreet ticks beside "Kavanagh" on the list. She knocked on the door of the next house as the bell seemed to be broken.

"Jeeze, would you give me a chance," she heard a voice mutter in the hall. Through the safety glass she could see a tall shadowy figure. "Who is it?" a male voice asked.

"Paige Brady, one of your local councillors."

"What do you want?"

"Would you mind opening the door, Mr Cole? I could explain then."

"How do you know my name?"

"I have a list of all the registered voters in the estate. Your name is on my list."

"It's like fecking *Big Brother*," he shouted at her. "Go away."

"If I could just . . ."

He opened the door and glared out at her. "Did you not hear me? I said go away. I have nothing to say to the likes of you."

"What do you mean — the likes of me?" Paige asked in astonishment. "I'm an Independent candidate, Mr Cole. I don't belong to any political party."

"I'm not talking about politics. I'm talking about women!" he practically spat at her. "No bloody good — the whole lot of you. Spawn of the devil. Go to hell!" he slammed the door in her face.

Paige stood on the doorstep for a moment in complete shock. He was obviously quite barmy. She shook herself, took a deep breath and crossed a heavy line with her pen through his name. "Mad!" she wrote to the far right of the line.

The next few houses had more normal occupants thankfully — even if two of them were staunch People's Party supporters and had already promised their votes to Paddy Burns.

"How's it going, Paige?" Tom crossed the road to talk to her.

"Not too bad." She looked down at her clipboard. "Five definite yesses, two for Paddy, seven undecided and one mad man." She told Tom about her experience with Mr Cole.

"Take care of yourself, Paige," Tom said with concern when she'd finished. "There are a lot of nutters out there. Maybe we should do the next set of houses together."

"It would take twice as long that way," Paige pointed out. "I'll be fine, honestly."

"If you're sure."

She nodded. "And how are the others getting on? Have you heard from them?"

"Harry rang to find out about your policy on the proposed 'Educate Together' school for Burnaby. Oh, and Molly got several requests for a playground for the estate. Apparently they're building on the green where the kids used to play."

"Interesting," Paige said. "I got the same request. There might be something I can do about that."

He linked her arm. "You're going to make a great Deputy, Paige. Do you know that? You really care, don't you?"

"Of course." She widened her eyes. "What are you suggesting, Tom? That not all politicians care?"

"Not at all." he winked at her. "Would I?"

"No comment," she smiled. "Now let's get back to work. We have a long evening ahead of us."

Paige sat down at the kitchen table the following morning. Tom had already got Alfie and Callum up and was feeding Alfie in his highchair.

"Morning, Sleepyhead." Tom smiled at her as she poured herself a bowl of cereal.

"Thanks for letting me sleep on," she said. "I just couldn't get out of bed this morning."

"How are the feet?"

"Not the best," she admitted. "I could do with a foot rub. Any offers?"

"I'll do it," said Callum, immediately jumping under the table and crawling to his mother's feet.

He took her left foot out of its slipper and held it in his small hand.

She winced. "Callum, your hands are freezing. Warm them up, please."

"How will I do that?" he asked from under the table.

"Blow on them and rub them together," Tom suggested.

"OK."

Tom looked over at Paige and smiled. She smiled back, put her chin in her hands and waited. A few minutes later she felt a slightly warmer hand on her foot.

"Is that better, Mummy?"

"Yes, thanks, Callum."

"Now what do I do?"

"Rub your mum's foot gently but firmly from the heel to the toes," said Tom. "Don't tickle her, OK?"

"OK."

Callum stroked his mother's foot as directed. Paige was surprised, he was actually quite good.

"How is it?" Tom whispered.

"Not bad," she whispered back.

"Will I pull your toes a little, Mummy?" Callum popped his head up from under the table. "Kind of stretch them. I saw a lady on *Richard and Judy* doing that to someone's toes."

"*Richard and Judy*?" Paige asked. "When were you watching that?"

"When Angus and me were making toasties last night. They were talking about modern art and Angus

248

told me to watch and tell him what I thought of the pictures."

"Really?" Tom asked. "Did you like them?"

"I liked the one of the snail by the French guy. The one made from all the bits of paper. Angus said the man did it like that because he was sick and his fingers couldn't hold a paintbrush properly. I think his name was Massey something or other."

"Matisse?" Paige asked.

"That's it," Callum said. "Matisse."

Tom shook his head. "Amazing," he murmured. "Our son the art critic."

"We're going to go to the gallery next week," Callum continued. "Angus said there's lots of pictures of animals and a cool computer thing that explains the paintings. Have I been to the gallery before, Mum?"

"No, I don't think so. But you've been to the stuffed animal museum and it's right beside it."

"Maybe Angus will bring me there too. How's your foot, Mummy?"

"Better," Paige said truthfully, wiggling her toes. "You're doing a great job."

"I'll do your toes." He popped back under and after pulling Paige's toes gently for a moment asked "Will I do the other foot now?"

"Please."

"And will this get me an extra star, do you think?"

"It just might." Paige laughed.

While Tom dropped Alfie over to his mother's, Callum sat on the end of the double bed watching his mother dress. She was currently standing in her bra, pants and tights, trying to decide what to wear.

"When will Angus be here?" he asked impatiently.

"Soon," Paige promised. She looked at her watch. "Very soon, hopefully." She was due in the *Now TV* studios at half past nine and it was now five past. With Dublin traffic the way it was, she'd be lucky to get there on time. She breathed a sigh of relief as the doorbell rang.

"I'll get it!" Callum ran out the door and thundered down the stairs.

"It's a man," he shouted up to Paige. "He says he's your taxi driver. What will I do?"

"Nothing!" Paige shouted back. "I'll be down in a second."

"I'm here too, Paige," Angus shouted up. "Sorry I'm late. I asked the driver to wait in the cab for two minutes. Is there anything I can do to help?"

"No, thanks. I'm almost ready." She looked in the mirror again. "Thank goodness Angus is here," she murmured. She quickly pulled a black top out of her wardrobe, held it up against her body, decided it would be too much with her black suit and threw it down on the bed with the other tops. "Why didn't I choose my outfit last night?" she asked herself as she rummaged through the tops hanging on the rail. "Damn, damn, damn!"

She picked up her mobile and keyed in Molly's number.

"Hello, Paige?"

"Molly. You've got to help me. I'm on *Now AM* this morning and I'm running late. What the hell will I wear?"

Molly thought for a second. "Is your dark pink trouser suit clean?"

"Yes, but is it not a bit . . ."

"Wear it with a plain white top and some heels. You don't want to wear black on the television — everyone does and it's instantly forgettable. You want people to sit up and remember you."

"I suppose."

"What time are you on at?"

"Ten."

"I won't keep you, so. Are you taping it?"

"Yes."

"Cool, I'll be over later to watch it this evening. Good luck."

"Thanks."

Paige pulled a plain white top over her head, and stepped into the dark pink trousers. She hoped Molly was right. Paige usually wore this suit at parties, not for work. Still, she didn't really have time to think about it. She threw on the pink jacket, wiggled her feet into her matching dark pink court shoes, grabbed her large brown leather bag, ran into the bathroom and swept her make up and hair brush into it.

"Mobile, wallet, keys," she muttered as she collected them all together and threw them into the bag. She looked at herself in the mirror. Her cheeks were flushed from all the rushing around, matching her suit. But she had to admit she looked pretty good. Luckily her stomach was still reasonably trim, otherwise she'd never have been able to wear the closely fitting trousers.

She walked quickly down the stairs into the kitchen, her heels clicking noisily on the tiled floor.

"You look nice, Mummy," Callum said, looking up from the table-top.

"Thanks." She smiled at him and ruffled his hair. He was playing a game of Junior Scrabble with Angus. "Be good now. I'll see you later."

"*Now TV* this morning, right?" Angus asked.

Paige nodded. "Ten o'clock."

"We'll be glued. Hope it goes well."

"Thanks. I have to run. See you later."

"We'll be watching you, Mummy!" Callum shouted as she closed the hall door behind her.

She opened the door of the taxi. "Sorry to keep you."

"Not at all, love," he said, folding away his paper. "We'd better get going though. We have to pick up Ms Higgins on the way."

Paige's heart sank. That was all she needed. She pulled her bag onto her knee and rummaged through it to find her foundation and her powder compact. She didn't want Annette to see her looking like a dog's dinner. She carefully poured some creamy base onto her fingers and holding the small compact mirror in front of her face, she began to smooth it onto her skin, taking care to cover the pasty, greyish skin around her eyes. Heavens she looked tired. She pulled out her tube of liquid concealer, dotted it on the dark circles and patted it in gently. Then she finished with some powder, mascara and lip-gloss. She looked at herself critically. She'd do — thank goodness for make-up. She knew she'd be given the full treatment in the make-up room of the studio, but she didn't want to go in there looking like death warmed up. Now at least she looked slightly presentable.

"Feel better now?" the taxi man asked.

"Sorry?"

She caught the taxi man's eye in the rear-view mirror.

"A lot of my fares do their make-up in my cab." He smiled kindly. "I think it helps them to wake up. Must be important in your line of work too. First appearances and all that. You're standing in the next election, aren't you?"

"That's right."

"My wife says she's voting for you. She likes your policies on childcare."

"And what about you?" Paige asked. "Who will you be voting for?"

"Haven't really decided yet. Paddy Burns has always been a decent sort. Says what he means. I like him."

"Would you think about giving me your second preference?" Paige asked directly.

"Sorry?"

"Putting me in as number two."

"Ah, I might. I'll certainly consider it."

"Thanks."

"But what would you be doing for the average working man like myself?"

"That's a good question," Paige said, wishing she'd never started this conversation. "A lot of my policies relate to childcare, funding for schools, improved services — water supply, upgrading roads . . ."

"Upgrading roads?" he asked. "Like making the roads better to drive on?"

"Exactly. Some of them are in a right state and I think it's unacceptable. And something positive has to be done about traffic congestion."

"I think you're dead right. Let me tell you a story about traffic congestion . . ." he began. Paige sat back against the seat to listen. She'd obviously hit the right note. After a ten minute monologue, he pulled up outside a red brick townhouse and beeped the horn.

"The wife's not that keen on your one Higgins," he admitted. "She thinks she's stuck in the Dark Ages. And she wouldn't be my choice either."

Paige smiled to herself.

Annette opened the door and walked towards the taxi. She was immaculately turned out in a sombre navy suit with a frilly white blouse underneath. Her hair was perfectly set in a static halo around her head.

She climbed into the front seat of the car. The taxi man said nothing. He knew this one all right — she was the old boot who had called taxi drivers "lazy" last year. How could he forget? He pulled swiftly out into the Dublin traffic.

"How are you this morning, Paige?" Annette asked crisply, turning around to face her.

"Very good, thanks."

"You look a little tired. Not sick are you?"

Paige could have hit her. "Not, I'm fine. Just canvassing until late last night, you know how it is."

254

"Oh, I leave a lot of that door-to-door stuff to my supporters," Annette said breezily. "Too busy myself. Far more important things to be doing."

The taxi man grunted.

"Sorry?" Annette asked him icily. "Did you want to say something?"

"No," he muttered. He didn't like this one's attitude at all. Snooty cow. Too busy to meet the common people — like himself.

"Who else is in the studio, do you know?" Paige asked Annette.

"Jackie and Hilda." Hilda Murphy was another Independent. She wasn't expected to win a seat, but had appeared on many radio chat shows expounding her rather extreme right wing views. She could always be relied upon to get under the listeners' skin.

"Just the women?" Paige asked.

"Just the women."

"Should be interesting."

"Quite."

Paige looked out the window as they approached Dundrum, where the studio was based. As they pulled up outside the buildings, she rubbed her finger over her teeth to check for any stray lip-gloss and pulled the hairbrush through her hair.

Stepping out of the taxi, she thanked the driver.

"Not at all," he said. "And I'll give you my number two," he promised her.

"Thanks," she smiled.

"And I'll get your number one, I presume?" Annette asked arrogantly, listening in to their exchange.

"Are you joking?" he snorted. "You're the one who was giving out about taxi drivers, last Christmas in the *Southside Sentinel*, remember?"

Annette's face reddened. "That was a long time ago. Besides, you can't believe everything you read in the papers," she said sniffily.

As they walked into the lobby, Paige could feel butterflies in her stomach.

"Those taxi drivers," Annette muttered as they approached the large curved desk. "Not to be trusted."

Paige ignored her and smiled at the receptionist. "Paige Brady and Annette Higgins. We're here for *Now AM*."

"Please, take a seat. A researcher will be out to you in a moment."

"Thanks."

Fifteen minutes later, Paige was sitting in the brightly lit *Now AM* studio, her lips sticky with freshly applied gloss and her short dark hair neatly stuck down by a generous soaking of hairspray, which had nearly asphyxiated her in the small make-up room. Her eyelashes felt heavy with mascara and her hands were hot and clammy with nerves. This was the very first time she'd appeared on national television. Jackie leant over and squeezed her clasped hands.

"Don't worry," she said kindly. "Once we're on air you'll forget your stage fright. Anyway, a bit of adrenaline never hurt anyone. Better than being as cool as a cucumber and dead on the screen." She gestured towards Annette pointedly who was sitting calmly on the sofa opposite them.

"Thanks," Paige said gratefully.

A moment later the presenters — Frank Ryan and Dee Kelly arrived and sat down.

"How are you all this morning?" Frank asked, smiling at the four would-be politicians.

"Fine, thank you," Hilda replied for them all. "And I hope this is going to be a fair and equal debate. I know this station is very left-wing and I want to —"

"This station isn't left wing, Hilda," Dee cut in. "Or right wing for that matter. It has no political allegiances whatsoever."

"And we're not really having a debate, Hilda," Frank explained. "This is breakfast television after all. We'll be keeping it light."

Annette muttered something under her breath.

"Sorry, Annette?" Dee asked. "I didn't quite catch that."

Just then the female floor manager strode over. "We'll be on air in two minutes, after the news headlines. Is everyone set?"

They all nodded.

"And everyone's been wired for sound?"

More nods.

"Good."

"They're all very young in here," Jackie whispered to Paige.

"And mostly women," Paige replied. "Great isn't it?"

"Absolutely!" Jackie said. "Wish more companies were like that."

Dee looked at Jackie and put her finger to her lips.

"Oops, better be quiet," Jackie said to Paige.

Paige stared at the coffee table in front of her which held two bright yellow *Now AM* coffee cups. The weather had just come on and she knew their slot was next. She raised her head and tried to stay calm. Her stomach was doing somersaults and she could feel a dull flush spreading down her neck and face. Hopefully the heavy television make-up would stop it being too noticeable. Damn, her cheeks would clash with her suit. She should have worn black — it would have been safer. What was she thinking of?

"And welcome back." Dee smiled at the camera. "We are very privileged to have the four women who are standing for election in the Dun Laoghaire Rathdown constituency in the forthcoming general elections — Deputy Jackie Pile of the New Alliance, Councillor Annette Higgins of the Democrats, Ms Hilda Murphy, an Independent, and Councillor Paige Brady who's also an Independent. Welcome to you all."

"Thank you." They all smiled and nodded.

"Let's start with Deputy Pile," Frank said. "Deputy, you've held a seat in the government for the past ten years, is that correct?"

"Eleven years," she corrected him.

"Eleven years," he continued. "And in that time you've seen a lot of changes, especially for women. Could you tell us a little about your work on the Women's Health Bill and what that will mean for the women of Ireland?"

"Certainly, Frank," Jackie said.

As Jackie explained the proposed bill, Paige's mind drifted. She watched Jackie as she talked and wondered if she'd ever be so poised and so confident in front of the cameras.

"And Councillor Brady, many of your policies involve women's issues of various sorts. Am I correct?"

Paige took a deep breath and looked at Frank. "That's right, Frank. Ireland is way behind most other European countries when it comes to the provision of childcare facilities. If I win a seat, I intend to lobby the government to provide affordable childcare for all those women who wish to work. I also intend to lobby for funding of the 'Educate Together' schools. I think it is important, especially in this day and age, that our children are educated with other children of different religions and different cultural backgrounds."

"That would be a complete waste of money!" Hilda Murphy interrupted. "We already have a fine network of primary schools in this country who all could do with extra funding. It would be foolish to start funding new schools."

"But most of the traditional schools are run by the churches," Paige pointed out calmly. "Both Catholic and Protestant. I'm talking about a different sort of education — where all children can be taught together, no matter what religion they are."

"What's wrong with religion?" Hilda spluttered. "Do you have something against it, Councillor Brady?"

"Of course not," Paige said, sounding calmer than she felt. "But just because something has always been done in a certain way, it doesn't mean it's right."

"Quite." Jackie nodded. "I think Councillor Brady has a good point. There is certainly a place for 'Educate

Together' schools in Ireland and her ideas on childcare are spot on."

"Two opposing candidates agreeing," Dee said. "How unusual."

"Well I don't agree at all," Annette said firmly. "I think Councillor Brady should stop trying to encourage mothers back into the workforce. A lot of Ireland's current social problems stem from mothers going out to work."

"That's ridiculous!" Paige said. "There are no approved statistics to back that up. How can you say that?"

"Look at your own son, Callum," Annette looked Paige straight in the eye. "I hear he has a lot of behavioural problems. Am I right?"

"That's unfair!" Paige raised her voice. "There's nothing wrong with my son, how dare you?"

"Ladies," Frank interrupted. "I think this is all getting a little personal. Let's concentrate on your polices, not on your private lives. Oops, it's time for a break. We'll be back in a few minutes with more of this election special on *Now AM*. Don't go away now."

As soon as Paige heard the ads come on she glared at Annette.

"How could you, Annette?" she asked. "How could you drag my son into this? There's nothing wrong with him."

"That's not what my contact at his crèche said. She told me all about his terrible record at Little Orchard. Calling the teachers names and running riot. Oh, I know all about Callum's behaviour, Paige, believe me."

Paige was dumbstruck.

"That's all a bit below the belt," Jackie said. "Let's keep this clean. I have no time for dirty politics and I don't wish to be associated with them."

"I'd have to agree." Hilda nodded.

Annette pulled herself up bolt upright on the sofa. "All's fair in politics, ladies."

"If you don't mind me saying, I don't think it shows you in very good light, Annette." Dee joined in.

"Really?" Annette raised her eyebrows and said nothing further.

As soon as they were back on air, Paige's heart sank.

"Now we have a viewer on the line who'd like to ask Councillor Brady a question." Frank looked at Paige. "Will you take the question, Councillor?"

"Um, I suppose so," said Paige nervously.

"Hello, my name is Peggy and I wanted to ask the Councillor if she's having a baby. I saw her in Holles Street last week and I was just wondering."

"Um, well . . ." Paige took a deep breath. Tom has told her to be honest and open if this ever came up, so that was how she was going to play it. "Yes, yes I am. I haven't made the news public yet because . . ."

"I think it's a disgrace," Annette piped up. "Mothers should be at home with their children, not gadding about the place looking for votes. She's putting the baby's life in danger."

"Yes, yes," Hilda agreed. "Women of Ireland, listen to me. I'd like to talk about the rights of the unborn child. In my day . . ."

261

Paige felt like crying. First the comments about Callum, now this. It was most unfair.

"I'd like to say something." Jackie leant forward, interrupting Hilda's rant. "We are not here to discuss Councillor Brady's personal life. What's Irish politics coming to if that's all we think the voters are interested in? Let's not insult their intelligence. Let's talk about what really matters — how we can get this country back on its feet. How we can improve the standard of life for the large percentage of the country who are living below the poverty line. How we can educate our children better. These are the things that matter, not the Councillor's personal life."

"Well said, Deputy," Frank said. "And now we have another call. This time for Councillor Higgins. And I believe it's someone you know, Councillor."

"Hello, Mum," came a voice down the line. "It's Chantal, your daughter. Remember me?"

"Um, yes, hello Chantal. And what are you doing, dear? Why are you ringing?" Annette's face began to pale and her eyes flicked around the studio nervously, before settling on her knees.

"I've been watching the programme and I'm ashamed of you, Mum."

"Chantal!" Annette said. "What are you saying?" She looked at Frank. "I think you should cut her off. This is not my daughter. This is an impostor."

"Mum, it is me. You know it is. And how can you be such a hypocrite? You worked the whole way through both your pregnancies and we never saw you when we were small because you were always at some meeting or

262

other. Dad brought us up. And how could you say that about that woman's little boy? What kind of person have you become? We don't even talk, Mum. You haven't said one word to me in over two years, maybe you'd like to tell everyone why."

"Um, yes, well, I've learnt from my mistakes, haven't I? And I don't think they'd be interested at all in our little stand-off. Goodbye, Chantal." Annette looked visibly shaken.

"But —" Chantal said.

Frank stepped in, worried about the legal implications of what she might say. "I'm afraid we'll have to leave it there as it's time for a commercial break. Thank you, ladies, for coming into the studio this morning. It's been most, um, interesting."

"Join us after the break for the amazing story of Gina, the surrogate chimp mother." Dee smiled broadly at the camera.

"Talk about getting personal," Jackie whispered to Paige as soon as the ads had come on. "I've never known an election like it. Remember Miles laying into Mark on the radio the other week?"

Paige nodded. "How could I forget?"

Frank looked at all the candidates. "That was quite something. I don't know what to say really."

Annette stood up. "You should never have accepted my daughter's call. It was most unprofessional of you. I'm, I'm . . ." With that she stormed out of the studio.

Hilda, looking almost as pale as Annette for some reason, followed her out.

"Phew!" Dee said. "I wouldn't be surprised if some of that ends up on this evening's news. Explosive stuff. What do you think her daughter was going to say?"

"Who knows?" Frank shrugged his shoulders.

"Thank you for having us on," Jackie said. "Sorry it all got a little heated."

"Not to worry, it's good for the ratings," Frank said.

I'm sure it is, Paige thought to herself. But it's not good for my nerves.

CHAPTER
THIRTEEN

Molly

"Are you expecting someone?" Paige asked Molly who's eyes kept flitting towards the door of Coffee Heaven.

Molly looked at her. "No, why?"

"You keep staring at the door, that's all."

"Oh, do I?" Molly drained the last of her coffee. "Would you like another cup? I'm getting one."

"Please. And a chocolate muffin if there are any left."

Molly pushed her chair out and made her way to the counter. Alex flew past her with two heaped plates of salad and a steaming bowl of soup.

"Back in a second," she told Molly. Alex placed the food in front of its owners and bustled back to Molly. She blew a stray piece of hair out of her flushed face.

"Busy?" Molly smiled.

"No kidding. I hate lunchtime. Especially when it's raining and everyone wants to eat in. What can I do for you?"

"Two coffees and a chocolate muffin."

"No problem." Alex glanced over at the door, looked back at Molly and grinned.

"What?" Molly asked.

"Nothing. I'll bring your coffees over in a few minutes."

"Thanks." When Molly turned around, she understood why Alex had been smiling. Sam was now sitting at the table with Paige. Alex had it in her head that there was something going on between herself and Sam. Try as she may, Alex just wouldn't believe Molly when she explained that they just enjoyed having lunch together, that was all, nothing more.

"Oh, yeah?" Alex had asked. "Every day? And coffee too?"

"We just get on well as friends, that's all!" Molly had protested. But it hadn't done any good. Alex still had the two of them pegged as the next Rhett and Scarlet. She just wouldn't listen.

"Hi, Sam," Molly said as she sat down beside him. "I thought you were on a day off today."

"I am, but I got these this morning and I knew you'd want to see them straight away. But I don't have long I'm afraid, I have to collect Hugh soon." He patted the large brown envelope which was resting on the table.

"What's that?" Molly asked.

"The designs for the Book Festival," Paige said excitedly.

"Have you already seen them?" Molly asked a little miffed.

"No, we were waiting for you, of course," Paige said. "Will you show us now, Sam?"

"Certainly." He opened the envelope and pulled out three sheets of A4 paper. "My friend, Dora did three different designs. She said there's no problem changing

266

anything you're not happy with — the colour, lettering, lay-out, that kind of thing." He spread the three sheets on the table. "What do you think?"

Paige looked at Molly. Molly was smiling broadly.

"They're great!" Paige said. "Just what we wanted. Bright and fun, with a romance theme. Which one do you like best, Molly?"

Molly studied the three designs carefully. They were all very different. One was an old fashioned design in the shape of a heart with a lacy border and filled with what looked liked pink and red pick and mix sweets. The next was more modern — another heart, this time filled with tiny books, all spilling over each other. The third was very striking — little pink cherubs flying up and down the page, their hair highlighted in gold, each holding a book.

She pointed at the cherubs. "That one."

"My choice too." Paige nodded.

"What do you think, Sam?"

"I'm not really your target market, am I?" he said. "But I'd have to agree with you. The cherubs are really eye catching. And the lettering and the slogan in the cloud is a great idea."

Paige read it aloud. "The Burnaby Book Festival in association with Happily Ever After Bookshop. Bringing Books Alive."

"And best of all," Sam said, "Dora showed the designs to her boss in the design house who turned out to be a dedicated reader. Her boss offered to sponsor the printing of the posters and flyers for the event if we bung some free tickets her way and put their company's name on all our promotional material. And Ink Press offered to print the programmes for free as part-sponsorship."

"Really?" Molly asked. "That's excellent news. Thanks, Sam." She felt like kissing him but thought against it.

"How can we thank you?" Paige said. "That's the best news I've had all day. No, all week. You're an angel."

"A cherub?" Molly laughed.

"Exactly." Paige smiled. "A cherub."

After Sam had left, Molly and Paige finished up their coffee.

"He's so nice," Paige commented.

"Sam?"

"Yes, Sam."

Molly looked at her and smiled. "I know. He's lovely, isn't he?"

Paige leaned closer towards her. "Has anything happened that you haven't told me about?"

Molly shrugged her shoulders. "Unfortunately not. But we're going out to the cinema on Saturday, so you never know. Fingers crossed."

"How did that happen? Did he ask you out again?"

"Not exactly. He mentioned there was a film that he'd like to see and I said I'd love to see it too but that no one would ever go to subtitled films with me. Not even you."

"Liar!" Paige snorted.

Molly laughed. "I had to think of something."

"What are you going to see?"

"A new French film. It's supposed to be really romantic."

Paige raised her eyebrows. "Did he choose it?"

Molly nodded.

"Sure, you're away on a hack, girl, in that case. I look forward to hearing all about it."

On Saturday night, Molly started getting ready early. She wanted to look her best but she didn't want to look like she'd put too much effort into it. If only men knew how long it took to apply "natural looking" make-up, they'd be shocked. She'd fake tanned her body earlier and had spent most of the last hour walking around the house half-naked, worried that it would streak if she got dressed. Luckily, Kate was out for the night, though she'd been very coy about where she was going. All that she'd divulge was that she was meeting an old friend and wouldn't be back until the following afternoon. Molly was intrigued but try as she might, she couldn't get any more information out of Kate.

"I'll tell you when I can." Kate had kissed her on the cheek, her eyes dancing with happiness.

"It's good to see you in such flying form," Molly had conceded. "But could you not just tell me his name, please?"

Kate had smiled and shaken her head. "You'll be the first to know, I promise. OK?"

Molly smelt her arms. They still reeked — the sweet acidic smell of flesh turning golden brown she hoped. She'd wait for a little while longer, then have a shower. She studied her legs carefully, turning them this way and that. They seemed a little browner all right, but it was hard to tell really.

Striding down the stairs two hours later in a flowery summer skirt, dainty slip-on sandals which flattered her feet, a white vest top and her fitted denim jacket she felt great. She'd piled her hair on top of her head, allowing a few tendrils to falls down on either side of her face to soften the effect, and her make-up was deceptively natural.

She waited for Sam in the living room. He'd kindly offered to collect her at home. Molly was delighted with this — it made it seem like a real date, not just two friends going to the cinema together. After spending a few minutes watching television, the doorbell rang.

Molly jumped up and went into the hall to answer it. As soon as she opened the front door she instantly regretted not checking through the tiny security peep-hole first.

"Hello, Molly," said Denis. "Can I come in?"

"What are you doing here?" she demanded, still holding the door half open.

"That's no way to greet an old friend."

"Denis, I'm sorry but I'm on my way out. I'll ring you tomorrow, how about that? We can talk."

"Why not now?" he asked persistently. "I miss you, Molly. I can't get you out of my head. I'm so sorry things turned out the way they did. But if you'll only . . ."

"Denis, please stop." Just then a car pulled up outside the gate. "I think this may be my lift. It's better if you . . ."

270

Sam walked in the gate. Molly waved at him. "I'll be with you in a second," she said loudly. "Denis," she said, turning her attention back to him, "you have to go now."

"I see," he stared at her, and she felt as if his cool, blue eyes could cut her in half, they were that sharp. "Am I that easily replaced?"

"It's not like that," Molly said. "Sam is a friend from work. We're going to the cinema together, that's all."

"Why are you so dressed up then? You never wore skirts when we were together."

"Yes I did, you're being ridiculous," Molly said. "Now I have to go, I'm sorry." She closed the door in his face, not knowing what else to do, grabbed her bag and waited a few seconds. Denis was still there when she opened the door again. "I'll walk you to the car," he offered.

She said nothing. There was no point in arguing with him, it would only make things worse. As they approached the car, Sam stepped out and held the passenger door open for Molly.

"Quite the gentleman," Denis observed. He held out his hand formally. "I'm Denis, I don't think we've been introduced."

"Sam," Sam said without betraying any emotion at all. "Nice to meet you. And that's my son, Hugh, in the back of the car."

Molly looked into the car in surprise. "Oh," she said waving at Hugh who waved back in reply. "I didn't realize he was coming with us."

"A family outing," Denis said, an unpleasant look on his face. "How sweet."

"We'd better get going, Molly," Sam said glancing at his watch. "Nice to have met you, Denis."

"And you."

As the car drove away, Molly breathed a sigh of relief.

"Sorry about all that," she said.

"Not to worry." He lowered his voice. "And I'm sorry I had to bring Hugh. His mum was called away on a voice-over job unexpectedly. Some ad she'd recorded got accidentally wiped by the studio and they have to re-record the whole thing. And his grandparents are away. I did try Dad but he's busy."

"It's OK. But he won't be able for the subtitles, will he? And the film's not really suitable anyway."

"Um, no. I was hoping we could go to the new Harrison Ford action film instead. Would that be OK? I know I should have rung you first but we were in such a rush and . . ."

"Sam, that's all right, honestly. We can go to the French film next week or something. I'm quite partial to Harrison Ford to tell the truth." She turned around. "Do you like Harrison Ford, Hugh?"

"Is he the old guy who plays Indiana Jones and who was in *Star Wars*?"

"Yes, that's right. I wouldn't have thought of him as old though."

"He's got white hair, like Grampa."

"But with a much younger girlfriend," Sam added.

"Grampa has a girlfriend?" Hugh asked with interest.

272

"No! Harrison Ford." Sam laughed. "You have to watch what you say with Hugh," he whispered to Molly.

"So I see," she whispered back.

"What are you saying?" Hugh asked.

"Just talking about the film."

After dropping Hugh back to his mum's, Sam drove back to Burnaby along the coast road.

"How's the writing going?" Sam said. "Or am I allowed to ask?"

"You are this week." She smiled. "Because it's actually going all right, fingers crossed. I've almost finished the story I've been working on. I just have to get the ending right. I always find endings so difficult."

"They are kind of important, aren't they?" He smiled back. "But I'm glad it's going well."

"Thanks." Molly looked out of the window. Sam was very easy company. She never felt she had to fill the silences with him. If they didn't feel like talking they didn't seem to need to. "Look at that moon," she said staring up. "Isn't it amazing? So bright."

"We should take a walk along the beach," Sam suggested. "It's such a beautiful evening."

Molly's heart leapt. "Yes, why don't we?"

Sam drove down the slip road to the beach and parked the car. "You won't be too cold, will you?" he asked as they stepped out of the car. "I have a jacket in the back if you like."

"That would be great. Thanks." He handed her a dark blue fleece and she put it on. The sleeves were much too long for her so she rolled them back. "I look huge in this," she laughed.

"No you don't, it suits you." He locked the car and took her hand. The steady heat of his skin against hers made her feel safe and warm.

They crunched down the shingle towards the edge of the sea and walked along the firmer, damp sand. The waves were lapping at the shore, with gentle wet swishes, and the moon illuminated the water, giving it an otherworldly, unearthly glow.

"About Denis," Sam began nervously. "I'm not causing any problems there am I?"

"Not at all. He's having problems accepting that it's over between us, that's all. We were together for ten years on and off and I guess he figured we'd end up together eventually. But it's definitely over."

"If there's anything I can do — talk to him for you, keep out of the way . . ."

"There isn't, but thanks for offering. He's harmless, just annoying. Anyway, let's not talk about him this evening. Did Hugh enjoy the film do you think?"

"Yes. He was a bit freaked out by the giant spiders, I think. He was gripping my hand so hard I thought he'd break my fingers at one stage, but he seemed to like the rest of it. Thank you for being so nice to him."

"He's easy to be nice to," Molly replied. "He's a good kid."

"He really took to you. He's not always that chatty with people. Actually he's usually quite shy."

"We were talking about books mainly. He's quite the little reader, isn't he?"

Sam nodded. "He started reading at four and he's been flying through them ever since. He's reading *The Hobbit* at the moment."

"So he told me. That's quite some child you have, Sam."

"I know, I'm very lucky." He lifted her hand towards his face and kissed it softly. "But thank you. And you're quite something too, you know."

Molly didn't know what to say. She could feel her face redden but hoped Sam wouldn't notice in the half-light. "Um, thanks."

"You're not used to compliments, are you?" he asked.

"I suppose not."

He stopped walking. "Come here," he said quietly.

Molly's heart leapt. His eyes were warm and kind and they drew her in, encouraging her to move towards him. He put his arms around her, touched her cheek tenderly, then ran his arms up and down hers, warming her through the fleece. "You're cold," he said. "We should go back to the car."

"I'm OK," she protested, not wanting him to stop. "Really."

He smiled at her. "Really?" he cocked an eyebrow.

I could drown in those eyes, she thought, staring into them. His blonde curls were falling over his face and he looked edible. Kiss me, she urged. Go on, kiss me.

He stroked her face again and ran his fingers over her lips. Molly thought her legs would melt from under her. She couldn't take much more of this. She could feel her breath becoming faster, and her heart skipped a beat as he planted a tiny kiss on the edge of her mouth. That was it — she'd had enough. She put one hand behind his head and pulled his lips towards hers. They kissed gently at first, exploring each other's mouths, growing more passionate with each lingering lip caress. Molly pressed her body against Sam's and felt him respond instantly, tightening his grip on her. They kissed for what seemed like hours, before drawing away and holding each other, Sam's firm hands cupping the hollow in Molly's lower back.

"You really are something," he whispered into her ear.

"You're not so bad yourself," she whispered back.

They walked back towards the car, lingering to have one final look at the beach before driving away.

"My house is just up the road," Sam said as they pulled out of the side road. "Would you like some coffee or something?"

Or something, Molly felt like saying but she refrained herself. "Sure," she said instead. "That would be nice."

As soon as they stepped into his house she knew he wasn't like other men. For one thing, from what she'd seen of the house so far it was incredibly tidy, except for an area of toys to one side of the living room, and shelves and shelves of slightly disorganized-looking books of all shapes and sizes. Children's books, Molly decided on closer inspection.

"Sorry, that's Hugh's play area," Sam explained. "It's always a bit of a mess."

"It's a lovely room," Molly said. She unzipped the fleece, pulled it off and handed it to him. He hung it on

276

the back of the sofa. "Sit down," he said. "I'll put the kettle on. Or would you like a glass of wine? I've a bottle of white open in the fridge."

"I'd love a glass of wine." She smiled up at him. "Thanks."

After he'd left the room, Molly had a good look around. The black fireplace had an intricate boarder of patterned tiles to either side of it and above the mantelpiece was a most unusual mirror, framed in what looked like driftwood. On either side of the fireplace were white wooden built-in shelving units, filled with all manner of objects — small wooden sculptures, a silver tankard, silver candlesticks, framed photographs of Sam and Hugh, some ornamental glass paperweights and a small block of wood decorated with painted-on primroses and forget-me-knots.

Sam came back in holding two generous glasses of wine. He handed one to her, put his own down on the wooden coffee table between the two cream sofas and sat down on his hunkers in front of the fireplace. He began to build a fire, placing firelighters on the grate and putting pieces of wood and small logs around them.

"I love real fires," he said as he worked. "They're a bit of a pain, but worth it."

"We don't have one in our house, and I do miss it," Molly said. "We have a gas one in the living room but it's not really the same, is it?"

"It's a good substitute." Sam stood up, brushed his hands on his jeans and picked up his wine.

"I love your mirror," Molly said as he sat down beside her. "Where did you get it?"

"I made it," he admitted. "I made most of the furniture in the house."

"Really?" Molly said in surprise. "Even the coffee table and the shelves?"

"Sure." He nodded. "They were quite easy. Hugh's bed was the hardest. He had a very fixed idea of what he wanted."

"What did he want?"

"Harry Potter's castle." Sam grinned. "Complete with spiral staircase and turrets."

"No! And you made it? Hogwarts isn't it?"

"That's right. I did, my impression of it anyway."

"Can I see?"

"OK." Sam stood up and held out his hand for her. He led her down the narrow hallway, opened a door and flicked on the light.

"Sorry it's such a mess."

Molly stepped over the Lego pieces and walked towards Hugh's bed. It was one of the most incredible things she'd ever seen. It reached from the floor right up to the ceiling, two dark green towers with purple turrets and a bed perched in between. Below the bed was a desk and a wardrobe, and against the far wall was a wooden puppet theatre, the puppets in an adjacent open wooden box.

"It's amazing!" Molly said. "I've never seen anything like it. Are the towers hollow?"

Sam nodded. "One has steps and the other has a spiral slide. Hugh loves sliding down it in his pyjamas when he's supposed to be in bed."

"I'm not surprised, what fun. And you made all this?"

Sam nodded and shrugged his shoulders modestly. "It took me a while, but yes, yes I did. I'm quite good with my hands."

"I'm impressed."

"Thanks. Now let's go back into the sitting room. Knowing my luck, the fire will have gone out."

They sat back down on the sofa and Sam put his arm around Molly's shoulders. The fire hadn't gone out, as Sam had feared and they sat in companionable silence gazing into it and sipping their wine.

"Thank you for a lovely evening," Sam said after a while.

"My pleasure."

He leaned over and kissed her again, trailing his hand down her cheek and caressing her neck and shoulder.

Sam's right, he really is good with his hands, Molly thought as they kissed. Damn good.

The following afternoon, Kate still hadn't arrived home. Molly tried her mobile but she wasn't answering. Molly had also rung Paige this morning, bursting to tell someone all about her evening with Sam, but Tom had answered the phone and said Paige was writing up some report for the County Council meeting on Monday evening and had asked not to be disturbed.

Molly toyed with the idea of visiting her parents — but why spoil a great weekend she decided. She would have loved to have spent the day with Sam but he was working in the bookshop. They'd have to start getting their rotas in synch, she thought. Thinking about Sam she smiled. She could still feel his lips against hers. He had dropped her home at four in the morning, after waking her up. She'd fallen asleep on the sofa, head resting on his shoulder, lulled to sleep by the warmth of the fire, the wine and the heady passion of the evening. He'd offered her a bed, but she wasn't quite sure what he'd meant by this and had opted to go home instead. She hated waking up in someone else's bed after spending the night unexpectedly, last night's make-up sunk into her pores, yesterday's stale clothes, no clean underwear. She never felt at ease in someone else's shower either — if it worked that was — she liked things to be clean and had had horrible experiences of standing on the slimy, hair ridden shower tray in Denis's house. She always ended up cleaning out that particular shower before daring to step into it. Yes, boys' bathrooms could be a downright health hazard, although Sam's, from what she'd seen of it, was remarkably clean, except for some toothpaste residue on the sink and the mirror which were only minor hygiene crimes in her book.

After having a shower in her own, ultra-clean bathroom and getting dressed in her most comfortable grey tracksuit bottoms and an off-white fleece, she walked to Burnaby Village to pick up a bagel and the papers.

Sitting down at the kitchen table half an hour later, she started flicking through the *Sunday Times* supplements while munching on her cream cheese and salmon filled bagel, washed down with some freshly squeezed orange juice. After she'd finished eating she looked at her watch — three o'clock. Still a large part of the day to fill. She thought about catching the afternoon showing of the French film at the Cineplex in Dun Laoghaire, but she had promised to go with Sam. She could always see it twice she supposed — no, that would be stupid. She knew damn well what she really should be doing and going to the cinema would just be a delaying tactic. She stood up, cleared away her plate and stacked the papers neatly on the table. She poured herself a glass of water, and made her way out of the kitchen, up the stairs and into her bedroom. She stared at her desk for a few seconds before sitting down.

As she turned on her computer and waited for it to boot up, she thought of Sam again. Sam walking on the beach, the wind in his curly hair, Sam paddling in the sea, Sam on his hunkers, building a fire, Sam's lips on hers . . . If she wanted to get any work done, she'd really have to stop. Think of your story, she admonished herself, not Sam.

She clicked on Microsoft Word for Windows and opened the short story she was working on — "The Fisherman". She read over what she'd written, changing words or sentences here or there and trying to get into the story. It was almost finished but she was having problems with the ending. For almost an hour she tried to think of some sort of logical and fitting conclusion, but ultimately failed once again.

She sighed deeply, began to bite at the skin around her thumb before picking up a pen and fiddling with that instead. "Come on," she told herself. "Think of something." She was about to turn off the computer in disgust when an image came into her mind, an image of a laughing, smiling man. Who is he? She asked herself. What does he look like? He's called Arthur, she decided. Arthur, um, Arthur, what? She tapped her teeth with a pen. Arthur Logan, Art for short. And he's tall, with messy black hair and dark blue eyes. Well built. She began to form his character in her mind. He works in the local library but he's also a painter, no a sculptor. A girl joins the library staff, Lisa. She's extremely quiet and no one can get much out of her, except for Art. They become friends and gradually he finds out why she's so quiet — her daughter died over a year ago and she hasn't even started to deal with it. Art helps her to come to terms with her loss and they fall in love.

Molly smiled to herself as she typed her notes frantically onto the keyboard. The story seemed to flow out of her from nowhere. The story of a woman and her road to recovery through the love of a good man. Sure, it was sentimental and maybe a little over optimistic, but hell, why not? People needed a bit of light relief and a little hope. Life was hard enough without having to read depressing stories all the time. There was definitely a place for some optimism in the world. Not to mention love.

She jotted down some more notes on her characters and her plot and then began to launch into the opening paragraph.

Molly read over what she'd written and smiled. Not a bad opening if I say so myself, she thought. She continued typing, drawing out Lisa and Art's story. By the time she looked up again, she was astonished to find it was almost seven o'clock in the evening. Over the last while she'd found writing a bit of a chore to tell the truth, but today the story had just told itself. Once she'd started, the characters had simply taken over, telling their own tale. Something that hadn't happened to Molly for a long, long time. She stretched her arms over her head and yawned. She saved her work and shut down the computer, happy and content. As she collected up her laundry — one of her usual Sunday chores — her mobile rang. She checked the screen — it was the shop. Sam was closing up today — she hoped there wasn't any problem.

"Hello?" she answered tentatively.

"Molly," Sam said warmly. "It's me, Sam."

Her heart leapt. "Hi, Sam." She sat down on the bed, all thoughts of laundry forgotten.

"Sorry I didn't ring earlier," he said, "but it was really busy in here. You know how it gets on a Sunday."

"Don't I just. Are you only closing up now?"

"Yes, unfortunately. Listen, what are you up to? Can I call over?"

"Sure, that would be nice. Would you like something to eat? I was just about to start making something."

"If it's not too much trouble."

"No trouble at all."

"I've been thinking about you all day," Sam said.

"I've been thinking about you too," Molly admitted, surprising herself. "See you in a while."

"Would you like me to bring anything?" he asked.

"Just yourself." She smiled as she put down the phone. Sam was delightfully straightforward and didn't seem to believe in playing games which was refreshing after Denis, who seemed to think that their relationship was a protracted game of Snakes and Ladders with a little Poker and Cluedo thrown in for good measure.

CHAPTER
FOURTEEN

Kate

On Sunday morning Kate woke up and opened her eyes. Feeling the unusually firm mattress beneath she remembered where she was — in the Presidential Suite of the Killiney Arms with Jay. Jay was lying beside her, on his back fast asleep and snoring gently. The previous week had gone by in a blur and she couldn't think when she'd last felt so happy. After a remarkably civilized dinner the evening after the hot tub incident — where she and Jay had talked and talked all night, ending up in bed together again — Kate had decided to take each day as it came and, after some initial reservations, concluded that maybe Jay had changed. She'd decided to give him the benefit of the doubt and to enjoy the short time they had together. Because once he left, it was over for good. They would just have this one last week, that was all she promised herself. Just one last, very final fling. To get him out of her system.

Jay had stayed in Dublin for four extra days just to be with her, and he'd already asked her to spend Christmas with him in Boston, which she had no intention of doing, of course. Christmas. As Kate lay in bed, thinking about Jay her mind drifted back to last

Christmas Eve, a day she'd tried to block from her memory and had almost succeeded.

They'd intended to spend last Christmas together but on Christmas Eve things had taken an unexpected turn. On that fateful day, Kate had finished up work early and joined her colleagues for drinks in the local watering hole. She'd tried ringing Jay several times as they were due to meet that evening, but his mobile had been turned off. Up until then they'd always met at her house, and looking back on it of course it seemed strange to Kate, but caught up in the romance of their relationship, it was one of many signs she hadn't spotted until it was too late. Her place was nearer where they both worked and it suited Kate well — it meant she didn't have to remember to bring fresh underwear and toiletries in her bag every time they met. But that particular evening, tired of waiting for him and sensing that something was up, after some dithering she made up her mind to call into Jay's apartment. It was a good half an hour's walk away from the bar but it was a fresh, crisp night and she decided she could do with the fresh air after the hectic day she'd had and the smoky atmosphere of the bar. She said goodbye to her colleagues and left, looking forward to seeing Jay.

Kate approached his apartment, her cheeks tingling from the cold and pressed his bell. No answer. She tried his mobile again — it was still off. Where the hell was he? A tall dark-haired woman approached the communal door and opened it with a key. She looked at

Kate for a moment as if deciding whether she was dangerous or not.

"Are you all right?" the woman asked Kate.

Kate nodded. "Visiting a friend. He's late."

"Wait inside, it's a chilly night." The woman held the door open for Kate.

"Thanks," Kate said gratefully. She was beginning to get cold.

Kate walked inside, took a seat on the red couch in the lobby and watched as the woman's back disappeared into the lift. All around her was deathly quiet. She pulled out her mobile and tried Jay's number again. Nothing. She sat there for a few minutes turning over the mobile in her hands, hoping it would ring at any moment, not knowing quite what to do if it didn't. Since meeting Jay she hadn't seen much of her other American friends and now she was beginning to regret it. She could always go back to the bar, she supposed, but she knew she wouldn't.

Just then, she heard a car pull up and voices outside the door. She looked out. A dark-coated man was stepping out of a yellow cab. It was Jay! Kate jumped to her feet to get the door for him as his arms were laden down with multi-coloured shopping bags. So that's where he was — shopping — of course! She was relieved and delighted to see him. As he approached the door he saw her and his face froze. He stared at her and then looked behind him at the elegant blonde woman, also holding several shopping bags, who was leaning over, paying the cab driver. Kate's heart sank. Who was the woman and why was Jay frowning like that?

Kate opened the door and held it for him as he walked through into the lobby.

"Jay?" she said quietly. "Are you all right?"

"No." He looked at her intensely. "I'll explain everything later, I promise. Right now please don't say anything to . . . um . . ." He gestured towards the woman. "Stay right here and I'll be down in a moment, OK?"

Kate was too shocked to answer.

"Sit down," he commanded. "I'll only be a moment."

Kate was so dumbfounded and so confused, she did as he requested. Surely there was some rational explanation for all this — an out of town college friend back for the day, a long lost sister . . . but why hadn't he introduced them? Kate feared the worst. Still, she just sat there, silent as stone.

As Jay and the woman walked past her, Kate watched them like a hawk.

"I'm exhausted," the woman said in a strong Boston accent. "I could fall asleep on my feet, honey. No more shopping, ever, OK?" She put her head on his shoulder as they stood and waited for the lift.

"Sure," Jay replied. They both stood with their backs to Kate and it suddenly all fell into place. He had another girlfriend. He'd replaced his little "Cat" with a more glamorous model. How could she have been so stupid? Jay was much too good for her, she'd known that all along.

She strained her ears, trying to hear what Jay and the woman were saying, but to no avail. She watched them both step into the lift and as they turned towards her,

Kate looked at Jay's face. It was betraying no emotion whatsoever. Kate felt a sharp stabbing in her chest. How could he ignore her like that? What was she doing sitting there, watching him when he had another woman by his side? She stood up abruptly, determined to say something. But it was too late, the lift doors closed just as she was galvanized into action. She waited for the lift to come back down, determined to follow him up to his apartment. But as soon as the doors opened again she realized to her surprise that Jay was still in the lift.

As he stepped out she began to flood him with questions.

"Where were you, Jay? I've been trying to ring you all afternoon. Who was that woman? Why is she in your apartment? What's happening? You were supposed to —"

"Cat," he interrupted. "There's a perfectly good explanation for all of this. Let's take a walk." He put his arm around her but she shrugged it off.

"No! I want to see your apartment. Do you realize in all this time that I've never been inside it? You've always had some excuse or other for me not to see it."

"You're being silly," he said smoothly. "Let's go outside and get some air. Have you been drinking?"

"No, not really. Stop trying to twist things. Jay!" He was walking towards the door.

He turned around and smiled at her. "Come on," he said. "Join me."

She followed him, not knowing what else to do.

"Who's the woman?" she asked again as soon as they were outside. "Tell me now, Jay, I need to know."

Jay said nothing for a few minutes, just kept walking towards the end of the block. Kate walked beside him. "Jay?"

He stopped and looked at her, his eyes dark and restless, unable to focus on hers for more that a brief moment. Kate knew immediately that it was over. He was smiling but his eyes were cold. "I don't know how to tell you this . . ." he began. He put his hands on her shoulders and rested them there. Kate could feel them pressing down on her, like a dead weight. "She's my wife."

"What?" Kate could feel the blood draining from her face and she began to feel quite faint. She shrugged off his hands and took a step back from him. "I don't understand. You never told me you were married."

"It never really came up."

"What do you mean?" she said again. "Never came up. You're joking, right?"

Jay shook his head. "I never meant to fall in love with you, Cat. But I did. And it's changed everything. My marriage was rocky before I met you but now it's practically over. But I can't leave yet, Cindy's . . ."

"Cindy?" Kate demanded sharply. "Is that her name? Cindy?" She snorted. "As in Sindy doll?"

"You're overreacting, Kate. As I told you, my marriage is over, we haven't been close for a long time. But this week she . . ."

"I don't want to hear it," Kate said icily. "You're married and your wife is waiting for you. It's Christmas

290

Eve, why wouldn't she be waiting for you? God knows where you've told her you've gone, you lying bastard. So go on, go back to her." Kate turned to walk away from him but he held on to her upper arm tightly.

"Cat, please let me explain."

"No! Get your hands off me!"

"There's no need to be like that. If you'll just listen . . ."

"I've been listening to your lies for quite long enough. I don't want to hear another thing from you."

"I understand that you're annoyed with me but . . ."

"Annoyed? Annoyed doesn't even begin to explain how I feel. I'm so angry, Jay I could hit you."

He looked at her in alarm.

"Don't worry, it's not really my style. I just want you to leave me alone." She turned away from him again and began to walk quickly down the street, not looking back.

"Cat! I can explain," he shouted after her. "Cat! Don't leave like this."

But she ignored him. As soon as she'd turned the corner of the block she stopped and put her back against the cold grey concrete wall of an anonymous apartment block. Only then did she allow herself to cry in huge, heaving sobs, engulfing her whole body.

Kate sat alone in her Boston apartment that evening, staring at the large package wrapped in jaunty Christmas paper still sitting under the small artificial tree. It was Jay's carefully chosen present — a simple but hideously expensive black cashmere scarf. Jay had rung both her mobile and her apartment several times but she'd eventually turned the mobile off and taken the other phone off the hook. Her eyes were red and swollen from crying and her heart felt torn to shreds, so torn that it would never heal. She wanted to go home. Back to Dublin, back to people she could trust.

"Cat?" Jay murmured and her thoughts were dragged back to the present.

"Hi, Sleepyhead," she said, trying to forget what she'd been thinking about. "I was just about to have a shower."

"I'll order breakfast and then I might join you." He grinned. "What would you like?"

"I'm pretty hungry," she admitted. "I fancy some scrambled eggs with salmon and some toast. And coffee, lots of it."

"Your wish is my command."

As she stood under the shower she heard Jay talking on the phone but she couldn't quite make out what he was saying. Must be ordering breakfast she mused, putting her head under the hot jets of water and letting it stream down her face and hair. God, she loved hotel power showers. Moments later Jay joined her, his tanned naked skin a sharp contrast to her paler body.

"Hello, stranger." She smiled through the steam.

He moved towards her, a bar of soap in his hands. "You look a little dirty," he smiled back. "Let me fix that." He lathered up the soap and began to smooth it all over her shoulders and her upper arms, moving slowly downwards towards her chest and stomach.

"Turn around," he said, "I want to do your back."

She did as requested and gasped as he ran his soapy hands up and down her legs, lingering deliciously on the tops of her thighs. He stood closely behind her, so close that she could feel his breath on the back of her wet neck.

"You're amazing," he whispered. "Do you know that?" He began to caress her stomach, moving his hands in tantalisingly slow circles on her skin. She began to turn around but he stopped her with his strong arms and pressed her gently against the white tiled wall in front of them. She put her hands against the tiles, feeling the damp coolness on her palms. He held her firmly, one hand circling her waist and resting on her stomach, the other free to caress her most intimate area. She surrendered to the sensation, her heart beating faster and faster and her legs almost buckling weakly beneath her.

He took his hands away, turned her around smoothly and entered her, making her gasp in surprise.

"Did I hurt you?" he asked tenderly, wiping water away from her face.

"No, don't stop," she whispered back.

"I won't," he promised. He was as good as his word.

"That was amazing," Jay said as they tucked into breakfast, wrapped in the hotel's fluffy towelling bathrobes. "I can't believe I have to go this evening."

"Then don't," Kate suggested. "Stay another night."

"You know I can't." He took her hand and stroked it gently. "I have to get back to Boston — I have a big meeting with one of the sports wear companies tomorrow. I'm sorry. But I'll be over as soon as I can."

"Jay!"

"I'm coming back to see you, you know I am. I keep telling you . . ."

Kate groaned. "And I keep telling *you*, this has to stop. I want to get on with my life and you're just confusing things."

"Really?" he asked with a smile. "You didn't seem too confused in the shower, Cat."

Kate blushed and ignored him. "I'm serious, Jay, OK. I don't want to see you again after this week. We've both had our fun and now it's back to real life."

"Is that really what you want, Cat?"

"Yes," she said definitely. More definitely than she felt. "It is."

"I'm going to ring you every day," he said. "You'll change your mind, I know you will. I know you."

"No, you know the old Kate, not the new one."

"Kate?" He laughed. "I guess my little kitty Cat has all grown up then?"

"Don't make fun of me!"

"I'm not. You're just being so serious."

"Life is serious, Jay, for some of us at least."

"It doesn't have to be." He leant over and kissed her on the cheek. "Life with me would be a whole lot of fun, Cat, sorry, Kate. You'll miss out."

"I'm willing to take that risk. I don't just want fun, Jay, I want something more."

"Like what?"

294

Kate looked at him and then looked away. She wasn't quite sure. But being with Jay didn't feel safe, she could never really relax around him. "I can't explain," she said finally. "Just something."

"Ok, I'm not going to push you. Let's just enjoy the remainder of the time we have together." He kissed her hand. "What will we do this afternoon? I have a few presents to buy, but apart from that, I'm all yours."

"Presents? For who?"

"My secretary, she's expecting another baby in a few weeks. And I might even get you one if you're good."

"Oh, I'll be good," Kate said seductively, glad that he'd stopped grilling her about the future.

"Really?"

Kate nodded. "Oh, yes."

The following day, Kate was lying in her own bed again, in the doldrums. Jay was gone, her whole life had been turned upside down and being on her own again was a huge anticlimax. The previous week seemed like a distant dream. Had she done the right thing by letting him go? Her head said yes, but her heart . . . she was trying not to think about it.

Molly had been sweet to her this morning, bringing her a cup of tea and toast in bed. Kate still hadn't told Molly about Jay and she was sorely tempted to, but she didn't want to talk about it in her current fragile state. She missed him so much and they'd only been apart for mere hours. How was she going to cope? She began to think. What if she'd made a huge mistake? What if he had changed? He wouldn't be single for long, not a man like Jay. In a few months' time he'd probably be married again, or engaged at the very least. She had to know for sure. Maybe seeing him on his home territory in Boston would help her decide. She'd never met his family for goodness sake, or his friends for that matter. If he really was serious about loving her, surely he'd introduce her to them all — it stood to reason. Then she'd know for sure. Kate sat up. That was it. That was how she'd know if Jay really had changed. He'd bring her to visit his family. Ha! She'd book a flight for the very next weekend and surprise him. She began to feel instantly better.

"I saw you yesterday," Lily said, looking at Kate carefully.

"Oh, really? Where?"

"On the main street, you were coming out of Presents of Mind."

"Oh." Kate knew that if Lily had seen her she'd also seen Jay, as they were holding hands at the time. He'd just bought a gorgeous silver picture frame for his secretary and a wooden toy for her little son. They should have been more careful — shopped in Dun Laoghaire or Bray — she should have known someone would spot them in Burnaby.

"The man with you — was that Jay?" Lily asked calmly.

Kate sighed. There was no point lying to her granny and besides, she was dying to tell someone. "Yes."

"You looked very happy," Lily observed. "Is he still here?"

296

Kate shook her head. "No, he left yesterday."

"Missing him?"

"Yes." Kate stared out of the window. It was the early evening and they were sitting in her granny's kitchen, drinking tea.

Lily said nothing.

"Before you say anything, he's changed, Gran, he's not the man he used to be. He's so much more caring, more considerate . . ."

Lily snorted. She couldn't help herself. "Is he still married?"

"Don't be like that, Gran, please."

"Well, is he?"

"He's almost divorced. His wife moved back to Maine, she's with someone else, a dentist actually. Does that satisfy you?"

Lily again said nothing. She wondered why her perfectly reasonable granddaughter was so blinded by love.

"Gran! Don't look at me like that."

Lily sighed. "Be careful, Kate. I don't want to see you hurt again, that's all."

Kate smiled. "I won't be, Gran. I'll make sure he's serious this time, before I get involved."

Lily felt uneasy. Why would a man who had just come out of a bad marriage want to get involved again so quickly? It didn't make sense. Lily had a bad feeling about all this, a very bad feeling. But she held her tongue. Kate had to find her own way in the world. She wasn't a little girl any more and Lily couldn't protect her.

"Say something, Gran, please."

Lily reached out her hand and placed it on Kate's. "I just want you to be happy."

"I am, very happy."

"Good."

"In fact, I'm going over to Boston next weekend to see him. It's pretty quiet in the shop and I'm going to ask Trina and Cathy for a few days off and cancel my dummy dates." Kate seemed so elated that Lily didn't have the heart to caution her.

"I hope you have a lovely time, dear," she said instead. "Take care of yourself. Boston's a big place."

"Gran," Kate smiled, "I lived there, remember? Don't worry, I'll be fine."

I hope so, Lily thought. God I hope so.

"I'm worried about Kate," Lily said to Angus the following morning, handing him a mug of tea. They'd become firm friends in the last few weeks, and this week Angus had taken it upon himself, with Callum's "help", to repaint her hall in a glowing yellow, replacing the rather drab white which had become decidedly off-white over time. He'd decided this was a good project for his young ward to undertake and a nice thing to do for Lily, who he'd become terribly fond of.

Callum was delighted with this of course, he'd never been allowed near the walls when his own house was being painted, in fact he'd been banned from the house outright when he'd trod in the paint tray and walked red footprints all over the beige carpet on the stairs. But today he had his own small paintbrush and mini-roller

298

and he was dressed in an old dress shirt of his dad's, an old pair of ripped-at-the-knee jeans and a baseball cap, turned backwards to protect his hair. He was merrily and carefully applying the primrose yellow paint to the edges of the walls and the corners, taking extreme pains to "stay within the lines" as Angus called it — on the walls and not on the skirting boards.

Angus sat down on the stairs and gingerly took a sip of the steaming hot tea. "Why?" he asked. He glanced over at Callum to check he wasn't listening.

Lily sat down beside him.

"It's a long story," she said. "But I think she's involved with a less than honest man."

Angus raised his eyebrows. "I didn't know Kate was seeing anyone."

"She wasn't until the last week or so, from what I can make out. Then this man reappeared, a man from her past. But I'm afraid his intentions are not honourable."

Angus tried not to smile at her old-fashioned phraseology. "Is there anything you can do about it?" he asked kindly.

"I don't think so. Just be there to pick up the pieces I suppose." She told a little about Jay and what had happened on the previous Christmas Eve in Boston.

"Poor Kate," Angus said when she'd finished. "Maybe it will all work out this time, you never know. Maybe he has left his wife."

"Maybe," Lily agreed. She didn't believe it for one second. "Oh, I'm sorry, I shouldn't have burdened you with all this. And I know you like Kate, I can see it in your eyes. What was I thinking of?"

Angus shrugged his shoulders. "That's all right. Anyway, I don't think she's ready for someone like me," he said evenly.

"Someone decent you mean?" Lily said astutely.

Angus shrugged his shoulders.

"Maybe not quite yet," she agreed. She looked over at Callum who was still stuck into his painting. "So, have you any spare rollers? I thought I might give you a hand."

"Lily, you're supposed to be resting." Angus smiled.

"Resting, pah!" Lily swatted the air. "You're only young once. Besides, I've my old worn-out tracksuit on, you don't think I'm dressed like this for nothing, do you?"

He laughed and handed her a fresh roller. "OK, but take it easy. You'll have to share a paint tray with Callum though."

"That's just fine. And how was your date last weekend? The ball?"

"How did you know . . . ?"

She tapped the side of her nose. "I know everything that happens in Burnaby."

"It was terrible to tell the truth. Patricia is stunning looking but she's . . . how will I put this? Difficult."

"Selfish and demanding?" Lily asked. "I remember her as a small child — always terribly spoilt. I'm afraid she hasn't really changed."

"It was an experience anyway," Angus said. "The meal was nice and I had fun dancing with some of the other book trade people. They're a nice gang."

"Were Molly or Anita there?"

"No, but the guy who owns Happily Ever After was — Milo. He was sitting at our table. Interesting man."

"Yes, so I hear." She rolled her brush in Callum's paint tray. "That's great, Callum," she said, studying the work he'd already done.

"I'm being real careful, like Angus said," Callum said.

"Yes you are, poppet," she ruffled his hair affectionately. "You're doing great. I'll tell your mum and dad what a good little painter you are the next time I see them."

After painting a large section of one side of the hall, Lily took a break and made more tea for her and Angus. He followed her into the kitchen to collect it, glad of the break. His shoulders had started to ache from lifting his arms over his head to reach the high spots.

"Would you like me to talk to Kate?" he asked as Lily put fresh tea bags in their mugs.

She looked over. "About Jay?" she asked.

"Yes."

Lily thought for a second. Her first reaction was to say no, but something made her change her mind. Maybe this gentle man would be able to get through to Kate. It couldn't do any harm — could it?

"You could try," she said finally. "I'm not sure if she'd listen to you though."

"You never know."

Kate opened the door early that evening and was surprised to find Angus standing there smiling at her.

301

"Hi, Kate, have you got a second?"

"Um, yes, sure. Come in." She stepped back from the door, let him in and closed it behind them. "Would you like some coffee?"

"Thanks." He followed her into the kitchen and sat down at the table.

She flicked on the kettle and stood leaning against the counter. "So, what can I do for you? More dating advice? I hear you've been seeing Patricia. How's it going?"

"I went to a work do with her," he said evenly. "That's all. We didn't really click to be honest."

Kate felt strangely relieved. "Oh, I see."

"I'll get straight to the point, will I?"

She nodded, her curiosity piqued.

"Your granny is worried about you and the American guy. She told me a little about last Christmas. She doesn't want to see you get hurt again you see and —"

"The American guy, as you so delightfully call him, is called Jay," Kate interrupted. "And what right do you have to come here and lecture me about my choice in men? So Gran put you up to this. I can't believe she told you about me and Jay."

"No. It was my idea. I just thought you might want to talk about it, that's all. Sometimes it's easier to talk to someone on the outside . . ."

Kate looked at him incredulously. "I know damn well what you're doing here and it won't work. Coming over here all kind and caring. Trying to muscle in on another man's territory. You're just as bad as the rest of them. And I thought you were different."

Angus was taken aback. That thought hadn't even entered his mind. He really did just want to help. "No, Kate, you've got this all wrong. Lily was worried about you, that's all. I thought I could help. I'm sorry if . . . maybe I should leave. But I'm always there if you need to talk, remember that. I'm there for you no matter what."

"Isn't that a boy-band song?" she asked disparagingly. "I can look after myself thank you very much. I'm going over to see Jay this weekend and . . ."

Angus raised his eyebrows.

"Don't look at me like that," she continued. "You'll see, you'll both see. Now I think it's best if you do leave."

Angus stood up. "I'm sorry if I upset you. I didn't mean to question your judgement."

"Yes, well, that's not what it sounded like to me. And you can tell Gran to keep my private life just that in future — private."

After she showed Angus out, Kate leant her back against the door. She was furious with both Angus and Lily. She grabbed the phone from the hall-stand and dialled Jay's mobile number. His mobile was turned off. Typical! She dialled her gran's number instead but cut it off after two rings. She was too annoyed to speak to her. Still, at least she only had three more days until she saw Jay again. Three long, lonely days.

CHAPTER
FIFTEEN

Paige

"And this morning I'd like to welcome Finbar White, Chief Political Correspondent of the *Irish News* for our election special," Wella announced on Chat FM.

"Shush, Callum!" Paige hissed. He was singing "Twinkle, Twinkle Star" to Alfie at full volume.

"Sorry, Mummy. I'll go up and get dressed, will I?"

"Yes, good lad," she said distractedly, trying to listen to the radio.

Tom turned the volume up, sat back down beside Alfie and began to spoon mashed apple and banana into his eagerly waiting mouth. Finbar White was the single most important and most highly respected political commentator in Ireland and his opinion counted. With only one week to go until the election, what he said this morning could sway the public's vote. Paige hadn't been able to sleep last night and was on tenterhooks this morning, waiting for his verdict on her possible election result.

"We'll start with the North Dublin constituency. Finbar, who's in the running there?"

Paige turned towards Tom. "This is agony," she said.

"Don't take what he says as gospel," Tom advised. "He's only one person. You have thousands of supporters out there, you know that, Paige."

"I know, but so many people listen to him."

Tom nodded. "But at least he tends to be fair. And he has no bias towards the male candidates like some of the commentators. Or towards the People's Party."

"I suppose so." Paige chewed the skin around her thumb and listened again.

"And Dublin West, Finbar?" Wella asked.

The doorbell rang. Paige stood up quickly. "I'll get it."

Angus was on the doorstep.

"Hi, Angus," she said.

"Are you all right, Paige? You look a little anxious."

"I'm listening to Finbar White on the radio. He's predicting the outcome of the elections."

"Phew!" Angus said. "Are you sure you should be listening?"

"I don't know. At least this way I'll hear it from the horse's mouth. It'll be all over the evening papers later and I'd prefer to know the worst before that."

"Or the best," Angus pointed out. "He might say that you're bound to get a seat."

"He might," Paige said doubtfully.

"I'll help with doorstepping this week," he offered. "And I could galvanize a few others too."

"That would be great," Paige said. "Thanks. It all helps."

"Paige!" Tom shouted from the kitchen. "Dublin South after the ads."

"Coming!"

"Welcome back," Wella said. "And this morning I have Finbar White from the *Irish News* with me, making his election predictions."

"Get on with it," Paige muttered under her breath.

"Dublin South next," Wella said. "Now that's an interesting one, isn't it Finbar?"

"Yes, certainly, Wella. Some changes could well be seen there."

Tom looked over at Paige. "Breathe," he told her.

She smiled at him.

"There are four seats to be filled there and the first two, in my opinion, will certainly go to Deputy Paddy Burns, the People's Party stalwart and a very popular man. And Deputy Jackie Pile, another popular name with the punters. They have both been good, solid representatives and I can't see them losing their seats."

"And Miles McGreinna?"

"I think Deputy McGreinna has had his day to be frank. From what I've observed over the last year, he's lost a lot of his support. I can't see him being re-elected."

"And of course, Deputy Ryan, of the Green Party is retiring so he's not standing this time around," Wella observed.

"Quite. I'd be surprised if Mark Tine didn't win the Green seat back. A bright young man, and a popular politician. The Green Party could do very well in this election if they play their cards right."

"So that leaves McGreinna's seat," Wella pointed out. "Who's in the running?"

"Well there's Annette Higgins of the New Democrats, already a well-known Councillor in Burnaby. She is, of course, Ray Higgins' daughter. She has a good chance on the back of that alone."

"Even after her father's tax scandal?"

"Yes, he's still fondly regarded by most, even after the revelations in the last tribunal."

"And Rex Reximus?"

"Ah, good old Rex is back again, on his usual 'Legalize Cannabis' ticket," Finbar said. "I don't think so, Wella. Do you?"

"I'm sure you're right," she laughed warmly. "And Hilda Murphy?"

"Again, she's not a runner. Too right wing for most people's taste."

Paige looked at Tom. "They've forgotten me."

"No, they haven't," he said reassuringly. "Keep listening."

"And finally, Paige Brady," said Wella. "Another Burnaby Councillor, running as an Independent. What do you make of her chances?"

"Reasonably good," Finbar replied. "She's very popular on the ground, she's not afraid to voice her opinion and she will certainly be in line for a good chunk of the liberal vote. I'd say she has a good chance of taking the fourth seat. It's between her and Annette Higgins."

"Interesting. Now let's move out of Dublin and on to Tipperary South. Feelings on that, Finbar?"

Paige unclenched her hands and sat up.

"That was great!" Angus said. "Your man said you have a good chance of getting elected. You must be pleased with that, Paige."

"I suppose," Paige said thoughtfully.

"What is it?" Tom asked. "There's something on your mind."

"If Finbar's calling it correctly and it is between me and Annette, I just wonder . . ."

"Yes?" Tom said impatiently.

"Whether she had anything else up her sleeve," Paige sighed. "I'm not sure if I can cope with any more surprises."

Tom noticed that Paige's face looked pale and drawn and she had dark circles etched under her eyes. He put down the small plastic spoon he'd been feeding Alfie with and put his arm around her. "Don't worry," he said. "It'll all be over soon. Just one more week to go — hang in there."

Paige gently shrugged off his arm. "I'd better go upstairs and get ready. I'm presenting the prizes for the Ladies' Cup at the Burnaby Sailing Club today. And I have a meeting with Connie before that."

"She's not still on about the Art's Centre is she?" asked Tom.

"No, she wants a word about environmental waste charges apparently."

"Exciting stuff." Tom grinned. Just then, Alfie started to grizzle.

"Will I have a go at feeding him?" Angus offered.

"That would be a help, if you don't mind," Tom said gratefully. "I have a few things to go over for Paige in the office."

"Not at all. Where's Callum? Is he still in bed?"

Paige smiled. "He's upstairs getting dressed. He's been rather a long time though. Heaven knows what he's getting up to." She walked towards the kitchen door and shouted up the stairs. "Callum! Callum! Angus is here. Come down, please."

A moment later she heard him dash across the landing. "Slowly, please," she said firmly.

As he appeared at the top of the stairs Paige had to hold back her giggles. He was wearing the most mismatched outfit she'd seen for a long time. Stripy blue and white trousers, with a red and white short-sleeved gingham summer shirt over a long sleeved black T-shirt.

"Angus is waiting for you in the kitchen," she said and followed him in.

"Hi, Angus," Callum ran over. "Can I help you feed Alfie?"

Angus nodded. "If you're careful."

"I got dressed all by myself this morning," Callum said proudly. "Mum hadn't left any clothes out like she normally does so I got them out of the wardrobe all by myself too."

"Well done," Angus beamed. "And you didn't pull everything else out too, did you?"

Callum looked a little worried. "Um, not really. Some shirts fell down but that's all."

Angus said nothing and continued to feed Alfie.

"Do you think I should put them pack in the wardrobe?" Callum asked after a moment.

"Are they still on the floor?" asked Angus.

"Yes," Callum admitted sheepishly.

"I think you should," Angus said gently. "That would be very helpful."

"I'll give you a hand, love," Paige said, smiling gratefully at Angus. "I have to go up and get changed anyway. I can hardly go out in my pyjamas now, can I?"

"You could, Mummy." Callum laughed. "Sometimes I leave my pyjama bottoms on under my tracksuit bottoms if it's very cold."

"Do you now?" Paige smiled grimly. "I didn't need to know that. Come along, young man. Let's go upstairs and sort out these shirts, will we?"

Callum nodded solemnly.

After a brief tidy-up in Callum's room and another type of wardrobe crisis in her own room, Paige was finally ready to leave. She'd decided to play it safe and wear a plain black suit today — she didn't want to upstage any of the lady sailors after all. Unbeknown to Tom, she was actually squeezing in a trip to her GP, Dr Adams, this morning before meeting with Connie. She didn't want to worry Tom, but she'd been having sharp pains in both her sides and she wanted to get it checked out.

Dr Adams, or "Jilly" as Paige called her, having been in school with her, gave Paige a thorough examination — blood pressure, weight, glands, stomach — before sitting her down in the old-fashioned dark red leather chair.

"Now, Paige, I don't think there's anything to concern yourself with. As there don't seem to be any other symptoms like bleeding or nausea, the pains sound to me like your pelvic muscles moving and stretching. It's perfectly natural during pregnancy. It's caused by the pregnancy hormones surging around your body at the moment, and it can cause some discomfort. But as long as you take it easy and don't go overdoing things, you'll be fine. Are you taking your iron tablets?"

"When I remember."

"Well, remember," Jilly said firmly. "It's important or you'll become anaemic. Your iron count is quite low as it is. And have you been getting enough rest? Or should I ask?"

"Probably not," Paige admitted.

Jilly looked her in the eye. "I know it must be hard, what with elections coming up and everything, not to mention Callum and Alfie, but you must take it easy. Promise me you will? You'll put the baby's health in danger otherwise, not to mention your own health."

"I promise." Paige smiled.

"Good. And if the pain moves or gets worse, or you have any other worries ring me immediately."

"Thanks, Jilly."

As Paige walked out of the surgery and unlocked the door of her car she sighed. Take it easy, Jilly had said. How on earth was she going to take it easy over the next week? Let alone after that. Maybe Annette was right, maybe she was wrong to be contesting the election when she was pregnant. She tried to block the thought out of her mind as she stepped into the car. As she drove towards Burnaby Crescent to meet Connie, she listened to Wella's morning show.

"And after the news we'll have more details of the shock exposure which will appear in this evening's papers. Orla Murphy, daughter of the election candidate Hilda Murphy has given an exclusive interview to the *Evening Tatler* on her relationship with the daughter of another candidate, Councillor Annette Higgins and their foreign adoption hopes. This is not good news for either of the candidates."

Paige couldn't believe her ears. If it was true, no wonder Annette and her daughter didn't get on. She pulled the car over and dialled Tom's mobile number.

"Did you hear the news?" she asked.

"I'm just listening to it on the radio. It's unbelievable, isn't it? This country gets stranger and stranger every day. What possessed the girl to talk to the papers?"

"Who knows?" Paige asked. "Sick to the teeth of her mother's piety probably. But it might mean Annette will stop digging up my past. From all accounts she has plenty of her own skeletons to contend with."

"No kidding. How was the meeting with Connie?"

"I'm just on my way. I got talking to an old school friend in the street. You know what Burnaby's like."

"Don't I just. I'll ring you if there's any more news."

Paige felt bad about lying to Tom but there was no point worrying him unnecessarily. She'd tell him about her visit to the surgery later.

That afternoon Angus brought Callum to the park. Burnaby Park was in an idyllic location at the bottom of Burnaby Hill, stretching down to the sea. The

312

playground in the park was a credit to the community council who funded it, recognizing the need for such a facility in the child-packed constituency. There was a wooden adventure playground for older children, and a brightly painted metal climbing frame, a set of miniature swings and a snake-like curving slide for the younger ones. It was a fine, if cloudy day, and they'd brought marshmallows to roast over the campfire that Angus had promised to help Callum build on the shore.

While collecting driftwood to make their fire, Callum saw a boy sitting on the steep rocks down by the sea. Callum was most impressed, he wasn't allowed to climb on those rocks alone as Angus said they were too dangerous. The boy looked familiar — white blonde hair and little round glasses. I've seen him somewhere before, Callum thought.

"Hello," he called over. "Want to help me collect some wood? We're making a campfire."

The boy stared at Callum for a few moments, then nodded and climbed carefully down the rocks towards him.

"Are you here on your own?" Callum asked as they gathered up driftwood in their arms.

The boy shrugged his shoulders.

"Are you here with your mum and dad?" Callum tried again, not one to be ignored.

He shrugged again and then shook his head.

"I'm here with my friend, Angus." Callum pointed up the beach where Angus was putting the fire together. "Well, he's my minder really but he's not bossy like normal minders. We do cool things together like bungee jumping and snorkelling."

The boy stared at him. "Bungee jumping?" he asked in a quiet voice. "Really?"

"Yes." Callum chatted away as they collected more wood, stopping every now and then to make sure the boy was listening. After their arms were full, he started walking towards Angus.

"Come on," he said to the boy who seemed reluctant to follow him. "Are you not hungry? We have marshmallows and sausages and bread for toasting."

The boy's eyes lit up. He was rather hungry. He hadn't eaten since this morning and his stomach was starting to make strange gurgling noises. He nodded at Callum.

"Come on then!" Callum powered on ahead, dropping some of his wood as he ran.

The boy bent down, collected up the wood and walked slowly towards Angus.

"Hello," Angus said, sitting up on his hunkers. "What's your name?"

The boy said nothing.

"This is my friend," Callum explained. "He was on the rocks over there. All by himself too."

"Really?" Angus asked. He looked at the boy carefully and then looked around. There didn't seem to be anyone in the park except themselves. "Are you on your own?"

The boy said nothing, nodding slightly and staring at Angus, his light blue eyes shining a little behind his

314

rather severe glasses. Angus decided not to push it. Maybe the child was lost.

"Can he have some of our campfire food?" asked Callum.

"Of course," Angus said. "I've started building the fire, we just have to light it now."

"Can I do it?" Callum asked hopefully, fearing the answer.

"Yes, if you're very careful with the matches," Angus said. He knew Callum would want to impress the other boy and he wanted to build his self-confidence.

"Cool!" Callum grinned. "I'll be real careful."

Angus showed him how to strike the match safely away from his body and how to light the firelighters. He knew firelighters were cheating a bit, but the kindling he'd found was a little damp and he knew only too well how short Callum's attention span was. If the fire wasn't lit within minutes, Callum would lose interest.

When the fire was burning successfully, Angus turned his attention to Callum's new friend.

"Do you like this beach?" he asked the boy.

The boy looked at Angus, nodded and went back to staring at the fire.

"Are you lost?" Angus tried again.

He shook his head.

"Do you live near here?"

The boy thought for a moment. "Daddy does. He lives near the other beach."

"Sandybay beach?"

Another nod.

Callum was watching the boy with interest. "I met you at the puppet show," he said, suddenly

315

remembering. "You were there with your dad. Molly works with your dad, doesn't she?"

Another nod.

"Molly from the bookshop?" Angus asked Callum. "Molly who lives with Kate?"

"Yes, silly." Callum laughed. "I don't know any other Mollys." He knew he'd been a bit rude but luckily Angus didn't seem to notice.

Callum smiled. "Hugh! Your name is Hugh. I remember now."

"Is your name Hugh?" Angus asked gently.

Hugh nodded and stared at the fire.

Angus could sense that something was wrong. The boy was practically on the verge of tears. Had something happened to him? Why was he on his own — he couldn't be much older than Callum.

"Before I ring your dad," Angus said gently, "is there anything you'd like to talk about? Did someone upset you?"

Hugh scrunched up his eyes. He wouldn't cry, he wouldn't. But tears began to cloud his eyes and he pushed up his glasses and brushed them away.

Angus put his arm around the boy and gave him a gentle hug. "It's OK," he whispered. "You're safe with us now. Let's have something to eat and then you can tell me what's wrong."

Hugh looked at him gratefully. "Do you have anything to drink?" he asked. It was a warm day and his throat was parched.

"We have fizzy orange," Callum said, oblivious to the boy's tears. "I'm not normally allowed it, Mum says it makes me hyper. But Angus said I could have it today as a special treat. I'll share my can with you if you like."

"Thanks," Hugh said quietly.

Angus smiled at Callum. "Good lad. Let's start cooking the sausages. I think Hugh could do with something to eat."

"Me too!" Callum grinned. "I'm starving!"

Paige winced. Her right side was aching badly and she couldn't do a damn thing about it. That was one of the downsides about being pregnant. She normally relied on heavy doses of pain killers to see her through her aches and pains, but this time she could take nothing. Stress headaches were her body's speciality, those and an occasional searing pain in her right knee from an old soccer injury.

She put her head in her hands and tried deep breathing for a few minutes. It didn't help. She stood up, went into the kitchen and flicked on the kettle. Maybe a hot water bottle would help. She pulled it out of the cupboard under the sink and put it on the counter. Waiting for the kettle to boil, she bent over the kitchen counter and put her forehead on the cool surface, which gave her some relief.

"Paige? Are you all right?" Tom walked into the room and stared at her. "What are you doing?"

She straightened up a little too quickly, causing blood to rush to her head, making her feel dizzy.

Tom looked at her in alarm. She was very pale and seemed wobbly on her feet. He put his arms out and guided her firmly into a chair.

"Sorry, I just feel a little faint," she said, trying a smile. "Nothing to worry about."

"If that's the case," he said, "why did you just wince?"

"I didn't," she lied.

"And why is your hot water bottle on the counter? Do you have a stomach ache?"

She shook her head. "I'm fine, honestly."

"I'm not convinced." The kettle boiled and clicked itself off. "Will I make you some tea?" he offered kindly.

She nodded. "That would be nice, thanks." The pain came again and she took a sharp intake of breath.

Tom looked at her in alarm. "I'm not stupid, Paige! What is it? Please tell me."

"It's nothing, just a little twinge. The doctor said . . ."

Tom stared at her. "What doctor? Jilly?"

Paige sighed. "I didn't want to worry you . . ."

"Well, now you are worrying me. When were you at the surgery?"

"This morning," Paige admitted. "I've been having this pain in my side off and on the past few days and I wanted to talk to Jilly about it."

"And?" Tom asked impatiently.

"She said there was nothing to worry about, it's hormonal. My pelvic muscles are stretching apparently — it's quite normal in pregnancy."

"What else did she say?"

"Nothing really."

"Paige, you're keeping something from me, I know you are. If you don't tell me I'll just ring Jilly and ask her myself."

Paige sighed. "OK. She said to try and get more rest, that's all."

"And?"

"To remember to take my iron tablets."

"Anything else?"

"No, OK, that's it," Paige snapped. "Now could you please stop harassing me? I have enough on my plate without this."

Tom raised his eyebrows but said nothing. He made her a mug of tea and put it down on the table in front of her. "Drink this. Then I think you should lie down for an hour or two, Paige," he said evenly. "The dinner this evening will be easier to deal with if you get some rest beforehand. I can deal with Callum and Alfie when they get back."

Paige glared at him. "As I keep telling you, I'm fine. I don't need a rest. Just leave me alone." She shoved the mug away from her and stood up, slopping some on the table in the process. "Stop treating me like some sort of invalid. I'm not sick, I'm just pregnant."

"I know that," Tom said gently. "Sit down, love, and drink your tea."

"No! I'm going to the study and I don't want to be disturbed. OK?"

She strode out of the room leaving Tom staring at her back in disbelief. Paige was prone to the odd mood but she hadn't snapped at him like that since Alfie was a few weeks old and she was over-exhausted.

"Paige!" he said loudly but she ignored him. A few minutes later he decided to check that she was all right. As he opened the door to the study he heard a strange noise. He stepped in. Paige was collapsed over her desk, sobbing as if her heart had broken.

"Oh, Paige. What's wrong?" He walked towards her and began to stroke the back of her head.

She looked up, her eyes red, puffy and full of tears. "I can't do this any more," she wailed. "I'm so bloody tired all the time. And I never see Callum or Alfie. I'm a bad mother." She began to cry again, heavy tears falling down her cheeks.

"Don't be silly," Tom said. "You're a great mother. You're just under a lot of stress at the moment. Things will get better after next week, you'll see. You'll get elected and . . ."

"That's just it!" Paige interrupted. "I don't know if I want to get elected. What about the boys? And the new baby? Maybe I'm not being fair to all of them. I'm a selfish person and I don't deserve children."

Tom thought for a few moments before saying anything. "Paige, I understand what you're saying, really I do. But you've worked so hard over the last few years to make this happen. Being a Deputy is all you've ever wanted. Burnaby needs you. Hell, the country needs you."

Paige smiled at him through his tears. "I know, Tom. But Callum's been so happy over the last few weeks. Maybe all he needed was some one-on-one attention, like Angus said. I'm scared he'll go back to Little Orchard in the autumn and he'll regress."

"That's not going to happen," Tom put his hand on hers. "Because we won't let it. Politics is part of who you are. You can't abandon it because you feel guilty.

I'm sure a lot of working mothers feel just like you. Think about it. The kids will be fine."

"I just don't know," Paige said. "I'll be working such long hours and it will put a real strain on our family life."

Tom said nothing. He stared straight out the window, a strange look on his face. He had a habit of staring into space when he was thinking.

"Tom?" Paige asked gently. She wiped the tears from her eyes. "What is it?"

"I was just thinking," he said, then smiled at her. "No, ignore me, it's nothing."

"What?" she demanded.

"It doesn't have to be you," he began tentatively. "I have equal responsibility for this family. I could take leave of absence for a year — the building society are quite flexible that way. I've been thinking about it for a while now. I could look after the baby and Alfie, bring Callum to school . . . no, it's a stupid idea, forget it."

"Why do you say it's stupid?"

"It would never work. We'd be completely broke for one thing."

Paige shrugged her shoulders. "Money isn't everything. Besides, Deputies get paid reasonably well."

Tom smiled. "So you've come around to the idea?"

She shrugged again. "Maybe. If I do get in, would you really take a year off?"

Tom nodded. "Yes. If we could afford it, I think I would. Do you think I'd be able for it? I've never really looked after a baby on my own before."

"Of course you would. You're great with Alfie." Paige smiled. She was beginning to feel a whole lot better. Her tears had stopped and the heaviness in her heart had started to lift. Maybe there was a way they could make things work. "And you'd take over all the household jobs too?"

"Like what?" Tom asked.

"The washing, cleaning, cooking, gardening . . ."

He laughed. "Paige, give me some credit. I already do a lot of those — the cooking and the gardening anyway."

Paige considered for a moment. "I suppose you do. Except cleaning the bathrooms of course."

Tom grinned. "I keep telling you, you're far better at that than I am."

"Excuses, excuses." She smiled back. "Tom?"

"Yes?"

She threw her arms around him and gave him an almighty hug. "I'm lucky to have you. You're a wonderful man."

"Why thank you, Deputy."

"I'm no Deputy yet."

"You will be, Paige. Trust me."

She smiled at him. Suddenly everything began to click into place.

"What do you think Callum will say?" Paige asked. "About you staying at home."

"I'm not sure. I hope he'll be pleased. Angus has news for him too. He rang me this afternoon as soon as he heard."

"What news? Why didn't you tell me?"

Tom smiled. "I didn't exactly get the chance."

"Sorry," she said, contrite.

"Not to worry. Angus has just been appointed as a teacher in Burnaby National School. And guess what class he'll be taking?"

"Not Junior Infants?" Paige asked in amazement.

Tom nodded. "Callum's new class. Isn't that great?"

"It's bloody brilliant! The best news I've heard all day. And it's been quite a day. Callum will be over the moon. He adores Angus. We're blessed." She looked up at the ceiling and put her hands together. Tears threatened her eyes again, this time tears of joy. "Thank you, God. I don't know what we've done to deserve this, but thank you."

CHAPTER
SIXTEEN

Molly

Molly looked up from her computer screen for the first time that morning. She wasn't due in to work until after lunch as she'd taken a half day to try and get some writing done. Luckily her phone had been quiet — up until now that was. She reached down, grabbed it from the floor beside her and answered it.

"Hi, Molly, it's Sam," said the familiar voice.

She felt a warm glow in the pit of her stomach. "Hi, Sam."

"I'm not interrupting anything, am I?"

"No, not really. I'm writing but I should probably take a break." She glanced at her watch. "I've been at my desk for almost three hours."

He whistled. "That's impressive. It's only half nine. That means you must have got up at about six o'clock. There's dedication for you."

"Don't remind me," she groaned. "It nearly killed me. But I was fine once I'd had some coffee and toast. How's the shop?"

"Grand. I was just ringing to say that a researcher from the Pat Bolan radio show rang to ask about the Book Festival. Her name's Julie. They want to interview some of the authors and talk about romance books in particular. She wants you to ring her back this morning. I hope you don't mind."

"Not at all, that's great news. I'll ring her back right now. Do you have the number?"

He read it out to her and she jotted it down.

"I'll see you at one in Coffee Heaven," Sam said. "And Molly?"

"Yes?"

"Are you dressed yet?"

"Mind your own business," she laughed. She was still in her pyjamas. "See you later."

After talking to Julie, a lovely woman and a huge Rose Lovett and Jennie Tracker fan, Molly went back to her short story. She found it difficult to concentrate after the interruptions, her mind was jumping all over the place. She read over what she'd written earlier that morning and noticed several spelling and grammar mistakes, highlighted on her screen by green and red squiggly lines. It was funny, she never noticed them when she was writing, only afterwards. She clicked on the spell check and began to correct them.

Her short story, which she'd given the working title of "Concrete Pictures", was really coming along. Her two main characters — Lisa and Art — had started to take over, telling their own stories almost without her help. Most importantly of all, for the first time in a long while, she was really enjoying writing. Her fingers clicked over the keys as fast as they could to keep up with the pictures and images that swarmed into her head. She had no idea where the story or the characters had come from. Often, listening to writers talking about their work she scoffed when they said that the characters just took over and told their own story. But in "Concrete Pictures" this seemed to be exactly what was happening. Maybe she was finally discovering the secret of writing. Maybe not. Maybe Sam was spurring her on to achieve greater things with his gentle encouragement and support. Whatever was happening, she thanked her lucky stars for it.

She read over the second section one more time. It wasn't bad at all — pretty readable Molly thought. Although she might need to pick the pace up a little, it was dragging a bit. Heaven knows what anyone else would think of it though. Then she had an idea.

"Have you seen Hugh, Molly?" Sam asked Molly later that day in Happily Ever After's office. His face looked pale and his wild eyes scanned hers hopefully.

"Hugh?" Molly was confused. Why would she have seen Hugh? "No. Is something wrong?"

"Yes. Brona dropped him off half an hour ago. I've just got off the phone to her. She said she was in a hurry and dropped Hugh outside the door. There was a tall man with glasses at the front of the shop and she presumed he worked there. She told Hugh to go inside and ask the man where I was. I must have been in here with you at the time."

"Glasses?" Molly asked. "Felix doesn't wear glasses."

"I know." Sam clutched the back of her chair as if he was about to fall over.

Finally Molly clicked. She gasped. "You don't think the man . . ."

"Don't," Sam said. "I'm already thinking the worst."

"Maybe the man was a customer and Hugh just wandered off."

"That's what the guards said. They're on their way. I've already tried Burnaby main street but there's no sign of Hugh. Can I take Felix and try the back streets?"

"Of course." She stood up. "I'm coming with you."

"What about the shop?"

"I'll close it. This is far more important. Your dad will understand."

Sam nodded curtly.

Molly grabbed her bag. "Let's go."

They walked out and Molly immediately spotted Denis loitering outside Coffee Heaven. As soon as she saw him a terrible thought crossed her mind. It was him — the tall man with glasses. What had he done with Hugh? She ran towards him. Sam and Felix followed her.

"Where's Hugh?" she asked angrily. She held both his arms and began to shake him. "What have you done with him? It was you in the shop, wasn't it?"

Denis stared at her in alarm. "What are you talking about, Molly?"

"Were you in the shop about half an hour ago?"

Denis said nothing and stared at the pavement in front of him.

"This is serious, Denis, were you?"

He nodded nervously. "I just wanted to see you. I only stayed a . . ."

"Did you see a small blond boy with glasses?" Felix asked calmly.

Denis looked at Felix. "Actually I did. He walked in and then . . ."

"You bastard!" Molly shrieked, thumping Denis on the chest. "I knew it was you as soon as I saw you out here. Where is he? I can't believe you've stooped this low. You evil . . ."

Denis put his hands in the air. "Hold on just a minute. What are you accusing me of? Child abduction? Molly, are you mad? Is that what you think of me?"

"Well, you've been stalking me for weeks now, you creepy shit," Molly said angrily, unable to stop herself.

Denis looked at her in alarm. "Stalking you? But . . ." He broke off and stared at the ground again. "I've been out of order, haven't I?"

Yes!" Molly said. "Way out of order."

"Listen," Sam interrupted. "This isn't really helping us find Hugh, is it?"

"Sorry," Molly said quickly. "Of course, what am I thinking?" She turned towards Denis. "You said you saw Hugh."

"Hugh was the blond boy in the shop?" Denis asked.

"Yes! What happened exactly?"

Denis thought for a moment. "He walked in the door, waited until the car outside had driven away and then walked straight out again. I thought it was a bit strange at the time so I watched him out the window."

"And?" Sam asked impatiently.

328

"He started walking down the main street and off to the right, towards the sea."

"Did you follow him?" Molly asked.

"No, of course not. Why would I follow him?"

"Thanks," Sam said. He turned towards Molly and Felix. "We'll try the Strand Road area." They both nodded in agreement.

"I'll come with you," Denis added.

Molly glared at him but said nothing. They could use all the help they could get. As they split up to search around Strand Road — Felix and Denis went to the left and Molly and Sam to the right. Molly was glad Denis hadn't insisted on going with her. She'd finally had enough of his erratic behaviour. It had to stop. He was lucky she hadn't shopped him to the guards yet. Speaking of which, a squad car pulled up alongside Molly and Sam.

"Are you Sam Devine?" the guard asked levelly.

Sam nodded.

"We haven't had any luck with your son yet but we'll keep looking."

"Thanks. Someone saw him walk down this way," Sam explained. "Maybe he was headed towards the sea."

"There's not much we can do at this stage, I'm afraid," the guard said, "except keep looking. We'll keep you posted on your mobile. If you hear of any other sightings please ring us."

"Of course," Sam nodded.

As the squad car drove away Sam looked at Molly and ran his hands through his hair. "This is hopeless," he said. "We'll never find him. And it's all my fault."

"It's no one's fault," Molly said. "Things just happen sometimes. We'll find him, don't worry."

"What if we don't? You hear such awful stories . . ."

"You've got to stop thinking the worst. He's a smart boy, he'll be OK. We'll find him, I know we will."

They walked down the road, scanning every garden and every car that drove past. In less than five minutes they'd reached the sea, which stretched out in front of them, winking in the sun, as if mocking them with its beauty.

"I suppose we'd better try the beach," Sam said, despair creeping into his voice. There were miles of it to comb — from Sandybay right down to Wicklow.

Molly didn't like to ask if Hugh could swim.

As they stepped onto the beach, Molly's phone rang in her bag. She was tempted to ignore it but something told her to answer it.

"Molly?"

"Yes?"

"It's Kate. Angus just rang me. He was looking for Sam's number. Do you have it? He's got Sam's son Hugh with him."

Molly almost fainted with relief. "Wait one second," she said to Kate.

She turned to Sam. "Hugh's with Angus, a friend of Kate's. He's safe."

Sam began to cry. "Thank God," he whispered.

As Molly hugged him tightly, she could feel the tension melting away from his body.

"I'd better ring Brona," he said, pulling away after a few minutes. "She's worried sick." He looked at Molly before punching in Brona's number. "Thanks," he said, brushing away the last of his tears.

"For nothing," she smiled at him. "I'm just glad that Hugh's safe."

They ran the whole way back to the bookshop where Angus had arranged to meet Sam. As soon as Sam saw Hugh he ran towards him and threw his arms around him.

"Where were you?" Sam asked, drawing back and looking at his son severely. "We were so worried about you. Why did you go off on your own like that?"

Hugh looked up at Angus who was standing beside him. Angus nodded at him and smiled.

"Hugh asked me to talk to you on his behalf," Angus said. "But let's go into the coffee shop first and have something to eat. The boys ate all the sausages and marshmallows and I'm starving."

"Good idea," Molly said.

"But . . ." Sam began. Molly took his hand. "The shop can wait. Everything can wait. Come on." She led him inside.

A few minutes later Brona rang Sam. "I'm outside the bookshop but it's closed. Where are you? Have you found him yet?"

Sam explained everything and a moment later Brona came bustling into Coffee Heaven.

"Hugh! You naughty boy!" she said walking towards him. "How could you put your dad and me through this? Have you no sense? We were worried sick."

Hugh looked at her nervously.

"Sit down, Brona," Sam said levelly. "Apparently Angus has something to tell us."

Brona stared at Sam. "Who's Angus?"

"I am." Angus smiled at her. "I found your son on the beach. Actually Callum did to be precise. To cut a long story short, he's a bit worried himself. Aren't you, Hugh?"

Hugh nodded solemnly.

"Would you like to tell your mum and dad what's worrying you?" Angus asked.

Hugh shook his head.

"Would you like me to tell them for you?"

Hugh nodded, staring at the table.

"Tell us what?" Brona asked.

"Why don't you go and play with Callum at the next table?" Angus suggested to Hugh. "Look, he's making a pie with all the sugar sachets. That looks like fun." Normally he'd stop Callum from making a mess on the tables, but today he was glad of the distraction.

"Callum? What are you building?" Angus asked.

"A sugar igloo," Callum replied. "But I need some more napkins." Angus passed him some. "I'm going to soak the napkins in milk and stick them on the top of the cup and cover it in sugar, like an igloo."

Hugh looked on with interest and then got up and joined Callum at the adjoining table.

"Well?" Sam stared at Angus impatiently.

"To get straight to the point," Angus said, "Hugh is worried that he won't be able to see you any more, Sam, now that his mum's boyfriend has moved in. That's why he ran away."

"Moved in where?" Sam asked Brona in confusion. "What boyfriend?"

"Glen," Brona said quietly. "You met him a while ago, remember? He only moved in last week. I was going to tell you but . . ."

"But what?"

"Oh, I don't know. I thought you might be funny about it, that's all."

"If it affects Hugh then you should have told me."

"I know and I'm sorry. But nothing will change. You can still see Hugh whenever you like. He needs you around."

"Have you told him that?" asked Sam.

"What?"

"That nothing will change."

"Not exactly. I didn't think I needed to."

"I see." There was silence for a moment.

"And he's also worried about you and Molly," Angus said to Sam. "He thinks you like her more than you like him."

"That's just ridiculous!" Sam said. "I love Molly but he'll always come first. He knows that. Why would he think that?"

"He's young," Angus said evenly. "You both need to talk to him and tell him how much you love him. Reassure him that he's important in both your lives. He notices a lot more than you think and he's feeling a little left out at the moment. He needs more stability, I think."

Brona nodded. "You're right. Angus, you talk a lot of sense. Thank you. Are you a psychiatrist?"

Angus laughed. "No, I'm a primary school teacher."

"Thanks, mate," Sam said. "Now I think we have some talking to do with our son."

Angus smiled. "Why don't I take Callum home? I think he's caused enough mess for Alex to clean up already."

"And I'd better reopen the bookshop," Molly said glancing at her watch. "Ring me later, Sam."

"I will. And thanks, Molly. Thanks for being there."

"Talk to you later." As Molly walked out of the shop her mind was racing. Sam had said he loved her. He'd also said that Hugh was the most important person in his life, more important than her. She wasn't sure how to feel about that.

"Molly!" a familiar voice called her from outside the book shop. It was Denis. The last person she wanted to see right at this moment. She walked towards him.

"Hello, Denis," she said, resigning herself to the fact that she'd have to talk to him sooner or later. "I have to open up." She put the key in the lock.

"I won't keep you," he said following her inside.

"I'm not really in the mood for talking —" she began.

"I understand," he interrupted. "I just wanted to tell you that from today on you won't be hearing from me. I've decided to move on. I still love you, I probably always will, but it's time I found someone else. Sam seems like a decent man. I hope you'll be happy together."

Molly stared at him in shock. "Um, well, thanks Denis. I appreciate that."

"I'm sorry I wasn't more helpful with finding Hugh. Maybe I should have followed him but I wasn't thinking."

"You weren't to know," she said kindly.

"Did you really think I'd abducted him?"

Molly shook her head. "Not really. I was upset and worried. I shouldn't have said that."

"It's OK. I've put you through a lot recently and I'm sorry."

"That's all right, Denis."

"Bye, Molly." He leant over and kissed her on the cheek. "Have a nice life."

"You too," she said as he walked away.

She sat down on the stool at the front desk, leant forward and put her head in her hands. All in all, it had been quite a day. And next weekend was the Burnaby Book Festival. She had so much to do it was scary. But right at that moment all she could think about was Sam.

CHAPTER
SEVENTEEN

Molly

"Why do they have to make these book posters so damn big?" Molly complained to Anita as she fought to keep another Bonnie Evans poster on the wall of the Burnaby Arts Centre.

"Blu-tack won't hold it," Anita said trying not to smile. "Here, try these." She handed Molly some drawing pins.

"Is it OK to use them? They'll make holes in the walls, Anita, maybe . . ."

"Stop fussing, I'm sure Tara won't mind."

"Tara won't mind what?" Tara, the arts administrator of the centre asked as she walked in the door of the lecture room.

"Sticking drawing pins into your newly painted walls," Anita explained.

Tara shrugged her shoulders. "Go ahead. The walls are there to be used. I'd love to get notice boards put up eventually but money's quite tight at the moment. Is there anything I can help you with?"

"Yes," Anita said. "The PA system. You'd better show me how to use it in case it acts up. In my experience, microphones never work when you want them too. Especially those clip-on ones."

"You shouldn't have any problems with ours," Tara said. "Touch wood." She touched the back of a chair and smiled. "They're all brand new."

"Excellent!" Anita said. "One less thing to worry about."

As Tara showed Anita how to work the PA system, Molly finished putting up the posters and resting the show cards on the windowsills and on the long speaker's table which was on a raised platform at the top of the room. Tara had already put all the chairs out, facing the platform, and had decorated the table with elegant flower arrangements. With the posters and balloons, all provided by the various speakers' publishers, the room was starting to look pretty good.

Sam and Felix were setting up the mini bookshop in the smaller room next door. Down the corridor, a journalist from *Sunday Ireland* was waiting patiently to interview Bonnie Evans who was currently on the way back from the RTE radio studios where she'd caused quite a stir on one of the morning radio shows. Molly and Anita had listened to it while setting up, horrified yet delighted with the controversial things Burnaby's most famous daughter was saying.

In the space of twenty minutes Bonnie had managed to criticize just about everyone in Ireland — from crooked business men, to politicians, publicans, farmers, housewives, working mothers, students and rude children — the whole gauntlet of Irish society in fact. Not to mention other writers. She hadn't made herself popular on air, the average listeners ringing in to complain about her harsh views attested to that. But it was compulsive listening and great publicity for the Book Festival.

One besotted man had even rung in to ask Bonnie to marry him. He admired her fiery temper and her outspokenness, he said. Bonnie had thanked him but then gone into a tirade against marriage and why it was a raw deal for any woman. The man, give him his due, took it all in his stride and said he'd happily take her on if she changed her mind. It was quite a show!

As Molly placed the last show card on the table, her phone rang.

"Molly?"

She recognized the voice immediately. "Paige, where are you?"

"Don't ask, I'm sorry but I'm running incredibly late and the battery's gone on my mobile. I'll be there in ten minutes."

"Not to worry, we've done almost everything now, so don't rush."

Paige sighed. "I'm so sorry, I really did mean to be there to help . . ."

"Paige, get a grip. The election's in three days, you're not Superwoman. See you in ten minutes. I'll be in the cafe helping Alex set up the table for the literary lunch."

"See you then."

"Was that Paige?" Anita asked.

Molly nodded. "She's on her way."

"I'm now fully trained to work the PA," Anita said. "So what's left to do?" She glanced at her watch. "Maybe I should get back to the shop. I'm sure Milo's fretting by now, stupid man."

Molly stifled a smile. They'd bullied Milo into looking after the shop for the afternoon, well Anita had anyway. His soft spot for her hadn't abated, which was coming in quite useful.

"You do that," Molly said. "He's probably dying for some designer coffee at this stage. I'll stay here. If we need you I'll give you a ring."

Anita kissed her on the cheek. "I'll be back once we've closed up the shop. See you later."

Molly walked her out, then strode into the Arts Centre cafe. It looked fantastic. Tara had hired tables, chairs and all the table settings from a local catering company, who had kindly given them everything free of charge. All they had to do was get the table linen laundered before they returned it. Harry was pottering amongst the tables, putting finishing touches to the simple yet stunning central arrangements.

He smiled at Molly as soon as he spotted her. "What do you think?"

Each round table was covered with a simple white cloth and set with gleaming cutlery and starkly white plates. The glasses had been polished to perfection, and shone as if they'd been lit from inside. In the centre of each table was a glass bowl surrounded by brightly coloured exotic flowers in mini vases. As Molly looked closer at the bowl beside her, she realized that each

339

bowl had a healthy looking goldfish in it, swimming away merrily in the clean water.

"Fantastic!" she beamed. "Where did you get the goldfish?"

"From the pet shop in Sandybay. They're on loan. We have to take very good care of them, I gave my word."

"Where's Alex?"

Harry smiled. "Where do you think? In the kitchen. She's checking out the facilities for tomorrow."

"What's on the menu?"

He thought for a second. "Let me see — soup made by Matty, I'm not sure what kind, smoked salmon, salads, home-made bread and lots of delicious looking sweet things."

"I can't wait," Molly said feeling decidedly hungry. She'd brought a cheese sandwich for lunch but had forgotten to eat it in the end. It had been such a busy day. But everything was almost in place. "Do you need any help?"

"No, I'm almost finished."

"I really appreciate all your hard work. You and Alex have been fantastic."

Harry shrugged his shoulders. "Thank Alex. She bullied me into it. She's got a good heart and she likes helping people."

"She's a great girl, isn't she?" Molly smiled. Kate had told her all about Harry and Alex's romance and she was delighted for both of them. Even though they were like chalk and cheese they seemed to get along famously and Harry had calmed down a lot since meeting Alex. She was obviously having quite an effect on him. Molly had always found him a little difficult to talk to, but he'd been positively charming all day. He'd even turned down a television appearance to help.

Molly stretched her arms over her head. "I'll go into the hall and set up the registration table and the notice board then. Call me if you need me."

"Will do." Harry went back to his beloved flowers.

Molly met Tara in the corridor.

"There are masses of calls on the answering machine about the festival," Tara said. "I've checked some of them and they are all asking if the event's booked up. What will I tell them?"

"We have room for about twenty more at the talks but the lunch is completely full," Molly said proudly. "Would you like me to ring them back for you?"

"Not at all, I'll do it," Tara said kindly. "It's going to be some weekend, isn't it?"

"It sure is," Molly agreed.

"There you are, Molly," Paige interrupted them. "Hi, Tara."

"If it isn't the Councillor herself," Tara said. "How's tricks?"

"Good," Paige said. "Busy but good. Now put me to work."

"Gladly," Molly said. "What are you like at photocopying? We need some more programmes."

"A whiz." Paige laughed. "Lead on."

"Who is that?" Anita asked Milo, gesturing towards a tall, blond man at the back of the shop. He was wearing black trousers, a black long-sleeved T-shirt and trendy steel-rimmed glasses and was talking notes on a palm pilot. "He doesn't look like a customer."

"Oh, pay no attention to him," Milo said, drawing her attention away from the back shelves. "He's from the council. Something about moving a water mains. Um, Anita, an order just arrived. It's waiting to be priced in goods-in. Would you like to see the new titles? There's a beautiful looking hardback Margaret Atwood."

"I've been waiting for that." Anita smiled. "Thank you, Milo."

He led her towards the goods-in area and followed her in. "I'll see you in a few minutes," he promised. "I'll just finish with the council guy." He went back out onto the shop floor and shut the door firmly behind him.

"Fine," Anita said absently, her hands stroking the deliciously cool blood-red matt jacket of Atwood's new book. She couldn't wait to read it again. She'd been given a proof copy but it hadn't looked nearly as elegant as this finished product.

"Well?" Milo said, approaching the man, his voice low. "What do you think?"

"It has possibilities," the man replied. "Distinct possibilities."

"Any sign of Rose?" Molly asked Kate the following morning. Kate was manning the Book Festival registration desk, with the help of Cathy and Trina.

Kate shook her head. "Nope. But Jennie's in the office with Tara and Anita."

"Well, that's something I suppose."

"Don't worry, she'll be here any minute," Kate said. "I'll come and get you as soon as she does."

"Thanks." As Molly walked back towards the lecture room, where Paige was waiting patiently to launch the event and introduce the speakers, she saw many familiar faces among the crowds and nodded and smiled at them in recognition — regular customers from the shop, two librarians from the local library, Connie Calloway and some of her cronies. As she made her way past the on-site bookshop she spotted Sam talking to Angus.

"Hi, Sam, hi, Angus." She smiled at them both. "I didn't take you for a romance fan," she said to Angus.

"I'm not really. Lily mentioned it and I thought I'd come along just for the morning as it sounded interesting. She knows Bownie from way back."

"Of course she does," Molly said. "Lily knows everyone."

"How's everything going?" Sam asked. "Will you be starting on time?"

"I hope so," she said. "We're still waiting for Rose to arrive from the airport."

"I think she may just have arrived," Sam said gesturing with his head to the doorway. Kate was standing there waving at them, the tall, red-headed Rose to her side.

"Thank goodness," Molly said with relief. "Let the show begin. See you both later."

"Call into the shop when it's all over," Sam said. "I'll be there this afternoon to help Dad. Felix said he'd hold the fort here."

"Great, see you later then." She gave him a wide smile. He really was lovely. She walked towards the door.

"Rose, I'm Molly, one of the organizers, and you've already met Kate." Molly held out her hand politely.

"And I'm Rose." Rose smiled warmly at her and shook her hand firmly. "And I met Anita and Tara in the office. And Jennie of course. I believe you're anxious to start. So lead on, I'm ready when you are."

"Are you sure?"

"Absolutely."

Molly felt a surge of adrenaline rush through her body. "Right. Let's get started then."

"That was brilliant!" a woman enthused to Molly after Rose and Jennie had received their second standing ovation. "Such interesting women, and such accomplished speakers." She touched Molly gently on the arm. "Thank you, my dear, for arranging this Festival. I'm having such a good time."

"I'm glad. And are you staying for the lunch and the afternoon session?"

"Of course, my dear, I wouldn't miss it for the world."

Molly looked around the lecture room and was delighted to see so many smiling faces.

"They were great," Paige said, stepping down off the platform where she'd been sitting with Rose and Jennie. The two authors were surrounded by fans, signing books like there was no tomorrow.

"Weren't they?" Molly agreed.

344

"It seems to be going well so far. Who am I sitting with at lunch?" Paige asked.

"Millie from the *Burnaby News*," Molly replied deadpan.

Paige groaned. "You're not serious. I was hoping never to meet her again after all that photograph business."

"I'm joking," Molly replied. "You're sitting with Connie Calloway."

Paige stared at her. "You're not funny, you know that?"

"Sorry, couldn't resist. You're at the top table with me and Anita."

"Good." Paige smiled and took Molly's arm. "I'm starving."

"How's the bump today?" Molly asked.

"Fine. I was feeling a little ropy yesterday but I cancelled a dinner last night and went to bed at eight."

"Good woman, you have to take care of yourself, Paige."

"Don't you start. You're as bad as Tom."

"It's only because we love you."

"I know, I know. Now where's the food?"

Molly led her to their table and they sat down. The room was already filling up with people, almost exclusively women, and there was a buzz of excitement in the air. A little while later, when Rose and Jennie walked into the crowded room, followed by RTE television news cameras, everyone stood up and clapped again.

"Hey, we might be on the telly." Paige laughed and nudged Molly. "Smile!"

Sure enough, the cameraman swung the camera around the room and rested the lens on Paige's smiling face. As an election candidate, with a fair chance of a seat, she was certainly worth capturing on film.

As everyone settled down into their seats, Anita stood up and addressed the room. "Welcome to the first Burnaby Book Festival Literary Lunch," she began. "As you'll notice there is a vacant seat at every table. As the lunch progresses, you'll get the chance to meet different authors as they take that seat. The authors will move anti-clockwise around the room every fifteen minutes. At least that's the idea. Whether it works or not remains to be seen." Everyone laughed politely. "And now I'd like to introduce the authors and ask them to take a seat at a table. In no particular order — you've already met Rose Lovett and Jennie Tracker." Another deafening round of applause and many cries of "Sit here, Rose", "Over here, Jennie". "And our very own Bonnie Evans." More applause. "All the three C's — Clare Connolly, Ciera Donald and Catriona Reilly." Applause and whistles. "Tina Laycock and Antonia Ash." More applause. "Cleo Holmes, Nancy Dealy and Peggy Walsh." More applause. When Anita had finished her introductions she sat down again.

"Well done," Molly said. "Do we not get an author?"

"We already have one," Anita replied. "You."

"I'm not an author," Molly snapped.

"You will be," Anita said, ignoring Molly's sharp tone. "Now let's eat. Paige had already demolished all the bread rolls on the table. She must be famished."

"Sorry," said Paige, "blame the baby."

Molly sat between Paige and Kate for the afternoon session on "Getting Published", with Anita to Paige's left, who was ignoring Milo Devine to a spectacular degree. Milo had arrived just in time for coffee and had found a spare chair and squeezed himself in beside Anita, much to her chagrin. He had then followed her like a puppy dog into the lecture room and sat down beside her.

"Who's on the panel?" asked Kate.

"You could read the beautifully and tirelessly photocopied programme," Paige suggested.

"Or you could tell me and save me trouble. I'm feeling very lazy after that glass of wine at lunch."

"Are you sure it was only one?" Molly smiled. "I distinctly saw you order another bottle for your table."

"Well, it might have been more like three," Kate grinned back. "But no more, mind."

"Did you enjoy meeting the authors?" Molly asked her.

"Yes! Some of them were a riot. And others were really smart and well read. And so nice. You'd never think they were famous authors. Cleo Holmes has a real thing about shoes too, so I was talking to her for ages. In fact, I think she missed a table change because of me. It was a great success, well done to all of you.

Now will you tell me who the speakers are or do I have to batter it out of you?"

"I think they're about to tell you themselves," Anita said jumping to her feet. She was supposed to be introducing the speakers who were seated on the platform waiting patiently to begin.

"Welcome back, everyone," Anita began. "I hope you all enjoyed your lunch. Now I have the great privilege of introducing the panel who will talk to you this afternoon on the subject of 'Getting Published — Tips from the Top'. From Trinity Publishers in Dublin we have Maggie Stevens who is the Sales and Marketing Manager; next up is Bonnie Evans, who I'm sure you all know is originally from Burnaby and now lives in the South of France and is one of the world's best selling romance novelists; Cleo Holmes, another highly successful writer from Dublin; and last, but certainly not least, the only man on the panel, Gerry Begley, from the highly respected Begley Literary Agency. And first up will be Cleo." Anita sat down as everyone applauded.

"Phew," she whispered to Paige. "I'm glad that's over."

"You were great," Paige whispered back as Cleo stood up and began to talk.

"Hello, everyone, I'm Cleo Holmes and I'm delighted to be here today with so many readers. I met some of you at lunch and it was lovely to talk to the people who appreciate my work. Writing is quite a solitary occupation and I don't get to meet many readers face to face. So I'd like to quickly thank the

organizers here today for this fantastic Book Festival."
Everyone clapped enthusiastically. "Now getting published
can be a very frustrating business for new authors,"
Cleo continued. "Many of you here may be writers
interested in seeing your own work in print, members
of writers' groups or simply readers who are interested
in the whole book world, including publishing. I hope
you all find this session on getting published interesting
and stimulating." Cleo then went on to talk about her
own experience — how she found an agent and got her
first book published by Trinity Publishers in Ireland.

Paige turned to Molly. "She's a good speaker isn't
she?" she whispered. "Very clear and easy to listen to."

Molly nodded. From what Cleo was saying, having
your first book published was pretty miraculous
considering the competition. In fact, Cleo was making
Molly feel downright despondent. What chance did she
have if it was so difficult — less than none, she figured.

Cleo continued. "You have to enjoy what you're
writing and your heart must be in it 100 per cent." She
went on to explain the different genres and which
genres were particularly popular at the moment.

"She's very thorough," Kate whispered to Molly. "I
never knew there was so much to it."

Molly nodded in agreement and went back to
listening.

Anita was watching Molly with interest. Molly was
totally focused on what Cleo was saying and was even
jotting down some notes on her programme. Anita
smiled to herself — maybe Molly was finally taking her
talent seriously. Unbeknown to Molly, Anita had read

several of Molly's short stories which had been stored on the computer at work. Molly's home printer was always playing up and she often saved and printed out her writing in the Happily Ever After office. Anita knew Molly had the potential to be a great writer, if she'd only believe in herself enough. But she knew Molly would have a fit if she thought Anita had betrayed her trust and read her stories, so Anita could say nothing.

"I wish all the writers in the audience the best of luck," Cleo said, concluding her talk. "And the best advice I can give you is don't give up. If you really want to be published you will. You just have to believe in yourself."

"Hear, hear," Anita murmured.

Everyone clapped enthusiastically. As the applause died out Maggie stood up.

"Hello, I'm Maggie Stevens, from Trinity Publishers, Cleo's Irish publishers. I'm going to explain what Trinity are looking for from new writers and how prospective writers should submit their book. Practical things like presentation of manuscript, how to send it in, how long you can expect to wait for a reply and so on." Maggie was as good as her word and gave a slick, well-prepared talk.

Next up it was the agent, Gerry Begley. "Most UK publishers expect writers to have an agent. In fact, the odds on getting published from what we call "the slush pile" in the trade — the unsolicited manuscripts sent in by authors directly to the editor of a publishing house — are tiny. So that's where I come in." He explained his role in the whole publishing business.

"Seems like a nice man," Paige said to Molly when Gerry had stopped talking. "Maybe you should ask him to be your agent."

"Get real!" Molly laughed. "He wouldn't be interested in me."

"You never know," Paige replied mildly.

"Shush, it's Bonnie next," said Molly.

Paige studied Burnaby's most famous daughter with interest. She was wearing a flamboyant wine-coloured cardigan, over a floor-sweeping black velvet dress. Her thick, rich dark red hair was piled on top of her head in an elaborate chignon.

"Attractive woman," Kate whispered to Molly and Paige. "Great cardigan."

"Shush," someone behind them muttered.

They grinned at each other and stifled the laughs.

"I'm Bonnie Evans," she began, then snorted. "As if you needed to be told. I am one of the world's best-selling authors and I think most of what is published today is unadulterated crap." Several members of the audience gasped. The journalists at the back of the room began to scribble furiously. "I think any writers out there who want to be published need to think long and hard." She stared at the audience intensely, making eye contact with some, making them jump. "Are *you* good enough? Is *your* work crap? Because if it is, don't bother trying to get published. And I think writers' groups are evil." More gasps. "Filling people's heads with silly notions of grandeur. Most people *can't* write. And you cannot be taught to write — I believe it's something you are born with. It's

351

as simple as that. I have the gift, a very special gift. But most don't."

A woman at the back of the room stood up, collected her things together and walked out, banging the door behind her.

"I've offended someone!" Bonnie clapped her hands together with glee. "Excellent! Now what I have to say is very important so please listen carefully." She looked around the room again. "If you do have the gift, you must use it. Indeed, if you have any creative gift you must use it. If you can write you must put your whole being into your writing and produce the very best book that you can. I will now tell you how I discovered my own talent and how it has changed my life."

"Powerful stuff," Paige said after she'd finished and Bonnie had received a rapturous standing ovation. "She's some woman."

The three women watched as Anita stepped onto the platform and began to thank all the speakers, shaking their hands warmly. Within seconds the platform was surrounded by people, most wanting to meet Bonnie. She'd made quite an impression.

"No kidding." Molly smiled at Paige.

"I found her quite inspirational," Kate said thoughtfully. "And she wasn't afraid of upsetting people, was she?"

"Quite the opposite," said Molly. "Most refreshing. And speaking of which, who's for a drink? There's a press reception in the cafe now to announce the winner of the writing competition and you're both invited of course. I'd better stay here and see if Anita needs anything done."

"Is there food?" asked Paige.

"You've only just eaten," Molly pointed out.

"It's not for me, it's for junior," Paige said, rubbing her stomach gently.

Molly smiled. "Good excuse. There's finger food and wine. Will that do you?"

"It will," Paige replied.

"Excellent!" Kate stood up gingerly. "My bum's killing me. These seats aren't exactly padded."

"Maybe it's you who isn't exactly padded," Paige pointed out with a smile. "So quit complaining."

An hour later, Anita stood in front of the crowd at the reception. She tapped the microphone head softly to check it was working and took a sip of water before starting. She stood up tall and addressed the crowd. "I'd like to welcome you all to the prizegiving of the Burnaby Short Story Competition which has been run in association with the *Burnaby News*. Beside me are the two other judges, Millie O'Shea, the Editor of the *Burnaby News* and Bonnie Evans. The winner gets their story published in the newspaper as well as five hundred euro, kindly sponsored by Star Insurances in Burnaby, and just this very afternoon Gerry Begley has also kindly offered to represent the winning author. Quite a prize for a new writer. Judging this competition was very difficult. The standard of entries was very high." She half-expected Bonnie to snort at this, but thankfully she didn't. Anita continued swiftly. "But there was one story which really stood out from the rest. It was a story about starting again, about getting one's life back after a terrible tragedy — the death of a young child."

Molly caught her breath. Did Anita just say the death of a child? Surely not? She listened to Anita carefully.

"The writer's prose style draws you into the story and the characters are extremely well rounded. I'd like to ask Bonnie to announce the winner."

Bonnie cleared her throat theatrically. "The winner is Mary Parker with her story 'Concrete Pictures'." Everyone began to clap and looked around the room for Mary Parker.

"Could Mary Parker please come up and collect her prize," Bonnie continued.

"What's wrong?" Paige asked Molly who had lurched sideways into her, spilling the last of her drink. Luckily Kate had gone to the bar for more. Molly's face was as white as a sheet. "Molly?"

Molly looked at her, a strange expression on her face.

Suddenly Paige clicked. "It's you, isn't it? Mary Parker. Molly, how exciting! Go up and collect your prize!"

"I can't," Molly hissed. "They've made some sort of mistake. I can't have won."

"Is your story called 'Concrete Pictures'?"

Molly nodded.

"Well then, it's not a mistake. Go on." She pushed her gently towards the stage.

At that moment Kate came back, two glasses of red wine and one of sparkling water balanced in her hands.

354

"Have I missed anything?" she asked. Paige gestured towards the top of the room.

"What's Molly doing up there with Bonnie and Anita?" Kate asked in confusion.

"She only won the writing competition."

"But they just said someone called . . . Oh, I see . . . Mary Parker *is* Molly Harper. You think she could have made a bit more of an effort with the pseudonym."

Paige laughed. "She never expected to win. I wonder what she's saying to Anita."

"Let's get closer and see," Kate suggested.

They wound their way through the crowd, towards the top of the room.

Molly was actually trying to persuade Anita to give the prize to someone else. Anita was having none of it.

"You won it fair and square," Anita said firmly to Molly's protests. "In fact, it was Bonnie who insisted that your story won the prize. She said she'd leave the judging panel if you didn't win."

"But . . ." Molly protested.

"Is this Mary Parker?" Bonnie asked.

"Yes, and she won't accept the prize. She says she doesn't deserve it."

"Don't be silly, girl. Some of the stories were rubbish. Yours wasn't. You have real potential. In fact, I think you may have the gift."

Molly looked at Bonnie in surprise. "Really?"

"I always tell the truth," Bonnie said evenly. "I'm renowned for it. Now stop being so stupid and accept what's your due."

Whatever she felt about Anita, Molly was far too scared to say no to Bonnie.

"OK," she said quietly.

"Excellent." Bonnie stood beside her and faced the audience again. The room became quiet.

"And here is Mary Parker." She handed her an envelope. "Well done, Mary. Would you like to say a few words?"

"Um, no, thank you." Molly's hands were shaking and she felt very faint. She hated public speaking and hated all those upturned faces watching her.

"Go on," Paige encouraged from the floor.

"You can do it." Kate smiled up at her.

Molly looked at them both and smiled back. She took a deep breath. Maybe she could.

"Um, I'd just like to say thanks to the judges for choosing my story. I've been writing for a few years now but I thought I was one of the crap ones, as Bonnie so succinctly calls them." Everyone laughed. "But I guess I'm not. And as some of you will know, my name is not Mary Parker, it's Molly Harper and I work in Happily Every After. I used another name because I didn't want anyone to know I'd entered the competition. I just wanted some feedback on my writing. But I never expected to win. But, um, thanks very much. I'm, um, delighted. And in complete shock to tell the truth. Thanks." Everyone clapped warmly.

Anita stepped up to the microphone. "Well, done, Molly. And now I'd like to ask Councillor Paige Brady to close the Burnaby Book Festival for us."

"Oh no!" Paige whispered to Kate under her breath and handed her her glass. "I forgot I was doing this. I've nothing prepared."

"Not you as well." Kate laughed. "You and Molly really are a right pair."

CHAPTER
EIGHTEEN

Kate

Kate gazed out the window at the fluffy, candyfloss clouds, illuminated by the blazing sun — the whole scene like something out of a Hollywood movie about heaven. The pilot had just announced that they were less than twenty minutes from Boston's Logan Airport and Kate could hardly contain herself. Her stomach was fluttering in anticipation at seeing Jay again. The fact that he didn't know she was coming only added to the drama. She rested the back of her head against the headrest and closed her eyes. In less than two hours, she'd be safely in his arms, cocooned by his love, basking in his admiration. She couldn't wait. She dozed off, into a deep dreamless slumber.

As the plane landed smoothly on the Boston tarmac, Kate let out a sigh — she'd never been the world's greatest flyer and was always relieved to be on solid ground once more. As soon as they'd pulled into the terminal, she gathered together her jacket, handbag and compact travel suitcase. As she was only flying over for a long weekend, she'd decided to travel light.

Walking smugly through the terminal with her hand luggage, past the poor souls in the huge, bustling baggage reclaim hall, and out through one of the entrance doors, she hopped straight onto one of the "Massport Shuttles" like a real native. From here she was swiftly delivered to the Airport "T", where she sat and waited for an underground train to take her safely to downtown Boston. As always she sent up a prayer for the efficient city transport network. It was one of the things she'd missed after moving back to Ireland.

It was Saturday afternoon and as she sat waiting for the train, she rang Jay's mobile. He tended to be busy at weekends — catching up with friends, shopping (unlike Irish men Jay liked to shop), and taking day trips out of the city. He was also a big Boston Red Sox fan and liked nothing better than to spend time in Boston's famous baseball park, Fenway Park, watching his favourite team compete. His mobile rang out. He probably can't hear it, Kate thought. Or maybe he's left it at home. His home number had changed recently and he hadn't remembered to give the new one to her yet, so she couldn't try there.

Kate tried to remember their exact conversation the previous evening. He'd said he had no definite plans but would probably meet a friend for lunch and go shopping for the afternoon. Then he might go out for dinner in the evening. It seemed a little strange to Kate who happened to know that his weekends were usually planned weeks in advance, but as he kept impressing on her, he'd changed. Maybe this weekend spontaneity was part of the new Jay. Perhaps she should have told him she was coming over, he could have met her at the airport, but, no, Kate thought, that would have spoiled the surprise.

A little later, after a pleasant enough "T" ride and a ten-minute walk, Kate stood outside his apartment building. She rang his apartment on the huge brass intercom board beside the front door. There was no answer. Damn! She tried his mobile again — again no answer. Well, he's bound to be back at some stage, she reasoned, thinking again that surprising him might not have been the best idea in the world after all. What was she going to do now? She was overheated from walking in the early afternoon sun, and her hair had begun to stick to her forehead. In fact, she could do with a shower. Failing that, she needed to go somewhere cool and spacious, somewhere with a good air conditioning system, somewhere with a left luggage department so that she wouldn't have to drag around her wheelie suitcase all day. Not that it would be all day, she hoped.

She racked her brains for inspiration. She'd love to browse the clothes shops on Newbury Street or even visit Filene's Basement, but both would be incredibly hot and crowded on a Saturday afternoon. She could visit one of the huge bookstores — Barnes and Noble or Borders but that wouldn't keep her occupied for more than an hour or two. Then she had a thought. All the time she'd lived in the city she'd never visited the famous art gallery — the Boston Museum of Fine Arts. Well, she had no excuse this time — it was cool, spacious and air conditioned; they would look after her suitcase while she was there and it also had a cafe and toilets. Plus it was only two stops away on the "T".

Delighted with her decision she tried Jay's mobile one more time. Still no answer. Half an hour later, stepping through the doors of the rather grand museum building, she tried once more with the same result, then turned her own mobile off and plunged it into her handbag, determined not to try Jay again until later.

As she strolled through the huge exhibition rooms, unencumbered by her bags and jacket, she drank in the art and ancient objects surrounding her. Mummies, hieroglyphics and Old Kingdom sculptures in the Egyptian rooms, Buddhist sculptures, Chinese ceramics and the huge array of strikingly familiar Impressionist pictures from Monet to Renoir to Gauguin.

Several hours later, calmed and soothed by the art and the surroundings, and physically refreshed by a nice salad lunch and lots of chilled fruit juice, she collected her bags, promising herself that she'd visit again very soon. Maybe she'd even drag Jay along next time.

She walked out the door and tried his mobile again — still no answer. At this stage she was getting a little worried. Maybe he'd gone away for the weekend with friends unexpectedly. What would she do then? She rubbed her temples, feeling a tension headache coming on. I'll go back and wait for him outside his apartment, she decided. I don't have any other choice. He has to come back sooner or later.

Sitting on the steps of the apartment she felt a shiver of déjà vu which she tried to banish as soon as it wiggled its way into her head. This is just like last Christmas Eve, a voice said, waiting for Jay outside his

361

apartment. Wondering where he was, what he was doing. Yes, but this time, she reasoned, it's totally different. Completely different. He's not married any more and he even offered to move back to Dublin to be with me. She took out the museum guide from her handbag and began to fan her face. She tried not to look at her watch but she couldn't help it. Almost six. He had to be home soon.

She heard voices behind her and swivelled around. A tall dark haired man was walking towards her. There he is! Kate grinned. That's Jay walking in front of that woman with the buggy. She felt a huge rush of relief spread through her body. Thank goodness! She jumped up and waved.

"Jay!" she shouted excitedly. "Jay!"

He put his hand over his eyes to shield them from the sun. Then he stopped dead. He stared at Kate in amazement as if she was some sort of alien from another planet, complete with green skin and stun gun. The woman stopped beside him and said something. Kate couldn't hear the conversation as she wasn't close enough. He said something back to the woman. Kate began to walk towards them. Jay put up his hand as if to say "stop", but Kate continued unabashed.

"Jay?" she said as she approached him. "What's wrong?"

As soon as Kate looked at the woman's face she realized what was wrong. Because the woman pushing the buggy beside Jay was his ex-wife, Cindy. Kate recognized her immediately. And to top it all she looked at least four months pregnant, her rounded belly protruding proudly beneath a tight white T-shirt.

Kate stared at Jay in confusion.

"What's going on here?" Cindy asked. "Who's this woman, Jay? She looks kinda familiar."

"Just a friend from work," Jay said, resting a reassuring hand in the small of his wife's back.

"Hi." Cindy smiled at Kate uncertainly. "I'm Cindy, and you are . . .?"

Kate looked at Jay. She felt her blood falling like a sheet from her face and upper body into her feet. Her palms began to sweat and she felt unable to say anything. "Jay?" she managed finally in a weak, whispery voice before her body felt freezing cold and the whole world went blank.

"Granny, are you in?" asked Kate, gripping her mobile tightly. She'd turned it on as soon as the plane had landed on Irish soil.

"I am," said Lily. "And where have you been all weekend? I was looking for you yesterday but your mobile wasn't working."

"Can I call over?"

"Of course, love. Is anything wrong? You sound a little strange. Where are you?"

"Dublin Airport."

"The airport? But it's not even nine. What are you doing there?"

Kate gulped back the tears. "I have to go, Gran. I'll see you in a while, OK?"

Lily sensed that this had to do with Jay but kept her thoughts to herself. What had the rat done now to upset her darling granddaughter? Had he stood her up?

"Take care of yourself, poppet. Granny Lily's here for you, understand?"

Kate clicked off her phone and immediately began to cry. It was such a relief to talk to her granny. She felt such an almighty fool.

"Kate," Lily said as she opened the door. "Come here and give your old granny a hug." Kate dropped her bags and lunged immediately forward, hugging Lily with all her might and breathing in the familiar scent of rose water.

Lily was shocked at Kate's appearance. She looked like she hadn't slept for days — her eyes were sunk into dark grey sockets and her face was red and blotchy as if she'd been crying for hours without stopping. Her breath was ragged and irregular and she was shaking.

"Come into the kitchen and we'll have a cup of tea. I'll put some brandy in it for you, pet, that'll help." She led Kate towards the back of the house, sat her down at the kitchen, then went back into the hall, moved the bags and closed the hall door behind her firmly.

Back in the kitchen, Lily clicked on the kettle and stood waiting, leaning against the kitchen counter. She knew better than to ask too many questions. Kate would open up in her own good time. There was no hurry.

"He's still married, Gran," Kate said immediately without prompting, unable to keep it in any longer.

"He's not separated at all. And they have a second child on the way."

Lily stared at her in shock. After the episode last Christmas she'd thought she'd heard it all — but this was worse, much worse. How could a man behave in such a way?

"He lied to me, Gran. About his wife, his son . . . everything. He even told me that she'd lost the first baby — his son. How could he say such a thing?"

Lily stood behind Kate and put her arms around her and kissed the top of her head.

"It's all over now," she crooned. "You're safe with your Granny Lily, now." Kate gave a huge sob. "That's it," she continued. "Let it all out, love."

Kate cried for almost ten minutes without stopping, huge gut-wrenching sobs. Tears rained out of her eyes in a deluge, spilling onto the kitchen table in splashes. Lily rubbed her back, then held her firmly as she wept. "It'll be all right," she whispered to Kate. "You're home now. Home with Granny Lily. Try to take deep breaths now, there's a girl."

After a little while the sobs grew further and further apart and Kate's breathing began to go back to normal.

"I'm sorry," said Kate, wiping her eyes and face with the large man's handkerchief Lily had given her.

"Sorry for what?" Lily asked gently. "None of this is your fault. You've nothing to be sorry about."

"But I feel such an idiot. How could I have let this happen? I should never have trusted Jay again. I'm so stupid." She held her head in her hands and rocked backwards and forwards.

"Don't be too hard on yourself," Lily said. "It happens. Everyone makes mistakes, especially where love is concerned."

"And she was so nice to me," Kate said, starting to cry again. "I feel so terrible."

"Who was nice to you?" Lily asked gently. "Maybe you should start at the beginning. Tell me everything."

"I can't," Kate whispered. "I just can't." Tears began to roll down her face again.

Lily patted her hand. "Try. It will make you feel better. Then we never have to talk about it again."

"Promise?"

"I promise."

"OK." Kate wiped her eyes and took a deep breath. "I met him in the Killiney Arms the week before last," she began slowly. "He was over on business and he'd asked to see me. I should never have gone but I did." She told Lily the whole sorry story — from that first heady evening with Jay, to fainting at his feet outside his Boston apartment block.

"Oh, Gran, I was mortified. I must have been out of it for several minutes. When I opened my eyes I found Jay standing over me and Cindy kneeling down beside me. She'd put the baby's blanket under my head and was wiping my forehead with a damp babywipe." Kate cringed inwardly at the memory.

"What happened then?" Lily asked gently.

"They took me into their apartment. Once we were inside Cindy asked Jay to make some coffee. He seemed a bit reluctant to leave us alone together, but he wasn't really in a position to argue. When he was in the kitchen, she looked at me and asked me straight out was I having an affair with her husband. I nearly died. I didn't know what to say. I couldn't look her in the eye, I just nodded and stared at the carpet. I expected her to hit me or shout at me at the very least."

"What did she do?" Lily asked.

"She started to cry. It was awful, Gran. She said she knew something was going on, that things hadn't been right between them for a long time — his mind seemed to be somewhere else. Cindy said he'd been carrying on with a girl from the office called Tammy for a few months but she'd confronted him about her and he'd stopped seeing her. She said she was sick of it and couldn't live with him any more. She'd stopped trusting him. I was so ashamed. I said I was sorry, that he'd told me he was separated. And then she said in this really sad voice, 'They always say that, don't they?' Oh, Gran, I felt so bad. She was being so decent to me and then Jay . . ." She shuddered at the memory. "He'd been standing at the door listening. He walked in and started telling Cindy how much he loved her right in front of me, how I didn't mean anything to him, how he couldn't live without her, how she had to give him one more chance. Cindy stood up and slapped him on the cheek. And then she told him to get out. At this stage the baby was crying in the buggy, I was crying, Cindy was crying and all Jay could do was stare at me. 'You've ruined my life,' he said to me. 'I'll never forgive you.' Then Cindy said 'Jay, you've no one to blame but yourself. This woman isn't to blame. You are. Now get out. You'll be hearing from my lawyers in the morning.'"

"It's like something from a novel," Lily said before she could stop herself.

Kate looked at her and then began to smile through the tears. "Gran!"

"I'm sorry but you know what I mean," Lily said. "It's all very dramatic. What happened after he'd left?"

"Cindy made us some coffee and we talked while she fed the baby. She asked me what had happened with Jay and I told her everything. I reckoned I owed it to her to be honest. We got on pretty well, to tell the truth, in the circumstances. After we'd talked for a few hours she booked me on a late flight and I came home."

"You must be wrecked," Lily said. "Would you like to lie down? The spare bed's all made up."

Kate shook her head. "I'm not tired. Maybe later. I slept a little on the plane. The air hostesses were so kind. I kept crying — I couldn't help myself. One of them sat with me for a little while to make sure I was all right."

"The kindness of strangers," Lily murmured.

"I really loved him, Gran," Kate continued. "He asked me to marry him only last week. He even said he'd move to Dublin to be with me but he was obviously lying the whole time. Just like he did before. I feel such a fool. How could I have trusted him?" She thought for a moment. "But, you know, Gran, in a strange way, I don't feel as bad as I did the last time he crushed me. It's as if my heart will never hurt as much after that. Jay hardened it last Christmas."

368

Lily smiled at her. "Your heart isn't hard, Kate. Believe me, I know. But that Jay has a lot to answer for. At least you weren't married to him and suffering all those affairs. Poor Cindy. What's she going to do now?"

Kate shrugged her shoulders. "She said she's going to divorce him. But who knows? They may be able to patch it up. There are children involved after all."

"Sometimes it's not in the children's best interest for the parents to stay together," Lily said thoughtfully.

"I guess not." Kate yawned. "Maybe I am a little tired. Can I take you up on the offer of a bed?"

"Of course. And when you've had some sleep I'll make us some lunch. How about that?"

Kate gave Lily a hug. "Thanks. I don't know what I'd do without you."

"Go and get some rest now," said Lily. "You've had a right old shock to your system."

"Thanks, Gran."

As Kate made her way upstairs, Lily drained her tea, by now a little cold. She put her elbow on the table and rested her head on her hand. For some reason she wasn't worried about Kate this time. Kate was right — she was in a far worse state last Christmas. She'd been so distraught then that she couldn't talk about what had happened for days. Kate was in a much better place now. If only she'd find a nice young man, someone who'd care for her and nurture her. Someone she could trust. Someone like Angus. Lily had done all she could to help things along. If it was meant to be they would find each other. But maybe they both needed just a little more assistance.

"Did you have a nice break?" Molly asked as soon as Kate walked in the door on Monday night.

"Yes, thanks." Kate replied evenly, dumping her suitcase at the bottom of the stairs. She'd spent most of the previous two days wrapped in a duvet on her granny's sofa watching television and eating junk food. But considering everything that had happened she felt remarkably all right. Jay had rung her mobile countless times but she'd switched it off eventually. She had absolutely nothing to say to him. She'd listened to the first of his messages — saying how Cindy really was out of the picture now and how he and Kate could be together forever. Obviously Cindy really had given him the boot and he wasn't prepared to be alone for longer than a minute. Still there was always Tammy in the office, Kate thought wryly after she'd deleted the message. I'm sure she'll take you back you creep. It had hurt her to know that there had been other affairs, that hers wasn't "special". But however much it hurt her, she kept thinking about Cindy. It was a thousand times worse for her. Kate swore that she'd never so much as smile at a married man again, even if he had separation or divorce papers to prove that he was "available".

"You missed all the drama on Saturday," Molly said as Kate flopped onto the sofa.

"Really? What happened?"

"Sam's little boy went missing. It was terrible. Sam was in bits."

370

"I can imagine. With all the child abductions on the news, I'm not surprised. They found him though?"

"Yes, thank goodness. Your friend Angus found him on the beach and brought him back. The poor child had got it into his head to run away."

"Angus?" Kate asked with surprise.

"Yes, he was quite the hero. Managed to convince the little lad to come back home of his own accord. Poor mite had it in his head that no one wanted him around."

"I know the feeling," Kate murmured.

"Sorry, I missed that," said Molly. "What did you say?"

"Nothing, don't mind me. It's good to be back. How was your weekend apart from the drama?"

"Good thanks. But you have to tell me all about your holiday. I've never been to Boston. What was the weather like? Was it hot?"

Kate nodded. "Yes, very. Makes a nice change. I wasn't out in the sun much though. I spent a lovely day in the museum and um, saw my friend."

"How did that go? Was it fun?"

"Not exactly," Kate admitted. "It was a bit of a disaster to tell the truth."

Molly sighed. "I'm really sorry to hear that. I know you probably don't want to talk about it but I'm here if you need me." She was quite used to Kate's obsession with privacy.

Kate thought for a second. She felt bad. Molly was a good person and seemed genuinely sorry for her troubles. It wouldn't hurt to tell her what had happened, in fact, it might be just what she needed. Granny Lily had been great and she'd made her realize that talking to a sympathetic ear really was the best therapy. "You know, Molly, I do want to talk about it this time. I know I haven't always told you everything in the past." Kate smiled gently. "In fact, I'm sure I've been more than a little evasive. But if you have the time I'd like to tell you all about Jay."

"Is Jay your American friend?"

"Yes. At least he was."

Molly smiled back at her. "Kate, I've all the time in the world. Why don't we open a bottle of wine and settle in for the night?"

"You know, I'd like that," said Kate. "I'd like that a lot."

"Does this mean I can borrow your Jimmy Choo boots?" Molly tried her luck.

"Don't push it," Kate laughed. "Those boots are sacred. But we'll see."

CHAPTER
NINETEEN

Paige

Paige woke up. She felt terrible — her neck was stiff and her buttocks were numb. The inside of her mouth felt dry yet sticky and she had a desperate urge to clear the gunge by brushing her teeth. Her suit jacket had fallen off her while she slept, leaving her cold and shivery. She should never have taken Tom's advice to have a nap in the car. She wondered what was going on inside the polling station, the large town hall in Dublin city. When she'd left the election count it was two in the morning and it was now almost five. She stretched her arms over her head, as much as she could in the confined space and flexed her feet and buttocks. She'd better go back in. She flicked on the inside car light and studied her face in the rear-view mirror, wincing as she saw the pale, unkempt reflection. She licked her two index fingers and removed the black mascara stains from underneath her eyes, rubbing gently so as not to pull and redden the delicate paper-thin skin. She then pulled her bag from under the car seat and found her emergency make-up kit. A few minutes later she felt a little more presentable. She braced herself for the scramble through the crowds at the count. At least Tom and her supporters were easy to spot — to the very far left of the hall, against the wall and beside Jackie Pile's gang.

"How are you feeling, love?" Tom asked after he'd given her a huge smile and hug.

"Groggy," she said truthfully. "I'm sure I'll be fine in a few minutes though. What's been happening in my absence?"

"Mark's in and they're counting his second preferences as we speak."

"How's it looking?"

"Hard to tell. Annette seems pretty confident — she's already given RTE an interview about what she'll do when she's in government."

Paige bit her lip. "Really?"

Tom smiled. "Yes. But she'll look pretty stupid when you win the seat, won't she?" He squeezed Paige's hand.

"I can't bear all this tension," Paige said. "It's excruciating."

"I know," Tom said gently. "But it'll be all over soon."

"And we have a final count in Dublin North," a voice boomed over the PA system.

Paige and Tom listened as the official read out the final results.

"In the Dun Laoghaire Rathdown constituency," another official read a moment later, "we have eliminated Hilda Murphy, Miles McGreinna and Rex Reximus."

Tom nudged Paige. "There's just you and Annette left."

Paige's face was pale. She said nothing.

"I think you should sit down," he said. "I'll go and find you a chair. Back in a minute."

"Thanks," she said gratefully. She was feeling rather faint.

He pushed his way through the crowds.

Jackie Pile appeared beside Paige and touched her on the shoulder. "How are you bearing up?" she asked Paige kindly.

Paige shrugged her shoulders. "OK, in the circumstances. I'm delighted you got in again. Well done."

"Thanks. And I look forward to working with you."

"If I get in," Paige sighed. "It's going to be close."

Jackie smiled. "I have every confidence in you, Paige. You've worked hard and you deserve it. If there's any justice in the world, you'll be elected."

"Thanks."

"And we have a recount for the last seat in Dun Laoghaire Rathdown constituency."

Jackie whistled. "You were right about it being close, Paige. I hate recounts, I don't envy you."

"You're an old hand at all this," Tom said, overhearing Jackie's last comment. He opened the plastic folding chair he was holding and smiled at Jackie.

"It never gets any easier though," Jackie said. "Would you like some tea or coffee? We have some at our table.

And some sandwiches I believe, although I can't vouch for their freshness."

"That would be great, thanks," Paige said gratefully. Although sitting down now, she still felt faint and something to eat might help her blood-sugar level.

An agonizing hour later, Tom put his hand on Paige's shoulder. She'd been dozing in the chair, leaning against his side.

"They're about to announce the result," he said.

Paige raised her head, looked over to the right and tried to pick out Annette in the crowd. It wasn't hard. She was standing on a chair, craning to the see the stage, one steadying hand on her husband's shoulder. At that moment Annette looked over towards Paige, as if sensing Paige's gaze. She nodded in recognition, no emotion showing on her face, her eyes lingering on Paige for a few moments before swivelling back towards the stage.

"Annette looks very confident," Paige said to Tom in a low voice.

"That means nothing," Tom assured her, staring at the stage. "There's our official. He's been handed the result sheet. Here we go." The man walked towards the microphone. Paige took a deep breath and braced herself for bad news.

"And in the Dun Laoghaire Rathdown constituency on the second and final count, Councillor Paige Brady has one hundred thousand and fifty-six votes. On the second and final count Councillor Annette Higgins has one hundred thousand and forty-two votes. I hereby

376

elect Councillor Paige Brady to the fourth and final seat."

A roar of approval swept the hall and all around her people clapped and cheered.

"Well done, Paige." Jackie kissed her warmly on both cheeks.

"Where's the new Deputy?" Paddy Burns boomed as he made his way towards her. "Congratulations, my dear." He gave her a huge bearhug.

Paige was overwhelmed. She clung to Tom's hand, the tears freely flowing down her cheeks.

"Have you anything to say to us, Deputy Brady?" An RTE radio journalist thrust a large grey woolly microphone in her face.

"Um, yes," Paige said. "I'm delighted and I'd like to thank everyone who voted for me."

"Are you surprised that Councillor Higgins didn't get in?"

"Yes," Paige said honestly. "I suppose I am."

"How do you feel about her comments about you this evening?"

Paige raised her eyebrows and looked at Tom. He smiled at her and shrugged his shoulders.

"I wasn't aware that she'd made any," Paige replied evenly, refusing to be baited. "And it's all a little irrelevant now, isn't it?"

"I suppose it is," the journalist said reluctantly. "But I think you should know that she called you . . ."

Paige put her hands in the air. "I honestly don't want to hear, thank you very much. I think Councillor Higgins has her own problems to be getting on with, don't you? And I'm sure what she told you was said in the heat of the moment. Now would you like to talk to Deputy Pile? She's right beside me."

"Um, yes, sure," the journalist said and left Paige alone.

"Well handled," Tom said.

Paige smiled at him. "Hey, I won. There's no point in rubbing her nose in it." She yawned. "Now, let's go home. I'm exhausted. We can celebrate tomorrow night. Right now, me and the baby need some sleep — in a bed!"

"Anything you say, Deputy." Tom put his arm around her protectively. "Home it is."

The following morning Paige woke up and remembered instantly. A warm feeling flooded her whole body — she'd won the election and she was now a full-blown Deputy. The enormity of the situation began to sink in. She glanced at the clock radio beside the bed — almost eleven o'clock — she should have been up hours ago. It was all very quiet downstairs — maybe Tom had taken the boys out for a walk.

She pushed herself up in the bed. She was still exhausted, exhausted but elated. She wondered if everyone had heard the news yet. She'd texted Molly last night but she must ring her mum and Tom's mum this morning. Although by this stage they'd probably have heard on the news. She got out of bed, slipped her feet into her slippers and wrapped her towelling dressing gown around her. Her stomach was starting to round out now — soon she'd be in fully-fledged "preggy" gear, but for now her looser clothes sufficed.

"Tom?" she called as she walked down the stairs. "Hello? Anyone home?"

She heard a muffled giggle from the kitchen and smiled. Callum was probably in hiding — waiting to jump out at her from under the table or behind the curtains.

As she walked into the kitchen she was met by a host of smiling faces — Tom, Callum, Molly, Kate, Lily, Angus, Tom's mum and dad, and her own mum. And Alfie looked on with interest from his highchair in the corner.

"Surprise!" Callum said. "We're having a party for you, Mum."

Paige laughed and looked down. "But I'm still in my pyjamas."

"It's my fault," Tom said. "I invited everyone over. I thought we should celebrate now as I have a special surprise arranged for you this evening."

"What sort of surprise?" Paige asked with interest.

"You'll have to wait and see." He smiled.

"Have some cake, Mum," Callum insisted, pulling her towards the kitchen table by her dressing gown tie. "Come on. Granny made it this morning and it's still warm. It's chocolate!"

"Well in that case." Paige looked at the large rectangular cake which was sitting on the table. "Congratulations," it read in white icing surrounded by little silver balls.

"Thanks, Mum." Paige smiled at her mother.

"We're all very proud of you," her mother said. "I'm afraid the icing isn't quite set, but I'm sure it will taste fine."

Tom handed Paige a knife. "You do the honours," he said. "We're all dying for a slice."

"I can't believe you're a Deputy now." Molly grinned. "Does this mean we have to watch what we say around you?"

"Not at all," Paige said. "It won't change me one little bit."

"Will you be famous, Mum?" Callum asked.

She ruffled his hair. "No, Callum."

"But you'll be on the telly?" he asked hopefully. "On *The Den* children's show?"

She smiled. "Doubtful. Unless Dustin the Turkey invites me."

"I'll write to him and tell him all about you," Callum promised. "I'll tell him what a good mummy you are and then he'll have you on."

"You do that," Paige said.

Everyone laughed.

Tom organized coffee and tea for everyone while Paige talked to Molly, Kate and Lily about the nerve-wracking night.

"How did you feel when they announced the final count?" Lily asked.

"I was in shock to be honest, I was convinced Annette had pipped me at the post. And it came as a huge relief I suppose, after all the hard work."

"We all knew you could do it," Lily said.

Paige smiled. "Thanks."

"Sure didn't Gran cajole all her friends to vote for you," Kate quipped. "Which must be practically half of Burnaby."

Lily laughed. "At least three quarters, please."

Paige smiled. "I couldn't have done it without all of you. And without Tom of course. And Angus."

"I did nothing," Angus insisted, handing Alfie back his soggy Liga biscuit.

"You kept Callum entertained," Paige pointed out, "and helped with Alfie. That's hardly nothing."

Tom tapped his coffee mug with a tea spoon. "I'd like to propose a toast. To Deputy Brady. May God protect her and all who sail in her."

Everyone laughed.

"I think he's calling you a ship, Mummy!" Callum said delightedly.

"Tom!" Paige protested.

He grinned at her and winked.

"To Deputy Brady," he repeated. They all raised their mugs and clunked them together. "To Deputy Brady."

That afternoon Tom met with his boss in the building society. He'd been working for Hannah Brookes for over five years now and they'd always got on well. She was a kind, if somewhat formidable woman who kept her staff firmly in line and had a habit of being a little more abrupt than most would like. Walking into her office, Tom felt a little nervous. He had no idea how she would react to his request.

"Hello, Tom." She looked up from her computer screen and smiled. "Please sit down."

"Thanks."

"How's Paige? I believe she's our new Deputy. Do congratulate her for me."

"I will."

"Now what can I do for you?"

"I'll come straight to the point, Hannah. Paige and I have been discussing the coming year and we feel that the children need one of us around. Callum will be starting school next year and we'd like to be able to collect him every day and do his homework with him — that sort of thing. And as you know, Paige is expecting again next year."

"Go on," Hannah said evenly.

"Well, um, I was hoping to take a year's unpaid leave to stay at home with the kids. Paige will be working all hours and um, we thought this might be a solution."

"I see," said Hannah. She said nothing for a moment. "Have you taken parental leave before?"

Tom shook his head. "No. If I've needed any extra days I've taken them out of my holidays."

"You're a good manager, Tom. I'll be sorry to lose you."

Tom caught his breath.

"I'll rephrase that," Hannah said quickly. "I'll be sorry to lose you for the year, but I understand completely. My own are all teenagers now, but it's still a struggle to keep the house running smoothly. I know how hard it is when they're younger, believe me. Besides, according to European Law you're entitled to several months unpaid parental leave if you have children under four or five. I can't quite remember the details but one of the women in the Bray branch has just started three months' parental leave."

"Really?" Tom asked. "And my job is safe even if I take as much as a year off?"

Hannah smiled. "Of course, we'd hate to lose you permanently. And maybe you'd consider doing some consultancy work for us at home?"

"I'd be happy to," Tom said eagerly.

"You're a good man, Tom," Hannah said thoughtfully. "There's not many husbands who would put their wives' careers before theirs. I admire you."

Tom blushed. Hannah wasn't usually renowned for her compliments. "Thanks," he murmured.

That evening Tom arrived home early from work.

"Anybody home?" he shouted as he walked into the hall.

"Daddy!" Callum came careering towards him and threw his little arms around Tom's waist.

Tom picked him up and threw him in the air. "How's my best boy?" He grinned. "Have you been good for Angus today?"

"Yes! And he told me about being my teacher. Isn't it cool?"

"Very cool." Tom smiled. "But you'll have to be extra good for him in class."

"I will," Callum said solemnly. "Angus has already told me that I have to be a good mample."

"Mample?" Tom was confused.

"You know, show the others how to be good."

Tom clicked. "A good example." He tried not to laugh.

"Yes," Callum nodded solemnly. "A good mample."

They went into the kitchen where Angus was feeding Alfie some sort of mushy goo.

"Hi, Tom," Angus said. "Want to take over?"

"Sure." Tom pulled off his jacket and hung it over the back of one of the kitchen chairs. Tom removed his tie and shoved it unceremoniously into a jacket pocket. Won't be needing one of those soon, he thought. He took the plastic bowl and spoon off Angus and sniffed the bowl's contents. "Banana?"

Angus nodded. "Banana and apple. Paige made it."

"Where is Paige?"

"Upstairs having a rest. She was looking a little worn out so I took over Alfie's tea."

"Thanks," Tom said gratefully.

"No worries. So how was the office, dear?" Angus asked with a grin.

"Fine, thanks." Tom laughed. "Actually it was good. I asked my boss for a year's parental leave and she said yes."

"That's great! Callum will be thrilled to have you around more. He's always saying how he'd love to do more things with you."

"Really?" Tom asked. "You never mentioned it before."

Angus shrugged. "You and Paige have been under a lot of pressure recently. You didn't need any extra guilt trips."

384

"I suppose not. I look forward to spending more time with him. He's growing up so fast. And I believe you told him about being his teacher."

"Is that OK? I hope you didn't want to tell him yourselves."

"No, it's fine. And he's delighted." They both looked at Callum who was colouring in a picture of Spiderman with chunky crayons.

"He's a good kid." Angus smiled. "I look forward to teaching him."

Tom coughed. "Um, I know we've never really said it to you before, not properly anyway," he began, "but we really appreciate all the time and effort you've put into his nibs this summer." Tom gestured towards Callum with his head. "It's made all the difference. We really are very grateful."

"I know you are." Angus smiled at Tom. "And it's been a pleasure, really. He's a real little charmer."

"Well, thanks anyway." Tom punched Angus gently on the shoulder. "And are you sure you're OK to babysit this evening?"

"Yes, positive. I'm sure it'll be useful to the school to have Deputy Brady owing me a favour."

Tom laughed. "You're probably right!"

Later that evening Paige had her usual wardrobe dilemma, except this time it was worse. The dark brown suede trousers she'd intended to wear were far too tight around the waist. She'd tried leaving the button and zip undone and pulling a black jumper down over her stomach but that made her look bulgy and made the seat of the trousers bag unbecomingly. Besides, what if her trousers fell down during the night and she didn't notice? She sighed and put the outfit back in the wardrobe.

"What's up?" Tom was lounging fully dressed on their bed, watching her. He'd already changed out of his work gear, showered and shaved and was rearing to go. He hadn't had much for lunch and his stomach was starting to complain loudly.

"I can't find anything to wear," she complained.

"Can I help?"

She smiled at him. "I don't know, can you?" She put her hands on her hips provocatively and raised her eyebrows.

"I think you should go out just as you are," he said. "You look great."

She smiled at him and looked down at her black lacy bra, matching G-string and hold-up stockings. "I think I might get a little cold. Besides, unless we're going to a lap dancing club I don't think it's quite appropriate."

Tom got up and walked towards her. He stood behind her, wrapping his arms around her waist.

She flinched. "Your hands are freezing!"

"They'll soon warm up," he promised. He moved them up her body, lingering over her breasts. He unhooked her bra and deftly removed it, throwing it onto the floor.

"Tom, we have to go," Paige protested. "We'll be late. Besides, Angus is downstairs."

"There's no mad rush," Tom said. "And Angus has taken the kids out to the park, bless him." His hands caressed her breasts and he began to kiss the nape of her neck gently. She turned around and smiled at him. She was actually feeling quite good all day and Tom seemed to be in flying form, it would be a shame to stifle him. Besides, they hadn't had sex for weeks as she hadn't been feeling up to it. And once the baby came . . . she shuddered to think how tired they'd both be. They should grab every opportunity they could, especially if Callum and Alfie were otherwise occupied. "In that case . . ." She kissed him firmly on the lips, put her arms on his shoulders and pushed him backwards towards the bed.

"Deputy Brady." He laughed, as they fell onto the bed. Paige silenced him with another kiss.

"I had an interesting meeting with Hannah today," Tom said later that evening after they'd ordered their food. They were sitting at a secluded table in their favourite restaurant, Fallon's in Burnaby.

"Oh?" Paige took a sip of her wine and smiled at him. "What about?"

"Things." He smiled mysteriously.

"Go on," she said impatiently. "What things?"

"About taking a year off to look after the kids."

"Really? What did she say?"

Tom smiled again. "She said yes. She's going to promote Annie Jones on a temporary basis and take on a new trainee manager to replace her."

Paige looked at him with a strange expression on her face.

"What?" he asked. "Are you not happy? It's what we'd discussed, Paige, before the elections."

"I know. But we didn't really go over the details — the financial end of things for example."

"I've had a look at the figures and as long as we don't go wild we should be fine. It'll mean no foreign holidays for example, and we won't be changing the cars, but we'll manage."

She was quiet for a moment, her fingers running up and down the stem of the wine glass, her eyes fixed on the dark red wine.

Tom allowed her time to collect her thoughts.

"I guess I haven't had time to take it all in," she said finally. "I didn't expect it all to happen so quickly I suppose." She looked him straight in the eye. "To tell the truth, it makes me feel a little inadequate as a mother. I feel like you'll be taking over and that I'll just be in the background, plodding away at work." She sighed. "I'm sorry, I'm not being fair. It's what we'd agreed, I know. I just didn't expect to feel like this."

Tom put his hand on hers. "Paige," he said softly. "You'll always be their mother. Nothing can change that. You'll always have a special relationship with them. I'll just be the one doing the school run and changing Alfie's nappies, that's all."

Paige snorted. "And you're more than welcome to Alfie's nappies. You're right, I know you're right. But I just feel kind of, oh, I don't know — left out, I suppose."

Tom smiled at her warmly. "Paige, you won't be left out of anything, I promise you that."

388

"I'm sorry, I'm being really ungracious," she said. "Most women would be delighted to have such a supportive husband."

"That's what Hannah said." Tom smiled.

"I really am very lucky." Paige leant over and kissed him on the cheek. "And I do love you, Tom."

He stroked her hand. "And I love you too. More than ever."

Paige felt a warm sensation in the pit of her stomach. She knew the next year was going to be hard for both of them, but as long as they were together they'd get through anything.

CHAPTER
TWENTY

Molly

"Before we get started I'd like to apologize," Milo began as soon as the other Book Club members had settled into their seats and stopped discussing their favourite event at the book festival, which they'd unanimously declared a huge success.

"Why?" Paige asked.

"Yes, what have you done now?" Anita asked with a sigh.

Molly tried not to laugh. Anita was sitting beside Milo and from what she could see the cold war between them still hadn't thawed.

"I recommended *Bright Light of My Soul*," he said picking up that's month's book choice and turning the elegant-looking matt grey paperback over in his hands. "It got some great reviews in hardback and I thought it would be an interesting read." He stopped for a moment.

"Milo, are you saying that you didn't like it?" Paige raised her eyebrows.

"No I didn't, not really," Milo admitted. He put a finger under the collar of his trademark black polo neck, as if letting some air in. "It wasn't the easiest read, was it?"

Anita snorted. "But I thought you informed us at the last meeting that we should all be reading more literary fiction, that our tastes were too, how did you put it, ah yes, 'unformed' and 'unrefined'."

"I didn't say that, did I?" Milo asked, getting a little red in the face.

"I'm afraid you did," Harry said, smiling broadly at him.

"Dad!" Sam hissed at him. "I must have come in after that," he said to the table. "It's not as if he's the world's greatest reader himself. In fact up until he bought this shop . . ."

Milo coughed loudly. "Um, yes, well, I'm sorry if I caused any offence at the last meeting. I was wrong."

"We won't be reading any more of your recommendations for a while anyway," Cathy laughed. "I hated *Bright Light of My Soul* — it was so depressing. I don't mind depressing as such, but there was absolutely no hope shining through at all. It was a weep fest from start to finish. Nothing of any interest happened to the main character, Hoppy. And what kind of name is 'Hoppy' for a woman anyway?"

"I thought it was supposed to be a kind of twist on the word 'happy' myself," Trina said. "But that's probably a bit too obvious. It's her first book though, isn't it? Una Franklin's. Maybe she'll cheer up a bit in the next one."

"Let's hope so," Anita nodded. "She can't get any worse. And what about the men in the book? They were all totally nasty characters — from your man Frankie, her first husband, to that guy who killed her at the end, Joe. I know as a gender men are not perfect," she looked pointedly at Milo, "but they're not all bad."

"I agree," Sam said. "It was a pretty bleak reflection on men. But some of the women weren't any better. Didn't her own mother practically sell her to Frankie for a piece of land?"

"That's right! She was horrible to Hoppy," Molly agreed. "And her so called 'friend' Susan wasn't much better."

"The one who told the guards that Hoppy was a prostitute?" Kate asked.

"Yes." Molly nodded. "She was a nasty piece of work."

"What are you doing after this?" Molly whispered to Paige an hour later. The debate on *Bright Light of My Soul* was beginning to wind down and the group were now discussing choices for next month's book. "Going for lunch with you." Paige smiled.

"Great!" Molly squeezed her friend's arm. "I wasn't sure if you'd be free, Deputy."

"What do you think, Molly?" Anita asked her, interrupting them.

"Sorry?" Molly replied. "I missed that."

"Cathy was asking if we could order copies of an American title in time for next month's meeting?"

"Depends on the book," Molly said. "But it shouldn't be a problem if the American wholesaler we use has it."

"Well then, I vote we take a break from literary fiction," Anita glanced at Milo and he winced.

"Hear, hear," said Cathy.

"I agree." Trina nodded. "Let's have something with a real story this time. And a happy ending please, if it's not too much to ask. Optimistic at the very least."

"Well then, I nominate Bonnie's new book," Cathy said. "It's only available in the States at the moment so we'll be the very first people to read it. It's based in Burnaby apparently and we might even recognize some of the characters. She told me about it at the festival."

"Excellent!" Anita clapped her hands together. "Any objections?"

Everyone shook their heads.

"Back to decent fiction then," Anita said, her eyes lingering on Milo. "And about time too."

The following Monday, Molly lingered outside the Begley Literary Agency, her stomach twisted with nerves. She looked up at the imposing Georgian Merrion Square building and fished in the small pocket of her oversized red leather bag for her powder compact, flicked it open and checked her face. She hoped she was dressed appropriately. She'd spent ages last night deciding what to wear, with Kate and Paige's patient help, and had finally settled on a pair of old reliable black trousers, a white shirt (Kate's) and a dark red fitted cashmere cardigan (Paige's). She completed the outfit with a black beaded choker (Paige's), the red bag (hers) and killer Jimmy Choo black high-heeled boots, Kate's pride and joy, which she'd insisted on lending to Molly for good luck. She'd popped a pair of runners in the bag just in case her feet were crippled from the heels on the way home as she'd taken the Dart train to abate the extra stress of driving in the Dublin city traffic, not to mention finding an elusive parking space.

The three of them — Molly, Kate and Paige — had had a delightfully girly evening in the end and Kate, usually dismissive of "girliness" had really got into the spirit of things. Kate had turned out to be a dab hand at making pink cocktails complete with authentic blender-produced slushy ice, slices of orange and lemon, and tiny multi-coloured paper cocktail umbrellas that she'd discovered in the cupboard under the sink, left over from some party or other. Molly and Paige had been most impressed. Molly regretted drinking quite so many of the "Deputy Brady Delights", as Kate had christened one of her dark pink concoctions, not to mention the "Milly Molly Mandys" which were blood red and full of vodka, or the baby pink "Catikins" but it had been a great evening.

Molly glanced at her watch. It was just after ten and if she didn't go in now she'd be late. She smoothed her trousers down her legs, checked the eye and hook fastenings on her shirt, as Kate had warned her they had a habit of coming undone at inopportune moments, and walked up the steps towards the imposing red front door. She rang the intercom beside the discreet "Begley Literary Agency" brass nameplate and waited. A moment later, a friendly woman's voice answered.

"Hello? Begley Agency. Can I help you?"

"Um, it's Molly Harper."

"Hi, Molly, Gerry's expecting you. Push the door and go up the stairs. Our offices are at the back of the first floor, in the return."

"Thanks." Molly stepped inside and looked around. The hall was amazing — it had soaringly high ceilings, complete with what seemed to be original plasterwork. A large, ornate crystal chandelier hung from the middle of the space, dangling weightily from the most organic ceiling rose Molly had ever seen. It was made up of huge fronds of fern-like leafy foliage, all curving and twisting down from the horizontal plane as if growing towards the floor. The hall was painted creamy white and the black and white tiled floor set it off beautifully. As Molly walked up the stairs, she could feel the thick pile of the cream carpet under the thin soles of her boots. The Begley Agency was obviously a huge success judging by appearances and Molly was distinctly impressed and overawed.

"What would Mr Begley want with me?" she asked under her breath. "He obviously has more than enough clients to be going on with."

"Hello." As Molly reached the top of the stairs she was greeted by a small, dark haired young woman. "You must be Molly, nice to meet you." She held out her hand and smiled.

"Hi," Molly said, shaking her hand firmly. She followed the woman through a doorway and into a small, bright office, furnished with a simple mahogany desk, an armchair and an antique-looking coffee table stacked high with book trade magazines — *The Bookseller, Publishing Ireland, Inis,* and *Dublin Books.*

"Gerry will be ready for you in one minute. He's just on the phone to an editor at the moment. He spends most of his day on the phone — he gets hundreds of calls every day." She gestured at the chair. "Please, make yourself comfortable. Can I make you some tea or coffee?"

"No thanks, but I'd love a glass of water," Molly said.

"No problem." The woman came back a few minutes later with a tall glass and handed it to Molly. "I'm Julie by the way, Gerry's assistant and general dogsbody."

"Nice to meet you, Julie." Molly smiled shyly. "Quite some offices you have here."

Julie laughed. "Most of this building belongs to the accountancy firm Gerry used to work for. We just rent this bit off them. It's not as glam as the rest of the building but it's in a great location. We get to impress clients with the address," she lowered her voice, "and the accountants get to namedrop the literary agency to make themselves sound more interesting. Plus we recommend a lot of our clients to them. So, everyone wins."

Molly smiled again.

Julie noticed how tightly Molly was clutching the bag on her knee. "You're probably nervous, but don't be. Gerry's a lovely man and he's very easy to talk to."

"What were you saying about me?" The door opposite Julie's desk opened and Gerry himself stepped out. He smiled at Molly. "I hope it was nice."

"Of course it was, Gerry." Julie winked at Molly. "Sure why wouldn't it be? Great man like yourself."

"Indeed." Gerry laughed. "Sorry to keep you waiting, Molly. I'm sure Julie was keeping you entertained. Please come in." He held the door for her and Molly stepped into his office. Julie was right — it wasn't as glam as the rest of the building but it was still an impressive room. The end wall was made up of richly coloured stained glass depicting a phoenix rising from vivid orange flames. In the centre of the room was another large mahogany desk and to the left and right there were filing cabinets and shelves and shelves crammed with books of all shapes and sizes.

"Do sit down," Gerry said. "Have you ever talked to an agent before, Molly?"

Molly was taken aback. "Um, no," she murmured. "Never."

He looked down at the sheets of paper in front of him. "Am I the first person to read some of your stories?"

She nodded shyly. She hoped she wasn't blushing too noticeably, her cheeks felt decidedly pink.

"Your work has a lovely fresh feel," Gerry said. "I think you have real talent. Unfortunately there's no real market for short stories at the moment. And I think your *Price of Gold* saga is a little too ambitious for a first book."

Molly's heart dropped. He didn't want her. Of course he didn't — a highly respected man like Gerry Begley. What was she . . .?

"How would you feel about that?" he asked. "Could you try it?"

"Sorry?" she'd missed what he'd said.

"Writing a contemporary novel. What do you think?"

Molly looked at him in surprise. "Um, I could give it a go."

"Your short stories are excellent and I'm sure Julie could place them for you in magazines, say *Trend* for example and *Dublin Books*."

"Really?" Molly asked with delight. "That would be great."

"I liked 'Concrete Pictures' very much. How would you feel about expanding that story into a novel? The two main characters were very strong and I think there's a lot of meat to them."

Molly smiled. Meat? She wasn't quite sure what to make of that but it sounded like a compliment.

"How about writing five or six chapters and a plot outline and then we could put a proposal together for a publisher? How does that sound?"

"Fine," Molly said. "Great, I mean. I think I could do that."

"I'm sorry, I never asked if you wanted me to represent you. You may like to look around for someone else. There's Josie O'Hara of course, and Phelim . . ."

Molly didn't have to think. Gerry seemed like someone she could trust, plus he genuinely seemed to like her work. "No, I'd like you if you'll have me."

"Of course I'll have you, my dear." Gerry's eyes twinkled. "I'd be delighted to be your agent. I think we'll get along just swimmingly."

"So do I." Molly smiled back. "And I'll get writing straight away."

"That's what I like to hear," Gerry said. "Welcome to the family, Molly. I'll ask Julie to draw up the official papers allowing me to act as your agent. Maybe you could come in next week and sign them?"

"I'd be happy to."

"Good, and you can tell me all about your progress on 'Concrete Pictures'."

Molly skipped down the building's steps after the meeting, almost twisting her ankle in the process and causing her to lurch ungainly against the dark blue handrail. She straightened herself up, rubbed her side where she'd hit the solid metal and smiled. Nothing could dampen her mood at this moment, not even a large bruise

"So how did it go this morning?" Sam asked as soon as she'd stepped foot in the bookshop. He was sitting on the stool at the front till, keying some customer orders into the computer. There were a few customers browsing the shelves but all in all it was pretty quiet.

"Really well." Molly smiled and dumped her bag on the counter to the relief of her poor shoulders — she always carried too much junk "just in case". She hadn't bothered changing into her runners either and was starting to regret it. Kate's boots were killers in more ways than one. She was dying to take them off and give her soles and insteps a rub. "Gerry was nice, he wants to be my agent. He's going to place some of my stories with magazines, well, his assistant Julie is, and he asked me to try writing a book based on 'Concrete Pictures'."

Sam laughed. "Try stopping for breath, Molly!"

She smiled at him again. "Sorry, was I gabbling? I'm just so excited about the whole thing. I can't believe it's all happening. First winning the short story competition, now this."

He jumped off the stool, walked around the counter towards her and gave her a huge hug. "If anyone deserves it, you do," he kissed the top of her head. "Well done, you."

Molly felt on top of the world. Not only did Gerry want her, she had the kindest and nicest boyfriend in the world.

"Thanks," she said.

"Ahem," a customer coughed beside them. "Can I pay for this?"

"Sure." Sam grinned and winked at Molly. "Why don't you go into the office and put your feet up for a few minutes. I'll deal with this."

"That would be great if you don't mind. I'll be back out in a while."

Once in the office Molly flopped down in a chair and rang Paige again. She'd tried her on the walk down to the train station, positively hopping to tell her the good news, but Paige's mobile had been turned off.

"Molly, I was just thinking about you. How did the meeting go?"

Molly told her all the details.

"Fantastic!" Paige said enthusiastically. "He sounds like just the man you need. So, I guess you just have to get writing now."

Molly bit her lip. The reality of the situation was only starting to kick in. "What if I can't write a whole book? I've tried before and I've always come unstuck about halfway through. I've never finished a whole one before."

"This time it's different," Paige assured her. "You've just won a prize for you work and you've got an agent. Everything's changed. You're a real writer now and it's your job to write. Just like it's my job to stop dog owners from allowing their dogs to poop on the beach. I know which job I'd rather do right at this minute." Paige laughed. "And I thought being a Deputy would be much more glamorous than being a Councillor. How wrong can you get?"

"Right now, alleviating dog poop sounds much easier to me." Molly sniffed. "Paige, what have I done? I can't write a book. Who am I kidding?"

"Listen to me, Molly." Paige's voice sounded firm and unbending. "You most certainly can and you most certainly will. I want you to go home this evening, have dinner, go for a walk and then sit down at your computer. Read 'Concrete Pictures' again. Read it over and over as many time as you have to."

"Why?"

"To get it into your thick skull that you can write, dummy," Paige said. "I know you have a book in you and I bet Sam thinks so too. And Anita. And Gerry has confidence in you, and he's a professional who doesn't know you from Adam. It's about time you had a little confidence in yourself, Molly. Do you hear me?"

Molly nodded.

"Molly?"

"I was nodding."

"So you'll stop thinking negative thoughts?"

"Um, I suppose so."

"And you'll sit down this evening and write?"

"I will," Molly said.

"Promise?"

"Promise."

"I'll ring you later. Now, smile, Molly. You *can* do it, don't forget that."

"Thanks, Guru Brady." Molly laughed. "I feel much better now. Talk to you later."

Molly smiled as she clicked off her phone. Just then Sam popped his head round the door.

"Dad's here for the meeting. Are you ready?"

"Damn, I'd forgotten all about it. Is Anita here yet?"

"Yes, she's talking to Dad. From what I managed to eavesdrop, they're going to the theatre together this evening."

"Really?" Molly raised her eyebrows. "I thought she couldn't stand him."

"I know." Sam smiled. "Wonders will never cease."

"Give me two minutes. I presume the meeting will be in here?"

Sam nodded. "And Felix is covering the shop floor for an hour or so."

"We'd better get going then I guess," Molly sighed. "Lambs to the slaughter and all that." She looked at him carefully. "What has your Dad said to you? What do you know? I know you know something."

"As I keep telling you," he put on a feeble Italian accent, "I know nothing. Nothing I'm at liberty to tell you anyway. Trust me." Sam looked down at his hands. Molly sensed there was something he wanted to tell her but for some reason he couldn't.

Molly sniffed. "He's going to change the shop, I know he is. He's never liked the pink and purple shelves and quite frankly I think the whole 'romance bookshop' thing is just an embarrassment to him. I can see it now — 'Milo's Cool Literary Bookshop' — all black and grey shelves. Black leather sofas, jazz music, poetry readings . . .'"

"Hello, are you ready for the meeting, Molly?" Anita walked into the office, interrupting Molly in mid-flow.

"Um, yes," Molly said. She looked at Sam who was trying not to laugh. "Ready, Sam?" she asked pointedly.

"Sure, whenever you are."

They all sat down in the small office, Molly behind the desk, Anita and Sam on the sofa and Milo beside them on a fold-out chair. It was decidedly cramped.

"So, Milo," Anita began, "why are we all here?"

Milo cleared his throat theatrically. "As you all know the bookshop figures haven't been the best in recent weeks. But I'm delighted to say that the festival was a huge hit and . . ."

Anita stared at him, her eyes narrowing. "And what?"

"The figures in the last two weeks since the festival have been very strong. So, I've changed my mind. The bookshop can stay as it is for the moment."

Sam looked at him in surprise. This wasn't what he was expecting.

"No jazz music?" Molly asked.

"Well, maybe a little jazz," Milo said. "But no black shelves and you can keep the name."

"Thanks very much," Anita muttered. "Milo, what do you mean — 'for the moment'?"

"For the foreseeable future, does that clarify it?" said Milo.

"No," Anita said firmly. "It does not. I want you to guarantee that you won't change the shop, not now, not ever. Like you promised me when you bought it."

"But I can't do that!" Milo protested. "Something might happen, romance might go out of fashion."

"Romance will never go out of fashion." Anita glared at him. "Not that you've ever read any of it. So how would you know?"

He looked straight back at her. "For your information, I read one of Bonnie's books only last week."

"Really?" Anita was genuinely surprised.

"Yes, really. And I liked it. I'll be reading her next book, for the reading group. After that I thought I'd give Rose Lovett a go."

Molly looked at Anita, who had a strange expression on her face, Molly couldn't quite read it.

Sam whistled. "Three books in one month, Dad. You'd want to watch that. Reading's a dangerous thing. Addictive. So when are you going to tell them, Dad? Are you going to play at bookselling for another few weeks, another year, another two years? That wasn't

404

exactly the plan now, was it? Your architect was on the phone yesterday. He asked for Mr Devine so I took the call. I can't believe you've been lying to me, your own son. How could you?"

Milo looked at Sam in shock, his face growing pale. "I don't think this is the time or the place, Sam. Why don't we discuss this later. I think . . ."

"The plan?" Anita asked Sam, steel in her eyes. "What do you mean?"

"Ask him," Sam gestured at his dad. "I had nothing to do with it, Anita, believe me."

Milo looked sheepish. "Ignore Sam," he muttered. "He doesn't know what he's talking about."

"Milo," Anita said firmly, her voice dangerously low. "Go on."

"If you won't, I will," Sam said, a threatening edge to his own voice.

"But . . ." Milo looked at Sam. There was a dangerous glint in his son's eyes.

"I mean it, Dad."

Milo sighed. There was no way out, he'd have to come clean. "I bought the bookshop to knock it down and build offices and apartments. The architect was ringing to discuss the planning application. He needs to make one or two small changes to the plan. So it'll take a while to get the application passed. But in the meantime the bookshop will stay as it is, of course. At least that was the plan. But now . . ."

Anita slapped him across the face. "You nasty little man. How could you?"

Milo put his hands to his face. "I'm sorry, Anita. But I'm a businessman. At least I was."

"That's no excuse, Dad," Sam said. "Why didn't you tell me at the very beginning? You're unbelievable."

"I knew you'd never manage to keep it a secret. You'd too damn nice for your own good, Sam, that's your problem."

"And once the building started, you'd fire me, along with the rest of the staff, was that it?" Sam demanded.

"Of course not, I was hoping you'd manage the whole project. You did do two years of engineering, after all. I thought it would work out for the best. Your brother, Miles, is very happy working for me."

"I'm nothing like Miles," Sam said with icy calm. "I was happy, am happy working in the bookshop. I don't need a high-powered job like you or Miles, working all hours, never seeing my family. I'm ashamed of you, Dad. How could you dupe Anita like that? You promised her that the bookshop wouldn't change."

"And it won't," Milo said.

"What?" Anita cried. "Spit it out, man!"

"That's what I've been trying to tell you all," Milo said. "I've changed my mind. I'm not going to develop this site at all. It'll stay as a bookshop. I'm going to sign the deeds over to Sam. I want you to own it, son."

"I don't want your charity," Sam said angrily. "How dare you?"

Milo smiled. "I knew you'd say that. Which is why I'm going to take a good chunk of the profits for the next ten years until you pay back every penny."

406

"Sounds reasonable," Anita said. "Don't be stubborn, Sam, take his offer. Stupid man's trying to make amends for what he's done. Idiot that he is." She shot a withering glare at Milo. "And don't think you'll be taking me anywhere this evening, you damn fool."

"But Anita . . ."

"Don't but Anita me. You'll have to do a hell of a lot of grovelling to get out of this one, Milo Devine."

Milo stifled a smile. "Yes, Anita," he said meekly.

"So you'll accept your dad's offer?" Anita asked.

"I'll think about it," Sam said. "I'll have to discuss it with Molly first. If she'll manage the shop with me I'll consider it. It would have to be what we both wanted."

Molly's heart melted. "Oh, Sam," she said before she could stop herself. "I'd love to."

Anita looked at Molly and smiled warmly. "Good, that's settled then." She glared at Milo. "Count yourself lucky Milo that you're still standing. Now let's get back to work. We have a bookshop to run after all."

"I'm exhausted." Molly flopped onto Sam's sofa that evening and kicked her runners off. Her feet were still hurting. "What a day."

Sam handed her a steaming mug of peppermint tea and sat down beside her.

"Thanks." She smiled at him. "But I still can't believe you didn't tell me about that architect."

Sam shrugged. "Sorry, I thought it was for the best. He only rang yesterday and I thought you had enough on your mind to be honest, what with meeting your agent and everything."

"You're probably right, speaking of which," she looked at her watch, "I can't stay long, I have to go home and write. I promised Paige."

"Not to worry." Sam reached over, took the mug out of her hands and placed it on the floor. "But you have to do it for yourself, not for anyone else."

"I know."

He smiled. "But before you go there was something I wanted to ask you."

"Yes?" she said immediately.

"Don't be so impatient, woman. Follow me." He stood up and offered her his hand.

She took it and followed him out the door and down the corridor. He pushed open the door of the spare room.

"What do you think?"

Molly looked around. The late August sun shone through the windows, illuminating the new empty pine bookshelves and matching desk.

"Did you make all this?" she asked.

He nodded. "What do you think?" he asked again.

She smiled. "It's great. A home office. Now you can mull over all those exciting bookshop invoices from the comfort of your own home."

He said nothing for a moment, looked at her and smiled broadly. "It's not an office, it's a study. It's for you. To write your book in. I thought, um, in time, when things settle down with Hugh, that you might like to live here with me. So this will be *your* study, not mine. Well, say something."

408

Molly could feel tears prick her eyes. She looked up at him. "Are you sure?" she whispered.

"Yes, positive."

"I'd love to live here with you. I understand about Hugh, so whenever you think he's ready that's OK with me. Until then, you might even let me use the study. I think I could write a book here, in fact, I'm sure of it." She ran her hands over the smooth surface of the top of the desk.

"Of course, it's your room now."

"And this is the nicest thing anyone's ever done for me." She threw her arms around his neck. "Thank you, Sam."

"It's a pleasure," he said as she covered his face with kisses.

CHAPTER
TWENTY-ONE
Kate

"What are you doing here?" Kate asked Angus suspiciously as she walked into her gran's living room.

He looked at her, red paintbrush in his hand. "Same as you, I presume, painting — or are they your normal clothes?"

Kate looked down at her ancient navy tracksuit bottoms, complete with holes in the knees, paint-splattered runners and an inside out light grey sweatshirt.

"Of course not," she replied archly. "Won't you excuse me?" She flounced out of the room.

"Gran!" Kate said walking into the kitchen where Lily was having a cup of tea. "What's Angus doing here?"

"I must have forgotten to tell you," Lily said mildly. "He offered to help paint today."

Kate glared at her.

"Don't look at me like that," Lily said. "He's a nice lad and very easy to talk to."

"I have no intention of talking to him," Kate said sharply.

Lily tried not to smile. Her granddaughter really was very stubborn. But still, it was a good sign if she felt so strongly about Angus. Much better than apathy. "Why ever not?" Lily asked.

"Just because." Kate didn't feel like explaining right at this minute. Besides, she wasn't sure if she understood why Angus always managed to get under her skin — it didn't make sense. She'd had quite enough of men in the last while and however "nice" Angus was she had no intention of becoming involved with anyone ever again. It was time to start concentrating on her career. She had a lot of dummy dates to catch up on — that would keep her busy. She was far too busy to think about anything else. And she'd had a couple of ideas for leather baby shoes — not that she intended to do anything about them of course — but it was nice to know that her talent hadn't completely deserted her as she'd feared. After breaking up with Jay the first time around, Kate thought she'd never design again. Maybe finally her heart was finally starting to heal.

Lily watched Kate's face. She seemed lost in thought. "Would you like some tea?" Lily suggested. "Or coffee? Sit down and have a break before you get started with the painting."

Kate stared at her. "I'm not painting with *him* in the same room."

Lily laughed gaily. "Listen to yourself. You sound like a petulant teenager, Kate. It'll take half the time with the two of you and you can keep each other company.

Give it a go and if it's really awful you can leave after lunch, OK?"

Kate muttered something under her breath and walked out of the kitchen.

"I presume that's a no to tea, then," Lily said to herself. She smiled and hummed softly as she washed down the sink and the kitchen counter tops. Some days she liked cleaning, she found it cathartic. As she wiped down the cooker, she thought about Kate and about Kate's parents. It was no wonder that Kate found it hard to talk intimately to people — her own parents had spent their early married life screaming and shouting at each other. Billy Bowan had never been a nice man. Luckily his fiery temper had abated with age and nowadays he and Cleo, Lily's daughter and Kate's mother, seemed to live a reasonably stable life all things considered. About time too. Lily sighed. It was all in the distant past but Lily feared it had all left an indelible mark on her only grandchild, one which she'd carry for life. It was no wonder she'd always been drawn to attractive, powerful, older and bullying men who ultimately always treated her badly in the end. Men like her own father.

"You're back," Angus said looking up at Kate. He was kneeling down on the floor, painting carefully around one of the plug sockets with a small brush.

"Let's just get this done," she said shortly, not wanting to encourage small talk. "Where are the brushes or will I make a start with the roller?" She surveyed the walls. Angus had already painted the

412

corners, edges and around the plug sockets of three out of the four walls.

"The roller, I think. I'll finish what I'm doing and then I'll join you. What do you think of the colour?"

Kate considered for a moment. Lily had chosen a rich, warm red, very different to the previous creamy white. "I'm not sure, it's difficult to imagine the whole room red. Won't it make the space seem very small?"

"Maybe. But it's a decent-sized room so it shouldn't matter too much. And the light is very good."

"I'll guess we'll have to wait and see." Kate moved towards the paint tins which were resting on a large white dustsheet, aka one of Lily's old bed sheets, and crouched down. She levered the lid off one of the tins and moved the paint tray beside it.

"Let me help," Angus said. "Those tins can be a divil to pour."

Kate was about to refuse his offer but he was beside her before she could open her mouth. He gently took the heavy tin out of her hands and poured a generous amount of the viscous liquid into the tray.

"Thanks," she murmured grudgingly. She pushed back some stray hair behind her ears and stood up. Tray in one hand and roller in the other she began painting the opposite wall to Angus, as far away from him as she could get.

"How was Boston?" Angus asked after a few minutes. "Paige told me you were over there for a holiday, lucky thing. I spent a summer working there in college on a J1 visa. I loved it."

"Really?" Kate left it at that. She had no intention of discussing her trip to Boston with him but she didn't want to completely ignore him — she wasn't that rude.

"Lily told me you used to live in Boston," he continued unabashed. "How long were you there for?"

"A while."

"I see." Angus wasn't one to be put off easily. He soldiered on. "I stayed in an apartment near Fenway Park. Mad place. Underneath the apartment block there was a pizza restaurant — very handy, and this second-hand shop which only opened when the owner felt like it. But it had amazing things for sale, dirt cheap too. Old clothes from the '40s and '50s, records and tapes of really bizarre bands and weird hats and shoes. Hundreds and hundreds of pairs."

"I think I know the place," Kate said before she could stop herself. "I used to go there to buy shoes."

"I forgot about your strange collection." Angus laughed. "You'll have to show me it one day."

Kate went silent again. She hadn't meant to talk to Angus at all. She was letting her resolve slip. She loaded the roller with some more paint and concentrated on covering the wall.

"Little Callum will be in my class this year," Angus said, still unwilling to give up. "Did Paige tell you?"

"No."

"He seems to be really looking forward to school. When I was there on Friday he dressed up in his uniform for me. He was dead funny, parading around the house like a male model. You should have seen him, Kate. His grey trousers were far too big for him —

414

Paige hadn't had a chance to take them up yet. He was tripping over the ends."

Kate smiled. Callum really was a hoot. "I hear Tom's taking a year off to mind the kids," she remarked.

"I know, isn't it great? I think more fathers should do it. It makes sense if their other half has a good job. What do you think?"

"I suppose you're right," Kate said thoughtfully. "Although Irish men aren't exactly known for their love of childcare and housework."

"Hey, that's unfair!" Angus laughed. "We're getting better. I'd have no problem minding my own kids. I'd love spending time with them. It would be a privilege."

"You'd like your own then?"

"Of course, wouldn't you?"

"I'm not sure."

Angus stopped painting and looked at Kate but her back was still towards him. "Why ever not?" he asked gently.

"Not everyone wants them you know," she said quietly. "I suppose you had a happy childhood?"

"Yes. Most of the time. Didn't you?"

Kate said nothing. She continued to move the roller up and down the wall. Angus noticed that there was no longer any paint left on it. He walked over and lifted the tray off the floor for her.

"You might need some of this," he suggested.

"Thanks," she murmured, dipping the roller into the tray.

Angus noticed that her eyes were glittering. Surely he hadn't made her cry?

"Um, did you hear about Sam's boy, Hugh running away?" he said, changing the subject.

Kate nodded. "Molly told me the story. Sam must have been in bits, poor man."

"He was. But Hugh hadn't gone far, thank goodness. It all worked out all right in the end."

"And you were great," Molly said. "Talking to the lad and making him feel better."

Angus shrugged. "Anyone would have done it."

Kate considered this for a moment. "No, I don't think they would have. They might have brought the boy back to his parents but they wouldn't have stuck around to help sort everything out."

"Maybe not. But as I said, I like kids. I just wanted to help."

"Here," Kate thrust the roller into his hands, "I'm just popping out to the loo. Be back in a minute."

Sitting on the edge of Lily's bath and staring at the white tiled floor, Kate wondered why she was feeling so strange. Lily was right, Angus was a nice man. A very nice man. Not as charismatic as Jay maybe, or as good-looking as some of her previous boyfriends. But he had other qualities. Deeper qualities. Damn it, he was a kind man who cared about other people and he liked her. He'd as much as told her so, over and over again. So what was her problem? She put her head in her hands. Maybe it was finally time to break the habit of a lifetime. She took a few moments to collect herself and then walked back down the stairs to the living room.

"Angus, I've got something to say to you."

416

Angus looked over at Kate who was still lingering in the doorway. "Really?"

Kate smiled. He had red paint splattered in his hair and a large red stripe on his forehead where he must have brushed a painted hand. "Yes. I'm sorry if I've been a bit . . . um, funny towards you. But you were one of my clients you see." She stopped, feeling decidedly awkward. "Anyway, I'm sorry. You're a nice guy."

Angus sighed. "I see." He sounded disappointed. He began to paint the wall again.

"What?" Kate asked. "What did I just say?"

He raised his eyebrows. "Are you serious?"

She nodded.

"You called me 'nice'."

"So?"

"Kiss of death. Believe me."

"I really don't have a clue what you're talking about, Angus."

He snorted. "Yes you do. Let's just paint."

"No, I'm trying to talk to you. But you're not making any sense." She walked towards him. "You have paint on your forehead."

He reached his left hand up to touch it.

"It's worse now. Look at your hands."

Both his hands were covered in red paint. "What can I say, I'm a messy painter." He wiped both his hands on his jeans, leaving dramatic red smears all down the denim.

She put her fingers in his paint tray and touched his forehead gently. "You looked better with the red stripe." She smiled, backing away from him.

He stared at her, grabbed her hand and forced it onto her own cheek, leaving a blob of red paint.

"Angus!" she shrieked loudly. "What are you doing?"

"And you look better with red cheeks." He laughed.

She looked up at him. His eyes twinkled back at her. He was smiling broadly and still holding both her hands, his grip firm. Her breath began to quicken. Was he going to pull her towards him and kiss her?

"What are you thinking about?" he asked. "You have a funny look on your face."

"Do I now?" she asked, cocking her head to one side.

"Are you flirting with me, Kate? Because if you are . . ."

"Of course not." She shook her head. "Sure, why would I do that? But come to think of it, I do owe you a date."

"Really?"

"Yes. How about tonight?"

"Are you serious?"

She smiled at him.

Angus smiled back. "I think that could be arranged."

Lily backed away from the door. She'd been standing there listening since she'd heard Kate shrieking and had hurried up from the kitchen to check that they weren't killing each other. But from what she'd heard, killing each other was the last thing on their minds.

"So, how was your date with Angus?" Lily asked Kate on the phone the following evening.

"How did you know? Did he tell you, I'll murder him!"

418

Lily laughed. "I'm psychic, you know that. And to tell the truth, I also have a bad habit of listening through doorways."

"Gran!"

"Tush, child. Anyway, are you going to tell me about it or not?"

"I suppose so," Kate said reluctantly. She knew what Lily was like — she'd go on and on at her if she didn't spill the beans so she might as well. Besides, part of her wanted to tell her gran everything. She'd already told Molly all about it after all. She felt she had to after she and Angus had woken Molly up at one in the morning with their tipsy giggling in the hall.

"It went really well, Gran. We went out for dinner in Cicero's and then went for a walk by the sea. And that's all I'm telling you."

"Are you seeing him again?"

"Maybe." Angus was calling over that very evening as Molly was going to the pub with Sam, but she was damned if she was going to tell Lily that.

"I'm glad, he's . . ."

"Nice. I know." Kate laughed. "Now I have to go, Gran. I've something in the oven."

"Dinner for Angus?" Lily asked astutely.

"Gran! Goodbye."

"You look great," Angus said as Kate opened the door. "New shoes?"

Kate looked down at her precariously high-heeled strappy silver sandals, peeping out from under her denims. "Like them?" she asked. "You don't think they're too much with the jeans?"

"Not at all, they're great." He handed her a clinking bag.

She peered into it. "Three bottles!" She laughed. "Are you crazy? It's a Monday night."

"We're celebrating."

"Celebrating what?"

"The full moon." He grinned.

"You're quite mad, you know that?"

"I'll take that as a compliment." He looked through the open door into the sitting room. "Is Molly here?"

"No, she's already left."

"So just the two of us then?"

Kate smiled. "Yes. But don't go getting any ideas, young man. Follow me."

She led him towards the kitchen, plonked the bottles down on the counter, took two glasses off the already-set table and grabbed the corkscrew.

"Red or white?" she asked.

"Red please. Can I open the bottle for you?"

"No, I've got it, thanks."

Angus sniffed the air. "Something smells good."

"It's pasta with meatballs. I hope you like it. I'm not much of a cook but it's fairly difficult to mess up pasta." She pulled the cork out of the bottle with a resounding pop and poured out the dark red liquid.

"I love it," said Angus.

"Sit down, it'll be a few more minutes." She gestured towards the table.

420

"Thanks." He looked at the dark pink tulips in the vase at the centre of the table and the candles in their tall silver candlesticks. "You shouldn't have gone to so much trouble."

Kate blushed a little. "It was no trouble, really." She handed him a glass of wine and tipped her own glass gently against it. "Cheers! To the full moon."

"To the full moon and to us," he said.

After dinner, they slumped onto the sofa in the sitting room, bringing a fresh bottle of wine with them. They'd already shared one bottle and Kate was feeling comfortably relaxed. She'd kicked off her heels and was rubbing the ball of her foot with her fingers. She loved her new sandals but they weren't the kindest to her feet.

"Let me," Angus offered, putting down his glass.

"No, honestly, I'm fine," Kate began, but before she knew it he had her foot in his lap and had begun to massage it expertly.

"I used to give my mum foot rubs," he said, working his thumbs into the ball of her foot and almost making her groan with relief. He really was very good at this, Kate thought. She lay back and closed her eyes. "Tell me if I'm hurting you."

"No, that's great."

After a few minutes he moved onto the second foot. When he'd finished, Kate's feet felt wonderfully rejuvenated. She opened her eyes and smiled at him lazily. "Thanks, you're a star."

"No problem." He brushed a piece of hair away from her face. "You're beautiful, do you know that?"

Kate smiled. "And you're very good for my ego. You're not so bad yourself."

He leant towards her.

Kate's heart gave a tiny leap. He'd given her a gentle kiss on the lips last night while saying goodbye, but she wasn't sure how she'd feel about . . . He leant over again and gave her a firm yet tender kiss. She tried to block all her preconceptions out, and kissed him back, gently at first, then more strongly. To her surprise, he seemed to know exactly what he was doing. To be honest, she'd expected him to be an average kisser at most, but he was actually supremely talented. A little less forceful than Jay, which wasn't a bad thing. In fact, she thought, as he began to stroke her back through her cotton top, Angus was a bit of a natural.

"Are you OK?" he murmured into her neck. "Should I stop?"

She pulled him closer towards her. "Don't you dare!"

"You look very happy," Molly said the following morning over breakfast, instantly noticing Kate's wide smile. "Good night?"

"Very good thanks."

"And was that Angus letting himself out earlier?"

"I'm sorry, did he wake you up?"

"It's fine, I was already awake. So he stayed the night then?"

"Might have." Kate spooned a large amount of cereal into her mouth and crunched away.

"That's great." Molly smiled. "He's a lovely guy. Really cute too. Patricia will be livid. She's asked him out several times since the Booksellers' Ball but he's always said no."

"Really?"

Molly nodded. "Must have been saving himself for you."

"Must have, poor man."

Molly laughed. "Listen, I bumped into Alex last night in the pub. She said to ask you to drop into the coffee shop first thing, she has news for you."

Kate glanced at her watch. "I have a meeting with a client there at nine, so I'll call in a little early to say hi. I wonder what's up."

"Who knows? She was in flying form though. Harry was there too. They make such a darling couple, don't they?"

Kate nodded and stood up. "I'd better get a move on then." She rinsed her breakfast bowl in the sink and dumped it in the dishwasher. "See you later."

The coffee shop was quiet and Kate spotted Alex as soon as she walked in the door. She was making sandwiches behind the counter, her back to the room.

"Alex?" Kate said.

Alex turned around and beamed. "Hi, Kate. Give me one second." She rinsed her hands under the tap and dried them on her apron. "Would you like a coffee?"

"Love one."

"I'll join you if you don't mind. You sit down and I'll be over in a minute."

Alex brought two large mugs of coffee over with her and sat down beside Kate. She placed her hands on the table in front of her.

"So how are things?" asked Kate. "Molly told me you had news."

"I sure do." She picked up her mug and Kate suddenly noticed the large, sparkling ring on her ring finger.

"You're engaged!" Kate smiled. "I don't believe it. When did this happen?"

"On Saturday night. We haven't really told everyone yet, so I'll have to take the ring off now, but I wanted you to be one of the first to know."

Kate leaned over and kissed her warmly on the cheek. "I'm delighted for you both."

"And it's all thanks to you," said Alex. "I hope you'll come to the wedding."

"I'd be honoured. But you know, it had very little to do with me, Alex, honestly."

"But you gave me the confidence to talk to Harry. I would never have approached him without your help. I must recommend you to all my single friends."

"But remember I don't normally do girls, so to speak."

Alex laughed. "That sounded bad, but I know what you mean. But maybe you should. You have a gift for bringing people together, it's your duty to use it. Us Irish girls need you."

"Maybe you're right," Kate mused. "It might be fun. I'll certainly think about it. Now I think my client has just walked in. If you'll excuse me . . ."

"Of course." Alex stood up. "And thanks again."

A small, red-cheeked man with a receding hairline walked towards Kate. He was wearing a plain navy sweatshirt over what looked like billowing multi-coloured pyjama bottoms. She had her work cut out with this one. She smiled as he approached the table. "Paddy, I presume?" She stood up and held out her hand.

He nodded shyly, blushed and took her hand in his. He had a surprisingly firm handshake and kind eyes. Maybe there was hope.

"Nice to meet you," she said. "I'm Kate."

Kate swung open the door of Baroque and sauntered in. She'd had a very productive morning, managing to squeeze in three client meetings and a quick lunch with Molly. And Alex's news had put her in a great mood too.

"Hi, Cathy. How was your morning?"

"Fine, thanks. What has put you in such a good mood?"

"Just life in general," said Kate, dumping her bag on the counter at the back of the shop. "Beautiful day, isn't it?"

Just then Trina came bustling in the door. "I have news!" she shrieked. "I was just at the clinic and I'm pregnant. And the doctor says everything seems to be all right this time. I think I'm going to have a baby!"

Cathy shrieked with joy and immediately gave her a huge hug. "I can't believe it, that's fantastic!"

Kate watched a little shyly before moving towards Trina and kissing her on the cheek. "That's great. Well done. When are you due?"

"Around Valentine's Day — can you believe it? I'm so happy."

"You deserve it after everything you've been through," said Cathy.

"Thanks." Trina wiped the tears from her face and sat down. "Now you'll have to get on with those baby shoes," she smiled at Kate. "You have no excuse."

"Actually I did come up with a few designs," Kate said casually. "Would you like to see them?"

"Of course!" Cathy said immediately. "You're a dark horse, Kate."

Kate pulled her sketch book out of her bag. She'd intended to work on them a little bit more before showing them to Trina and Cathy but it felt like the right time to share them. It was turning out to be quite a day.

CHAPTER
TWENTY-TWO

Epilogue — A Year Later

Paige

"How's my favourite god-daughter? Behaving yourself, Jess?" Angus rubbed the baby's cheek tenderly and gently with his fingers. "How's she been?" he asked Tom.

"Pretty good, touch wood," Tom said still standing in the doorway. "Come in, Callum will be delighted to see you."

"Mr Cawley!" Callum tore down the hall and threw himself at his favourite teacher.

"You can call me Angus now," Angus laughed. "Except in school, of course."

"But you're not going to be my teacher in September, are you?" Callum asked dejectedly.

"No, you'll have Miss Peters. She's lovely. I hear she gives treats on Fridays to the best table."

"Really?" Callum couldn't hide his interest. "What kind of treats?"

"Special pencils, I think. And stickers."

"And sweets?" Callum asked hopefully.

"I don't think so," Angus said. "But you never know."

"Would you like a cup of tea?" Tom asked him.

"If you're not busy . . ."

"Not at all. It gives me a good excuse not to hang out the baby's washing."

Angus followed Tom into the kitchen. "Here, give me Jess while you put the kettle on."

"Thanks." Tom handed her over and began to rub his right shoulder. "She's getting really heavy."

"Where's Alfie?"

"At Granny's," Callum interrupted. "It's just me and Daddy today."

"And Jess," Tom reminded him.

"But she doesn't really count," Callum said patiently. "She doesn't do anything. Just eats and cries and poos."

"Callum! He's very taken with his new baby sister as you can see." Tom laughed.

"After I've had my tea, why don't I take you out for a while, Callum?" Angus suggested. "Give your dad some peace. What do you think? If that's OK with you, Tom."

Tom grinned and gave him a thumbs up. "That would be great."

"Cool!" Callum practically jumped up and down on the spot. "Can we go to the zoo, Angus, please?"

Angus looked at his watch. "Sorry, Callum, we'd never get across the traffic in time. But what about the pet farm in Bray?"

"Yes! I'll just go and get my wellies." He dashed out of the room. "And don't worry. I'll tidy up my toys before we go."

"Hasn't lost any of his energy I see." Angus smiled at Tom.

"No kidding."

428

"So, how are things? Still enjoying being at home? I haven't seen you since the summer holidays kicked in. Sorry I haven't called in sooner."

"Not to worry," Tom said. "Things have been busy but I'm enjoying being with the kids. Most of the time at least. Although I'm not sure about next year. We may need extra help then."

"Really?" Angus was curious. "Why so?"

Tom grinned and pushed his hair off his face. He really did need a haircut but with the three kids to keep under control it was hard to find a slot. "We haven't told many people yet, but Paige is expecting again."

"No! Are you serious?"

"Couldn't be more so. It's a little sooner than we might have liked, but hey, four is a good-sized family. And they're opening a crèche in the local government offices in Dun Laoghaire which will make life much easier. We've already put Jess and the baby down for it next year. I'm hoping to work in the mornings and look after the gang in the afternoons."

Angus whistled. "You'll be busy."

Tom nodded in agreement, poured boiling water from the kettle into two large mugs and added tea bags. "Milk and sugar?"

"Both. Two sugars."

Tom put the steaming mug down on the table in front of Angus.

"Thanks."

Just then Paige walked into the kitchen. "Is there enough water for another mug, I'm dying for a cuppa?"

429

Tom smiled at her. "Of course, Deputy." He prepared her a mug, added a dash of milk and handed it to her.

She kissed him on the cheek. "You're a honey. Hi, Angus. A natural with Jess as always. Would you like to keep her?"

Angus laughed. "What would you do if I said yes?"

"The way she's been sleeping, I might take you up on the offer."

"How's work?" Angus shifted Jess a little as his cradling arm was starting to go dead.

"Will I take her for you?" asked Paige, noticing his discomfort.

"Not at all, she's grand."

"To answer your question, work's great. Busy, but great. I have a meeting in Blackrock this evening so I'm only home for an hour or two."

"Tom told me the good news," said Angus. "About the baby. Congratulations."

Paige looked at tom and back at Angus, grinning ruefully. "In for a penny, in for a pound as they say. We must be mad."

"Mad but happy." Tom wrapped his arms around Paige's waist.

She turned a little and kissed him on the cheek. She felt truly blessed.

Kate

"Do you want them painted?" asked Angus, staring at the new shelves on Kate's living room wall.

430

Kate thought for a moment. Molly had recently moved in with Sam, leaving Kate with the lease, so she'd decided to live in the townhouse on her own for a while. Her new dating cum matchmaking service for men and women — "If the Shoe Fits" was doing very well, her baby shoes for Baroque had been a great success and rent money wasn't a problem. Angus was angling to move in with her, but she was enjoying living alone and being self-sufficient. Still it might be nice having him to cuddle up to when the nights got longer. Maybe she'd ask him to move in at Christmas. A new beginning for them both and a good way to banish any lingering Christmas Eve skeletons.

"What about white?" he asked.

"Against the blue? Do you think?"

He nodded. "Might be quite striking."

"I think I'll leave them plain wood for the moment. I'll put the shoes out and then we can see."

"So I'm finally going to see this famous shoe collection," he said. "I'm most privileged."

"Better believe it, Buster." She smiled. "I might even let you see my own designs. I won an award for my green 'Emerald City' trainers I'll have you know."

"No!" he joked. "Not the 'Emerald City' trainers!"

She elbowed him in the side playfully. "Stop slagging me."

"Ow," he protested, grabbing her around the waist and pulling her towards him. "That's how you treat me, after my long weekend of hard work."

"And Sam had nothing to do with it?" Kate laughed.

"Well, he might have helped a little," Angus conceded.

"You couldn't have built the shelves without him," she said. "Admit it."

"You're probably right. But I was the one running all the errands to the DIY store when we ran out of things."

"You were, pet." She patted his hand.

"I think we should christen the new shelves," he said, kissing her firmly on the lips and pushing her towards the sofa.

"You don't christen shelves, that's beds."

"Who says?"

"I suppose you could have a point." She kissed him back enthusiastically. Angus Cawley had been a revelation to her. Not only was he kind and considerate, he was also passionate, spontaneous and fantastic in bed. To top it all he'd proposed marriage every day since last New Year's. One day in the not too distant future she could even see herself taking him up on the offer.

Molly

"And this is my office," Molly said proudly to Paige. "Sam built all the units for me, and the desk."

"It's fantastic," Paige said enthusiastically. "What a lovely place to write. And what a view."

They both stared out the window. The early evening sun was bouncing off the waves and the sky was still eggshell blue.

432

"Would you like a glass of wine?" asked Molly.

"Love one." Paige followed her into the kitchen.

"Sam and Hugh won't be back for ages," said Molly. "They've taken Leon for a long walk on the beach to try and tire him out a little. Puppies are a lot of work. But Hugh adores him."

Paige laughed. "Wait till you have a baby to contend with."

"At least babies don't chew the legs off your furniture," Molly pointed out, "and you can put them in nappies to avoid all those delightful 'accidents'."

"True." Paige laughed.

Molly handed her a large glass of red wine. "Cheers!" she said lifting her glass to Paige's. They clinked glasses gently.

"Cheers," Paige said. "To you in your new house."

"Thanks." They sat down at the kitchen table.

"How's the book doing this week?" asked Paige.

Molly smiled. "It's doing well from what I can gather. And there were nice reviews in *Dublin Books* and in *Taste*." Molly's first book, the extended version of her "Concrete Pictures" story had been published at the beginning of the month. Renamed *Just in Time*, with a show stopping red and white cover, it had already sneaked into the bestseller lists at number five and was the talk of Burnaby. It was hard to miss the dramatic window displays in Happily Ever After, Baroque, Slick Harry's and in Coffee Heaven. Alex and Harry were now married and living in domestic bliss in Wicklow with two black Labradors and a huge black

Land Rover and were delighted to support their friend's book.

"And Anita loves it," Paige reminded her. "She told me yesterday — I saw her at that new Irish art exhibition in Halo."

"Was Milo with her?" Molly asked with a smile.

"He most certainly was. Following behind her like a puppy dog, as per usual."

Molly laughed. "She still claims she can't stand him."

"They're as bad as each other," Paige said. "And speaking of Milo, how's his son, your other half?"

"Don't call him that!" Molly protested. "It sounds awful."

"OK, then, how's your partner?" Paige said in a terrible fake American accent.

"Stop!" Molly giggled. "Sam's just fine."

"Good." Paige smiled at Molly. "I'm glad you found him. He's a lovely guy."

"I know." Molly smiled back. A moment later she gazed into her wine glass. Paige is right, she thought, I am lucky. I found Sam and somewhere along the way I also found myself. I'm Molly Harper, and I'm a writer.

Also available in ISIS Large Print:

Red Letter Day

Colette Caddle

The No.1 Irish Bestseller

Tipped as one of Ireland's top young designers and recently married, Celine Moore is relaxed, happy and looking forward to an exciting future.

When tragedy strikes in the violent loss of her husband, the dreams she aspired to melt away and are replaced by aching loneliness and anger.

In trying to bury the past, Celine embarks on an affair and attempts to make a new life for herself away from local gossip. But eventually she has to face her demons and to seek the happiness that was once hers.

ISBN 0-7531-7205-4 (hb)
ISBN 0-7531-7206-2 (pb)

Something Borrowed

Tina Reilly

Fresh, frank and funny tale of loves lost and found

Adopted as a baby, Vicky McCarthy's curiosity about where she came from has finally got the better of her: she wants to trace her birth mother. If that doesn't cause friction enough, there's a new face to contend with at work: Ed O'Neill, whom Vicky is convinced is being groomed for her job as manger of Dublin toyshop Toys Galore. Sal, Vicky's best friend, thinks Ed is gorgeous and that if Vicky doesn't bag him, she will. But Vicky is going out with Marti, manager of an up-and-coming boy band, with a six-year-old son and complications of his own.

ISBN 0-7531-7131-7 (hb)
ISBN 0-7531-7132-5 (pb)

Singled Out

Trisha Ashley

Cassandra Leigh's long-term partner, Max, is handsome, charismatic, sophisticated — and married. Cass always dreamed that one day she and Max would be wed, but now she's waking up to reality like an elderly Sleeping Beauty and realising that not only is the prince missing, there isn't even a half-way decent frog in the offing.

Meanwhile, Jason, one of her oldest friends, has developed a crush on her and she's had an encounter of a closer kind than she bargained for with Dante Chase, new owner of the UK's most ghost-infested manor house.

Now the vicar wants to sell Cass off to the highest bidder at the local charity slave auction, and Max, Jason and Dante are each determined to bid for her. And somehow Cass knows that they're all after more than a little light dusting . . .

ISBN 0-7531-7421-9 (hb)
ISBN 0-7531-7422-7 (pb)